Praise for the Novels
of Scott Mackay

"Scott Mackay can always be counted on to create a work that is original in design."　　—BookBrowser

"A terrific book, from first page to last: big ideas, believable characters, great action—it's all here."
　　　　　—Robert J. Sawyer, author of *Mindscan*

"Mackay writes with impressive grace and clarity."
　　　　　　　　　　　　　　　　—*Locus*

"Very suspenseful, a good scientific puzzle, and enough plot twists to give the entire novel an original feel."
　　　　　　　　　　　　　　　　—*Chronicle*

"A decidedly different 'what-if.'"
　　　　　　　　　　—Science Fiction Weekly

"Mackay deserves your attention."
　　　　—*The New York Review of Science Fiction*

"[A] satisfying action SF, quite suitable for a weekend's entertainment."　　　　　　　　　—*Booklist*

"Mackay's newest has everything we expect of good sci-fi."　　　　　　　　　—*The Davis Enterprise*

PHYTOSPHERE

Scott Mackay

A ROC BOOK

ROC
Published by New American Library, a division of
Penguin Group (USA) Inc., 375 Hudson Street,
New York, New York 10014, USA
Penguin Group (Canada), 90 Eglinton Avenue East, Suite 700, Toronto,
Ontario M4P 2Y3, Canada (a division of Pearson Penguin Canada Inc.)
Penguin Books Ltd., 80 Strand, London WC2R 0RL, England
Penguin Ireland, 25 St. Stephen's Green, Dublin 2,
Ireland (a division of Penguin Books Ltd.)
Penguin Group (Australia), 250 Camberwell Road, Camberwell, Victoria 3124,
Australia (a division of Pearson Australia Group Pty. Ltd.)
Penguin Books India Pvt. Ltd., 11 Community Centre, Panchsheel Park,
New Delhi - 110 017, India
Penguin Group (NZ), 67 Apollo Drive, Rosedale, North Shore,
Auckland 1311, New Zealand (a division of Pearson New Zealand Ltd.)
Penguin Books (South Africa) (Pty.) Ltd., 24 Sturdee Avenue,
Rosebank, Johannesburg 2196, South Africa

Penguin Books Ltd., Registered Offices:
80 Strand, London WC2R 0RL, England

First published by Roc, an imprint of New American Library,
a division of Penguin Group (USA) Inc.

First Printing, June 2007
10 9 8 7 6 5 4 3 2 1

Copyright © Scott Mackay, 2007
All rights reserved

 REGISTERED TRADEMARK—MARCA REGISTRADA

Printed in the United States of America

PUBLISHER'S NOTE
This is a work of fiction. Names, characters, places, and incidents either are
the product of the author's imagination or are used fictitiously, and any resemblance to actual persons, living or dead, business establishments, events, or
locales is entirely coincidental.
    The publisher does not have any control over and does not assume any
responsibility for author or third-party Web sites or their content.

To Katie

ACKNOWLEDGMENTS

The author would like to thank the following for their contributions to this novel: Anne Sowards, Joshua Bilmes, A. V. Phillips, Ian Mackay, Joanie Mackay, and Claire Mackay.

PART ONE

1

From his eighth-floor room in the Nectaris Buena Vista Hotel and Gambling Casino, Gerry Thorndike watched the shroud form over Earth. It moved with the slowness of a minute hand sweeping around a clock. He tried to view it as a scientist might, struggled to bring to bear his scientific education, training, and experience, but was hard-pressed to make any substantive observations about the Tarsalan-created phenomenon, knowing he was up here on the Moon, and his wife and children were still down there, on Earth.

He turned from the unsightly thing, angry that the aliens should resort to such an insidious measure, wondering why after nine years in orbit they should now suddenly decide to change their political approach to the immigration question. He checked his waferscreen notes. If the shroud's current growth rate remained the same, it would reach North Carolina in less than a day. He thought of Glenda in their house on the outskirts of Raleigh; of his two children, Jake and Hanna; and of how he had been a fool to jeopardize everything he had ever valued with this questionable trip to Nectaris.

He walked to the pressurized observation deck and looked at the wasteland of gray regolith below, much of it churned with rover tracks and footprints, looking like a beach after a busy Saturday afternoon. He pulled out his fone and tried once more—as if coming out onto the observation deck might make a difference—but the computerized voice from AT&T Interlunar told him for the seventh time that service between Earth and the Moon was currently unavailable, that they had technicians working on the problem, and that they hoped to have service restored shortly. Yet how could AT&T Interlunar work on the problem when the communications disruption was yet another pressure tactic on the part of the Tarsalans? In a fit of frustration, he threw his fone against the polycarbonate pressure glass. But fones were hard to break, and after a defeated sigh he picked it up, inspected it, and put it back in his pocket.

He glanced once more at Earth—and at the green thing that grew over it like a fungus. The unnerving scene came to him slightly warped, the result of the man-made magnetic field around Nectaris that protected its citizens from solar wind and electron-stripped galactic radiation. What could he do? The shroud slithered across the western hemisphere like a garden slug, rippling at the edges, pitted with brown specks, mottled with even darker spots that looked like mildew. He glanced at North Carolina and saw clouds—a June storm whirling up from the Gulf. Was Glenda being smart about it? Was she driving to Raleigh and stocking up on canned goods? Was she purchasing candles, matches, and batteries? Was she maxing out their credit cards, buying time, hunkering down, preparing for the worst? Or was she talking over the back fence with Leigh Phelps? He cringed as he thought of Leigh, wondering how his suspicions could have blunted his judgment so badly. Just because the rest of his life was falling apart didn't necessarily mean his wife was sleeping with the neighbor.

He placed his hand against the pressure glass, sadly realizing that his blowup about Leigh was just a symptom of a larger problem, a growing malaise in their marriage that seemed to be creeping into his and Glenda's life the way the Tarsalans were making this bizarre shroud creep around the Earth. He flexed his fingers against the polycarbonate. He wanted to touch Earth, embrace it, save it, stop this sickening green pall from enveloping it. But the shroud persisted, and as he glanced toward the East Coast he saw, for the first time, an opposite edge, and understood that east would meet west, south would meet north; all the various blooms would join up, and darkness would entomb the Earth.

For several seconds he fought to control his panic. He had failed his family so often in the past, and he didn't want to fail them now. But no flights in and no flights out—not with this Tarsalan shroud.

His panic ebbed and he went back to his room. He switched on the TV and watched the news, the Nectaris local broadcast. The news team had some breaking information. Three fresh blooms had formed: one over the Indian Ocean, another over South Africa, and a third above Bermuda.

Before he could get the details, someone knocked on his door. He walked over and answered, knowing who it was, full of mixed emotions, and not sure how he would react.

Ian Hamilton stood there. "I don't know about you, but I'm bar-bound. I've been watching the news all morning. It's depressing the hell out of me."

"You know I don't drink anymore, Ian."

"Gerry, drinking is the chief reason people come to the Moon."

"I'll have a cranberry juice."

"With vodka."

"With ice."

Ian shook his head. "You sure have changed."

"I can't go carousing like I used to."

"So you're going to pull a Neil on me?"

"Actually, I'm going to pull a Gerry."

The hotel lounge, Tranquility Base, served drinks to a large, mixed crowd. Gerry and Ian found stools at the bar with a good view of the TV. People negotiated the weak Moon gravity with varying degrees of success, the native Moon workers managing with ease, but the visitors from Earth overstepping themselves, crashing into tables and chairs. Most of the furniture was padded and bolted to the floor. Many Earthlings restricted themselves to Velcro paths.

On TV, the Lunar Broadcasting Corporation played live pictures of Earth taken from the Lunette Surveyor Satellite. The image of the shroud, like a diseased piece of flesh, reminded Gerry of the rot he sometimes found in the deepest corners of his refrigerator. What in God's name was he going to do? It was real. It was happening. And he was stuck on the Moon, as powerless as could be.

It left him in a piss-poor mood, and questioning the motive behind Ian's knock and subsequent invitation to Tranquility Base. Ian ordered drinks, a Jack for himself and a cranberry juice for Gerry. To make matters worse, his old friend ordered a shot of Smirnoff on the side for Gerry, as if he wanted to tempt Gerry any way he could. Conversation between them froze. After a minute Gerry did the repetition-gets-the-message-across thing one more time.

"I'm not drinking, Ian. These aren't the good old days anymore."

"Is it going to kill you?"

"It just might."

"I know you're worried, but maybe if you had a drink—"

"Ian, no. I've been sober for two years. I'm not going to blow it now. Especially not with that thing around the Earth."

"Then why the hell did you come to the Moon in the first place? Without your wife." He laughed in the old boisterous way. "Come on. Let's party."

"I don't need alcohol to party."

"Yes, but this is the first time we've seen each other in seven years."

"I had no idea you were here."

"But surely to God it calls for a drink. After all the great drinking times we had?"

"Ian, as I much as I like you, I regret all those times we got drunk together. Thanks for the vodka, but I don't think so."

Ian shook his head in a hard-done-by way. "I wish I was rich enough to say no to free booze. I may have to take her off your hands, if you really don't want her."

"Be my guest."

Ian considered. "We'll leave it by your glass for the time being. You might change your mind. If you're not going to drink . . . if you want to celebrate our reunion with just a crummy old cranberry juice, and not remember all those good times . . ."

"Ian, I want to remember all those good times. But there were some bad times too. Times that hurt Glenda. Times that hurt my kids. It's going to take me a long time to face up to that, but it starts without drinking an ounce."

Ian looked away and sighed, gripping his Jack Daniel's as if it were the last one he would ever have. "The truth is, Gerry . . . I don't care if you drink or not. I just want to talk to you. I've got something on my mind, and I thought if you had a drink . . . you'd be a little more receptive. What I've been meaning to tell you . . . ever since you got here, but didn't have the guts . . . God, it was crazy seeing you in the civic pool the other night. After seven years! And up here on the Moon. That was really something. And I didn't want to put a damper on things at that particular moment, so I thought I would wait a couple of days . . . but I was meaning to ask you . . . even despite the recent circumstances you told me about . . . I mean . . . how good, really, is your financial situation? The reason I ask is that AviOrbit's reducing my retainer. They do that to pilots who turn fifty in the calendar year . . . it's just their policy, and there's nothing I can do about it, but it still caught me by surprise, even though I knew it was coming, and now . . . now my own personal budget . . . I find I'm running a bit short, so I was just wondering . . . If you can afford a trip to the Moon, you must be doing something right. Especially if you're staying at the Buena Vista."

"Ian, it's really nice meeting you here, and it was a big surprise . . . but the only reason I came to the Moon, and didn't go somewhere else, was because my parents bought the trip for me years ago, when the Buena Vista was having a big promotion. Package-deal vouchers with no time limit. My parents gave me the voucher when I graduated. Neil got one too. Without the voucher, I wouldn't be here. As for my money . . . I already told you, North Carolina State let me go six months ago. Glenda and I are hardly making our mortgage payments, Hanna's asthma medication is killing us, and my severance pay is running out."

Ian now looked hangdog. "I just thought if you could afford a trip to the Moon . . . I didn't realize you had the voucher."

Gerry had a closer look at Ian and could hardly believe his old friend was here. He wore a rawhide jacket with huge shoulder pads and silver-flake detailing. Old Ian Hamilton, the god of good times, the prophet of empty pockets, with his seat-of-his-pants religion. And was he truly surprised that money had finally found its way into the conversation? It was always money with Ian. And with him as well, come to think of it. And now this ridiculous trip to the Moon. He regretted the old package-deal voucher. He wanted to be with his family.

His anxiety came back. He couldn't stop thinking of Glenda. He looked at his watch. It was ten-thirty in North Carolina. What was she doing? She would be getting ready for bed. Was she thinking about him? Or, after his most recent performance, did she even care about him anymore?

"You're worried about her, aren't you?" asked Ian.

For someone so insensitive, Ian sure could be sensitive at times.

"All the things we fought about, Ian. . . . Do you know I actually had the gall to accuse her of fooling around with the neighbor? You see what a ridiculous man I am? And it wasn't only about the neighbor. The finances . . . the move to Old Hill . . . never having enough time for each other. And the drinking . . . it's still like a nightmare to both of us, even after two years." Gerry shook his head. "She really took it badly when I blew up about the neighbor. God, I regret it. Now I'm up here, and she's down there, and I have no way of getting in touch with her. Did you hear anything on TV about AT&T Interlunar getting things up and running again? I don't understand how they can get things going if the Tarsalans are causing the problem."

Ian raised his eyebrows. "I understand Mayor Hulke's office is getting official communications. Us plebs, though . . . forget it."

"I sure would like to talk to Glenda and get it straightened out. We walked right to the brink, Ian. I told her I was sorry before I came up, and we both thought it was a good idea I use the old voucher so we could have some time apart, but . . . she had this look in her eyes, like she was making plans—like she just wanted out—and it's scaring the hell out of me. You don't know what you have until you're in danger of losing it."

A special report came on the TV. Both men looked up.

Mayor Malcolm Hulke was making an announcement. The anchorman disappeared, and a shot of the Nectaris Civic Center's Council Hall came onto the screen. It was a round chamber three times the size of the Buena Vista's largest meeting room, blasted right into the gray rock of the Moon, the surface laminated with polycarbonate, the space lit by a galaxy of halogen lights. Various council and media members sat in the chamber. Locals and visitors filled half the public gallery.

Hulke emerged from a doorway to the left. He wore shorts and a T-shirt emblazoned with the latest tourism logo for Nectaris: a crescent moon drinking a piña colada with a big smile on its face, and some dice in the foreground with the dots made to look like craters. Hulke was a slightly overweight young man with a patch of tawny hair combed over his narrow pate, close-set eyes that reminded Gerry of mole eyes, and the oddly smooth complexion of a man who had spent his entire life in the Moon's weak gravity. He climbed the steps with an ease of motion an Earthman simply wouldn't have on the Moon, his slender bones the product of Ossimax—the low-grav anti-bone-leaching compound they put in the water here. He stopped at the podium, took a waferscreen from his pocket, unfolded it, then tapped his temple three times to activate his automatic contact lenses.

The mayor looked at those in the public gallery, then turned to the cameras, to his waferscreen, and at last to the members of the media. "Just before we get started, I want to say I won't be answering any questions about the alleged Oxygen Production Unit kickbacks, so if you've come to dog me with that old horse you might as well go home. I've surrendered all appropriate documents to the special investigator's office, and until he makes an evaluation, I'd appreciate it if you'd just drop it for a while. We've got real news to talk about tonight, this whole shroud thing around the Earth."

The noise in Tranquility Base subsided as people turned to the TV.

"The Tarsalans unilaterally suspended immigration negotiations a couple weeks ago, and now they've gone and put this shroud around the Earth, and who knows when they're going to take it down? Generally, communications are intermittent. We're getting a few special drops from the United States, messages-in-a-bottle-type things, and we're doing our best to reply . . . so it's not like we *can't* talk to them, and find out what's really going on . . . because we can, at least on a limited basis. And I see Richard Glamna already has his hand up, but I'm going to ignore you, Richard, because I can tell you've been saving up another OPU zinger, and if you go ahead, you'll just embarrass yourself. So put your hand down, and let's concentrate on what's important. Like I say, some of these drops are making it through, so we're getting the . . . the gist of things. And I guess the gist of things . . . how can I put the gist of things?"

Hulke paused, and his face settled into a slightly comical, questioning, but ultimately benign expression of disbelief, as if he were surprised and even mildly amused by the gist of things.

"The Tarsalans are telling us . . . or at least the U.N. is telling us . . . that our good buddies in the Tarsalan mothership won't come back to the table until they get their way." Hulke had to pause again, his shoulders rising, his brow pinching with incredulity, as if he found this notion ridiculous. "The G-15"—and he said this with a kind of ass-kissing reverence—"along with the other developed nations of Earth, have made a final offer: the Kanem Region of Chad, the Arnhem Land Reserve in the Northern Territory of Australia, and the Chattahoochee National Forest in the state of Georgia." He looked around, his face frozen in a mask of beneficence, as if the offer of these small land packages to the aliens was the best deal anybody could ever hope for, like getting a complimentary night in the presidential suite at the Buena Vista. "Unfortunately, the Tarsalans aren't playing ball. It really makes you wonder, doesn't it?"

Lisa Rand, of the Lunar Broadcasting Corporation, stood up. Why the mayor let her get away with it, and not Richard Glamna, Gerry couldn't guess. Maybe because she was a lot prettier than Glamna. "Mayor, have the Tarsalans made any moves against the Commonwealth of Lunar Colonies, and can we expect a similar shroud to develop around us?"

The mayor nodded, as if he had been anticipating this question right from the start. "I don't have any concrete information on that right now, Lisa. But according to our customs records, all Tarsalan visitors to the CLC returned to their mothership three weeks ago, well before their negotiation team said sayonara to Earth. So does this mean they're planning something for us? I don't know. At this point I think we should be prepared for anything."

The young LBC reporter persisted. "But as far as you know, we're not looking at a shroud."

"The real problem for us right now, Lisa, is this blockade of weaponized satellites the Tarsalans have deployed around the Earth. Earth can't send us any supplies. So there's nothing in the way of food coming in. Which means we *do* have a situation, but a situation revolving mainly around food. We could start to feel the pinch in as little as a few weeks. Bear in mind that the summer is our busiest season. We've got more mouths to feed. I've sent some guidelines to the hotels. Nothing too drastic. At least not right now. A bit of rationing. Shorter menus. I think all of us on the Moon could benefit from cutting back, especially on the rich desserts. I know I could stand to lose a pound or two. I understand how some of our hotel guests . . . how they came up here to splurge and have a good time, and now I've got to throw a wet blanket on the whole shebang, and I guess they'll end up being mad at me. But we have to watch ourselves if we're going to be serious about this thing. I know that's not our specialty on the Moon, being serious, but we have no idea how long the Tarsalans are going to go on with this."

The mayor looked at his waferscreen, tapped it a few times to change text, then faced the cameras once more.

"You'll want to know if the U.S. fired at the shroud. As a matter of fact, they have. But their missiles had little effect. They made a number of temporary holes, but that's all. Secretary of Defense Sidower said it's a bit like fighting a ghost; that you go to punch it and your fist goes right through. Anyway . . . since current military options seem to be limited right now, Sidower says it might be a good idea to take a scientific approach. And I say *wunderbar*, fantabulous, and *muchas gracias*, Mr. Secretary, for finally coming up with an idea that might actually work." He raised his index finger. "Not to be outdone . . ." The self-immolating smile Hulke was so well known for came to his face. "But I think we should try to do the same thing here. We've got a lot of scientists on holiday here." He let his finger settle to his side, and the holopaint on his T-shirt made the crescent moon wink. "So . . . to all you scientists out there, please give us a hand. Please join us. I've booked Section A of the H. G. Wells Ballroom at the Armstrong Convention Center for six-thirty tonight. I thought we all might sit around and talk. Shoot the breeze, so to speak. See what we can come up with, rather than give Earth all the honors as usual. If nothing else, it should be a good time."

2

Neil Thorndike sat on his yacht, the *Escapade,* his feet
in braces, strapped into his casting chair, his fishing rod
bent against the weight of a freshly hooked blue marlin.
Louise stood next to him, a daiquiri in her hand. Pedro
expertly maneuvered the yacht so the fish wouldn't swim
beneath it. Neil's three daughters, Melissa, Ashley, and
Morgan, leaned against the taffrail, watching. Things
would have been perfect if it weren't for the green storm
approaching from the west.

Here in the West Indies, in the U.S. Virgin Islands off
the coast of St. John, with Trunk Bay visible over the
southern horizon, the sky was sunny and it could have
been any June—oh, those two last glorious weeks in
June, when he went on holiday with his family, when he
was done with the school year, and hadn't yet embarked
on his summer research. The only time during the whole
year he felt free. As usual, he had a blue marlin on his
line. His luck with the great blue never failed.

Only what was he going to do about this green
storm . . . this emerald shroud drawing ever closer to
the sunny shores of Trunk Bay?

He wondered what effect it would have on the gardens
of his fifteen-room vacation home overlooking the bay.
Would all his beautiful tropical miracles wither and die?
The marlin offered slack and he reeled it in. What kind
of effect was the shroud going to have on his holiday?
How long before Tony Bayard issued an executive order
from the Oval Office to track him down? He wasn't

going to think about it. The shroud. The media name for it. Still, he was curious. The Tarsalans never ceased to amaze him. It was like the old saying: What would they think of next?

The marlin jumped out of the water. Morgan clapped her hands. Melissa and Ashley looked bored. But Morgan—she was still young enough to appreciate the thrill. Poor Morgan. What was he going to do about her? The fish arched on its side and splashed spectacularly into the water. His line tightened and he braced against the resulting drag. Gabriel and Raymondo stood ready at the back with grappling hooks. He wondered what they made of that green storm up there; whether they were concerned about their families or trying to figure out how they were going to cope with it. The marlin offered slack again and Neil relaxed. The *Escapade* shuddered as it plowed into a large wave. An explosion of spray rained down on the boat.

As the spray cleared, he saw a Coast Guard vessel approaching from Trunk Bay.

He sagged in his chair.

"Neil?" said Louise.

"Here they come," said Neil.

"Who?" she said.

He pointed. "I knew it couldn't last."

She turned and watched the vessel. He glanced at Louise, the love of his life, and saw a slackening of her jaw.

He called out in Spanish, "Raymondo, it looks like you're going to have to get in the chair and take over." Raymondo glanced at Neil, then out at Trunk Bay. He put his grappling hook on the deck and helped Neil out of the straps. Neil got out of the chair and helped Raymondo strap himself in. He gave the man a benevolent grin. "Get some good pictures of it. And make sure you record its weight. I keep a log."

He walked over to Morgan and stroked her light brown hair. "It looks like Daddy's going to have to go."

"You're always going," said Morgan.

"Not always."

"But this was going to be special. You said you weren't going to let them bother you, no matter what."

"I know, sweetie. But Daddy's going to have to deal with all those . . . green clouds up there. It looks like it's turning into a big emergency. So I really have to go."

"You were going to help me with my reading."

"Mommy's going to do that."

"When will you be back?"

He kissed her forehead. "As soon as I can, sweetie. In the meantime, have fun. Ashley, Melissa, I want you *including* Morgan while I'm gone. And please don't tease her." He glanced at the sky, then turned to Louise. "I'm going to finish this up quickly. The Tarsalans think they're smart, but they're not that smart."

There it was, his usual bold confidence—the certainty that he could do anything, beat anything, and win anything.

Louise came to his side. "What do you think it's made of?"

"I have no idea. But I'll find out."

A worried look came to her face. "We're going to be all right, aren't we?"

He had to think about that. "*We're* going to be all right. People with money are going to weather this thing just fine. It's people like . . . Gerry and Glenda, for instance, who might be . . . inconvenienced by it. Why don't you give Glenda a call when you get back to the house? I worry about her. Especially now that Gerry's run off to the Moon. See if you can figure out a way to give her money without making her feel like she's begging."

"But is that thing . . . do you think it's going to . . ."

"I don't know. And I'm not going to worry about it. My guess is that I'll beat it in a week or two. I've got the low-temperature superconductivity thing starting in the middle of July, and I've got to have this cleared up by then. It's probably some simple compound that's going to break easily. The Tarsalans haven't come here with massive resources, so they can't afford something complex, or particularly resistant. This is just a scare tactic. And the president will give me carte blanche, like he always does. In a few weeks, all this stuff will fall harmlessly to the Earth like . . . like . . . what's that book by Dr. Seuss? The one Morgan loves so much? The one where it rains all the green muck?"

"Bartholomew and the Oobleck."

"Oobleck. Right. That's all this stuff is." Neil's brow furrowed. "I forget how that story ends. It's been so long since I read it to Morgan."

"The king says he's sorry for having his magicians conjure up Oobleck, and the Oobleck melts away."

Neil nodded. "Right. That's how easy it's going to be. I'm going to look up at the sky, I'm going to say I'm sorry, and it's going to melt away."

3

Glenda Thorndike's alarm rang at seven in the morning, but through the fog of her sleep she thought it must have gone off early, because when she opened her eyes it was still dark outside. Then it all came back to her. The shroud. Her body tensed. She reached for Gerry's side of the bed and, even though it was cold and empty, she left her hand there for a long time.

At last she pulled it away. As she pushed her covers off, she felt a distinct chill in the house. The house should have been warm on a June morning. She should have heard cardinals outside her window—oh, how she loved the song of the cardinal. But it felt like the beginning of winter.

She maneuvered her feet into her slippers—sturdy Cree moccasins Gerry had bought for her last Christmas—pulled on her housecoat, and walked to the window. She drew the sheers aside and looked upward. The sky roiled, stitching itself together in an ever-thickening patchwork of green, light in some places, dark in others, like the smoke from a genie's bottle—magical and impossible, terrible yet wondrous. She weakened in fear.

She could make out the woods behind the house, and saw a deer nibbling the grass. The deer didn't seem bothered by the shroud. But the birds. Where were the birds? The feeder should have been Grand Central Station at this time in the morning.

She walked to her dresser and lifted her fone. An

expensive device. Gerry had one too. Rented units, because how often did they speak to each other on an interlunar basis? She pressed the automatic redial and the fone beeped through the digits of his number. As usual she got the same infuriating message: Interlunar communications were currently unavailable, they had technicians working on the problem, and they hoped to have service restored shortly. Then she heard a new addition to the message. "Due to the length of the service interruption, AT&T Interlunar will be sending each of its valued customers a twenty-five-dollar gift certificate, redeemable at any Hutton-Lewis Beauty Spa location." She clicked off in anger. She didn't want a beauty spa. She wanted her husband.

Missed him.

Had to say she was sorry.

Loved him after all, and wanted him back.

She kicked off her moccasins, let her nightgown drop, peeled off her underthings, walked to the *en suite* washroom, and got in the shower. She felt as if she were taking a shower in the middle of the night. She washed her hair and body, then got out, dried off, and wrapped a towel turban-style around her hair. She walked into the bedroom naked, and tried the fone again—couldn't help it—hoping against hope that this would be the minute, the second, the precise moment when the techies at AT&T Interlunar would work their magic and restore her service. But it was *nada, nyet, impossiblé*—then the offer of a twenty-five-dollar gift certificate to a Hutton-Lewis Spa.

She clicked off.

She got into her nursing home uniform, blow-dried her hair, and went to wake Jake and Hanna for their third to last day of school.

Jake was out of bed in seconds, happy and excited. He ran to the front window and threw open the curtains. He looked up at the sky. He sank to his knees, as if praying to God, lifted his hands to his cheeks, and said, "Wow," his voice suffused with a soft and quavering reverence. "It's gotten a lot thicker overnight, hasn't it, Mom? Isn't it cool?"

"Jake, it's not cool."

"It's cool, Mom. I don't care what you say."

"Go pour some cornflakes. And go easy on the milk. We have to make it last."

"I'm going to turn on the TV and see if there's anything new."

"There won't be anything new. Just eat your cornflakes and get ready. You always have to scramble for the bus."

She continued down the hall and went into Hanna's room. Hanna had a poster of Beethoven on the wall. An electronic piano rested on a stand below it, and Glenda saw that Hanna's music was turned to the "Moonlight Sonata." Hanna's clarinet sat on its bell next to the piano. Hanna slept deeply. Glenda shook her daughter, who opened her eyes and turned her head. She looked at Glenda as if she were still in a dream, and made an unverbalized noise that was meant to acknowledge her mother in a nonchalant and uninterested way, as if Glenda were the most boring and annoying spectacle in the world. Then she turned over, closed her eyes again, and slipped back into oblivion.

"Hanna, come on. The bus is going to be here soon. You need a shower. Your hair's a mess."

"I'll wear a scarf around my head."

"Hanna, you need to wash your hair. You should try and get into these habits before you go to college."

"One more minute?" Hanna bargained.

"Your voice sounds a little rough."

"I need my puffer."

And as if she had just now remembered she was afflicted with chronic asthma, Hanna reached out her long, skinny arm so that it double-jointed backward, fumbled for her bronchodilator, put the mouthpiece to her mouth in a greedy gesture, and gave herself three good blasts. Glenda made a mental note. Had to get more. Hanna was running out. But where was the money? And that

thing in the sky. Plus the pills. And that thing in the sky.
Hanna sat up and coughed—coughed long and hard like
she did every morning. With that thing still in the sky.

"That's it, honey. Get it all up. Then get into the
shower. You know the steam does you good."

"One more minute?" Hanna said between coughs.

"You've had a minute."

"That didn't count. Give me *five* more minutes."

"Let's not make the bus wait this morning. Come on.
Out of bed." She gripped Hanna's ankles, playing with
her like she was a kid, even though she was sixteen.
How did her little Hanna grow so tall? Just like her
father. Hanna tried to pull her legs away, but it made
her laugh and she finally sat up. She looked around the
room, and at last out the window.

"Is it ever dark."

"I know."

"I wish Daddy was here. He never should have gone
to the Moon."

"Your dad's had a rough year."

"Yes, but he should have taken us with him."

"The voucher was his from a long time ago. And he
needed some time alone."

"I've never been to the Moon. Half the kids in my
class have already gone. Why don't we get to go to the
Moon?"

"You know the answer. Get into the shower. And
don't forget to take your asthma pill."

"I've only got two left."

"I'll pop by the pharmacy after work."

"Is Dad going to get a new job?"

"He's going to worry about that when he gets back."

"How's he going to get back, now that the Tarsalans—"

"Hanna, let's live a day at a time. The bus is going to
be here in forty-five minutes."

She left her daughter and went into the kitchen.

The kitchen windows were big, and the presence of
that thing in the sky made itself felt in the hairs on the
back of her neck. She lifted Hanna's pill bottle from the

windowsill. Like a good boy, Jake was crunching down his cornflakes. She willed there to be more than two pills in Hanna's bottle, but willing things was so much magical thinking and, sure enough, only two remained.

She then checked the cupboards for food. Canned stew, soup, vegetables, fruits, and tomato sauce lined the shelves. How long was this thing going to last, and was food going to be a problem, and was she letting her imagination run away with her, like she always did?

She opened the fridge. Stocked full of stuff. But she needed more. People were hoarding, and the grocery stores around Old Hill couldn't keep up. She heard Hanna getting into the shower. Only where was she going to get the money to buy more groceries? And the fuel cell in the car needed recharging. And the car's software was due for an update, and how was she going to pay for that? She took a few breaths, trying to calm herself. If only she could get a few more hours at the nursing home; they just might make ends meet if she had more shifts at Cedarvale.

The phone rang, not the interlunar one but the regular one, the one spelled with "ph." She hurried over, thinking she might miraculously receive information about Gerry, but when she turned on the vidscreen, she saw Louise's face, sharp, crystal-clear—uncanny what a good transmitting set would do. She was sure Louise saw nothing but a blur.

"Glenda?"

"Hi, Louise."

"Can you fix your contrast? I can hardly see you."

Crappy Home Tech brand, fifteen years old; no wonder Louise couldn't see her. She was sick of having crappy things and living in a crappy house. She pressed the appropriate function key.

"Is that better?"

"You need a new set."

"Where are you calling from?"

"Trunk Bay."

"Oh. You're down there."

"Have you heard from Gerry yet?"

"No. AT&T Interlunar is still working on the problem."

"Neil wanted me to phone you. To see how you were doing. Is it dark there yet?"

"You can't see open sky anymore. The last of it disappeared a few days ago."

"It's worrisome, isn't it?"

"Does Neil have anything to say about it?"

Because surely her genius brother-in-law would save them from all this.

"The Secret Service came for him yesterday," said Louise. "I imagine he's been in meetings ever since."

"Oh . . . so he's going to . . ."

"They've drafted him for it."

"And does he have any ideas . . . I mean . . . about what to do?"

"He's confident he can get rid of it in as little as two weeks. You know Neil."

"So you think it'll be over in two weeks?" Her shoulders eased in relief.

"That's the timetable Neil's given himself. And you know Neil. How are the kids, by the way? How's Hanna's asthma?"

"It always gets worse this time of the year. All the pollen."

"And Jake's okay?"

"Jake's fine. He's loving all this . . . this craziness. He thinks it's cool."

"Did they give you more hours at the nursing home yet?"

She looked away. "The lady who was supposed to leave might not leave now."

"Oh . . . because if you need a little help . . . and I don't want you to think of it as charity . . . but with Gerry stuck on the Moon . . . Neil and I just thought . . . you know, if you needed a little extra help to tide you over, we'd be happy to . . ."

Glenda's lower lip stiffened. "No . . . I think I can manage." *Glenda, just cave in, swallow your pride, you need the money.* "I have a little put away for emergencies." *Lies, lies, lies.*

"And you've got enough to pay for Hanna's medicine?"

"Oh, yes . . . of course." *Shift away from your own neediness, Glenda. Focus on kids.* "How are the girls, Louise?"

"We're always worried about Morgan."

"Morgan's a sweetheart."

"I just wish she'd learn how to read. She's ten years old. She should know how to read by now."

"Kids have their own schedules for that kind of thing."

"Glenda . . . if you get into trouble . . . or if this thing goes on for any length of time and you need some help, just call us. Don't be proud. I can't stand the thought of you and your kids going without."

"We'll be fine, Louise. Really we will."

But as she disconnected the call, she felt worried again. Why did she have this senseless pride? Why was it so important for her to show Neil and Louise that she and Gerry could make a go of it, and that they could cope in the face of adversity? She pushed these thoughts from her mind, as they were the same old ones she always had, nothing new. Better to take a positive outlook; this whole thing was going to blow over, she was going to get more hours at the nursing home, Gerry was going to come home from the Moon and find a great job, and they would work it out and have the same kind of picture-book marriage Louise and Neil did.

But in the meantime . . .

In the meantime.

She went back to the cupboard and looked at the food. She had a vision. Of a green world turning brown. Of food disappearing. Of massive famine.

Surely it wouldn't come to that.

But if it did . . .

She walked to the basement door, opened it, went downstairs, glanced around at the junk, and spied Jake's old toy box, red and yellow, made of chipboard, with a

clown face painted on the front. The basement light
went on as she passed the sensor. She lifted the antique,
rolled-up maps, the ones Gerry had collected over the
years—not because he used them, just because he liked
them—opened the toy box, and saw a lot of action figures, toy vehicles, and a toy xylophone. She emptied the
toys on the floor, took the box upstairs, and placed it
on the counter.

"That's my toy box," said Jake.

"Do you mind if I use it?"

"What do you need it for?"

"I'm going to bury some treasure. You can help, if
you get ready in time."

"Mom, we don't have any treasure. We're broke."

"I think we should bury some food."

"Why?"

"Just in case we need it."

"Why don't we keep the food in the cupboard, where
it belongs?"

"Because I think we should have a backup cache."

She took cans and jars of nonperishable food from the
cupboard and placed them in the toy box. She glanced
over her shoulder and saw Jake staring at her, his cornflakes forgotten, a hint of fear tracing apprehension on
his smooth young face.

"Why bury food?" he asked.

"Just in case things get bad."

"Things won't get bad, Mom. You just have to believe
that they won't."

"You sound like your father."

"You don't have to bury food."

"I'm the mother. It's my job to look after you. And I
take the job seriously."

"But why bury food?"

"Because I don't want anybody coming into the house
and stealing it."

"Why would they steal it?"

"Jake, how many times do I have to tell you? There
are bad people in the world. And if bad people get desperate, they become extra bad. If this shroud lasts any

length of time, everything's going to stop growing and food's going to run out. You think anything's going to grow with that thing up in the sky? Plants need light to grow. Two weeks of total darkness, and that's it, there goes next year's crop."

"Uncle Neil will talk to the president before that happens."

"If you need me, I'll be in the backyard."

She finished stocking the toy box with jarred and canned foods, and was surprised by how heavy it was once she lifted it. She went out the back door and ventured into the yard. The green sheet of the shroud mottled its way from horizon to horizon. A few clouds floated beneath it. The green was so dark in spots that it verged on black. A raccoon lumbered by at the end of the yard and disappeared into the bushes, all mixed up about night and day.

She carried the box into the woods and found a spot among the sycamores. The leaves on the trees rustled in a cool breeze—too cool for this time of the year. How strange the trees looked, silhouetted against that green sky. She put the box down, walked back to the toolshed, and got the spade. She carried it to the spot between the sycamores, broke the earth, and dug.

The earth smelled rich with living things. She dug some more and, in digging, knew she had made an admission to herself. This wasn't like the regular and small disasters that befell people on a daily basis, making their lives miserable for a while, then finally drifting away like a bad dream. This was the Apocalypse. And she wanted food for when the Apocalypse finally came.

She arrived for her short morning shift at the Cedarvale Nursing Home and Long-Term Care Facility an hour later. Old people played chess in the hallways, the lights were up bright, and the inmates were dressed in sweaters or jackets and enjoying themselves, as if the shroud were cause for celebration. She nodded a polite hello to the elderly volunteers in the information kiosk, passed the coffee stand, continued down the hall to Section H, climbed the stairs, and finally reached the Palliative Care Department, where people went to die. She waved to Elma and Karen, two nurse-receptionists, but they were too busy with the phones and didn't notice her pass. Didn't matter. Had to speak to her supervisor, and speak to him fast.

She found Whit, a tall black man, at his desk going over the master schedule.

"You too?" he said.

"Pardon?"

"Everybody's asking for time off."

"No . . . I don't want time off. If you need me to work a few extra hours . . ."

"I just might." He motioned out the window. "Everybody's concerned about the weather."

She looked out the window and saw the shroud moving across the sky like a green shadow.

"You knew my husband was stuck on the Moon?"

"You were saying."

"And that the university let him go?"

"That's tough. I'm sorry about that, Glenda."

"It's just that I'm . . . I'm running a bit short. And Hanna's got her asthma prescription to fill. And I don't know what the policy is, but I just thought if I could . . . if you could give me an advance on my pay. Just to tide me over the next couple of days."

She hated this, begging for money. But better she beg Whit than Neil and Louise. Whit looked to one side and his forehead creased. He took a deep breath and sighed, then glanced up at her with sympathetic brown eyes.

"It's all automatic, Glenda. Payroll won't even accept hours worked—not from me, not from any supervisor— till the Thursday *after* the pay period ends."

Her lips tightened in irritation. "And there's not some special form you can e-mail them?"

"You have nothing in the bank?"

"I live paycheck to paycheck, Whit. That's the way it is."

"How much do you need?"

"Enough to buy Hanna's medicine and some extra food."

"Will two hundred dollars do?"

"I was hoping for three."

"I could make three." He took out his wallet.

She was disarmed by Whit's generosity. "Whit, I can't take your money."

He withdrew a touch-sensitive cash chit, keyed in the appropriate amount, and handed it over. "I don't want your kids suffering, Glenda. You can pay me back whenever. But if you're looking for groceries, you may have to go all the way to Raleigh. Dee was telling me there's nothing around here. The shelves are bare. People are hoarding."

"So I heard. I plan to make the trip after work."

"Then take my money, and think nothing of it."

4

The Armstrong Convention Center was seven stories underground, on the south side of the lofty Apollo Way. A scale model of Apollo Eleven angled upward through the brightly lit space above a fountain that was timed to shoot fifteen streams of water every three seconds. The convention center itself was a domed oddity, chiseled into the rock of the Moon, the rock laminated with polycarbonate.

Gerry and Ian entered via the center doors and passed a coffee shop, a money-exchange place, a travel office, and a number of clothing stores. They soon came to the North Atrium's moving walkway. The air smelled of marijuana and, glancing up to the next level, Gerry saw two showgirls in costume, rhinestones pasted to various suggestive parts of their bodies, passing a large zebra-striped joint back and forth as they chatted amiably to the cyber-enhanced security guard at the neon-outlined security kiosk.

He and Ian came to the end of the walkway and took three extremely long escalators down to the third lower level. Here they passed a gargantuan tank full of genetically enhanced dolphins, which would come to computer interfaces and conduct rote conversations with tourists for a few dollars. Gerry stared at the dolphins. He had a sudden urge to be near the ocean. He pictured the surf at Nag's Head, and wanted to be walking barefoot in its foam.

As they entered Section A of the H. G. Wells

Ballroom—the walled-off Section B was at present home to an A.A. meeting (he knew them well)—one of the mayor's aides came forward with a waferscreen and asked Gerry and Ian to write their names, a list of affiliations, areas of expertise, and educational credentials in the spaces provided. Gerry did this, then looked around the room. There seemed to be a preponderance of showgirls and tourist workers here. He was touched. People were eager to help Earth. In the far corner he saw technical types, several in suits, a number in lab coats, possessed of that curious brand of killer intelligence all technical types had, sitting in a circle arguing about something with the splitting-hairs vehemence customary to their tribe.

"Is that the AviOrbit contingent?" he asked Ian.

"That's them. They're all good guys. I don't see any of the new pilots, though."

"So these are engineers?" Gerry tried to keep the flagging spirits out of his voice.

"Yup."

"They build interplanetary spacecraft?"

"Right."

His voice sank into further hopelessness. "But have no grounding in pure, abstract science."

"Why don't you go over and ask them?"

"Let's just listen to what people have to say. I don't want to get into a big, long conversation with people I don't know."

The mayor's assistant walked to the podium and handed the waferscreen to Hulke. The mayor scanned the data, flipping through it electronically with a touch of his right index finger. He finally stopped at one page in particular. He then had a few words with his assistant, who pointed across the rows of brown stackable plastic chairs to Gerry. The mayor looked at Gerry, then at the waferscreen, and finally nodded to himself, as if he found Gerry's presence encouraging.

At last the mayor clapped and got everybody's attention.

"Thank you all for coming," he said. "I see here that

we have several extremely talented professionals from a variety of major organizations and institutions throughout the solar system. So I'll try to up my usual rhetorical style. I'll attempt to be a little more formal. I welcome you to the Moon. I guess I'll start with a few caveats, quid pro quos, and fine-print stuff, just because I know some of you must have some misconceptions about the Moon. For starters, we do things in a small way here. We're a tiny community; fifteen thousand permanent residents in Nectaris, and only another ten thousand in the secondary communities." He spoke as if by rote. "Which means we have nothing in the way of money. I just want to make sure you all understand—this thing is volunteer."

Several nods assured him that the volunteer nature of the effort was well comprehended.

"Good. I see we have some friends from AviOrbit. I knew Ira would come through for us. But I doubt AviOrbit can contribute much in the way of a budget either, so don't get your hopes up, just because the techies have arrived. And I see that Professor Luke Langstrom is visiting us from the University of Mars. Sorry, Dr. Langstrom, but the money for this project will pale in comparison to some of the legendary research grants you've worked with. It's the casinos that have all the money. Not us in council. Professor Langstrom, for those of you who don't know, was the first to isolate evidence of prehistoric life on Mars in a series of experiments he conducted forty years ago in the Pegasus Cavern System of the Valles Marineris." He turned to the gathered media. "You see, I know these things too. So the next time you call me ignorant, just remember that."

Gerry cast a curious glance at Langstrom, who was well into his seventies, had white hair, bushy silver eyebrows, and sat slouched in his chair with a confident but whimsical grin on his face, as if he found the whole lunar effort to destroy the shroud amusing. Langstrom would have been a kindly old grandfather type if it weren't for something bitter in the eyes, and stingy about his lips.

What kind of life had he lived on Mars, wondered Gerry? Did he even care about Earth?

"Also visiting us this week is Associate Professor Gerald Thorndike, of North Carolina State University." The mayor consulted a lot of additional notes. "Gerald Thorndike is the younger brother of Professor Neil Thorndike, a name many of you in the science community will no doubt know." Here it was again, his name, always linked to Neil's. "My assistant has written here that Neil Thorndike was the cowinner of the Nobel Prize in Physics last year, and also winner of the Davison-Germer Prize, and that he's one of the senior members on the United States National Science Board. We're extremely honored to have his brother here today. Gerry, welcome to the Moon."

Gerry felt uncomfortable with this backhanded introduction. People clapped. He couldn't count the number of times he'd been presented as Neil Thorndike's brother, not as a scientist in his own right. He stood up and took a perfunctory bow, wanting only to get on with things.

He sat down, and Hulke introduced some people from AviOrbit, rocket scientists the lot of them, but maybe a few, he hoped, who had knowledge of basic Earth sciences. Hulke then launched into a recap of everything that had happened in the last two weeks: how negotiations had broken off with the Tarsalans, how all Tarsalan visitors and delegations had returned to the mothership—the TMS as it was called—and how the shroud had grown day by day despite military attempts to destroy it.

"At this point, I'd like to let the scientists take the floor. Professor Langstrom, if you could go first. We'd appreciate any thoughts you might have."

Langstrom raised his hand dismissively, continuing to smile in his amused way. "I hardly think I'm the ranking scientist here," the Martian said, taking out a pipe and stuffing it calmly with marijuana. "Gerry Thorndike is. Let the man who has something in jeopardy speak first."

There was a tone in Langstrom's voice that Gerry didn't like, as if he were somehow blaming Gerry for the shroud.

"Dr. Langstrom, you flatter me," said Gerry.

"I'm a Martian. Have been for the last sixty years. I think we should hear from an Earthman. After all, it's Earth that's in peril." Again, that tone.

Gerry hesitated. "If that's all right with the mayor."

Hulke looked at Gerry the way a showbiz manager eyes new talent, with a mixture of hope and despair. "By all means, Dr. Thorndike. If you think you have something to say."

"Because I *have* been thinking a lot about the shroud lately."

Especially because his wife and family were still on Earth.

"Then come to the podium, and let's hear it."

With mounting confidence, Gerry rose from his seat and walked to the podium. He was conscious of his size, tall but lanky, six-four, and how his six-four frame couldn't seem to get the hang of lunar gravity. As he reached the mayor, he smelled alcohol. He shook hands with Hulke.

The mayor's hands were cold and moist. "Just give them something to hope for," he murmured, as if he believed the situation were already lost. "The rationing thing isn't as good as I'm telling everybody."

What he saw in the mayor's eyes was fear. Okay. So things were worse, a lot worse, if the mayor's eyes were any indication. Things had reached such impossible levels that they actually had to consult scientists. Gerry turned from the mayor, gripped either side of the lectern, and gazed out at his audience. He could see that they were all counting on him, not because he was Gerry Thorndike but because he was Neil Thorndike's brother; even the showgirls looked as though they had heard of Neil.

He cleared his throat.

"The shroud," he said, immediately slipping into lecture mode, as he had in Jarrell Hall at NCSU. "What is it?" He looked around his audience as if he expected someone to answer him, pausing on purpose to get their attention, then continuing with the obvious follow-ups. "Is it alive? Is it dead? Will all the blooms finally join up and cover the Earth? And if the shroud envelops Earth, will any sunlight get through? Will it let heat through? If it lets heat through, will it trap heat, the way greenhouse gases do on Venus? Will the Tarsalans employ the shroud for a fixed period, or will they allow it to remain in place indefinitely? If it remains in place indefinitely, what will the consequences be—socially, politically, and environmentally?"

He paused, and leaned more firmly against the lectern.

"You get up in the morning, and the sun doesn't rise, and the birds don't sing. It's dark, and it stays dark all the time. Today is June twenty-fourth. It's summer in the northern hemisphere. The last spring blossoms have left the trees and the leaves are out. The wheat is still green, and the spring rice in Asia is just partway along. The vegetable crops are no more than young shoots. Now there's no sunlight. What does that mean? I think this is what we have to concern ourselves with most. The immediate effect of the shroud is going to be on plant life. A lot of plant life is fairly resilient and can hang on through a lot of punishment. But depending on how long the Tarsalans decide to go on with this shroud . . . a farmer will walk into his field, and he'll see his wheat or corn growing weaker every day and starting to wilt in the darkness, and at some point he'll make the decision to plow it under because it won't be harvestable. You get enough farmers doing this, and the markets start to react, and consumers react, and panic sets in. And that's what I think is going to be the most negative effect of this . . . shroud . . . at least in the short term. This . . . unavoidable panic. People will hoard, and that will just make the situation worse. And really, the food-distribution system, at least in the U.S., isn't set up to take major or prolonged strain. There's about a one-week supply in the commercial food network, and as for national emergency stores, we've got a six-week supply.

But you have to remember that most of these emergency stores are in Western Secessionist states, so that's where we get a political factor, and the strain may be enough to worsen not only the panic, but also the hoarding."

He paused to register the effect he was making. Judging from the blank looks, it seemed many of them, especially the Lunarians, didn't know too much about the Secessionist Movement in the western United States. One middle-aged man, a doctor in a lab coat, looking as if he had just ducked over from the Aldrin Health Sciences Center, got up and asked him about it.

Gerry marshaled a few brief facts. "It's been building for the last hundred years or so, and finds its origins in the general political polarization of the United States into red and blue states. Also, over the past fifty years, as the Hispanic population in these states has shifted from the minority to the majority, the movement has gained a cultural and religious impetus. Make no mistake, the governors in these states are hard-core, and they know their grass-roots constituents favor eventual secession, especially after their long and fractious fight over illegal immigration with the Federal Government. A few of these governors are so archsecessionist that I'm sure they'll willingly blockade their emergency food stores for political gain. That's going to adversely impact an already tenuous U.S. food-distribution system. This means the Federalist states could be facing major food shortages sooner than we'd like to imagine. And these food shortages are going to be badly exacerbated by hoarding."

The doctor sat down, seemingly satisfied with Gerry's overview. Gerry continued.

"Western Secessionism is one of the reasons people are going to hoard. But if it gets dark and stays dark, they're going to hoard because they won't be sure if they can count on next year's crop. We don't know how far the Tarsalans are going to go with this shroud. Or if we can defeat it. As for third-world countries, the situation will be that much worse." He gave everybody a good glancing over. "And what about us here on the Moon?"

He caught the mayor shifting uncomfortably. "Given current stockpiles, and quick implementation of the mayor's rationing program, we're perhaps in a better situation than Earth. But I imagine things will go critical fairly quickly."

He paused.

"So that's why I'm really glad the mayor has called this meeting. Because we should get working on this right away. I haven't got too much else to say. But I think we should all try to appreciate how serious the situation can become. If the Tarsalans decide to go long-term with this, it could get bad. I'm talking *really* bad."

The usual party atmosphere of the Moon was gone.

There wasn't a rustle of sound anywhere.

It was like none of them could believe he was telling them this. As if they had come to party, but he had spoiled the mood.

He glanced around the room once more. And he had to wonder how his brother, Neil, would have handled the situation; whether he would have stood up here and listed problem after problem, as he had done, or if he would have tried to offer solutions. This was the essential difference between them. Neil had all the answers. All Gerry had were questions.

The mayor seemed to think so too, because he finally cleared his throat and got up from his chair. "Thanks for that insightful . . . uh . . . overview of the potential . . . should I call them problems, or disasters . . . thanks for that, Gerry."

He left the lectern and wasn't sure if he had added anything substantive to the discussion at all. He glanced at Luke Langstrom. Langstrom didn't look so amused anymore. He gave Gerry a solemn nod, then got up to say his own two bits about the shroud.

As Gerry sat down, Ian gave him a nudge. "Wow. Not exactly what I was expecting."

"It's not going to be a holiday, Ian. At least not if the Tarsalans keep it in place for a long time."

And Gerry felt like the most unpopular man in the room.

The death of the party.

The guy people avoided because he was such a downer.

He did, indeed, feel like Neil Thorndike's younger brother.

The meeting broke for refreshments an hour later. Mayor Hulke approached Gerry as he spigoted coffee into a Styrofoam cup. Nothing but coffee these days.

"Would you be willing to head this thing, Gerry?" asked Hulke.

"Me?" Gerry was surprised. "Wouldn't it be better if one of the guys from AviOrbit did, someone who's familiar with the scientific resources on the Moon?"

"We thought an Earthling might be more appropriate. And of course you carry the Thorndike name."

Gerry's lips tightened. "I'm not my brother, Malcolm. If they're expecting miracles just because I'm Neil's brother—"

"No one's expecting anything. But I touched base with the AviOrbit guys during the break, and they say they would be comfortable if you would . . . more or less direct things. All these guys from AviOrbit—they're just techies. They get their orders from Earth, and they build according to spec, and they don't know how to tackle a project like this, not if there's going to be a lot of pure science involved. Believe me, I know. I worked at AviOrbit for fifteen years before I became mayor. You're the only real, working scientist in the group. What I said on the TV about there being a lot of scientists here on holiday . . . that was just to boost morale."

"What about Professor Langstrom?"

"Professor Langstrom's been retired for years. I think you're the most suitable candidate, Gerry, and so do a lot of other people."

Gerry nodded, and couldn't help feeling flattered. He rarely got asked to be the head of anything. "If that's the way they feel, I'd be happy to give it a shot. But you were talking about budget. Do we have *any* budget?"

The mayor looked away. "Not really. The city has an emergency fund for fixing unexpected pressure leaks. We haven't had a leak in forty-five years, so we could dip into some of that. But it's not going to be much."

"I'm just thinking . . . we may need things . . . things that only the merchants here can provide. Some might donate. But others might be reluctant. We can't ask people for their livelihoods. Not if they can't afford it. So if we have at least a little leeway money—"

"I'll get council to release some of the emergency fund. But you have to understand, Gerry, our tax base is small. We'll be running things on a shoestring."

Gerry put a reassuring hand on the mayor's shoulder. "Malcolm, you don't have to worry. I've been running things on shoestrings all my life."

5

Neil sat in the Oval Office six hours later—with barely time to change into a suit. A Secret Service agent walked here and there through the Oval Office, aiming an aerosol can all over the place, spraying the corners, behind pictures, in the vents. The aerosol particles were charged with bug-disabling properties—the Tarsalans were fond of deploying flying listening devices throughout the White House, the Capitol Building, and the Pentagon. Once the Secret Service agent was done—the room turned out to be clean—National Security Advisor Julie Petrov launched into an overview of the situation.

"The Tarsalans still aren't budging."

President Bayard sat behind his desk, a lean man from New Mexico, tall, his cheeks lined and tanned, his hair nearly white, every strand combed meticulously in place. Vice President Ben Baldwin stood to one side with his hands in his pockets, rocking on his heels, chin thrust forward so his lower lip protruded over his upper one. Others present were the president's chief of staff, Holden Gregory, and Secretary of Defense Joseph Sidower. Here to represent the National Science Foundation were himself and Dr. Robert Cruz.

"We advised the president to reject the Tarsalan demands," continued Julie Petrov. "As far as this administration is concerned, all talks are at an end until the Tarsalans remove the shroud, call in their killer satellites, and restore our interplanetary communications. We've told them we consider the shroud an act of aggression." She turned to the secretary of defense. "Joe? Do you want to talk about the military option?"

Sidower shifted forward and tapped his waferscreen a few times. "The Joint Chiefs of Staff are having the Pentagon draw up war plans against the Tarsalan killer satellites, as well as the mothership. The Seventh, Tenth, and I think the . . ." He consulted his notes. "The Eleventh Orbital Squadrons of the 101st Airborne have been put on highest alert and are prepared to move against the TMS at any moment. My generals tell me that the main offensive strategy is not a direct attack against the TMS, but rather to establish a net of mines in a series of various orbits around the Earth, so that the whole forms a barrier the TMS will find extremely difficult to maneuver around. The mothership may heighten its orbit to avoid one string of mines, only to find itself smashing into another."

The president spoke up. "Joe, say I decide to give the order and send the 101st Airborne in." He tapped his cheek with two fingers. "What's to stop the Tarsalans from mounting a retaliatory strike from their homeworld at a later date? And how long would it take them to mount a strike from their homeworld?"

Sidower glanced at Neil. "I better hand this over. Neil, maybe you can give us—or the president—an overview on the likelihood of this potential response from the Tarsalans."

Neil nodded. "Tony, I wouldn't put the risk too high. We've been gathering a lot of data from various observatories, radio-telescope installations, and space-based observation posts for nearly eight years, trying to track back the route the Tarsalans took to get here." He motioned at the sky. "We've learned that the TMS traveled at up to and including—but not beyond—the speed of light." He leaned forward on the sofa, putting his elbows on his knees. "Their drive emissions stop forty light-years away, in the . . . it was the 51 Pegasi star system, wasn't it, Bob?"

"That's right," said Cruz. "My team made the preliminary findings. It's confirmed. The 51 Pegasi star system.

Previous observations tell us there's an Earth-like planet in that system."

Neil sat back, took his palms from his knees, and raised them upward. "If that's where they came from—and we're fairly certain it is—we hypothesize that the TMS took at least forty years to get here. Since that time, the technology on their homeworld may have improved. And we also have to take into consideration that the Tarsalans trade with numerous other species in several other star systems, and that such trade is bound to accelerate the rate of their own technological advancement." He paused, caught up in his own speculations. "But while it's . . . *possible* they may have developed a faster-than-light drive by this time—and that a retaliatory force could arrive here soon—it's highly unlikely. Even given their current capability to communicate instantaneously over large astronomical distances, the possibility of an attack is remote. Should they in fact decide to retaliate, it would take them four decades to get here, and only if they left fairly immediately after the first Mayday."

The president lifted his chin, leaned back, and put his hand against his desk blotter. "So in other words, we have forty years to prepare for a retaliatory strike?"

"From the homeworld, yes."

The president turned to the secretary of defense. "And based on current intelligence, Joe—on everything we know about their military capability—do you think such a retaliatory strike would be . . . could they make a go of it in any significant way, given the distance they have to travel? I mean, talk about fighting your long-distance war."

Two creases came to Sidower's forehead. He reached up and scratched his bald pate. "Tony, if you're asking me for my best guess . . ." His eyes narrowed. "Would they fight? Could they fight? From that distance? I'm doubtful. It's not beyond the realm of possibility that they just might pack it in and give up. Look at it this way. Are they willing to sink another forty years into gaining the right to immigrate to Earth? It doesn't seem worth it to me. Not really. Especially when we've played hardball with them right from the beginning. I can't speculate with a hundred percent certainty, but I believe a sustained military campaign against Earth from a distance of forty light-years would be like . . . like trying to write the history of the world with a broken pencil. It wouldn't work. They'd be fools to try. And if they do try, I believe they'll again use a passive weapon, like the shroud. Maybe they'll poison the oceans the next time around."

"And what's so passive about the shroud?" asked Ben Baldwin, stepping forward. The vice president glanced around. "All the Tarsalans have to do now is play a waiting game. I hate them for putting us into this position, but maybe we should draft a second counterproposal to their immigration demands. I know our policy is not to deal with blackmailers, but at the same time we might prevent massive loss of life if we go back to the table. Maybe, if we double the original offer, they might accept a compromise and dismantle the shroud. Maybe we should propose a special session of the United Nations and see if we can come up with something that will appease them for the time being. At least so we can buy some time. Because we need time. We've been rushed into this. We had no idea they were going to play this card."

"In other words, you suggest we stall," said President Bayard.

"Exactly."

"And if we come back with a second counterproposal, and they accept it—what then?" asked Sidower. "We open the door. They see that we're weak. That's sending the worst kind of signal, Tony. I personally think you should give the 101st Airborne the order. I think we should destroy as many of those killer satellites as we can. That will give us a freer rein to bust up the shroud with whatever means Neil and his team can devise. And we might even mount some kind of strike against the TMS directly. Because I think ultimately that should be our focus. They must have some means to control the

shroud aboard, and if we can get our hands on it . . .
That doesn't mean I think we should stop trying to figure
out a way to dismantle the shroud from the outside.
That's the whole reason Neil and Bob are here."

The president paused as he considered the secretary's
words, lifting his hand to his chin and resting it there in
a contemplative pose before taking it away and leveling
his blue eyes on Neil.

"Neil, could you give us an overview of both the long-
term and short-term effects of the shroud?"

Neil sat back as he considered the possible repercus-
sions. "Well . . . you have the obvious: no crop growth,
food shortages, and possible famine. But you also have
an overall breakdown in Earth's various ecosystems.
Starting with the oceans, there won't be any light to
generate plant life. That means many creatures will
starve. And if these smaller creatures starve, the larger
ones that feed on them will starve as well, and so on,
up the food chain. If it goes on long enough, atmospheric
deterioration might become a problem. Plant life sucks
in huge amounts of carbon dioxide and spits out oxygen.
So there could be a basic chemical change in our
atmosphere."

"So a greater greenhouse effect?" ventured the president.

"Not in the short term. Short term we're looking at a
significant cool-down. With heat and light from the sun
blocked, we could be looking at snow in July. But don't
get me wrong. Even though light won't get through, heat
still will, according to current analysis, and the shroud
will trap this heat over the long haul. Computer models
tell us this heat will begin to build. So while we might
start off cold, it will get hot fairly quickly. When you
take all these things into consideration, the socio-
political fallout might be immense."

The room grew still, and he could tell everyone was
thinking of the Western Secessionists.

The president continued. "Why do you think the Tarsalans have decided to use the shroud against us in the
first place? If they're so technically superior to us, why

don't they just mount a full-scale invasion? Why don't they just come in and take what they want instead of applying this slow pressure thing on us?"

"For one thing, they don't have the resources aboard the TMS to mount a full-scale invasion. Remember, there's only fifty thousand of them up there, and many of them are just immigrants who want to live on Earth. For another thing, it's not in their nature to be violent."

"You know this . . . this Kafis on a fairly personal level, don't you?" asked the president.

"He's one of their senior scientists. I've had him as a guest to Marblehill, my home in northern Georgia, numerous times. He's also one of their junior negotiators, and is responsible for establishing diplomatic relations with the inhabited moons and the inner planets."

"Is there anything you've learned from him that might help us in this particular situation?"

"Only that the shroud fits right in with the teacher-student emphasis of their whole culture. They don't want to *punish* us into accepting what they want. They want to teach us that, ultimately, Tarsalan immigration to Earth is the only logical and acceptable proposition. It's a known fact that Tarsalans have two brains. Many tests have been performed on them, in particular the Cameron Chess Study, and in terms of intelligence quotient it's been shown that they far outstrip even the most brilliant human being. They've come to the Earth with the notion that they can teach us quite a lot because they're more advanced than we are."

"I find that presumptuous as hell," said Sidower.

"Nonetheless, the teacher-student aspect of their culture, developed over a million years, is hardwired into the way they think about everything. Kafis has a phrase he uses sometimes: Instruction through discipline. They have an instrument on their home planet. It's called a cinerthax. On Earth we'd consider it an instrument of torture. Tarsalan students purposely tie themselves to the cinerthax while they study, and the cinerthax twists and turns their bodies in the most painful ways. It doesn't injure them. But it certainly motivates them to learn. That's their way. And that is, I think, one of the guiding principles behind their decision to mount this shroud around the Earth."

The president stared at his desk blotter, thinking. "What about the shroud itself, Neil? If we get rid of it, then the pressure's off, and we can turn the whole thing around."

Neil didn't hesitate. He never hesitated, always showing everybody, especially the president, that he belonged in the Oval Office. "If we take an aggressive scientific approach to the shroud, I think we can destroy it in as little as two weeks." Neil looked around, gauging reaction to this can-do proclamation—and saw hope. Now it was time to cash in. "But Mr. President, I'm going to need resources."

"Neil, you can have whatever you want. Make a list."

"For starters, I need a sizable sample of the shroud. We have to get a *piece* of it into the lab. We have to see what it is, and analyze it on a molecular level. Bob and I have talked about it, and we've decided that this is the way to go. You don't know what something is until you've looked at it under a microscope. I'm sure that once we examine it microscopically and analyze it in a number of different ways, we'll see that it's an extremely simple compound. I believe the Tarsalans are going to have to do things on the cheap because they don't have the resources to do things otherwise. And that means simple. Which means there should be an equally simple solution as well, perhaps a chemical one, something that will break the bonds that hold the shroud together. But as I say, in order to arrive at *any* solution, I need samples. And substantial samples."

"Any ideas on how we're going to get these samples?" asked the president.

"We get our friends at the National Center for Atmospheric Research involved. We ask them to loan us three of their HIAPER aircraft."

Everyone paused.

"And what exactly is a HIAPER aircraft?" asked Julia Petrov.

"HIAPER is an acronym." Yes, he had it all at his fingertips. Six hours between Trunk Bay and the White House, and he was formidably prepared. "It stands for High-Performance Instrumented Airborne Platform for Environmental Research. They're great little jets with suborbital capability, the best of their kind in the world. We usually use them for tracking pollution plumes, or collecting data from the tops of storms, or monitoring the lower edges of the stratosphere. They can attain altitudes most research aircraft can't—even spend brief periods in space—which makes them ideal for reaching the shroud. They're easily equipped with the kinds of scoops and intakes necessary for gathering our sample. They fly out of Colorado, and I think it would be a good idea to have them fly with military cover. Joe, what's the Air Force base in Colorado?"

Sidower squinted as he thought about it. "That would be Peterson," said the secretary of defense. "And come to think of it, Peterson's also home to the First Space Wing, so if the HIAPERs need any space support, they've got it."

"Good. Mr. President, I suggest we get our samples first, before you mount any definitive military action. Let's get that stuff into the lab and analyze it. Once we have samples safely returned to Earth, you can launch whatever strikes are necessary."

The president nodded. "Sounds like a plan." He turned to Sidower. "And Joe, I'm glad we can get Colorado in on this. These Western Secessionist states—this is just the kind of thing they'll capitalize on. And it worries me because if things get really bad . . . they've got a real breakaway mentality these past few years, and considering they house some of our largest food-supply depots—anyway, I'm sure you get my drift."

"We'll try to make the bastards feel as if they're helping."

Julia Petrov spoke up. "I should point out that we've received a communications drop from the Moon. It parachuted through the shroud without detection, and the Navy recovered it a thousand miles north of Easter Island yesterday. The mayor's office in Nectaris says the Moon is mounting its own scientific effort to neutralize the shroud."

Neil felt some alarm. "The Moon?" he said. "Why's the Moon getting involved? All they've got up there are gambling casinos, strip joints, and cannabis bars."

The vice president interjected, "They have some top interplanetary-spacecraft design engineers."

"Yes, but . . . we don't want them screwing up our own operations. I'm sure their interference is going to be misguided, to say the least. They don't have nearly the same expertise we do. Nor do they have the resources we have." Neil turned to Julia Petrov. "Any idea who's heading the project?"

"Your brother, as a matter of fact."

Neil felt his face warming, and was momentarily disconcerted by this odd juxtaposition; poor old Gerry, as a matter of fact, being spoken about in the Oval Office.

"My brother?" He shook his head in disbelief. "With all due respect to my brother . . ." His usual tact seemed to desert him. "They can't let Gerry take charge up there. I love him dearly, and he's brilliant in his own way, but he has an uncanny knack for making wrong decisions, and for taking the wildest kind of risks. Mr. President, you have to get the State Department to talk to this mayor in Nectaris and tell him . . . tell him . . ." He raised his palms in consternation. "I urge you to have a midlevel diplomat, or even a senior diplomat, send a drop to this mayor in Nectaris and tell him to . . . to stand down."

The president glanced around at his team, hesitant to give an immediate answer.

It was Chief of Staff Gregory who finally spoke. "But Neil, we can't dictate to the Moon. They have their own sovereignty up there now. And don't we need all the help we can get?" The chief of staff gestured out the windows behind the president's desk. "Look at that thing. All we have left is a bit of open sky far to the east. Don't you think we could use the Moon's help?"

"Yes, but the Moon *can't* help us," said Neil, now

exasperated with the thought of his brother balling up the whole effort. "They have no scientific expertise. Mr. President, if you want, I'll sign a recommendation against their interference, and we can send it to them in the next drop. Who knows? They just might end up provoking the Tarsalans. For the sake of their own safety—and ours—we should strongly advise Nectaris and the other CLC communities to butt out. Otherwise I can't guarantee the success of this thing."

6

Glenda's part-time shift ended at one.

She went out to the parking lot and asked her car to take her to the Stedman's at Rock Quarry Road and Tarboro Street, on the outskirts of Raleigh.

She saw only a few other cars on the highway. For the most part driverless transport trucks plied the route, their lights piercing the green gloom. She looked up at the sky as her car went on its way. Now, at midday, the verdurous murk was brighter, but still . . . still *unnatural*, not as dark as night, but darker than the darkest storm clouds. What worried her was the trend. It was getting darker every day. How long before it was completely dark?

She got to Stedman's and saw that hundreds of cars crowded the parking lot. The big lot lights were on, burning like blue sulfur and, in contrast, the sky looked black. She reluctantly shifted to the driver's seat and took manual control of the vehicle.

She had to scout fifteen minutes before she finally found a parking spot on a residential street five blocks away. She got out of her car. Not the best neighborhood. Houses were fifty years old, made of preformed Duratex. Most of the Duratex had minute cracks in it. Weeds grew waist-high in some front yards.

She finally reached the Stedman's parking lot. Not only was it crowded with cars, but with people as well.

Glenda walked to the shopping cart corral and discovered that all the shopping carts were gone. She looked around and saw an elderly couple unloading groceries into the back of their car.

She walked over. "Can I take your cart when you're through?"

The lady looked at her in sympathy. "We had to do the same thing. It's like dollar days."

Once the couple was through unloading, Glenda pushed the cart to the store, only to discover that there was a long lineup to get in. People waited with expressions of grumpy impatience on their faces. She peered to the front, where a pair of armed security guards regulated the flow. She looked in through the big front windows and saw that the lines to all the cashiers were backed up. She sighed. This was going to take forever.

She had to wait forty-five minutes before the security guards finally waved her through.

Inside the store, she immediately sensed that this wasn't a regular grocery crowd. There was an undercurrent of desperation, even fear.

To maneuver up and down the aisles, she had to wait a minute or two for other people to pass. The shelves were all but empty. Especially of canned goods. She got the last two-kilogram bag of rice. Also a nineteen-ounce can of stewed prunes. And some cat food, even though they didn't have a cat, but if worse came to worst . . .

She reached the bottled-water section but there wasn't any bottled water left. At the meat counter she got some pig's feet and spiced pork chops, the only things remaining. As for fruit and vegetables, she obtained the last bag of russet apples, two bundles of leeks, a turnip, some garlic, and three onions that were starting to sprout. She wanted cheese because cheese was protein, but there wasn't any left. She wanted juice because it had vitamins, but the cooler was empty. From the dairy section, she managed to get a jug of soy milk that was leaking. She now felt plugged in to the current of desperation and fear. She wouldn't have been surprised if the crowd rioted.

She approached a stocking unit and asked the machine when they were going to get more cheese.

"Current delivery date undetermined, pending emergency federal legislation, re: FEMA relief contingencies."

She grabbed a bag of sugar. A box of salt. Someone had spilled a package of spaghetti all over the floor. She picked up as many strands as she could and stuffed them into a loose plastic bag. She mentally tallied the groceries and knew she had at least a hundred dollars' worth. Not the two hundred dollars she had hoped for, but maybe it would be better to hold onto the remaining money for emergency backup. Who knew what was going to happen in the next week or two?

She struggled to the drugstore section of Stedman's.

As she waited to get Hanna's prescription filled, hundreds of nervous thoughts rustled through her mind. *Live a day at a time,* she kept telling herself. By tomorrow this whole thing could be over. Tomorrow was Saturday. In the bright sunshine, she and her kids would hike to Jordan Lake and have a picnic, and the Tarsalans would compromise, and so would President Bayard, and maybe they might have a few Tarsalans living in Old Hill, and wouldn't that be fun and interesting for the kids, having aliens living in the neighborhood? So everything would be all right, and she would live a day at a time, like her mother always told her to.

Only she couldn't stop thinking about how all the plants were going to die. What happened when photosynthesis stopped worldwide? What happened when every tree, flower, and blade of grass croaked?

She finally got Hanna's medicine, enough to last her daughter a month, went to a Customer-Assisted Checkout Line, and waited again. That's when she heard people yelling at the front. Then the smashing of glass. Then gunshots.

She dropped to the ground. So did everybody around her. But then other people came running down the aisle. And these other people were just normal, everyday Raleigh citizens, yet they had wild looks in their eyes and guns in their hands, and two of them came up to her grocery cart and emptied its contents into garbage bags.

"Hey! That's my stuff!"

"Lady, it's every man for himself."

They took everything.

But as they ran away, a hole developed in their bag.

Prunes. Salt. Pork chops. They were hers, but the people in front of her snatched them up. More gunshots. Some screaming. And sirens outside.

At least she still had Hanna's drugs—and that's what she had really come for anyway.

Glenda got home halfway through the president's speech—she didn't tell the kids about the looting because she didn't want to upset them—and caught bits and pieces of it as she got supper started in the kitchen.

"The United States and its allies view the shroud as a blatant act of aggression," Bayard was saying. "Despite our repeated attempts to open high-level diplomatic channels with the Tarsalan delegation to protest the shroud, all such attempts have failed. The Tarsalans say through their junior staff that until their immigration demands are met the shroud will remain in place. A lot of you have come to the conclusion that, should the shroud block out the light of the sun, it might have a direct and drastic effect, in the short term, on food supply, in particular on our crops next year. This is an unreasonable fear, and I can assure the American people that we have the situation well in hand. In spite of this, some of our citizens feel they must resort to civil disorder."

Glenda listened more closely.

"We've already seen numerous instances of looting. Let me assure you, my fellow Americans, and especially those of you who feel you must participate in this unlawfulness, there's absolutely no call for criminal activity. I warn you now—looters will be dealt with harshly." He raised his hands in a calming manner. "I can only say this to people who feel they must loot—everyone will be fed. Our response to this emergency has been quick and appropriate. What have we done? For starters, I've asked state governors to mobilize and make ready their various relief agencies. I've ordered my chief administrators at FEMA to study the feasibility of implementing contingency rationing plans on a nationwide basis, and have empowered the military to take control of and administer the commercial food-distribution system when and if it is deemed necessary. I've asked the National Science Foundation to make a full and complete study of the shroud. If we can dismantle the shroud in any reasonable time frame, my experts in the Department of Agriculture believe we'll still have our crops next year, and the food pressure will be off. So while we might have to tighten our belts in the short term, I believe in the long term we don't face any real, serious food shortage. I urge calm, and vow to you that your government, and governments all over the world, are working hard to solve this problem. I urge civic responsibility. I urge you to support your government—and your neighbor—any way you can."

Bayard gripped both sides of the lectern, and a conciliatory smile came to his face.

"And I especially appeal to those of you who are Secessionist Movement supporters, and I know there are a good many of you. Now is not the time to think of splitting up the country. Now is the time to show solidarity in the face of what is turning into a considerable national emergency. I know that in at least three states, Secessionist referendums have been proposed for the November election period. I would ask that supporters of these referendums put any and all such campaigns on hold for the time being. I would ask that we pull together and beat this thing as fellow countrymen. The color of your vote doesn't matter. Red or blue, we all have to stand together."

He let go of the lectern and squared his shoulders.

"In the meantime, the toughest decision your president faces is how to respond to this blatant act of aggression by the Tarsalans. Right from the start, we knew they were asking for immigration rights. They told us that they were a peaceful people and that they desired to conduct senior negotiations with us in regard to the possibility of immigration. This was reasonable. It was practical. And it promised mutual betterment to both our peoples. We in the United States have always understood immigration. We all come from immigrant ancestry. But we also understand that an immigration policy must be managed. It has to be based on common sense and sustainability. We know that to flood our shores with an uncontrolled influx of immigrants would not only be detrimental to the existing inhabitants, but also to the immigrants themselves. So we offered controlled immigration to selected islands in the South Pacific, with strict quotas on reproduction. That's when we learned their demands were unreasonable. They requested unlimited immigration anywhere in the world, with the right to decide their own birth policies. In the last nine years there have been a series of offers and counteroffers, and still the two sides remain significantly polarized. Now the Tarsalans have withdrawn from negotiations, and have mounted this shroud around the Earth. They've given us an ultimatum. Let me make this clear. The United States won't tolerate ultimatums, and will never give in to blackmail.

"And so I've had to make the toughest decision of my presidency. At twelve-thirty p.m., Eastern Daylight Time, today, I put the U.S. military on highest alert. I've sent a final message to the Tarsalans. This message is a counterultimatum. Dismantle the shroud within forty-eight hours or the United States and its allies will bring to bear against the Tarsalan mothership and its other deployed craft the full might of the world's military forces. So far the Tarsalans haven't responded. But I think this message has sent to them a firm comprehension of just where we stand. The United States and its allies will not be dictated to. And we will not have our sovereignty challenged. And if they don't dismantle the shroud, war shall and will be declared."

By this time Glenda was gripping the edge of the dining room table with white-knuckled hands. Her mouth had gone dry and her palms were moist. Wasn't it bad enough that they should have the shroud around the

Earth? Wouldn't it make things far worse to go to war with the Tarsalans? Yet she could see the president's point. They couldn't let the Tarsalans push them around.

"Mom, are the Tarsalans going to bomb us?" asked Jake.

"I don't know, sweetie."

"They probably won't bomb here," said Hanna. "Old Hill is the most boring place in the world."

"I don't see why we don't let them live anywhere they want," said Jake. "It's a free country. I wouldn't mind having one for a neighbor. I've only ever met Kafis at Uncle Neil's, and I'd like to meet a few more. I don't know why the president doesn't put out the welcome mat."

"Because they overbreed, stupid. They have four babies at a time."

"Hanna, don't call your brother stupid. And we don't know that they would overbreed. Yes, it's true they have four babies at a time, but everything I've read says they've really embraced birth control."

"But Mom," said Hanna, "they can tell us anything they want about what they do back on their homeworld, and we have no way of checking it out. I talked to Uncle Neil about it last Christmas. He says we can't verify anything about the way they do things on their homeworld, and that if we open the door to them, we could find ourselves in real trouble."

Glenda looked out the window at the shroud. "I think we're in real trouble already."

7

Gerry met with Mayor Hulke, Ian Hamilton, Dr. Luke Langstrom, and a fourth man, Mitchell Bennett, the appointed representative of AviOrbit, a day later. Mitch was a man roughly his own age, but he wore a suit. Gerry had his baggy old corduroys on. Mitch's hair was short, a tawny red shaved as closely as a layer of felt. Gerry became conscious of his own straying, long hair. Mitch maneuvered with feminine grace through the Moon's weak gravity while Gerry lumbered about like an out-of-control giant.

Malcolm Hulke held the document of contention in his hands, downloaded from Earth's latest drop. His jaw tightened and he scratched behind his ear, where Gerry saw an angry red patch of psoriasis. The mayor finished scanning the document a third time, then glanced at Gerry, puzzled.

"I don't understand why they would send this to Avi-Orbit's office, not mine."

"Neil's trying to undercut your authority," said Gerry. "It's his way of playing politics."

"Why doesn't he want our help? You'd think we could offer a unique perspective up here on the Moon. And it's not beyond the realm of possibility they just might fail. Wouldn't they want us as backup?"

"Considering my brother has the full resources of the United States at his disposal," said Gerry, "odds are he's going to come up with something sooner rather than later."

"And if he doesn't?" said Hulke. "What if he tries one thing, then another, then another, and none of them work? Why doesn't he want our help?" Hulke was obviously hurt by Neil's signed recommendation. "This whole section here—about working at cross-purposes— do you think he has a point? And Gerry, this bit about your qualifications. Or lack of them, as he puts it. That's not nice. Have you always had this . . . this *thing* with him? How can he say you have no qualifications?"

"I'm sure Dr. Thorndike is an excellent judge of qualifications," said Langstrom. "And I'm sure he knows his brother better than any of us."

Gerry glanced at the Martian sourly. "Neil's always been nervous about the way I do things."

"One thing you ought to know about Neil," said Ian. "He likes to steal the show. I say we don't even answer this. We've got our own sovereignty up here. It's not as if they own the shroud. If we go along with this ridiculous request to . . . to stand down, we might blow our own chances of getting rid of the thing. Why don't we just say that the Moon is Plan B? In my experience, Plan B is the one that always works." He took off his hat, a rawhide outdoorsman's hat, smoothed his shoulder-length hair, and bunched his lips, looking ready to spit. "I've known Neil and Gerry since . . . since a long time ago. We grew up in suburban Illinois together. At first I was best friends with Neil. I admired the hell out of the guy. He got good grades, and when it came time for college, he was accepted into the best of them on a full scholarship. But he's overconfident, and that's going to be his downfall. Then you take a guy like Gerry. He hasn't had the most stunning career. And he's flat broke most of the time. But Gerry looks at something, and he sees things other people don't. Gerry's got more patience in his baby finger than Neil has in his whole body. Have you ever had some kind of problem, and no matter how hard you puzzle on it, you can't come up with an answer? So you put it aside at the end of the day, then go to bed, and right when you're falling asleep you find a solution? That's the way Gerry's mind works all the time. Gerry is Plan B, and I'm telling you, Plan B is the one that's going to work."

"I don't think we should sell Dr. Thorndike short so quickly," said Langstrom. "He's won the Nobel Prize, after all. And, no offense, Gerry, you haven't."

"Prizes don't mean a thing," said Ian.

"They're a way of recognizing excellent work," said Dr. Langstrom.

"Not when it comes to Neil and Gerry."

"I think your bias is showing, Mr. Hamilton," said Langstrom.

"Let me give you an example," said Ian, leaning across the table toward the elderly Martian. "When we were kids, the three of us got stranded in Chicago. Neil immediately came up with a plan to panhandle money so we could buy bus tickets home. He took charge of the operation and we had the money in no time. But then, at the last minute, he got us on the wrong bus. I remember what he was like that day. He was *so* confident. But then he screwed up. We traveled all the way to the other end of Chicago before we figured out what he'd done. Who comes to the rescue? Gerry. He logs on to his laptop and determines we can connect with a southbound train if we change buses at a transfer point a few blocks ahead. We didn't even have to pay an extra fare. Plan B. Gerry rarely overlooks anything."

"Considering Neil Thorndike has a position as a special advisor to the president," said Langstrom, "I doubt he overlooks much either."

"Yes, but this document we have," said Ian, tapping the mayor's waferscreen. "It's nothing but Neil trying to take over like he always does. He's not even willing to consider that the Moon might have something to offer. I say we decide against him."

"Getting stranded in Chicago and having to raise bus money thirty years ago is one thing, but this is quite another. I should think Dr. Thorndike's come a long way since then."

The group fell silent. Gerry watched the mayor glance

at the waferscreen a fourth time. Hulke's face again took on an expression of puzzlement. He looked up from the document and inspected Gerry the way he might an unpredictable dog. What was Gerry going to do next? Was he going to roll over? Was he going to play dead? Was he going to shake a paw?

"Gerry," said the mayor, "the decision's yours. You're the head of this thing. If you think we should pull out . . . I mean, if you think you and your brother will be working at . . . *cross-purposes* . . ."

"I can understand some of what he's saying. They might use an agent against the shroud, but then we might go ahead and use a different agent, and the two might cancel out, or combine in some unexpected and dangerous way. But until we know exactly where Neil's research is going—until the NSF communicates that to us— I think it would be foolhardy to stand down. As for this thing about my qualifications . . . I haven't been a complete failure. I've had some small successes in oceanic research. I'm recognized as North Carolina's number-one hydrographer. And I've always believed in myself as a scientist." He motioned at the waferscreen. "No matter what anybody else says."

"If that's your decision," said the mayor, his brow rising.

"I just don't think we should stop when all we've got is a bunch of ifs, maybes, and mights. I believe we should go ahead and see what we can find out about this damn thing. At least for the next little while."

The way to go was small. Gerry knew no other way. But as he rode the sky elevator to AviOrbit's launch platform, he couldn't help noting the misgivings on the mayor's face. Mitchell Bennett, of AviOrbit, kept staring down at the Moon—which was now forty miles below— as if he, too, were embarrassed by the *Smallmouth*. Gerry inspected the probe one more time, and now he also had his doubts.

About three times the size of a bleach bottle, and roughly the same shape, its outer shell was matte black and composed of the most advanced stealth alloy Avi-Orbit had in stock. Airfoils jutted on either side. The instrument module, something he was extremely proud of, rode at the front, a payload of standard and advanced electronics that he'd ingeniously linked to some nifty software Mitch had helped him develop. Proton microthrusters—really braking thrusters from bigger craft—provided the primary means of propulsion and navigation. At the back . . . well . . . nothing more than a crude nuclear bomb, the thrust device for when the *Smallmouth* had to escape Earth's gravity well and return to the Moon.

"Why did you call it *Smallmouth*?" asked the mayor. "Other than the fact that it has a small mouth. I mean, no complaints. I like weird names, but I . . ." The mayor trailed off, all his doubt implied.

"In a lot of ways, the probe is going to act like a smallmouth bass," said Gerry, now feeling self-conscious about the name. "It's going to putter about like a smallmouth bass in a bunch of weeds, conduct its experiments, and then come back with its sample. I fish in Jordan Lake for bass, that's why."

"It's just that . . . I don't know . . . it doesn't seem like much of a spacecraft." The mayor turned to Mitch. "Mitch, maybe we should have tried something bigger."

"Trust me, it's going to work," said Gerry. "You know what I like about it? It's simple. It's cheap. And I think Mitch and his team did a great job."

"I hope it comes back," said Mitch, giving the probe a reluctant glance.

"The NSF already has their sample," said Hulke. "We got the drop this morning. They still want us to butt out."

"There's no harm in us taking our own look," said Gerry. "No one's going to notice the *Smallmouth*. Especially not the Tarsalans."

"Your brother sent three special atmospheric aircraft with Air Force cover. Apparently there were some casualties, but they didn't say how many."

Gerry turned his attention to the *Smallmouth*. "At least no one's going to get hurt if this probe goes down."

The sky elevator continued to rise until it was fifty miles above the lunar surface. At this altitude, Gerry saw the curve of the Moon, and the vast panorama of the moonscape below. The terminator cut a dark line over the surface, but beyond it craters, ejecta patterns, mountains, and plains came into sharp relief, lit by the sun.

The sky elevator at last came to the launch platform, and the doors opened on a large hangar area with a huge polycarbonate pressure door at the far end. Through this pressure door Gerry saw stars in the blackest sky he had ever seen. Was this black sky what the shroud looked like from Earth? he wondered. Had the green gotten so dark it was now black?

Technicians took charge of the *Smallmouth*, wheeling it away.

Gerry, the mayor, and Mitch found their way to the observation tower, where they saw the entire launch facility spread out below. Several interplanetary craft lay floating in orbit, tethered to workbays that were themselves linked to the platform by flexible pneumatic lifts. The launch facility, shaped like a kidney, measured two square miles, and had a number of hydralike extensions at the ends—tethers that were currently empty. The sun hit the facility with bristling light, but the yellow-tinted visor of Gerry's pressure suit blunted its brightness. He felt queasy because of the weightlessness, but not overtly so. Immediately below him he saw the small-components launch area. It was here that the *Smallmouth* would begin its voyage.

The technical crew wheeled the probe along magnetic rails to Platform 5. Once there, they unlatched the *Smallmouth* from its dolly and connected it to release hooks. They backed the dolly away and disappeared into a nearby hangar.

The countdown began, and when it was finished the probe puttered slowly upward, traveling at no more than a few miles per hour, at last disappearing out of sight as it angled into the transit orbit that would take it to Earth.

Gerry glanced at Hulke. "We have liftoff."

Hulke sighed. "In a manner of speaking."

PART TWO

8

Neil met with the president, the national security advisor, and the secretary of defense at Camp David. As Neil entered the meeting room, he saw that Tony Bayard was giving him a good looking-over, as if the president expected nothing but the best news from him. National Security Advisor Julia Petrov's lack of sleep was painfully apparent in her haggard appearance. Secretary of Defense Joe Sidower sat at the end of the table, his bald head bowed as he went over some waferscreen notes. The White House photographer took stills.

Neil's previous mood of unshakable optimism had now turned to one of cautious pragmatisim. He couldn't help thinking of the Cameron Chess Study, and how even the smartest human beings hadn't yet beaten a Tarsalan at chess.

The president sat, and Neil followed suit. Julia Petrov took her seat as well. One of the kitchen staff came around and poured coffee. A plate of Danishes sat in the middle of the table. The food-distribution network was breaking down day by day, its decline driven relentlessly by the growing certainty that there would be no crops next year, which in turn engendered mass hoarding, and people were already going hungry. Yet this morning he was having coffee and Danishes with the president.

"Neil," said the president, breaking into his thoughts. "Can you give us an update? Your original two-week deadline has come and gone, so I hope the news is good.

Your preoccupation . . . is making me . . ." The president trailed off.

Neil prided himself on always giving it straight to the president. Yet he began tentatively, and without his usual bravado. "My team and I . . . we've had some time to study the retrieved shroud samples, more than my original two weeks, yes, and the initial results show that the shroud is made primarily of plant material. On a chromosomal level—and I don't want to get too technical here—it resembles some of the more common forms of phytoplankton we have in our oceans. The shroud is a living, breathing, growing entity, Mr. President, and it knows how to heal itself."

The president paused to consider.

"If it's a living thing," said Sidower, "it can be killed."

Neil grinned at this characteristically hawkish response from Sidower. "One would think so. In fact, I had some of the top herbicide specialists in the country come to the lab in Miami to take a look at the specimen. We sat around and had a real bull session about the whole problem."

"And what did you come up with?" asked the president.

"Well, we hypothesized that we could use some commercially formulated herbicides because, structurally, the shroud is similar to many of the plant and weed varieties that these products are active against. But as we mapped out the specimen's chromosome, we began to see that some of its DNA sequencing differs from the more common forms of phytoplankton. It was a tough genome, but we finally got it all mapped out."

"And how, exactly, does it differ?" asked Julia.

Neil glanced at the national security advisor. "Some of the sequencing in the specimen comes directly from Tarsalan genetic makeup itself."

This, he knew, was the showstopper.

The president's eyes went wide. "You mean they've stirred some of their own genome into the mix?"

Neil raised his palms, as if he were as surprised as the president. "Their splicing techniques are far more . . .

advanced than ours." He sat back and consulted his waferscreen. "You might remember I wrote a paper on a subset of Tarsalan genes, ones with transmutational properties. These are the ones we're finding in our samples."

Sidower made a face as he glanced at the president, not looking too pleased about the growing complexity of the threat.

"If you could give us the essentials," said the president.

Right. Bayard liked the simplified version. But he wasn't sure he could simplify something that was so complicated. "Let me go into lecture mode here. The Tarsalans have a subset of genes in their makeup, and this subset of genes can mutate certain of their physical characteristics, depending on environmental circumstances. This is what's made the Tarsalans so . . . so adaptable, and it's why they've been able to live on so many different planets throughout the galaxy." He squinted as he tried to demystify the whole concept. "The simplest analogy would be the jackrabbit. It turns white in winter. Not that the mechanism in the Tarsalan is in any way the same, but it gives you an idea of what I'm getting at. Chameleon lizards turn from brown to green and back again. There's a transmutational component."

"So they've put some of themselves into the shroud," said Sidower. "Big deal. How does it affect our odds of defeating the goddamn thing?"

He glanced at the secretary of defense, who was cantankerous for obvious good reason.

"Eventually we *will* defeat it." He meant it to be a bold Neil Thorndike proclamation, but it came out sounding weak. "It's just that I think it will take a little more time than I originally thought. And that's because the shroud—and, by the way, I prefer to call it the phytosphere now, because that's what it is, a sphere made out of plant material." He felt his forehead moistening. "Anyway, the phytosphere seems to adapt to whatever we throw at it, most probably because of this subset of transmutational genes. Also, we're finding it hard to penetrate the individual planktons themselves because the Tarsalans have spliced resistant traits of the Martian paleo-organism, Aresphyta, into the mix, and this has created a kind of impenetrable shell around each individual organism. To give you a bit of history—"

"We get the picture, Neil," said Sidower. "This shell more or less acts as armor."

"Yes."

"And there's no way we can penetrate this armor with conventional herbicides?" asked the president.

"No. I've got one team working on finding a herbicide that will effectively destroy the phytoplankton component, another working on destroying the shell, or carapace if you will, and a third studying the Tarsalan genetic component. The main thrust right now is the carapace. We've got to find a way to break the carapace. Once we've done that, we can concentrate on the organism itself."

"Do you have any ideas about the carapace?" asked the president.

Neil squared his shoulders, forcing his confidence. "We've tried acids and other corrosive agents, but so far nothing has worked. We have to devise something that can compete against the carapace, in the Darwinian sense, and come up the winner every time. We need something that's adaptable and can shift strategies, depending on the situation. I believe the best answer is to develop some kind of omniphage, an organism that can eat through the carapace, and won't stop eating. If we develop an omniphage capable of penetrating the carapace, we can then use the same macrogen as a delivery module to carry a lethal dose of whatever toxic agent we finally develop to kill the xenophyta—that's what I'm calling the individual organisms."

"And is it possible to develop such a . . . hell, what do you call it? An omniphage?" asked the secretary.

"I have a team of geneticists working on the problem right now."

"So when you say it should be designed to carry a

lethal dose . . ." The president trailed off, trying to figure it all out.

"It would essentially be a workhorse macrogen engineered to penetrate the carapace and administer the necessary fatal agent. As for the fatal agent itself, my team is working on a hydrogen sulfide compound that's going to fool the xenophyta into thinking it's getting its usual supply of carbon dioxide when in actual fact—"

"But first we have to get this . . . this omniphage going, right?" said Sidower.

"Yes."

"And do we have all the best experts on board to help us build this omniphage?"

"In the case of the Aresphyta, all the best experts would be Martian."

"Wonderful. Let's send a drop to Mars right away."

Neil nodded, even as his confidence once again ebbed. "I've been having some of my people track these experts down. And they tell me that the top expert of all, Dr. Luke Langstrom, is currently on the Moon. As a matter of fact, he's part of my brother's team."

Neil couldn't help being galled by this. After advising strongly against his brother's involvement, and getting Gerry's flat refusal in a recent drop, his brother now held a trump. He glanced around at the other three, and knew they understood the implications. He had alienated all those working on the Moon effort, and now it was going to play against them. Neil couldn't help feeling like an idiot. And he didn't like feeling like an idiot. Especially in front of the president.

The president turned to the national security advisor. "Send a priority drop to the Moon. Do whatever it takes, but get this Luke Langstrom on board."

9

Gerry left the Nectaris Buena Vista after supper and strolled down Sagittarius Way, still trying to come to grips with all the wild and conflicting information the *Smallmouth* had brought back from the shroud. He looked at the vaulting underground dome of Nectaris, ten miles across and two miles high, most of it laminated rock, but with huge polycarbonate windows here and there. He headed downtown.

At this time of the day, the lighting technicians, probably zonked out on premium-grade bud, were having fun with their spots, floods, and lasers, choosing, for the most part, a mood indigo. The sky was a preternatural violet, intense in its dark luminosity, the epitome of dusk, peppered here and there with red stars. Food vendors were conspicuously absent, and as he reached Pisces Road, he realized that even the prostitutes weren't around, that all the curtains to the brothels were closed, and that despite the carnival indigo of the evening sky, there weren't many people about at all, as if the somber situation on Earth had cast its pall over the gay old Moon.

Yet a few cafés were open, and he saw couples sitting at tables drinking espresso and eating pastries. He remembered the old days, when he and Glenda had lived in the center of Raleigh, before the kids had been born; how they would go to cafés, just like these young people, and believe for a while that life had all the magic of an indigo sky with red stars.

He strolled down Pisces Road toward Möbius Lake.

Would he ever make sense of all the bizarre information from the *Smallmouth*?

Have a tough problem to solve? Go to the ocean and look at it for an hour. But all he had now was this artificial lake, which was really the town's main water recycler and Ossimax dispenser. He hoped Neil was making progress on Earth. He hoped that tomorrow he would wake up and look at Earth, and that the shroud would be gone. In the meantime, he had a lot to think about. He took a deep breath and focused his concentration.

He was just reaching Möbius Lake when Ian Hamilton came out of the nearby Nickel and Dime Cannabis Bar and Roti Shop; he could never go far in this city without running into Ian, it seemed.

"We were just talking about you," said his old friend.

"Who?"

"Me and the girls. And Malcolm. And Luke."

"I'm just out for a walk."

"Why don't you come inside?"

"As long as you know I don't smoke anymore. I never really did."

"Then have a coffee. It's on me."

He followed Ian into the Nickel and Dime.

Looking around, he saw that it was a cozy little place, all the furniture made of artificial wood, the Velcro trails decorated with designs of colorful thread, a lot of thick macramé tapestries on the walls, and aquariums filled with genetically enhanced Siamese fighting fish with fins and tails so long and so colorful he could easily understand why they were the chief objets d'art in this stoner bar. The fish bioluminesced, turning on and off like Christmas lights.

He and Ian went to a table at the back, really more a low platform surrounded by cushions, and there he found the mayor and Dr. Luke Langstrom, their eyes glazed, their mood placid, their bent philosophical. The air was sweet with the smell of hashish, and he had a hard time getting used to it because it was still illegal in North Carolina. The girls. He had forgotten their names. Only that Ian had been dragging them around for a

while. Twins? He wasn't sure. They looked much alike.
Pretty. Small. Fine-boned. Showgirls, but showgirls of
the Moon variety, born here, raised here, like elfin
queens in their delicacy, as tranquil and as still as a day
in the Mare Serenitatis.

"You remember Gwen and Stephanie?" asked Ian.

He waved. "Hi."

"Here's the man of the hour," said the mayor. "Have
a seat."

He maneuvered awkwardly—still wasn't used to Moon
gravity—and sat on one of the large, embroidered pil-
lows. He glanced at Luke Langstrom, who was grinning
with ruby red eyes over a bowl of Moroccan. Ian took
a seat beside him. The mayor had half his mind on some
kind of 3-D game involving holographic leopards and
parrots. So. Here it was. The perfect cross-section of the
lunar effort to destroy the shroud. His committee on all
things serious. Yes, why not? Neil had the president and
the president's closest advisors. It made perfect sense
that he should have potheads and showgirls.

"So you're him?" asked Stephanie.

And they would all speak cryptically, and answer cryptically, and no one would understand anybody else, but
somehow, through a series of non sequiturs and red her-
rings, they would get the job done. "Who?"

"The man who's going to save the world."

"I'm going to try, sweetie," he said, the sweetie coming reflexively because he always called Hanna sweetie.

"We don't talk to many Earthmen," said Gwen. "You
move funny."

"I know."

"I could teach you to walk right," said Stephanie.

He looked at Stephanie closely. She had pink hair,
and a makeup atomizer had misted her face blue. She
had plucked eyebrows, now lined with twinkling blue
sequins. She had painted her lips a shade of plum.

Before he could accept Stephanie's offer, Dr. Langstrom said, "I got the attachment you sent. The microscopic photographs were spectacular." Langstrom
glanced at Stephanie with marked disapproval, then

turned back to Gerry. "They brought to mind some of the Martian fossils I've researched. I would like to look at the samples firsthand, if you don't mind."

Gerry studied Langstrom. "Be my guest. What do you make of the photographs?"

"Rather a stark comparison between the ones taken in the lab and the ones taken in the shroud itself, isn't there? Microscopic section photographs right inside the foul thing. How did you arrive at such a technique?"

Gerry shrugged. "You've got to study things in their natural habitat, Luke. Studying it in the lab is only going to lead to a lot of miscues."

Langstrom's amused intolerance softened. He looked as if he had been given a fascinating new toy. "Interesting organism."

"You got my e-mail about the carapace?"

Langstrom's eyes narrowed. "Reminds me of the carapace of Aresphyta C-4721. If only Nectaris had a DNA sequencer." The Martian turned to the mayor, as if he were to blame.

"Anything like that is always done on Earth," said the mayor.

"Because it would be interesting to see if the Tarsalans used Aresphyta genetic strands to construct this organism. C-4721 is of course a prehistoric organism, and I've only ever seen fossil specimens. But it's not beyond the realm of possibility that the Tarsalans could have recovered a live specimen. They've been coring the Martian ice cap for the last several years, and C-4721 mimics certain present-day Martian organisms, especially in the growth of its carapace. Grows like a tooth, you know. Impervious to ultraviolet radiation. It wouldn't surprise me at all if the Tarsalans spliced C-4721 into their phytoplankton base."

The mayor spoke up. "Gerry, no pressure, my man, but any ideas on how we might . . . like . . . do a pest-control number on the phytosphere?"

"Phytosphere? Where'd you come up with a name like that?"

"Just what the Earth guys are calling it."

Gerry's confusion, ambivalence, and puzzlement over the shroud—phytosphere—came back. "I don't know what we're going to do." Phytosphere. That would be a Neil name. "Every time I think I have an answer, I run into a roadblock." Everything was Greek to Neil. "I'm thinking herbicide—get AviOrbit to design and build some applicator satellites—but I'm not sure it would work because many kinds of phytoplankton can absorb huge amounts of herbicide with little, if any, detrimental effect." He wondered if Neil was thinking herbicides. "Going the herbicide route might be counterproductive."

"It would be more than counterproductive," said Hulke. "It would be impossible."

"Why?" said Gerry.

"Because we have no herbicide or large-scale chemical production facilities here on the Moon. We don't even use herbicides here. We're a . . . a hermetically sealed community. Everything that comes to our customs depot is meticulously screened. We don't have any weeds in any of our gardens . . . or hydroponic acreages, because the seeds for such plants have never gotten past our teams in the first place."

So even if they wanted to go the herbicide route, it was out of the question anyway? "What's the latest drop from Earth say? Phytosphere. Who thought that name up?"

The mayor glanced away, as if he were embarrassed. "That would be your brother. He's in the news, Gerry." Hulke focused on him and folded his hands. "He's made a number of announcements to the media."

Gerry nodded stoically. "And what's he got to say for himself? I mean, over and above calling the shroud the phytosphere."

Langstrom piped in with an odd kind of glee. "He's calling the individual organisms xenophyta."

Gerry regarded the Martian evenly, then turned back to the mayor. "Anything else?"

Hulke's eyes narrowed. "Nothing specific about their plans to destroy the . . . the phytosphere." As if the mayor were reluctantly giving in to Neil's nomenclaturu-ral template. "Only that they've definitively confirmed that it is in fact derived from ocean plankton, just as we have, and a few other components that they wouldn't disclose." An expression of patient aggravation came to the mayor's face. "They've devised a . . . how did they phrase it . . . a three-pronged approach to dismantling the phytosphere. These drops from Earth . . . God, they're funny." Yet the mayor looked peeved. Was he wondering why Gerry hadn't devised his own three-pronged approach? "I asked them for a full scientific report but they . . . they more or less flipped me the finger. If that's the way they're going to play it—by the way, what about . . . like, a report from you, Ger?"

Gerry shook his head, momentarily distressed by how baffling he found all the *Smallmouth*'s information. "I haven't got any reports, Malcolm. All I've got are a lot of questions. I guess in their drop they didn't say anything about the way the xenophyta behaved in the lab as opposed to the way they behaved in the actual phytosphere."

The mayor paused, and he could see it in the mayor's eyes: Hulke thought that maybe—just maybe—Dr. Gerald Thorndike, formerly of the NCSU, might have something. "Why? Is there a big difference?"

"A *huge* difference. The xenophyta . . . they embrace each other when they're in the phytosphere. They have these two little flagella on each organism—tiny whiplike appendages, like the flagella on certain phytoplankton. When they're in the phytosphere, these flagella twine around each other to form long chains, and these long chains then go on to form huge mats, which then go on to the bloom phase. Then the blooms join to form the entire phytosphere. These flagella are extremely active in the phytosphere. But you take the xenophyta out of the phytosphere and put them in the lab and the flagella grow limp. The xenophyta still congregate in colonies, but they don't bind with their flagella. So far I've yet to discover any electrical or chemical stimuli inside the xenophyta that can account for the flagella becoming paralyzed like that. They seem to need the entire phytosphere to bind, and I can't figure it out."

Outside, the sky turned purple and now had orange stars. A waiter came by with a tray of smokables but everybody had had enough.

Gerry looked around at the group. In Stephanie's eyes he saw a burgeoning idolatry. In Malcolm Hulke he saw apprehension, as if the mayor were blaming him for coming up with yet more obstacles. Ian Hamilton wasn't even paying attention anymore, and was instead focusing on Stephanie, gazing at her as if she were the most beautiful creature on the Moon.

Luke Langstrom was the only one who looked fascinated by the problem. "So do you have any theories about it?"

Gerry's brow rose. "Only that there's got to be some trigger that's turning these flagella on and off, depending on where they are."

Later, as they strolled around Lake Möbius, Stephanie took his arm.

"Maybe I can sit in at some of your sessions," she said.

"If you'd like."

"Because I've been thinking about the shroud. The phytosphere. Whatever you want to call it."

"You have?"

"An outside opinion might help. Are there any showgirls on your committee?"

"No."

"Then don't you think you should have one?"

He gave her a smile. "I think maybe we should." To make things perfectly clear, he added, "I've got my wife down there. And the more people working on the problem, the better."

She paused. "I don't know many scientists."

"Perhaps you should count yourself lucky."

"You don't seem like a scientist."

He looked away. "No. And sometimes I don't feel like one, either."

"Except I can tell you're the most brilliant man on the Moon right now."

"And how can you tell that?"

She tightened her grip on his arm. "It's just something I can tell. This way I have. Ask Ian. He knows. I can tell you have a different way of looking at things than other people."

"And is that a curse or a blessing?"

She stopped and peered at him more closely. "In your case, I think it's a blessing."

He couldn't say why, but Ian seemed to be made extremely uncomfortable by Stephanie's friendliness toward him.

A short while later, as Gerry got into a more protracted conversation with Dr. Langstrom about the xenophyta and the flagella, he watched Ian pull Stephanie aside and separate her from the rest of the group. The two lagged behind. He glanced back. Stephanie looked so small next to Ian, her Ossimaxed bones slender; an impossible creature, growing up in this weak gravity as an entirely different species of human, moving with the grace of Peter Pan in Neverland. Tonight, she wore magenta contact lenses, and she reminded him of a cute blue lab mouse. He sensed a mild distress in her, and understood that Ian was a problem for her.

Neil and Dr. Langstrom strolled to a bench, where they sat. Dr. Langstrom suggested that he rather liked "being in the thick of it" again, and Gerry at first couldn't decide whether this was an appropriate remark or not, considering Earth's peril, and formed a new notion of the Martian professor—that within his grandfatherly exterior there lurked an immense ego, and that his interest in the xenophyta and flagella wasn't necessarily about the phytosphere, but more about Dr. Luke Langstrom showing Dr. Gerald Thorndike how smart he could be.

In any case, his true concern was for Ian and Stephanie, as they seemed to be having a real row back by the lake. He couldn't help wondering if they might be

lovers, and if he had inadvertantly been the cause of
their quarrel. As the recipient of Stephanie's overt
friendliness, he had to consider the possibility that he
might have precipitated a jealous tantrum in Ian. Ian
gripped her by the arm, and she tried to pull away. But
he had a tight hold on her. When she looked up at him,
he thought she might have been angry, but instead she
looked perplexed, as if Ian's words were now puzzling
her greatly. At last he let her go. The others had drifted
on ahead. Dr. Langstrom was still talking about the phytosphere and possible ways to destroy it, none of them
sounding the least bit plausible to Gerry. Stephanie became subdued, said a few quiet words to Ian, then
turned around and walked back up Pisces Road. Ian
watched her go, then came toward Gerry.

As his old friend closed the distance, Gerry excused
himself—rather abruptly, if Dr. Langstrom's surprise was
any indication—and joined the god of good times.

"Everything all right?" he asked.

Ian looked at him for several moments, apparently
fighting to contain a strong emotion. "She's tired, that's
all. She gets moody if she has too much excitement."

10

In the third week of July, Glenda stepped out her back door into the darkness and turned on her flashlight. The beam cut through the gloom and fell in an amorphous circle on the trees at the end of the yard. Nearly half the leaves had fallen; the other half hung limply from their branches.

Her watch said five p.m., and it should have been light, but it was dark, and the darkness was doing something to her. She didn't feel like Glenda Thorndike anymore. Glenda Thorndike was always bold as brass. But now she felt . . . perpetually unsettled.

Where the hell was Leigh? She swung her flashlight toward her neighbor's house. She shook her head. Was he hiding? Dead? Or had he just gone somewhere, maybe to his folks' place?

She proceeded across the patio onto the grass. The grass smelled funky and was slippery underfoot. It had rotted, like lettuce in a fridge. She walked to the toolshed and got the spade. With the spade in one hand and the flashlight in the other, she proceeded to the rear of the lot.

The woods looked like something out of a horror movie. Her heart pulsed with fear. She was afraid of bears. They got a few down from Jordan Lake every so often. With the forest dead, would the bears be hungry and come down into Old Hill looking for something to eat? Would a hungry bear consider her fair game?

"Live a day at a time," she murmured into the dark.

She shone her flashlight at a maple tree. After three weeks without light, the wilted leaves hung like sleeping bats, their green cellulose as pliant as limp balloons, the tree giving up the ghost as it eased into sapless purgatory. One maple might not look so strange—but they were all like that.

She stopped halfway to the woods. Did she want to go in there to get the toy box? She never went into the woods at night. But of course it wasn't night. It was five o'clock in the afternoon.

She glanced at Leigh's house once more. God, this darkness. It penetrated her with horrible imaginings.

She gave up on going into the woods and, leaning the spade against the fence, walked over to Leigh's house. If she knew her neighbor was there, maybe she wouldn't be so afraid.

His car sat in the drive, hooked to its recharge cell. The blinds on his living room window were drawn and the light was on, but the light had been on like that for the past five days. She was really beginning to think something had happened to him.

She went to the front door. The console scanned her and asked if she were the owner, a guest, or a delivery person.

"It's Glenda Thorndike."

She read the screen. *Glenda Thorndike: acknowledged. Please wait.*

So Leigh was inside? "Leigh?"

She caught movement at the side of house.

Leigh emerged from the bushes. She swung her flashlight in his direction. He carried a rifle. His face was slack, as if the last several days had taken their toll on him.

"It's you," he said with obvious relief.

She lowered the flashlight. "I thought you were inside."

"You're alone?" He peered past her shoulder. "Where are the kids?"

"In the house." She motioned at his weapon. "What are you doing with a rifle?"

"Turn off the flashlight." He cast a nervous glance toward the road. The corners of his lips turned downward and he raised his chin. His eyes narrowed in suspicious perusal of the thoroughfare.

"What's wrong? Why were you at the side of the house?" She glanced out at the highway. "What are you doing?"

He continued looking at the road. "Just being cautious."

She turned off her flashlight. "Have you been going to work? Your car's always in the drive."

"I've been off for a while now. I'm going to weather this thing at home."

She gave him a hint of her own apprehension. "I just wanted to make sure you were here. I thought something might have happened to you."

He turned to her. He tried to smile but his expression crumbled, and he looked as if he were going to be physically sick.

"Leigh, what's wrong?"

"I did something stupid."

"What?"

He looked away. "I told a couple of guys at work I had a stash."

"A stash? What kind of stash?"

"Food. Water. Basic supplies." He rubbed the back of his neck. "We were just sitting around talking about the shroud . . . and how people were preparing for it. And I let it slip." He shook his head. "I'm a total idiot."

She gave him a sympathetic grin. "I'm sure they all have their own stashes."

"Glenda . . . I saw this thing coming a long time ago. I never trusted the Tarsalans. I've been stocking up for the last three months, since the minute the negotiations got rocky. I knew they were going to try something. And these guys at work—they're always so full of themselves. We were talking about the shroud . . . and I had something to brag about for a change, so I bragged." He shook his head and glanced out to the highway again. "Now I realize it was a big mistake. I keep thinking they're going to come to my house and take everything I have. I haven't slept. My whole cycle is screwed up."

He lapsed into silence.

She tried to be helpful. "Where do these guys live? Do they live far?"

"In Raleigh."

"And you think they're going to come all the way out here and raid your house?" She shook her head. "Doesn't that sound a little . . . crazy?"

"It's just this one guy, Jamie . . . the last day I worked, the way he looked at me. He knew I was taking time off. Just the way he was looking at me. Like he had plans for me. Like he was going to hook up with these other guys, Lars and Perry, and they were going to come out . . . I wouldn't put it past them, Glenda. These guys are real assholes."

"Yes, but how much of a stash do you have? All the stores are closed. Would it be worth their while?"

"I've got two fifty-gallon barrels of fresh water. I've got candles, and boxes of ammunition for my rifle. I bought a lot of dried-food dinners from a specialty place in Raleigh, those little vacu-packed ones. I've got a hundred rolls of toilet paper. I know that might sound stupid . . . but toilet paper is something you don't want to do without."

"Jeez, Leigh. I really don't have more than enough supplies to last me a week now."

Leigh's eyes narrowed in speculation. "If you guys get hungry, I've got tons."

She nodded, trying to swallow her pride. "The government relief truck didn't come to the school yesterday."

"I've got an extra rifle, too. You know how to use a rifle?"

"My dad used to take me partridge hunting. Back when I was a kid in Kansas."

"Because you should really have a rifle in the house."

"I hate to ask you for a handout."

"The food reserves in this country have been horribly managed."

"Bayard's doing everything he can."

"Not really."

"He's downed a total of thirty killer satellites. We're chipping away at them."

Leigh shook his head. "That doesn't help the food situation, does it?"

His complexion was pale, and he had great dark patches under his eyes. Despite his boasts of more than enough food, he looked as if he had lost weight. He smelled like he hadn't bathed in days, and his face was unshaven.

"Leigh, why don't you come over and sit with us for a while?"

Leigh drifted for a few seconds, staring at the dead grass; then his eyes narrowed and the corners of his lips tightened. He looked like an entirely different man. "I would like to see Jamie try," he said darkly. He turned to her. "Let me get that rifle."

As he went inside, the lights turned on automatically. Their glow spilled onto the front stoop. The begonias in the terra-cotta planters had died. The ivy covering the side of the house was nothing more than a dry, spidery track.

Leigh came back a few moments later with the rifle and a plastic bag. "Here. I hope you won't have to use it, but you never know." He held up the plastic bag. "And here's three freeze-dried dinners and a few boxes of ammo. Put the freeze-dried dinners in boiling water and they cook up nicely. If you need more, let me know. I've got a stash in the basement, plus some stuff buried out behind the shed."

She took the rifle and bag. "Thanks." She inspected the rifle, a Remington. "It's pump action?"

"You ever fire one before?"

"No. Just bolt action."

He took the rifle and demonstrated how to use it, then handed it back. "It's got a four-round magazine. It's not the best rifle, but it's not the worst, either."

When she finally went back home with her rifle, food, and ammo, she had a lot of jittery new thoughts, ones she knew she wouldn't have if it were broad daylight.

Thoughts of Jamie, Lars, and Perry. Thoughts of Leigh going beserko on her. Of everybody going crazy because of the damn dark. But most of all she thought of how Leigh had a stash buried behind the shed. Because if worse came to worst . . . She nodded to herself. Yes, if worse came to worst.

She heard about people getting into confrontations. Fighting over food. Even killing each other for it. But she never got in a confrontation herself. She talked to Tammy St. Martin, who lived over the west hill, and learned that every single store in Old Hill had been looted clean and there wasn't even one can of beans left anywhere.

And then the mailman stopped coming and she phoned the post office, and the computerized voice on the other end told her that, because of labor difficulties, the post office would now implement a system of rotational mail deliveries, and that any given addressee couldn't reasonably expect to get their mail more than once a week.

She learned from Whit that fully half the Old Hill Fire Department had quit.

"Everybody's looking out for their own. Especially because this . . . this darkness is starting to go on for a while."

Other strange things happened, and these things told her that the whole country was being affected. Small, ridiculous things, details one wouldn't normally think of, but details that seemed to be more frightening to her than the larger calamities that might eventually come. For one thing, she stopped getting bulk or spam e-mails, as if the people or corporations who generated this crap now had much more serious things to worry about.

On the television, people were indignant about the nearly total lack of food relief and ranted against the Western Secessionists for being so tightfisted with the assistance. Why wasn't the government doing something to intervene?

Then there would be sound bites of farmers plowing

under crops, or killing their livestock because they had nothing to feed them with.

Shortly after that, she couldn't get any network television at all, just the Emergency Broadcast System, and that was too bad, because there was nothing but a test pattern on the EBS most of the time.

The radio still worked, though, and that's how she got her news.

There was news of how the electrical utility workers were deserting their jobs and management was struggling to hang on, but it was hard because people had to spend a lot of time looking for food and the other essentials of survival, and couldn't spend a lot of time at work. She got news from the Internet, and learned that there had been a cascading blackout in the West affecting forty million people. Then she got the scare of her life because the power went out in Wake County, and the blackout lasted five hours. Also, a few buildings burned to the ground downtown, set alight by looters, and no firemen came to put them out.

So, little by little things got worse, but out here on the highway she and her kids remained okay, because Leigh kept giving them food. She started filling empty pails and jars with tap water and storing them downstairs in the basement in case the water stopped working. She tried to get through to Gerry every day, but never could. The power went out again, and this time the utility told the customers it wasn't their fault; that they were caught in the middle of a cascade, and they were having these cascades because there simply wasn't the maintenance staff to keep the electrical equipment properly serviced.

And then the Internet went down, right around the time the radio went down, so she had no idea what was going on. The servers across the country weren't adequately connecting to each other. On certain evenings she couldn't get the news site, and finally she couldn't get anything at all, not even her home page.

This particular brand of Armageddon, at least at first, was of a slow and creeping kind, but it was pernicious. It was formally announced, on one of the few evenings the radio came back on, that fully ninety percent of next year's crops had been lost, and that many livestock had already starved to death. Things couldn't survive without light.

When Leigh told her that there had been several home invasions over in Willington—people just trying to find some food—she tried to buy stronger locks for her doors, and even traveled all the way to Raleigh to find a locksmith who was open. But it seemed as if locksmithing, as a profession, had entirely disappeared, and she was forced to make do with the crappy old locks she already had on her doors.

11

Are you afraid of the dark? This question kept parading through Glenda's mind once the rolling blackouts became a more permanent feature of their day-to-day living. And she was sure it was the same all over the country. Twelve hours of night was one thing. But at the end of that twelve hours, daylight was supposed to come back. Now it didn't. Not with the power off most of the time. It was dark twenty-four hours a day. The days had stretched into weeks, and the weeks had stretched into the first month, and they had received only occasional blips of power every now and again. They were officially at war with the Tarsalans, but most of it was happening up there, beyond the black skin of the shroud, while down here it just got darker and darker, and colder and colder, so that on a few occasions it had actually snowed, right here in North Carolina, in the middle of summer.

Her kids sat on the floor around the living room coffee table playing chess because it was the only "board" game they owned. All their other games were electronic, and with no electricity they couldn't play them. They played by candlelight and she watched them with low-level apprehension because everything was running out—food, medicine, electricity—and she didn't know how much longer she could hang on.

She could be grateful for one thing only: Leigh next door was providing them with food every now and again. But Leigh was getting that look in his eyes, like a boy who had a high school crush, and she was afraid that he was going to do something stupid, like make a pass at her, and then she wouldn't be able to accept his food anymore.

She hated it all. But mainly it was the dark. It was like a chronic disease, something that made her feel not only anxious but also under the weather, as if she were suffering from the weakness of persistent anemia.

Even worse was her loneliness. God, how she wanted Gerry. She sipped her cold chamomile tea. She wanted to be pressed against his tallness. She wanted to feel his arms around her. She wanted to tell him she was sorry for exploding like that.

She was just thinking she might try the fone again, which had become like a talisman of futility to her, when she noticed light coming through the front window.

She looked out the window and saw firelight far to the west. Something was burning? She walked to the door, opened it, and went out onto the porch. She gazed to the west and saw the glow of what must have been a considerable conflagration just over the hill. Was that Tammy St. Martin's place burning? Tammy with her two little girls, and her husband, Denny, who was with the National Guard and trying to keep the peace in Raleigh? Jake came out onto the porch and, after a moment, so did Hanna.

"Is it a house fire?" said Jake.

"I think it must be the St. Martin place. I hope Tammy and her girls are okay."

"Where's the fire department?"

It was a good question, but one she already knew the answer to. Who's afraid of the dark? They all were, including the men in the local fire department. People were afraid, and fear was driving them—driving them as much as the darkness. People weren't showing up for their jobs. She was going to the nursing home only when she felt like it. All the stores were closed. The banks were closed. Commerce, for the moment, had been suspended. And people were starting to fight each other. She glanced at Leigh's place. Leigh had the right idea. Stock up, hunker down, and hope for the best.

"Maybe we should go up and help," suggested Hanna.

Glenda looked around the yard, then along the highway, then out into the farms and fields beyond the highway.

"I think we should stay put."

"Are they going to let it burn to the ground?" asked Jake.

"Kids, we've got to be real careful with those candles."

She then saw another source of light, blue flashing police lights coming over the hill to the east, and a second later Sheriff Maynard Fulton's police cruiser appeared. It came racing down the highway at seventy or eighty miles per hour, and in addition to her fear of the darkness, she now felt her long-standing fear of the sheriff. An old truck, one that bumped and rattled along the road, followed the sheriff's cruiser, and she recognized the truck as that of the sheriff's younger brother, Buzz Fulton. She felt an additional old fear, the fear of Gerry's alcoholism. Because wasn't Buzz Gerry's favorite drinking buddy in Old Hill? And hadn't they gotten so magnificently plastered on more than one occasion that Sheriff Fulton had had to intervene? And hadn't Sheriff Fulton then eyed her in an uncomfortable fashion when she had come to pick Gerry up in the drunk tank?

"Kids, get inside. Don't let them see us."

"Mom, it's just the sheriff."

"Don't you think I know that?"

She herded her kids inside and shut the door, just as the Fulton brothers sped by.

She hurried to the kitchen window where, in a moment, she got a view of the cruiser and truck hurtling west on the highway toward Tammy's place. She gripped the edge of the counter for support.

She watched the fire burn for the next fifteen minutes, and her shoulders eased. At last she went back to the living room and sat in Gerry's easy chair. She liked sitting in the chair because it had his smell. She thought the emergency was over, and that they could go back to the apprehension and ennui of total darkness twenty-four–seven. But then, glancing out the living room window, she saw headlights swinging back down the highway, coming from Tammy St. Martin's place, and the two feared vehicles finally came up her drive; first the cruiser, then the truck.

Her body stiffened because she knew Fulton possessed all those characteristics you didn't want in a cop. He was a man who was liable to abuse his power at the first opportunity.

She sprang from Gerry's chair and rushed to the kitchen. She pulled their few cans of food from the shelves, shoved them into a canvas bag, quickly took it down to the basement, and hid it among all the boxes, then hurried upstairs just in time to hear Fulton knock at the front door.

"Kids, let me do the talking," she said.

She smoothed her hair, walked to the front door, and opened it.

Fulton looked thin. He was a square-jawed man with a mustache, and squarish aquamarine eyes atop squarish red cheeks. His flashlight printed a cream circle on the porch step, and in its glow she saw an expression of mistrust on his face. Buzz came up behind the sheriff.

"We thought we'd check up on you, Glenda," said Maynard.

"Howdy, Glenda," said Buzz.

"Buzz here was telling me you usually go down to Marblehill around this time of the year, so we really didn't expect to find you here."

"No, we're here."

"I guess you would be," said Buzz, "with Gerry stuck up on the Moon and all."

"Matter of fact," said the sheriff, "I'm glad you're here. Gives us a chance to tell you about the changes we've been making."

"Changes? What changes?"

"I wish they'd at least get radio up and running again," said Maynard. "Me and Buzz have been doing a lot of door-to-door. And I'm getting a bit tired of it. Mind if we step inside?"

"I'd prefer if you didn't."

"Now, Glenda, you got to learn to trust the sheriff. It wasn't your fault that I had to throw your husband in the drunk tank so often. I was only trying to help him."

"You insulted him repeatedly. You made passes at me. And now you think I'm supposed to trust you, Maynard?"

"Oh, come on, Glenda," said the sheriff. "Gerry can take a little kidding. That's all it ever was. And you should be thanking us for coming round. We thought you'd be in Marblehill. Why ain't you down there? That's where I'd be if I had half a chance. Buzz here tells me it's quite a place. Huge. With a pool and tennis courts."

"My husband's decision to take Buzz down there three years ago was a mistake. Buzz, you were a bad influence on him."

Buzz frowned. "He was a bad influence on his own self. He was the one doing all the drinking."

"He embarrassed himself in front of his brother, his sister-in-law, and their kids. All because you were there to egg him on."

"Let's not dig up old dirt," said the sheriff, breaking in. "We're just here to check up on you, Glenda, that's all. Because . . . truth be told, it's getting harder to keep the peace in Wake County. I've had to deputize some of the boys, Buzz here included. Lot of people don't know what's going on, what with radio and TV being down. So I might as well tell you; we're more or less on our own in Old Hill. Court's been closed down. All the stores have been closed down. And because of this Western Secessionist thing, the delivery of emergency food supplies has been reduced to a trickle. Mayor's gone away, we're not sure where. Fire department's gone AWOL. And I don't mean to alarm you, but there have been a lot of home invasions in this area lately. The murder rate has climbed a bit. And it's not because of the criminal element. People are trying to find enough food." He glanced over at Leigh's house. "How's your neighbor? He bothering you at all?"

"Why would he bother me?"

"Pretty woman like yourself . . . Everyone knows about you and Leigh."

"I resent that. There's nothing between us. I'm a happily married woman."

"Only your drunk of a husband has run off to the Moon."

"Maynard, this is why I don't respect you."

Maynard's face settled. "Well, Glenda, I think you better start respecting me soon. Because I'm the only one around here who can protect you. You're a target, you realize that, don't you? With law and order breaking down—and believe me, I'm doing my best to keep the peace—but with law and order breaking down, a lot of desperate young men, they find a pretty woman like you, and they realize they have nothing to lose, and they may want to have their way with you. So you've got to realize that you need a sheriff more than you ever have before. I don't have to keep sheriffing. I'm doing it because I feel a responsibility to the people of Wake County. Lot of people want a sheriff around. Only we're not getting any support out of Raleigh anymore. The chief is telling us we can walk if we want to, especially with the food situation getting so bad, and us having to look after our own families, but I feel it's my civic responsibility to stay on."

"Aren't you noble?"

He shook his head. "Why do I even try with you, Glenda? In any case, the nature of my job has changed. The Wake County Sheriff's Department has undergone a . . . a . . ." He scratched his head. "What would you call it, Buzz? A restructuring, I guess? Folks understand they need a sheriff, and I do what I can for the Old Hill area, only, like I say, we've got no support from Raleigh—no food, no nothing—so if people want a sheriff's department, they got to contribute. My officers need food. If you've got any extra food around—or maybe old Gerry has a couple stray bottles of bourbon."

"There's no alcohol in the house."

"Okay, okay. Don't get so defensive."

"And we don't have any food. We're starving like everybody else."

"Then you know . . . there are other ways a pretty young woman like yourself can contribute."

And here it was, what she knew he was going to get around to sooner or later—and Buzz, oddly, looking away, as if he were embarrassed by it but nonetheless willing to tolerate it.

"Get off my property, Maynard."

"It just comes down to a question of whether you want my protection or not. We got Tammy and her kids in the cruiser. Her house burned down and she has nowhere else to go. Denny is God knows where. A few days ago we asked her for food, but she didn't want to give us any, and now her house burned down, because, you know, we can't protect everyone; just the people who are willing to cooperate with us. Wouldn't it be a shame if your house burned down too?"

Her insides shriveled in fear as she understood the game he was playing. "Maynard . . . please . . . I've got no food. And for God's sake, I'm a married woman."

"That ain't stopping Tammy. She knows what she has to do to survive."

"Please . . . just go."

"You think about it, Mrs. Thorndike. Your situation's similar to Tammy's. You don't have your husband around to protect you. You have only the sheriff."

At work a few days later, Glenda pushed a food cart down the hall. The cart had stale tea biscuits on it, and an urn full of weak tea. The place stunk. The cleaning staff didn't come anymore. It was only her and Whit trying to keep the place running. She lifted a biscuit and shoved it into her mouth. The place was dark and she had to wheel the cart down the hall using a flashlight. She saw another flashlight up ahead. Her own beam sketched out Whit's tall figure.

As Whit reached her, he said, "Mrs. Waters is dead."

"Do you need help moving her?"

"It's already done. Help yourself to another biscuit. And take a few for your kids." Whit shook his head. "I don't know how much longer we can stay on, Glenda. There's not much we can do."

"So only twenty-seven residents left now?"

"Twenty-six."

"And you've tried contacting their loved ones?"

He didn't answer. In fact, he switched to another topic entirely, one he had grown obsessed with over the last couple of days. "I'm afraid those kids might come back. One of them has a gun."

"If you have to defend yourself . . . I mean, if they give you no choice . . ."

"Why are they coming here anyway?"

Glenda shrugged. "I guess they think we have food."

He motioned at the tea biscuits. "You call that food?"

"I wonder where their parents are?"

Whit reached in his pocket. "Take the keys to the dispensary. We've got asthma drugs in there."

She was elated by the offer because she had thought often about the Cedarvale dispensary. She took the keys, shoved them in her nursing uniform pocket, stood on her toes, and kissed him on the cheek.

"Thanks, Whit."

"Haven't been in touch with my family for years," he said. "I have a brother in Detroit. Maybe I'll head up there."

So. There it was. The inevitable. "That's it? I don't have to come anymore?"

He looked away. "I appreciate you hanging on as long as you have."

"It's just that . . . my kids."

"You don't have to apologize, Glenda."

"Then maybe after today—"

"I'm thinking of moving everybody up to 3C. To the single rooms. Everybody's too spread out now. I'm going to shut down the elevators and barricade the stairwells. We'll put all the food in the sterile room. If those kids come . . ." He trailed off, not finishing his thought.

"How long do you think the food's going to last?"

He shrugged and raised his eyebrows. "Maybe another ten days."

"Do you need help moving people? I could stay if you want."

"Go to your children. Leave this cart to me."

"Can I charge my car one last time?"

"You don't have to ask. And you can come back and recharge it any time."

She gave the cart to Whit, and hugged him.

She then negotiated the dark corridors with her flashlight.

She went to the dispensary and took all the asthma medicine she could find.

Next she went to the garage and charged her car. She checked the gauge on the generator and saw that it was good for another fifteen charges.

She drove the car herself—no satellite connections to drive the car for her anymore—and wondered if she would ever have to worry about getting another job again.

12

Having told everybody in the mayor's office of his defection, Dr. Luke Langstrom now sat on the edge of his seat, elbows resting on the table, his upper lip hoisted in a tight smile, his blue eyes sitting like insensible marbles behind his narrowed eyelids. Gerry had that old familiar sensation that, while he had been fogging his brain with the ether of his own confused musings, someone else had comprehended the situation with the crispness of a high-powered microscope and had then pulled the rug out from under his feet.

He glanced at Malcolm Hulke, gauging the mayor's reaction. The mayor gazed at the Martian with wide, perplexed eyes. Then it was over to Mitch Bennett, the AviOrbit representative. Mitch's lips had twisted into a tremulous pout, and he looked like a sensitive schoolboy who had just been teased beyond endurance.

Ian Hamilton, smelling of last night's drunk and sporting his rawhide cowboy hat, had his unshaven chin thrust forward and his brow set in an angry frown. "That's the biggest bullshit story I've ever heard, Luke. Did Neil Thorndike put you up to this?"

The Martian shifted. "I won't deny that Dr. Thorndike's signature was on the drop. I'm honored that such a distinguished scientist thinks he can put my modest talents to good use."

"So have they confirmed through genetic analysis that the chromosomal makeup of the xenophyta carapace might in fact be derived from the Martian specimens you've studied?" asked Gerry, wanting only to find out what he could.

"I'm not at liberty to say."

"Luke, we're a team," said Ian. "Just the other day you were telling me how you were personally behind Gerry a hundred percent."

"I am. And I wish Gerry the best of luck."

"Why can't you discuss the carapace with us?" asked the mayor, his tone sounding as if he had bitten a lemon.

"The National Science Foundation Task Force on the Phytosphere thinks it's better if we keep our research confidential. They prefer I use the American Legation's drop system now."

The mayor fought hard to disguise his disappointment. "I guess we can't stop you."

"The smug sons of bitches," said Ian. "Gerry, you should send Neil a drop and tell him to butt out. He realized you had a good thing, so he came in and took over, like he always does."

"I don't look at it that way, Ian. We're all in this together."

But Ian wasn't satisfied. "What did he give you, Luke? I know how Neil works. What's on offer here?"

The Martian scientist shifted again. "Can't we be civilized about this? Gerry's right. Ultimately, we're all trying to do the same thing. Defeat the phytosphere."

"What Neil can't steal, he always tries to buy," said Ian. "What was your price? Everybody's got a price."

Langstrom frowned again. "The point is, this whole lunar effort is ridiculous. You have no money. You have no resources. And your chief scientist"—he nodded at Gerry—"is stalled in his primary research. I'm not even convinced his primary research should be the main focus. I think the flagella will ultimately prove to be a side issue. Who cares if they behave one way in the lab, and differently when they're in the phytosphere? I don't think it matters." The Martian's tone grew defensive. "You've forgotten the most basic scientific principle, Gerry, that of Occam's razor. The simplest theory is the best theory. All I can see of your research so far is that you're trying to complicate—unnecessarily—what is really a simple problem. Take a page from your brother. The thing's an organism. Therefore, it can be killed. And yes, it's an interesting phenomenon to see the flagella behave differently in different environments. But solving that problem has no ultimate value, at least not in terms of destroying the phytosphere."

In spite of himself, Gerry couldn't help feeling hurt. "And my brother's approach is so much better?"

"I can only speak in the broadest general terms because of the confidentiality issue, but in the wide spectrum of things, yes, it is."

"And in the *wide spectrum* of things, what is he *generally* planning to do?"

Langstrom frowned. "For one thing, he *has* a plan. You don't. I would even go so far as to call his plan a procedure; one with clear directions and logical steps that technicians and military personnel can follow. Step one is to identify the chemical and biological makeup of the phytosphere, which he's done, right down to mapping its entire genome, something we on the Moon don't have the equipment or expertise to do. Step two is to break down its defenses; in other words, find a way through its carapace. That's where I come in with my omniphage. Step three is the introduction of a comprehensive toxic agent that will ultimately prove fatal to the phytosphere."

Gerry shook his head. "You see, Luke, that's where I disagree with my brother's approach. I've studied all kinds of phytoplankton. They develop quick resistance to any kind of toxin and, in many cases, certain toxins will promote their growth. And let's not forget, a toxin will be the first thing the Tarsalans look for. I mean, my God, here's a race whose individual members have two brains apiece. It's been proven by scientific study that they outthink humans again and again. And you honestly believe they haven't thought of a toxic approach yet? You can't fool the Tarsalans."

"From what I understand, your brother doesn't plan on fooling the Tarsalans. He plans on fooling the organism itself. And I believe he's going to be successful. Your brother's a brilliant scientist. He has the greatest minds behind him. He has the full resources of the United States at his disposal. He's had wide experience at managing large projects. Unlike you, he's a goal-oriented problem-solver. I'm sorry, Gerry, but you sit inside a problem, look around, admire the view, meditate . . . and nothing concrete gets done. I'll admit that perhaps at some time in the future, when this crisis is over, the flagella might bear a closer, if extraneous, investigation. But right now we have to focus on destroying the phytosphere, not just staring at it as if it were an intriguing plaything."

"This toxin is going to turn out to be the dead end, Luke, mark my words. And I don't see how you can't recognize the importance of the flagella. The flagella are where we should begin, because they're the only part of the xenophyta's body that function outside the carapace. And if I were going to use a toxin, I wouldn't waste my time trying to bite through the carapace with an omniphage. I would go directly for the flagella apertures, because the apertures offer an already existing means of ingress. Neil thinks he can bash his way in anywhere. He's always favored the frontal assault."

"That's because it works."

"I believe his methods often lead to blind spots. Sometimes it's better to step back. Sometimes it's better to take the wide view. The kind of science Neil practices may be *too* goal-oriented. You have to let the science speak to you, not the other way around. You can't dictate to the science, the way Neil does." He shook his head and sighed. "I'm sorry, Luke, but you're backing the wrong horse."

"At least your brother has a horse."

Gerry glanced at the others, then turned to the elderly Martian. "Then fine. Go, Luke. We don't need you. Getting through the carapace isn't going to make any difference in the long haul."

"It's Dr. Thorndike's belief that it might make all the difference in the world."

*   *   *

Gerry was in the Alleyne-Parma Observatory later that night. This . . . this *tourist* attraction was his primary research platform. Heaven's Eye rose beside him, done up like a sea captain's telescope, with gold curlicues and florets along the side. Maybe Luke was right. Maybe the Moon effort was ridiculous. The observatory staff had gone home. He glanced at his watch. Just past midnight. The best time of day to think.

He sat in front of the monitors—the special ones the techies at AviOrbit had hooked up to Heaven's Eye for him—and he had the distinct feeling, impossible yet magical, that Glenda would emerge from the shadows and tell him to come to bed. He was worried. If only he could get through. He thought of his den at home. She would come into his den, and she would say, "Come to bed, Ger, it's getting late." And . . . and . . . He looked into the shadows of the observatory and realized he would give anything to see her one more time.

He turned back to the monitors and concentrated. He had to go back to asking basic questions. And he guessed the most basic question was this: Why were some spots on the phytosphere dark while others were light?

Gerry's shoulders stiffened. He leaned forward and looked at the phytosphere more closely. "Good question, Gerry."

Yes, here it was, the quiet nighttime inspiration. He remembered Luke Langstrom's words. *You sit inside a problem, look around, admire the view, and meditate.* Maybe that was the only way. Maybe true insight came only to those who allowed their brains to function on several levels, in the wee hours of the morn.

The color variations proved elusive. He chose a couple of simple function keys and heightened the contrast. The difference between light and dark became more pronounced. Possible answers? Varying thickness. What would cause varying thickness in the phytosphere? Barometric pressure? Did the phytosphere have its own weather system? Sitting on top of the troposphere, with tentacles dropping down into the troposphere's cold trap for moisture supply, did the phytosphere possibly echo, in a faint way, the disturbances that were happening in that real weathermaker?

He shook his head. He didn't have the data to answer this question, and until he could measure the real-time weather in the troposphere against the mottling effect in the phytosphere, this particular hypothesis would have to remain in the realm of speculation.

Funny, the way the brain thought if you just let it go. Is this what the Tarsalans did? Let their brains go? Both their brains? When he let go, questions linked themselves in long chains. The next link in the chain of this particular problem came to him unbidden: Was there a pattern to the color variation?

He focused on the real-time footage that was coming in directly from Heaven's Eye.

He had to watch it for a half hour before he could say with any certainty that the shades were actually shifting—so slowly that the change was nearly imperceptible to the human eye.

He turned his attention to the archival footage of the shroud, over a month's worth of nonstop round-the-clock digitized images, the kind of long-term observations he liked to watch so much. He keyed in a command that brought it right to the start, two days after the initial meeting in the H. G. Wells Ballroom.

He played the footage, sped it up—sometimes patterns became more apparent when they were accelerated.

He watched for the next hour, compressing a full day into sixty minutes. And he definitely saw dark patches change into light patches, and vice versa, but the attenuations were too random for him to definitively conclude that there was any pattern.

So he compressed a week into sixty minutes, and by the time three o'clock rolled around he had seen it seven times, an amorphous band of lighter coloration passing from east to west in a definite pattern. Toward the equator, the band of lighter patches broke apart, and some even whirlpooled, as if caught in a weather system. He

was somewhat disappointed. He felt fairly certain that
what he had here was a kind of weather system inside
the phytosphere. That it seemed to be on a daily cycle
with a twenty-four-hour periodicity made him suspect it
might be artificial, and that the Tarsalans had created
it—maybe as a housecleaning tool for the phytosphere,
or perhaps as one of its operational aspects.

He shook his head. He wasn't sure how he could turn
this to his advantage. He sighed as his shoulders sank.
Was this another flagella-type dead end? Was the proper
approach just to kill the phytosphere any way they
could, rather than try to understand it first?

What could be another possible reason for the change
in coloration, other than an artificially created weather
system? A chemical change? What was an indicator of
chemical change? Heat. Bingo. How could he measure
heat? He would need to hook up some infrared equipment to this appalling tourist attraction.

He left the telescope and went to the circular hall
ringing the observatory. He passed the washrooms, the
gift shop, and finally came to the observatory office.

In the office, he phoned Mitch Bennett—he didn't
care what time it was; he had to talk to Mitch and find
out whether this was doable.

"Hello?" The tone of Mitch's greeting was worried,
as one might expect from a phone call at three o'clock
in the morning.

Gerry told him what he wanted.

"Infrared?" said Mitch, as if the request were impossible. "Have you met Ira Levinson? He's the one everybody's always mistaking for a brick wall."

"I just want to get a better idea of what we're looking
at in terms of temperature fluctuations in the phytosphere. I could be on to something here, Mitch." Or he
could be grasping at straws.

"Yes, but we don't have any infrared units out of
mothballs right now. Years ago we used infrared for
tracking, but since we upgraded to singularity drives, we
haven't used the infrared stuff in . . . in decades. And
I'm sure most of it's been sold off."

"Most?"

Mitch paused. "Ira and I have never gotten along."

"Yes, but is there any left?"

"Hang on, let me check my waferscreen . . . it's been acting funny lately. I'll see if I can . . ." Mitch disappeared from the vidscreen and all Gerry got for a few seconds was a view of rumpled sheets. Then Mitch came back, sat on the bed, adjusted the vidcam upward, and Gerry saw his sleep-swollen face. "I'm just looking at the record right now. . . . That stuff's expensive." Mitch seemed to be going through a long list. "Ira's not going to want us dicking with it. If there's any left, I'm sure he's planning to sell it. And anything earmarked for liquidation . . . He's obsessed with the bottom line, Gerry. We're in a competitive, high-stakes, frontier industry."

"Yes, but can you—"

"Hold on, hold on . . . I've got it, and it's . . ." He watched Mitch's brow fold with misgiving. "Ah, *shit*." As the diminutive AviOrbit representative hardly ever swore, the expletive indicated something truly awry.

"What?"

"We've got a unit crated in one of the orbiting warehouses. The retrieval expense . . . he's not going to like it."

"Can we take the sky elevator up and check it out?"

Mitch paused. "Gerry . . . let me be blunt." A look of intense skepticism came to Mitch's eyes. "Ira isn't so convinced by you."

Alarm pinched Gerry's chest. "Why? He doesn't even know me."

"It's just that there's this impression . . . and it's been going around . . . and he's gotten wind of it. Ira's a technocrat, an engineer. What do you expect? He thinks pure science is a waste of time."

"If it's just old junk, I don't see why we can't take a look at it."

"Yes, but this particular unit in the catalog here is a light-gathering optical refractor. We'd have to hook it up to an IR array and conduit, and that's going to take an engineering staff, which in turn means a proposal, which in turn means Ira. Remember Ira? He's the guy people mistake for a brick wall."

"Mitch, this is important. I'm not sure where it's going, but I know it's going somewhere."

"Now, *there's* a proposal Ira's going to like."

"Let me talk to him."

Mitch's face reddened. "No . . . no. I better do the talking. We might not get along, but I know how to handle him." He looked away with sudden despondency, as if he had abandoned all hope. "I'll get into my shark cage, and I'll make sure I have my stun gun, and that my will's in order, and I'll tell Ira that I'm not sure where we're going, but that I think we're going somewhere. And then I'll pray."

13

Glenda reached for Gerry's side of the bed. She peered toward the alarm clock, hoping to see its dim blue digits, praying that the utility company might have restored power by this time, because wasn't this going on a bit too long? Didn't they understand that the dark freaked people out, and that to make people live in the dark all the time was simply too much?

All she saw, as she stared in the general direction of the alarm clock, was more darkness.

She pulled her hands close to her collarbones, curling into a fetal position.

She lay there for close to an hour, and that's when the power came back on. She heard the electric baseboards crackling, heard her own voice on the answering machine, "Hi, this is the home of Glenda, Gerry, Jake, and Hanna Thorndike," et cetera, et cetera, and at last heard the television go on, the president's voice coming over the Emergency Broadcast System—yes, Bayard's measured game-show cadences.

She sprang out of bed and hurried to the living room. She blinked in the light. She wasn't used to seeing light. The lamp beside Gerry's chair was on. So was the porch light. The fluorescent light above the kitchen sink was on and spilled its bluish glow over the dining room floor.

"Units of the First, Second, and Eighth Infantry Units have been moved into place, and there have been fierce clashes along the state borders, but so far the Army has yet to break the stranglehold. These three states house some of our largest emergency food supply depots. You can rest assured that I'm doing everything in my power to keep the supply lines open, and I consider the unilateral actions of Governors Fitton, Peters, and Marles, as well as their Western Secessionist supporters, to be criminal. I can pledge to the American people that all three governors will be prosecuted to the fullest extent of the law, once the situation is brought under control. Until such time, our relief efforts will be severely hampered, and at this point we can't guarantee any of our previously scheduled relief drops, and ask you to bear with us while our military units attempt to regain control of these critical food stockpiles. Until such time, the First Lady and I offer our sincerest prayers, and urge you—"

And that was it, because with a percussive click and the trace flash of a sudden power surge, the electricity failed once again and the house was plunged into darkness.

"Mom?" Jake's voice.

"It's okay, sweetie."

"Was the power back on?"

"For a bit. Go back to sleep."

"I'm hungry."

"I'm going to ask Leigh if he can give us some more food tomorrow."

Because from the look of things, the government wasn't going to come through anymore. From the look of things, the Western Secessionists were at last ruining the country. Which meant the food situation had just gone from bad to impossible. And come to think of it, why hadn't the television woken Hanna up? Hanna was sleeping way too much.

Glenda waited for her eyes to get used to the dark, then felt her way through the living room and went down the hall into Hanna's room. Couldn't see a thing—it was truly an absence of all light, especially when the power was off, that made things so difficult.

She stumbled into Hanna's bed, her shin hitting its steel frame—a lot of bumps and bruises for everyone, wandering around in the dark all the time—and she heard Hanna's deep and heavy breathing, her lungs crackling, always half inflamed. She sat on the edge of Hanna's bed and put her hand on Hanna's leg.

That's when Glenda heard a truck coming down the highway. She thought it might be an Army truck bringing food relief. But then she recognized the steady *putt-putt* of a civilian truck, and wondered who would be driving down the highway in the middle of the night. The middle of the day? Which was it? Headlight beams made squares of light on the wall, and as the truck drew closer, the squares moved, passed over Hanna's shelf of stuffed animals, rested momentarily on her grade-five district-wide spelling bee plaque, and finally shifted obliquely as the truck pulled up Leigh Phelps's driveway.

She got off the end of Hanna's bed and walked to the windows. A pickup truck crunched up the gravel, two men riding in the back and one driving. They pulled up to Leigh's house and got out. They had rifles—hunting weapons that she could see in the glow of the headlights—and she knew that Leigh's fears had been justified after all, that the look he had seen in Jamie's eyes had been enough.

It was a crossroads for her, because she had the extra rifle now, and knew how to shoot—all those summers partridge hunting with her father in Kansas—and it was the moral thing to do, get her rifle and stand shoulder to shoulder with her neighbor against these men, especially because she was planning to ask Leigh for food again tomorrow. But the risk was too great. She had to survive. Not for herself but for her children. She would not put herself in harm's way, not unless it was for Hanna and Jake.

So she retreated from the window, fearful that they might have seen her face in the glare of the headlights. She sat on Hanna's bed, gripped her daughter by the leg, and shook her. Hanna moaned, then said her usual, "One more minute," but must have at last sensed something strange going on because she pushed herself up, cleared the hair from her face, and squinted at the glow of the headlights coming in through the windows.

"Sweetie, we have to go to the basement."

"Why?"

"Remember what we talked about."

Hanna's sleepiness immediately lifted and her blank look of slumber was transformed into one of alarm.

They left Hanna's room and walked down the hall to get Jake.

Jake was already up and looking out his own window, down on one knee, a yard back from the casement and well into the shadows so that any chance glare from the headlights wouldn't catch his face. He glanced over his shoulder as his mother and sister entered. He didn't say a word, but his expression, at once solemn and concerned, with a knit to his tawny brow, revealed a boy who simply accepted, who had made the transition, who understood and was now resigned to the ways of this dark world.

He got up and lifted his Handheld Sport from his desk, a game-playing device that no longer worked because it got its recharge from sunlight.

He followed them down the hall to the basement stairs.

They descended the narrow, steep stairs into the shallow basement—more a storm cellar—and, as was so often the case these days, especially since the power had become intermittent, Glenda found herself in a world of touch. The banister was smooth and cool against her palm. The dank smell of the cellar permeated her nostrils. Her children creaked down the stairs behind her. Her foot hit the basement's concrete floor with a light scuffing sound. She reached for her rifle, which she had leaned against the wall at the foot of the stairs.

And then it happened. What she had been dreading, but also what she had been expecting. The obvious outcome to all this buildup. Because hadn't it been a long time now, and wasn't the food situation just a bit much to take, especially when no one knew when it was going to end? Yes, the inevitable happened. Gunfire—like the barking of dogs—erupted from next door. It was a sound she at first didn't want to admit to herself, because it escalated the situation to an entirely new plane. The rifle shots made her skin crawl and her throat tighten, but at last she shook all feeling away because she knew she had to look after her children.

"Jake, will you hurry up?" she said in a small, panicked voice.

"I can't see where I'm going."

"Shhh."

"Mom," said Jake, "they're not going to hear us over all that gunfire."

How easily Jake accepted it all.

"Just move quickly and quietly to the back. Jake, grab onto my sleeve, and Hanna, you grab onto Jake's."

Forming a human chain, they walked in the darkness until they came to the back. More gunfire came from next door, and then a lot of shouting. Then there was one final shot, and all the shouting stopped. They listened for a while. Nothing.

The phone rang upstairs. Her body stiffened. Who could that be? Maybe somehow Gerry had managed to get back, and he was phoning from somewhere on the "ph" phone. She was terrified because she thought the men next door might hear the ringing. She was eager to go answer so she could see if it was Gerry, but hesitant to move from her safe basement refuge.

At last, Glenda bolted from her crouched position on the floor and, feeling her way through the aisle of junk, came to the foot of the stairs. She crawled up the steep steps on all fours.

She came to the kitchen, rose to her feet, and got no farther than the table when someone shone a flashlight in through the front window. She froze and quickly backed up against the wall.

The flashlight beam penetrated through the living room to the dining room, and into the kitchen, where she saw it brightening first the cupboards, then the sink, then the floor. And all the while the handset part of the vidphone continued to ring on the dining room table, set to sing like a cardinal because she loved the sound of the cardinal so much.

The flashlight beam swung away, and its peripheral glow grew dimmer and dimmer, until finally the kitchen was dark again. She sprang from her hiding spot against the wall, and headed for the dining room table, where the phone continued to tweet like a cardinal. She got halfway there when the phone stopped ringing. Even though her good sense told her she had lost her chance, she lifted the phone anyway.

"Gerry?"

All she heard was silence.

She selected the call list to see who had phoned but the little screen remained blank. Who could it have been? Neil? Louise?

She rested the handset on the receiver and went downstairs, disappointed and close to tears. She felt her way through the dark to the back. Her kids sat crouched next to the downstairs refrigerator.

"Was it Dad?" asked Jake.

"I didn't get it in time."

Her kids said nothing.

She sat down.

"Are they still out there?" asked Jake.

"One came to the window and looked inside."

All three lapsed into silence. She thought of all the other people hiding in the dark, in similar situations. And then thought of the Western Secessionists, now making everything a lot harder.

14

At what point does a man lose faith in himself?

This question gnawed at Neil as he sat in his Coral Gables dining room with the rest of his family, listening to the gunfire outside. They sat in the dark. Candles flickered on the table. Ashley read a magazine on her waferscreen, the glow of the thing lighting her face. Melissa sat on the chaise longue painting her toenails pink. Morgan, his precious Morgan, had her chair pressed right against his. He had his arm around her, and she was scared—constantly frightened now, morbidly terrified, as if the dark were a monster that was just waiting for the chance to kill her.

At what point did a man lose faith, and realize that the problem he had decided to solve was simply too big to solve?

Louise gazed at him stoically, enduring the gunfire outside, but with a look in her eyes that told him it was unendurable. The dark outside was like a thing alive. It pressed in on them with the unstoppable force of a bad weather front. A day, a week, even two weeks, okay, they all knew it was going to be dark for a while. But a month? And now even more than a month? He was second-guessing himself constantly, and he knew it was because of the dark. He didn't know what to tell his family about his progress, and he felt like he was letting Louise and the kids, the president, even the whole world down.

Outside, it was the haves against the have-nots. And

damn those Western Secessionists. It wasn't that there
was no food; it's just that there was no distribution. And
everybody knew—yes, right down in their stomachs—
that the existing food, the hoarded food, was indeed finite, and that next year's crop was gone. People fighting
over an ever-shrinking pile of food. The equation was
simple. Why hadn't the government prepared for it?

He got up and walked into the sunroom. He looked
out across his swimming pool and saw flames reflecting
on the water—a neighbor's house burned up the street.
Where were the firemen? He walked out the big French
doors onto the patio. All his exotic shrubbery was dead.
The ground stunk like rotten hay. He rounded the fountain and found the maid, Eva, boiling MREs on the barbecue because there was no electricity, at least not right
now. He hoped that the neighbors wouldn't smell them
and come over for a handout.

He approached her. "Eva, I want you to know—you
can go home to your people any time you like."

Eva looked up. Her face was a mask of fear. She was
neither young nor old, and yet her fear made her look
ancient. "You want me to go?"

"Only if you want to."

Even his manner of speaking had grown halting and
unsure, and it was because he was always creeping
around in the dark; he wasn't a man who liked creeping
around in the dark.

"What does ma'am say?"

"I just thought . . . a lot of people want to be with
their families . . ."

"My family is in Colombia. And things aren't so good
there right now."

The barbecue flickered and he saw the reflection of
the flame dance on her face. The black pall of the phytosphere hovered in the sky. "You're welcome to stay."

Tears clouded her eyes. "Thank you, sir."

As if he had offered her an ironclad guarantee that
she would survive the phytosphere.

He turned and walked back to the house. He pushed

his way in through the French doors only to find his wife coming out into the sunroom with that special phone they had given him, the one that sent its signal through a squadron of communications aircraft that were constantly aloft.

"It's Bob Cruz," she said, and hope danced in her eyes like a sad childhood remembrance.

He took the phone and pressed it to his ear. It was bulky and big, like a combat radio, and had a nubby black antenna. He had his usual reaction—a tightening of his esophagus, a spray of acid over the lining of his stomach, and a premonition of yet more bad news.

"Bob," he said, the name dropping from his mouth like a dead bird from the sky.

"We've got Luke Langstrom on board. He's working on the omniphage."

Here was a border—one between good luck and bad, and for a split second he was balanced on the infinitesimal edge of either. The cards had again been dealt in his favor, and he felt within himself the distinct quality of good luck, elation mixed with relief, like a chill mixed with a fever.

"How soon does he think he can do an initial workup?"

"He says a few days."

"And Gerry's reaction?"

Bob paused. "No word."

Neil hesitated, but then got down to business. "Does Langstrom have any preliminary ideas?"

"He's already selected a designer organism from his old files. Apparently he's designed dozens of omniphages like this. He uses them as surgical tools to study the guts of modern-day Aresphyta."

A little more talk about the chemical teeth of potential omniphages, just so when he briefed the president and the secretary of defense he could give them a cohesive overall picture, and then he thumbed his special phone off. He looked at the phone, contemplating it the way he might a strange artifact. He put it on the table.

"Good news?" said Louise.

"Langstrom is working for us." Neil shook his head. "I hope Gerry's not too mad."

Melissa looked up from her toenail painting. "Does that mean it's going to get light again, Dad?"

How to answer his eldest daughter? He gazed at her in the candlelight coming from the table, and he momentarily wondered about her inner life, how she was dealing with the phytosphere, second by second, minute by minute—how she was coping with that sporadic and unnerving gunfire outside. Just who the hell was shooting? And did Miami really have so many guns? Melissa was losing her tan. Even that was something she would have to deal with.

"It's a step in the right direction, hon."

He heard a strange sucking sound from the kitchen. His wife and daughters glanced that way, their heads flicking in unison. He lifted the flashlight, walked past the dining room table, and entered the kitchen. The sucking sound came from the sink. He walked over, and further pinpointed the sound to the faucet. He recognized the sound. It was the sound of water pressure fading away.

Louise and the girls came into the kitchen. He turned on the cold-water tap and the sucking intensified. He tried the hot-water tap, and the pipes below gurgled and burped, and the sound grew more and more distant as the pressure reversed itself and drained away into the main pipe outside.

He turned to Louise. It was a strange scene, Louise's blond hair backlighted by the glow coming from the candles in the dining room, her face barely illuminated by the flashlight, and the three girls gathered around her, watching him expectantly, looking to him as the authority on all things technical.

He could only state the obvious. "The water's . . . gone off."

He took a few seconds to connect in his mind the series of events that might have led to this circumstance. How did water get to his house? He wasn't even sure.

Only that during either the filtration or actual pumping process, power was needed, and power, at best, was an intermittent resource these days.

"We have the pool," said Louise.

Yes. And so they would drink pool water, and it would taste too much of chlorine, and it might make them sick, but what choice did they have? Pool water and army rations. This was the way it would happen. A slow and steady reduction, until the reduction was complete and life couldn't continue. Had to dig in. The thought came to him suddenly. Find a defendable position, stock it, and dig in. Flashback to medieval times, when might made right, and those who survived were the meanest motherfuckers in the valley. Go up to his home in northern Georgia, Marblehill—even its name was tough—and protect his wife and girls for as long as he could until the reductions reduced them to the final repose of death.

He shook his head. He had to stop thinking that way. Negative thinking never got anybody anywhere.

In the next moment he stopped thinking anything at all, was only an organism reacting, not even necessarily interpreting what he was reacting to, just jerking to the floor at the sound of all the windows breaking, ducking instinctively even as he saw his family do the same, and only in that moment, as he felt the cool surface of the ceramic tile against his hands, did he understand that the house had been peppered with a hundred or so rounds of machine-gun fire despite the Morrison fighting vehicles protecting them out front. Who the hell were they up against? A question of the haves against the have-nots. A question of either starving to death or not starving to death. Especially now that the Western Secessionists had fouled things up.

"Louise?"

"Neil?"

"Girls?"

"We're here, Daddy."

"Ashley? Morgan?"

Responses from daughters number two and three—

"I'm here, we're here, I'm okay, we're okay"—that he couldn't really hear, because at that moment there came the *chat-a-chat-a-chat* of return machine-gun fire from their front drive, the gunner phrasing his counteroffensive with a nearly calypso rhythm, little bursts of fifty-caliber rounds for the next twenty seconds until it finally stopped, and the only sound was some people yelling far in the distance.

"Everybody stay here," he said. "I'm going to see what's going on."

He crawled through the glass of the broken kitchen window, cutting himself, acknowledging the wetness of the blood on his hand, but too pumped up to feel the pain.

In the dining room, he got to his feet and ran hunched over to the den.

He got his gun, and he thought that this was the last thing he would ever have seen himself doing, skulking around his own house with a gun in his hand. He heard another burst of machine-gun fire, only this time it was several streets over—maybe gangs, maybe cops, rumors from the Morrison fighting vehicles out front, cops forming gangs, anarchy thriving in the growing lawlessness of the thickening phytosphere. How long before the Marines out in the Morrison fighting vehicles turned against them? How long before things broke down *completely*?

He left the den, walked back into the dining room, then turned right and went into the sunroom. Shards of glass littered the floor. He scanned the backyard down to the canal and saw the Coast Guard vessel at his dock, the *Escapade* puny next to it, but couldn't see any Coast Guard sailors aboard. Where had they all gone? AWOL? The flames from the house fire the next street over were bright now and, glancing to the right, he saw that the conflagration was flaming out of control. *And the dark.* An aging Martian scientist. That's all he had to offer against this darkness.

He opened the French doors and stepped onto the patio. The patio was like a jigsaw puzzle of broken glass. Goddamn it, his family was a *priority* family. They shouldn't have to live like this. Marblehill. Stock it. Block it. And dig in. Maybe phone some of his old Air Force buddies. He glanced at the pool and saw something floating in it. An alligator. Animals were acting bizarrely, boldly, because of the phytosphere. He saw the flick of a reptilian tail, the glow of alligator eyes; funny, the way the eyes glowed like that, even in the blackness of the phytosphere. And maybe, just maybe, the alligator smelled blood, because wasn't that blood over by the barbecue, and wasn't that Eva lying amid a constellation of glowing coals?

He rushed over. Called her name.

But she didn't answer, couldn't answer, was too badly torn up to answer—frightening, the damage machine-gun rounds could do. She was hit somewhere in the chest but he couldn't tell where. Her blood looked black on her black uniform, and the only blood he really saw was a spray of the stuff on her white collar. But he knew it had to be bad because a sucking sound came from her chest. Just like the sucking sound from the faucet. Alarm threatened to overwhelm him.

He had to grab onto her clothes because she was so limp, slippery with blood, and unable to brace herself. He carried her into the house, and as he entered the sunroom he heard splashing in the pool, the alligator now agitated. His family came out of the kitchen. Morgan cried. From the other two it was, "Oh my God," the all-purpose refrain of their teenaged lingua franca. Louise immediately dug through the drawers of the buffet and pulled out linen napkins to use as pressure dressings, her petite ballerina's body quivering like a leaf in the wind.

Neil felt as if he were in a dream, and that in this dream the things people said and did made no difference, that all the knee-jerk survival responses of the human race to this sinking ship of a calamity were going to add up to nothing. Nonetheless, he kept going. Even as Eva's chest sputtered weakly, and even as blood got all over the expensive Persian carpet out in the front hall. The maid's feet knocked over a vase. He opened the door.

What he saw before him was a scene of devastation. The soldiers had dug pits and were burning all the dead vegetation, so that, at the four corners of his once carefully manicured lot, smoldering craters sent ash and smoke into the air. Bullet holes riddled his sports car and the cherubs of the Italianate fountain now presided over basins that had been damaged by gunfire. In the light of the various neighborhood fires, his grass looked pale—not pale like the pale grass of August, but exsanguinated, as if the chlorophyll-carrying phloem within had been bled dry of their life-sustaining processes. The carefully stuccoed walls surrounding his property, painted an evocative shade of Tuscan gold, were now cracked and pocked, and great sheets had broken away to show the concrete underneath. Out beyond the gate he saw the Morrison fighting vehicles. Marines hid behind the vehicles, some on their stomachs, their rifles ready, another on one knee, all of them peering in the same direction, as if an intensely interesting spectacle unfolded down the street.

He walked with Eva in his arms, and he realized that he was tired. Physically exhausted, yes, but also spiritually drained, as if, like the phloem in his grass, he, too, had been bled dry. He glanced over his shoulder and saw his wife following, daintily picking her way down the steps, past the cars. He wanted to tell her to go back, but he found he didn't have the energy. He put one foot after the other and kept heading for the front.

"Sergeant?"

The streetlights were out. A barricade of burning cars flamed three blocks away, where the neighborhood of the have-nots began. The sergeant turned, a black man he had gotten to know fairly well named Baskerville, grim-faced and scared, and not much older than Melissa. He turned so quickly that the red pinpoint of laser light from his scope skidded across the outside wall of the compound like a maniacal scarlet fairy.

"Get down, sir. They've made a flanking move."

"Who?"

"We're not sure. Some renegade officers from Miami-

Dade, we think. They've got military-grade weapons. This whole neighborhood is sitting on a shitload of food, and I guess they want some.''

"Eva's been shot. She needs a doctor."

Baskerville crouched and loped over to the gate, his buddies letting go with a sudden and heart-stopping fusillade of gunfire to cover him.

Baskerville forcefully dragged Neil by the shirt back inside the compound. "Sir, I'm going to have to ask you to stay in the house. At least until we get this situation under control."

"She's bleeding to death. And the sailors from out back are gone."

Baskerville looked at Eva. The soldier unclipped a flashlight from his belt.

"I knew they were going to bolt. Put her there."

Neil put the maid on the ground. As he did so she quivered in pain. Baskerville shone the flashlight down the front of her uniform. He put the flashlight next to his knee and unbuttoned her blouse.

Louise approached from the house, and as she finally reached them she put her hand on Neil's shoulder. The sound from Eva's chest wound grew fainter. At what point did a man lose faith in himself? The sound from her wound stopped. At what point did he realize that the forces ranged against him were far too large to handle? Marblehill. Stock it and lock it. The immense stillness that could only mean the cessation of life crept over Eva the way the shroud had crept over the Earth. At what point did a man come to realize that the concerns of the world at large were of secondary focus, and that his main objective should be his family?

Baskerville looked at him just as his troops fired a field flare into the sky. The flare lit Neil's front yard with a flickering white glow and, as it sank in the direction of the poor neighborhood, gunfire erupted from beside the Morrison fighting vehicles, the age-old music of war, the beat and rhythm of *things breaking down*.

"We'll look after her, Dr. Thorndike."

"Look after her?" he asked. "How?"

In the light of the flare, Baskerville's face changed, hardened, his eyes narrowing, his lower lip curling a fraction of an inch, a hint of disrespect in his eyes as if he were wondering how Neil could ask such a stupid question. Neil sensed a schism between himself and Baskerville now.

"You know. Deal with her remains."

Louise gave him a tug. "Neil, let's go back in the house."

"You listen to your wife, Dr. Thorndike," said Baskerville. "Ain't nothing to see out here."

15

Glenda got up from her basement floor once the truck drove away.

"Stay here," she told her children.

She had to argue with them, because kids wouldn't be kids if they didn't argue, but at last she left them on the floor next to the refrigerator and moved through the darkness, touching her way along the piles of junk to the foot of the stairs, clutching her rifle in one hand and feeling her way up the steps with the other.

In the kitchen, she listened.

Usually there was the hum of electricity coming from the refrigerator, or the sound of cars out on the highway. But except for the ticking of the battery-powered clock in the dining room and the hush of fresh snow falling against the windows (yes, more snow, just in the last few minutes), all was silent.

She crossed the kitchen floor, now used to navigating in darkness. She veered left around the kitchen table, maneuvered to the right, went through the dining and living rooms, then stopped short, exactly at the front door, and clutched the doorknob.

She went outside.

She saw a light burning in Leigh's dining room window.

Using it to see her way, she crossed the yard to the hedge separating her lot from Leigh's. She squeezed her way through, the stiff, dead branches snagging her sweater. She walked down Leigh's driveway toward his house, pausing often to listen, the snowflakes crash-landing on her face.

Up in the hills she heard gunfire.

She continued down the drive through Leigh's carport and into his side yard. She heard the snow melting from the roof into the eaves, a steady trickle. Then more gunfire up in the hills.

As she neared the dining room window, she crouched. She double-checked to make sure her safety was off, felt her heart beating more quickly, was afraid that someone was still inside, and that she might have to kill them. She peered in through the dining room window and saw, in the light of a battery-powered lamp sitting on the table, three chairs toppled on their sides. The glass in the china cabinet doors was broken, and three bullet holes punctured the walls. She stared at the destruction and couldn't help thinking that it was an odd mix—this suburban dining room with its department-store furniture, such an everyday scene, now destroyed like this.

Finally she moved to the rear of the house. She looked through the back door into the kitchen.

The door had been broken open, and the security console smashed. The kitchen table lay on its side—she dimly perceived its outline in the light coming from the dining room. She stepped into the vestibule leading into the kitchen. She saw Leigh's hiking boots, garden clogs, and sandals sitting neatly side by side on an imitation Navajo mat.

"Leigh?" she called.

She got no reply.

She proceeded into the kitchen.

Her toe hit a can of something. She lifted the can and saw that it was instant milk. She couldn't help thinking how her kids could use this instant milk. Use anything. She put the can of milk on the table and walked into the dining room. She lifted the lantern, a neat little rechargeable unit that had a rustic look to it, like it came from a sailing ship of yore. She smelled cordite, and saw brass rifle shells on the floor. She lifted a shell, a .303;

a good hunting round, deadly enough to down a man in one go.

Taking the little lamp, she checked the whole first floor: Leigh's bedroom, where everything was tidy and the bed made; the second bedroom, which he had turned into his weight-lifting room; then into the third bedroom, where he had his computer and all his other electronic junk; then the bathroom, where, in the bathtub, behind the shower curtain, she found two fifty-gallon Duratex coolers of fresh spring water. Jamie, Lars, and Perry must have missed them.

She backtracked into the living room, then the dining room, then the kitchen, and stood at the top of the basement stairs. She held the rechargeable lantern high, but the light wasn't focused, and permeated only halfway down the steps. Nonetheless, it was strong enough to see footprints in blood on the risers.

She now looked at the kitchen floor. Blood was tracked everywhere. Her sneakers had left their own prints.

"Leigh?" she called again, hoping she would hear a groan, sigh, or cry for help.

She heard nothing. She stood at the top of the stairs for close to a minute as the anxious possibilities tumbled through her mind. She fought with her own conflicting impulses. Run? Investigate? She finally held the lantern up and went downstairs, trying as best she could to miss the blood on the steps.

In the basement, she found an extensive hydroponics installation. Leigh had never brought her down here before, and she was surprised to see all this stuff. She saw tomatoes, zucchini, and carrots growing in long, narrow planters, and an array of grow-lights overhead, all of them now off. She saw a hydrogen-powered generator in the corner. The final third of the basement had been bricked up and turned into a large cold cellar. She walked over and had a look. Thick Styrofoam insulated the inside of it. As she entered, she held the lantern high. Shelves lined every available square inch of wall.

The shelves were bare. Jamie, Lars, and Perry had made a considerable haul.

She turned around, and that's when she saw Leigh. He lay behind the door on his back, head tilted to one side, feet splayed, wearing a camouflage hunting vest that was dark with blood. He looked like he was sleeping. For such a violent death, his final resting position was one of peaceful repose. Blood trickled down the drain in the corner. The blood had been stepped in, and the chaotic footprint pattern reminded Glenda of the finger paintings kindergartners did.

She stood there for several seconds.

Then she heard the sound of a car in the distance—far up the highway, at the top of the east hill.

She immediately bolted.

She switched off her lantern and exited by the back door. Was it Jamie, Lars, and Perry coming back?

She ran all the way to the bottom of Leigh's backyard, and now felt Leigh's death coming to her in a blur of tears. The falling snow was cold against her face. She turned around and looked toward the highway. She saw through her tears the blue flash of police lights a quarter mile up the road. A new fear exploded through her chest. It was Maynard Fulton, coming to investigate. He would see her footprints in the blood.

She opened Leigh's back gate and hurried over to her yard. The flashing police lights now lit up the whole neighborhood, even though the two cars were still a couple of blocks away.

She went through her own back gate, ran up the yard and in through her back door. She closed it, locked it, then hurried into Hanna's bedroom. From the window she saw Leigh's house, with the angle wide enough for a partial view of the front drive. The two police cars pulled up and came to a stop.

She saw Brennan Little, one of the sheriff's deputies, get out of one car and walk up the side of the house, shining his flashlight into the dead bushes and along the window casings, his gun drawn. She saw Sheriff Maynard Fulton get out of the second car and walk to the front of the house, quickly disappearing from view behind the carport.

"Mom?" Hanna called from the top of the stairs.

Glenda left Hanna's bedroom and went into the kitchen. Flashing police lights now partially illuminated the inside of the house.

"Go back downstairs."

"Is Leigh dead?"

"Yes."

"Really?"

"Go downstairs. The police are here."

The new logic: *The police are here. Hide.*

Glenda followed her downstairs, and the police lights strobed throughout the basement. Jake had taken advantage of the unexpected light to find an old toy, an alien action figure, only this alien was nothing like the aliens up in the TMS. It wore medieval armor and had a big laser gun, and everybody knew real aliens didn't wear medieval armor and shoot laser guns.

She sat there with her children for a few minutes, Jake playing alien, Hanna starting to wheeze despite the nursing home medication. Too much of the damp basement for her. Glenda heard the muffled chatter of the police radio through the cheap Duratex windows.

A few minutes turned into ten. She thought Fulton might go away. Maybe she wouldn't have to look into those eyes of his—those mocking blue eyes that constantly undressed her. She hoped that he would simply take what he wanted from Leigh's house, add it to whatever hoard he was building—because it was all about the building of hoards these days—and never come back.

But . . .

The knock came at last . . .

A loud knock.

The knock seemed to squeeze her heart so that the passage of blood through her chest felt painful. The knock came again. She thought she might *will* Fulton to go away, but *knew* her own footprints were in the blood, and *knew* that Fulton wouldn't go away no matter how hard she willed him to.

"You two stay here."

She went upstairs, answered the door, and saw Fulton standing there in the dark. He wore his uniform jacket and hat, and he looked cold. The snow behind him was stopping.

"You heard the noise next door?" he said.

He always tried to trap her with his questions, she knew that, but as she didn't see a trap in this particular question, she answered truthfully.

"I heard it."

His mistrust deepened. "And you didn't call? Some local calls are still going through."

"I've been hiding in the basement all this time."

He shone his flashlight at her shoes. "Is that so?"

She looked down and saw Leigh's blood. Damn. Trapped. Even though it was snowing outside, her face felt hot. "I went over there to check things out after his killers left." Because there was no denying it now.

Fulton's face settled and he contemplated Glenda for close to five seconds. "You see his basement?"

Another trap, because her footprints were on the stairs as well. "I saw it." She wasn't going to fall for this one.

He lifted his chin. "What do you suppose he had on all those shelves?"

"Is that a serious question, Maynard?"

He shook his head. "Always the tone, Glenda. In case you didn't know, I'm here to serve and protect."

"That's what your mouth says. But your eyes tell a different story. Please stop looking at me like that."

He shook his head a second time, but he was grinning, as if he were enjoying this. "And after all the help I gave you with your husband."

"Leigh didn't tell me anything, if that's what you want to know."

"So you have no idea who his killers are?"

She brushed the hair from her forehead and felt her expression sink, not in fear but in anger, and had the damnedest impulse to order Fulton off her property and tell him never to come back. "Jamie, Lars, and Perry. Work buddies. That's all I know."

"No last names?"

"No."

"Found your footprints in that basement room, Glenda. Were you looking for food?"

She went all innocent. "Was that what he had in there?"

"Old Leigh wasn't going to let you starve. Everybody knows about you and Leigh."

She frowned. "Why don't you act like a sheriff for a change, Maynard?"

"Leigh didn't give you any food? Because it looks like he had a lot down there. Then all those vegetables he was growing. He was planning for the long haul, wasn't he?"

"He never gave us any food."

His eyes widened. "Is that so?" He shone his flashlight past her shoulder. "Do you mind if I come in and look around?"

He tried to get around her, but she blocked his way.

"I'd prefer it if you didn't."

"I think I better," he said.

"Maynard, I'd appreciate it if you didn't."

"Seems to me you should be glad to have me around, Glenda, now that Gerry's gone and run off on you."

"Gerry hasn't run off on me."

"What do you suppose he's doing up there on the Moon right now?"

"I told you, he doesn't drink anymore."

"Glenda, I've got to take a look around. Police business."

"Then show me a warrant."

"Ever since the . . . restructuring, we don't need warrants. We're streamlining our jurisprudence as we go along, on account of the courts being closed."

He used his great physical size to push past her.

"Maynard, stay out of my house!"

"Sorry, ma'am, but I'm investigating a murder."

He walked into the living room, got down on one knee, and looked under the couch. He then went into the dining room and opened the cupboards under the china cabinet.

"You're looking for food, Maynard. Leigh's murder has nothing to do with it."

"Ma'am, if you don't calm down, I'm going to have to cuff you."

She followed him around the house, knowing she was powerless to stop him.

He went into the kitchen and opened the cupboards. He walked to the fridge, even though it wasn't working, and shone his flashlight in there. He shut the door and shone his flashlight directly in her face.

"Where are you hiding it all, Glenda?"

"Will you stop shining that thing in my face?"

"You got it all in the basement, like Leigh did?"

"Got what?"

"Your food cache."

"Maynard, I don't have a food cache."

"You've already lied to me once."

"And you said you were investigating a murder, not looking for food."

He shook his head. "You're too smart for your own good, you know that?"

He walked across the kitchen to the cellar door.

"My kids are down there. Please don't scare them."

"I'm the sheriff. Why would they be scared of me?"

She followed Fulton down the stairs. "Kids," she cried. "It's just the sheriff. He's coming down. No need to be afraid."

Fulton got to the bottom and shone his flashlight at all the boxes of junk in the middle, then at the tool bench, then at the washer and dryer, and finally at Jake and Hanna.

Glenda's rifle leaned against the wall next to Jake.

"You've got a rifle?" said Fulton.

She scrambled for the quickest dodge. "It's just an old thing my Dad gave me."

"You got a license for that thing? You need a license in Wake County."

"Somewhere. In all these boxes."

He walked over and lifted the rifle. "Hate to tell you this, but the Wake County's Sheriff's Department is confiscating all firearms at the present time. I'm going to have to relieve you of this firearm for the duration of the emergency. Got any ammunition?"

She couldn't hide her desperation any longer. "Maynard, please don't take my rifle. It's the only thing I've got to protect me and my children with."

"Ma'am, I repeat, got any ammunition?"

"Just what's in the rifle."

"That's twice you've lied, Glenda."

"Please leave the rifle. I hear shooting in the hills. I need my rifle in case any of that comes down here."

Fulton lifted his chin and contemplated Glenda. "You come over and see me sometime, Glenda." His implication was clear.

"Maynard, please."

"You want your rifle back or don't you?"

"Okay, okay, I'll come over and see you sometime."

Just then, Little called from upstairs. "Maynard?"

"I'm down here."

"We found crates and crates of stuff up in his attic. Canned goods and everything."

"I'll be right up." He turned his attention back to Glenda. "Now you listen to me, Glenda. I'm in charge now. I'm running the town *independent*. You just remember that. Me and the boys, we're more or less operating the whole show out of Old Hill right now. Ain't going to be no more government help. So it's about time you start being nice to me." He gave the rifle back to her. "You come round and see me, you hear? Gerry won't mind. Gerry's all the way up on the Moon getting drunk. I'm the only one you got to look after you now."

16

At the daily meeting the next morning, Gerry insisted that Stephanie, the showgirl, fill Luke Langstrom's chair—and it was agreed by the others that a tourist worker should have representation on the committee.

Gerry outlined his latest finding to the group, and was glad to see that at least Hulke showed some interest, his small gray eyes focusing with curiosity.

"So, this . . . this band—a band is what you're calling it?"

"It's more amorphous than a band," said Gerry, "but I guess we could call it a band if you like."

"So, you can . . . like, see it? It's there all the time?"

"Yes. I'm hoping to get a second *Smallmouth* off the ground so we can fly in and take a closer look. This second *Smallmouth* will be specifically designed to follow the band, and I think the readings we'll get from it will be markedly different from the ones we've obtained from the first *Smallmouth*. Plus I've got Mitch working on the infrared angle for me. It will be interesting to see if there's any heat fluctuation."

Gerry glanced at Mitch. Mitch's face was pinched, and the AviOrbit representative wouldn't take his eyes off his waferscreen. The small, intense man spoke without looking up. "I was just thinking that maybe we can analyze the visual-light data more thoroughly . . . just so we can confirm for Ira that any resources he puts into an infrared array might in fact yield some usable results. Because, to tell you the truth, he really doesn't see what you've done with the results from the first *Smallmouth* yet . . . so he asked me why we even bothered with the *Smallmouth* in the first place if you weren't going to use . . . you know . . . the data in any constructive way."

Gerry's frustration simmered. "I'm still analyzing it, Mitch. Believe me, I'm going as fast as I can. If anybody's got anything at stake here, I do. My wife and kids are down there. But there's a wealth of information the *Smallmouth* brought back with it, and I'm only one scientist, and I have hardly any lab staff, and no proper equipment. I've had to borrow equipment from the high school. I'm using *high school* stuff, for God's sake."

"It's just that Ira, he gets in these rhetorical moods. And he was in a really bad one this morning."

Gerry turned to the mayor. "Malcolm, I'm asking you to put pressure on Ira."

"Me?" The mayor seemed flustered by the notion. "Gerry . . . let me explain something to you. As mayor of Nectaris, I don't have any say over what AviOrbit does."

"But surely you must have some clout. Talk to Ira. Tell him we need to find out what's going on with this band. Tell him we have to get this infrared array up and running. Tell him we even need a second *Smallmouth*."

"Gerry, he's not going to go for another *Smallmouth*," said Mitch.

Gerry felt himself losing heart. "But we might need it."

"You haven't analyzed the data from the first one."

Gerry glanced at Ian, then at Stephanie, and while both looked at him in obvious alarm, neither of them seemed to know what to do.

At last he turned back to the mayor. "I thought I was in charge here."

"You are. But can't you see Ira's point? Sending the first *Smallmouth* cost a fair nickel, and—not to sound like the city's totally down on its luck . . . but Ira, he's a bit of a bean counter, and he wants the council to fork over at least a sizable chunk for that particular mission, especially now that it's starting to look like a bust."

"A bust?" said Gerry, wondering how the mission could be characterized that way. "It's not a bust at all. And a second *Smallmouth* would follow the band, so it's going to be different."

"He's also a bit reluctant—and I also was on the phone to His Majesty this morning—but he's also a bit, uh, hesitant, to open the coffers at this particular moment because there's now the feeling . . ." He turned to Mitch. "I guess it's more than a feeling, right, Mitch, because we've got some reasonable intelligence to back it up. So . . . there's now the feeling that the Earth is on the verge of doing something in a . . . a *grandissimo* way about the shroud, and if Earth is going to go ahead and get rid of it for us, why waste money when we can save the funds for, like, a festival or something?"

"And what are they going to do?" asked Gerry.

"Something along the toxin line." The mayor raised his palms, widened his eyes, and shook his head. "At this point, it's probably more cost-effective to hold off a bit."

Stephanie leaned forward beside him. "That's exactly the opposite of what we should be doing."

The mayor turned to the showgirl. "And why's that?"

"Because once Earth blows it—and I'm convinced Earth is going to blow it—we should move fast with whatever we have so we can still catch the Tarsalans off guard."

A paternal grin came to Hulke's face. "Ah, yes . . . but hon, I don't think Earth's going to blow it. You're just showing your Moon bias. They've got the fantabulous Dr. Thorndike as their ringmaster. He's got the . . . the top eggheads in the country backing him up. He's got the . . . ." And here he mimicked the overblown diction of the official drops. "The entire resources of the United States of America at his disposal." The mayor glanced at Gerry and, with a glibness that was slightly drawn, added, "Gerry, you've got only high school stuff."

The rawhide hat twitched menacingly beside Gerry.

"Before you can kill something," Ian said darkly, "you've got to understand it."

"Now, Ian, my man, I'm sorry, but you must have lifted that from a movie somewhere, and I don't know how seriously I can really take you when you start talking like that. We can't be thinking Hollywood. We've got to look at the fiscal side of things. That's all I'm trying to do here. I'm trying to do what's right for the city. If we *knew* the toxin wasn't going to work, it would be a different story. We'd be throwing every last penny into our own effort. But because the toxin is in fact going to work . . ."

"But it's not," said Stephanie. "Gerry already said so."

The mayor turned to Mitch. "Should I go into specifics, Mitch? Just so we can convince them?"

"If you think it will help."

"So you got a drop?" said Gerry.

"Correcto-mundo, my friend. As a matter of fact, we received it at 0500 hours this morning." The famous self-immolating grin came to the mayor's face. "Listen to me. I'm starting to talk like them."

"And what's my brother got to say for himself this time?"

"Ah . . . now Gerry, I'm not a technical guy."

"I thought you said you worked for AviOrbit."

"I did. In public relations."

"Then just give me . . ." The mayor's phrase came back to haunt him. "The gist of things."

The mayor raised his eyebrows. "All I know is that they're going to fool the phytosphere in some way. It's the old ace up the sleeve. The old switcheroo. Something like that." The mayor squinted as he concentrated harder. "Was it . . . hydrogen sulfide?" He shook his head. "Jeez, all that chemical stuff. I don't know how you guys keep it straight. Anyway, they're going to flimflam the phytosphere somehow." He turned to his assistant. "Damian, didn't we make a note of the specifics somewhere?"

The mayor's young assistant looked up from his waferscreen. "They're going to starve the phytosphere of its carbon dioxide supply by fooling it with hydrogen sulfide."

Gerry thought it through and was able to put the rough idea together. Neil was going to use hydrogen sulfide as a carbon dioxide substitute—fool the phytosphere into thinking it was getting the right nutrient, and thereby starve it of the same. It was an ingenious idea. Of course it was ingenious—his brother was no slouch.

Yet he still had doubts. "I hope it works. But I don't think we should sit around and wait to see if it does. Mitch, if Ira won't go for another *Smallmouth*, at least get him to go for the infrared array. Because as much as my brother's idea sounds like a good one, the Tarsalans might find a way to neutralize it. We'd be fools to stop our own research and put our eggs into Neil's basket."

He looked at the mayor, then at Mitch, and he saw that he had made at least some small impact.

The mayor turned to Mitch. "Tell Ira that we'll partially underwrite the infrared array if we can later incorporate it as part of the tourist attraction at the Alleyne-Parma Observatory."

Mitch nodded, the expression in his eyes like the flat line on a heart monitor. "I just hope he doesn't go rhetorical on me again."

17

Neil and his family sat huddled in the back of an armored limousine heading through the dark streets of Miami. They were leaving town. Many buildings were now gutted. Others continued to blaze. The fire department was nowhere in sight. He heard the rumble of their escorting Morrison fighting vehicles outside the car. A priority family. At least they were getting the hell out of here. At least the powers that be finally understood they couldn't stay in Coral Gables anymore.

Would it work? His mind circled back to the question of the hour. Would the omniphage munch through the carapace, and would the compound then mimic carbon dioxide appropriately? In the lab, yes. But in the phytosphere itself? The whole thing left him unsettled.

They soon reached the highway and traveled south.

Halfway to Homestead, he got a call. On his phone. *The* phone.

Secretary of Defense Sidower sounded tired but satisfied, his voice rough, as if he were recovering from a cold. "We've launched, Neil. South Dakota went first. Then Texas. Then Guam. Florida should be next. You might see a few missiles from where you are. I can't tell you how goddamned relieved we are. I've read your reports. So has the president. I know we're going to beat this thing." Then, after a pause, he added, "You've done it again, Neil."

Here it was, the basic integer of his life—people in power telling him he had done good. Yet he couldn't help thinking of Kafis, the Tarsalans' chief scientific envoy, his Tarsalan counterpart, and how Kafis, on his many visits to Marblehill, had always surprised him with peculiar ways of looking at things, and of thinking about things—as if the alien could rotate a problem in his mind, view it from all sides, and see every possible permutation and variation. The chess game. Was he going to win? Or was he going to lose?

"I think the hydrogen sulfide thing is sly enough to beat them."

"I think so too."

"It's just a question of understanding the way they think. I'm lucky in that I've had many one-on-one sessions with Kafis. I know how sly he can be. He's always seven steps ahead of the obvious. But I think the hydrogen sulfide is eight steps ahead."

"If you're going to beat a Roman, you have to think like a Roman."

"Yes. And I think I've come to a real understanding of the . . . the Tarsalan mind-set."

"I wish I could say the same, Neil. He's a formidable adversary."

"As formidable as Kafis can sometimes be, I don't think he necessarily views the phytosphere in an adversarial context."

"If the phytosphere isn't adversarial, I don't know what is."

"As I said to the president, it's a teaching tool. Or at least that's the way I think Kafis views it."

"Right," said the secretary. "The cinerthax, or whatever you call it. The only thing it's taught me is how to hate them more than I already did."

"Hating an enemy and understanding one are two different things." Neil felt he had to expand. "Children on the Tarsalan homeworld don't live with their parents. They live with their teachers."

The secretary of defense considered this. "I always hated school."

"Kafis tells me the quest for knowledge is like a religion on Tarsala. Whenever he came to Marblehill, he was always trying to teach me things. Particularly with a variety of Tarsalan games. He says that in harmless games, especially where strategy is involved, we can learn a great deal about ourselves. From a military standpoint, that's something you should keep uppermost in your mind."

"And does Kafis think the phytosphere is a harmless game?"

"All I'm saying is that he understands things best through teaching protocols. They all do."

"Then I guess we're teaching them a lesson." The secretary paused. "How soon can we expect to see some light?"

"Our best estimate is forty-eight hours. Maybe sooner."

"And you're sure it will start in alpha bloom first?"

"Yes."

"Because it . . . it can't come soon enough, Neil." Sidower hesitated. Neil braced himself for yet more bad news. "Never mind the civilian side of things, I'm talking about the military." It was like a personal admission of failure.

"Is the president safe?"

"He's in lockdown."

"And the vice president?"

"In a secure location in Key West."

"And the president pro tem?"

"We've lost the president pro tem," said Sidower. "He was assassinated in his home state. We think by Western Secessionists. It's a tough thing, being a federal democrat in the West right now."

Neil took this as a personal blow because he had been good friends with the president pro tem. "And the speaker?"

"Still safe."

"And what about military bases?"

"We've had some problems."

"But Homestead is safe."

"Would I send you and your family there if it wasn't?"

"So no problems at Homestead at all."

"The rationing's tight, Neil. There's been some minor insubordination. But that's it."

"When was the last time you spoke to Greg?"

"Leanna spoke to him a couple of hours ago. He knows you're on the way. He remembers you well."

"I should hope so."

"There's nothing like the bond of the military. He's got a nice place set up for you and your family in the Officers' Compound. We've had laboratory units airlifted in, and bunks made ready for whatever personnel you think you might need for a second line." The secretary put out a feeler. "The president wants to know if you've had any more thoughts about a second line yet."

Neil glanced at the dark sky outside the limousine window, and again thought of Kafis. "I've drawn up the main, broad principles. If the omniphage and toxin don't work, we develop a virus. We've already tested a few, and we've had some initial success against what's turning out to be a fairly strong immune response on the part of the Tarsalan component in the xenophyta. We hope to have something workable, at least on paper, by the middle of the month. Is it possible to get help with a second string of biological launches from our allies?"

"You're kidding, right?"

The seriousness of the situation seemed to color everything the secretary said.

"So they have no launch infrastructure intact?"

"If you think the U.S. is bad, you should see other countries."

In the secretary's terse utterances, he saw Armageddon's remorseless agenda. "Are we talking horrific?"

The secretary cast around for the proper words. "It's been going on for a while now, Neil. The surgeon general has advised us that the population has reached a nutritional threshold." The implication was clear. "As well, he's reported outbreaks of cholera, diphtheria, and typhoid. Horrific would be understating the case."

Neil regarded the faces of his wife and daughters sitting in the seat opposite him. They stared at him, wondering what he was talking about. Their eyes prospected for hope, the strain apparent in the way they had all lost weight.

"And what about the Tarsalans?"

Sidower paused again. "We're having great luck with their satellites. We've downed fully seventy-five percent of them. We're planning a major offensive in the coming days. We're going directly for the mothership."

"Anything on the diplomatic front?"

"Neil . . . the diplomatic front's been abandoned for the time being. We're going to board the TMS and take control of the phytosphere's control mechanism." The secretary paused again. "Your toxin and virus . . . we'll try those. But I wouldn't be fulfilling my obligations and responsibilities as secretary of defense if I didn't militarily try to get my hands on the damn thing's control system. I guess you'd call it my own . . . cinerthax. If I've got to put them on the ropes to teach them a lesson, then that's what I'll do. It's my little contribution to this whole hellish mess."

A short while later, after he had ended his call with the secretary, Neil saw several flashes to the west. These flashes resolved themselves into pinpoints of flame, and they rose steadily into the sky. He had thought he would feel a sense of accomplishment. But instead he thought of Kafis once more, and of the way he and Kafis would sometimes play chess together at Marblehill. He could see the pieces on the board, remembered the many occasions when he had been on the verge of winning only to have Kafis surprise him with an unforeseen countermove. The faces of his wife and daughters flickered in the glow of the distant launch flames. Was it a question of his own mind-set? Of actually being able to put himself in a place where he could be the teacher, and Kafis the student? He knew that Kafis was infinitely more intelligent than he was. And compared to the human race's scant few hundred years of technological culture, the Tarsalans had had a million years of it. The Tarsalans were superior to humans in every way.

"He doesn't get it," he said, out of the blue, with no context.

"Who?" said Louise.

"Kafis. He doesn't get that we'd sooner make our own history, and not become a part of Tarsala's."

Louise looked away. "Let's just hope he doesn't end history."

PART THREE

18

Sunlight came to Wake County two days later. Glenda squinted as it streamed through her kitchen window. Hanna and Jake stood at the back door peering at the woods behind the house. Glenda left her spot by the kitchen sink and joined them.

The world looked frightful. Everything was dead. Grass brown. Trees bare. Not like winter, because even in winter she could tell the trees were still alive. In this phytosphere season, the browns and grays of the dead things had a whiteness to them, the telltale sign of a plant's inability to produce chlorophyll. The forest looked like a dirty rag. The sun lit it up like a spotlight. On some trees the leaves still hung as if glued in place, only they didn't look like leaves anymore, but more like spent coffee filters or bits of yellowed newspaper. The pine trees reminded her of the Christmas trees people threw out after the holidays, dry and brittle, their needles fleeced. Her lawn was a damp morass of dead grass and mud.

She saw Leigh's shed.

Yes, Leigh's shed.

One of those tin ones, bought in a long, flat box and erected one sheet at a time, white, with a green roof. Some dead ivy clawed its way up the side. Ivy. That was Leigh's thing. Poor dead Leigh. If Sheriff Fulton had been good for nothing else, he had at least buried Leigh.

Her stomach groaned. The sun shone through a hole in the shroud, and its bright intensity was hurtful to her eyes. The sky on the horizon was dark green. This horrible parody of a North Carolina woods looked preternaturally bright against the lugubrious backdrop of the thinning phytosphere.

Her kids stunk. She stunk. There was no running water anymore. When they bathed at all it was in the nearby Taylor Creek, and that was full of dead things.

She saw smoke in the hills. Something was burning.

She opened the door and stepped outside.

Far in the distance, she heard a bird singing. A cardinal. Singing by itself. The sound filled her with hope.

"Come on, kids. Let's go dig."

They got the shovel and spade out of the garden shed.

And then she stopped. How could she have been so stupid? She let the shovel fall and hurried to the back door.

"Mom?" said Hanna.

"I've got to fone your father. I'll be able to get through now."

She tried because, now that there was a hole in the shroud, surely communications would be restored.

But she got the same heartless message.

She resolved to periodically keep trying while the hole was there.

She went back outside. "It's still down. We might as well dig up Leigh's stuff."

They walked to the back fence and went through the gate. Then they walked through Leigh's gate into his yard.

Jake went into the dead man's shed, got one of his shovels, and came back out.

All three started digging.

The soil felt loose. She kept looking out to the highway, fearful that at any moment she might see a police cruiser. But all she saw were the neighboring houses stretching out along the highway, some traditional ranch styles, others conglomerations of geodesic domes, and still others molded in the fanciful shapes the more up-to-date residential architects employed. This whole end of town looked deserted. They were the only ones about.

She dug, and was surprised by how weak she felt, how bony her wrists looked, and how easily she ran out of breath.

Hanna started coughing.

"Hanna, sit for a while."

Her daughter sat on the ground.

Glenda was also alarmed by how hot it was, as if with this sudden burst of sunshine the world had ignited. No more snow. No more winter in summer. Instead it was summer with a vengeance. She stopped digging and checked the thermometer on the side of Leigh's garden shed. Ninety-two Fahrenheit. Was that possible? Could the temperature rise so dramatically? Or was this but another phase in the shroud's evolution?

She went back to digging. After a while, her shovel hit something hard. She looked at her children. Jake stopped digging. His blue-and-red windbreaker hung from his bony shoulders.

"You hit something," he said.

"I think so."

She cast another nervous glance toward the highway.

Jake sank to his knees and shoved dirt out of the way with his hands. Hanna looked at her brother as if she didn't fully understand what he was doing—she was all doped up on the asthma medication from Cedarvale. Glenda got down on her knees beside her son and helped.

In a few moments they uncovered a crate—it looked like Leigh had made it himself out of sheets of four-by-three Duratex, the white sheen of the material smudged with dirt. Jake used his fingers to uncover the outlines of the crate, digging steadily, and at last found a rope handle. He yanked, then yanked again until some dirt shifted.

"Jake, move," said Hanna. "Let Mom get at it with the shovel."

Jake moved, and Glenda stuck the spade down the

side and levered the crate. It still wouldn't budge. So she dug some more. Then she helped Jake with the rope handles.

At last, they yanked it loose. "It's heavy," she said.

With a little more yanking they finally pulled it out of its hole onto the surrounding lip of ground. Glenda lifted the lid and saw several cans inside.

Jake pulled one out. "Irish stew! And look at this. Chicken noodle soup. And chili. And this one . . . it's mandarin oranges!"

Glenda cast another nervous glance toward the highway. "Let's get this stuff inside before someone comes. We can't let anybody know we have it."

"And look, here's some flashlight batteries," said Jake. "And candles."

"Let's just get it inside."

Over the next hour they dug up the surrounding area and found five more crates. They took them inside. They were filled with a variety of canned and dried goods, as well as, ominously, a handgun and three boxes of ammunition.

Most puzzling of all were some keys.

"What do you think they're for?" asked Jake.

"I don't know," said Glenda. "Maybe his cabin. He has a cabin on Jordan Lake."

"Do you know where?"

"No. He wanted to take me up once . . . when your dad was in the hospital. . . ."

"He had the hots for you, Mom," said Hanna.

Glenda shook her head. "No . . . no, I don't think he did. We were just good friends, that's all."

"But you never went up, right?" said Jake.

"No."

"Because you love Dad, right?"

"Yes."

Jake motioned at the keys. "You think he might have food stashed in the cabin?"

"I don't know. It doesn't matter. I don't know where it is."

While they dug out the sixth and final crate, Buzz

Fulton, the sheriff's brother, drove by in his truck, the old junk heap bumping and rattling along the road. He slowed as he passed the house, and Glenda knew he could see what they were doing. He came to a brief stop as he passed in front of the house, but then continued into the hills, his vehicle looking lonely, as if it didn't belong in the sunlit stillness of the dead woods.

"Mom?" said Hanna.

She watched Buzz go until he disappeared over the west hill. Then she looked down at the handgun. Then at her son. "You want to learn how to use this, Jake?"

19

As Gerry and Ian rode the train out to the Alleyne-Parma Observatory to take their first look at the perforated phytosphere, Gerry held his fone tightly to his ear, even though he had just ended his call to Glenda. Miracle of miracles, they had at last gotten through to each other.

He took the fone away and looked at it, then put it in his pocket.

He went over his conversation with Glenda carefully, even as Ian gave him an apprehensive glance. That desperation in her voice. He had never heard her like that before. That bit about the stew, and how they were cooking it on a fire out back because Hanna wouldn't eat it cold. And how Buzz Fulton had driven by a few times. Good old Buzz. He had shared more than a few drinks with Buzz. And the Cedarvale asthma medicine making Hanna high all the time. And Jake learning how to use a pistol. It was all so . . . unsettling.

A snippet of the conversation came full-blown to his mind.

"I'm working on a plan," she had said.

"What kind of plan?"

"I'm going to disperse the food in the woods out back. And we're going to run watches. Me and Jake. Hanna's too stoned from the medicine. If anybody gets too close to the house, that's it, Gerry, I'm not asking any questions."

In the shrillness of this last statement, Gerry had

heard his wife's true anxiety, her tone a revelation, her sentiment a measure of just how bad things had gotten. He stared at the bleak lunar landscape as they passed a spur line that led to an oxygen production facility—three great white spheres on the otherwise gray horizon. He understood—with chill finality—the jeopardy his wife and family faced. Armed men might come to the house and take their food away. Possibly kill them. And Glenda and Jake were going to fight them with a rifle and a pistol, no questions asked. He had to find a way to beat the phytosphere and beat it fast.

He glanced at Ian.

"So?" said Ian.

"She's not doing too good." And he had to struggle to keep his emotions controlled.

"But she's keeping it together, right?"

He thought of her plan. "In a manner of speaking."

"Because I always knew she was a strong woman. Right from the moment I met her."

"The neighbor got murdered."

"Really? What happened?"

"He had a food stash. Some guys came to his house, killed him, and took it. He had an extra stash buried out behind his shed. That's what Glenda and my kids are living on right now."

Ian lifted his chin. "She'll get through."

Gerry swallowed against the growing lump in his throat. If he talked too much about this, he might lose it. He decided to change the subject.

"I was in the mayor's office this morning for an update." He bolstered his voice with a businesslike tone. "Neil's toxin not only seems to be working, but the U.S. military and its allies have destroyed fully seventy-five percent of the Tarsalan killer satellites."

Ian raised his brow. "So maybe ships will start getting through again. Maybe you'll go home soon, buddy."

Gerry felt himself getting shaky again because Ian was suggesting home. "They're telling us to stay put. I think the military's got something planned, Ian. Over and above the toxin thing. Something big."

Ian shook his head. "You mean something stupid."

They reached the observatory a short while later.

For Ian, it was an occasion to take a nip from his flask and light up a joint.

Gerry, on the other hand, went directly to Heaven's Eye.

Rather than look at Earth on the monitors, he studied it through the telescope's actual lens.

The terminator curved along the Earth's meridian like a black fingernail, the planet in gibbous phase, looking like a partially closed green eye. At first he didn't see any imperfections in the uniformly emerald pall, but soon, as the Earth rotated, he discerned an ill-defined black pupil. The muck of the phytosphere was a beryl pudding, and invisible fingers tore it apart. The ragged edges around the pupil had the whiteness of a plant that could no longer produce chlorophyll.

"Do you want a hit off this?" asked Ian.

"Take a look at this. See what you think."

Gerry moved out of the way.

Holding the joint—a merry little smokable in pink paper—between his thumb and middle fingers, Ian leaned down and looked through the eyepiece. Gerry, meanwhile, considered what he had seen. He had to admit, it looked as if Neil was having some success.

Ian lifted his head. "Looks like it's doing something."

Gerry's eyes narrowed. "Yeah."

"You think it will work?"

"I hope so."

"But?"

Gerry shrugged. "Maybe he's got it."

"But?"

It was indeed a piece of work that such a colossal structure could be dismantled this way, and he felt nothing but keen admiration for his brother.

"We'll just have to wait."

"Wait for what?" asked Ian.

"Seems like a slow process."

"And?"

"The Tarsalans could respond."

"Respond how?"

"With a neutralizer, or antidote, or some such other molecular or nanogenic agent. If you're going to fight the Tarsalans, you have to be smarter, stronger, and sooner than they are."

"Sooner?"

"You have to hit them all at once, like Stephanie says."

Three technicians delivered infrared equipment to the Alleyne-Parma Observatory the following day.

Gerry was surprised, and also relieved. He had thought for sure that he wouldn't get any of this new equipment until Neil's toxin attempt had unequivocally failed. That he should see the equipment so soon made him think his arguments had, after all, carried weight, and that even the rhetorically minded Ira Levinson had at last seen reason.

The apparatus, in its entirety, was a boxy unit about the size of a refrigerator, and reminded Gerry of a giant multilens camera. One of the lenses stuck out further than the others, protruding from the white casing about six inches, while the other two lenses remained recessed into the instrument, covered with special optical filters made of blue glass.

The technicians took the whole afternoon to install the unit, and to download software into the accompanying computer.

When they were done, they gave Gerry a rundown, and by the time they left he was fairly adept at imaging, enhancing, and analyzing the infrared views of Earth.

The mayor came a few hours later. "How's it working?" asked Hulke.

"You pulled some strings."

"It was more than strings, Ger."

"Malcolm . . . thanks."

"Just do something with it. Give Ira a bone or something."

"I've been studying the new images for the last few hours."

"And so, like, your brother's thing . . . is it working?"

Gerry shrugged. "As far as it goes, I guess. But the evidence is inconclusive yet."

"Even in the new images? Does this . . . does it help get a better look at what your brother's toxin is doing? Because I had to use that . . . that line of reasoning with Ira, even though I didn't know what the hell I was talking about. Otherwise you would have been waiting forever."

Gerry sighed. So. Here it was again. The hidden agenda. The new apparatus wasn't meant to further his own research, but to confirm his brother's. What else was new?

He glumly told the mayor the truth. "I'm not sure."

The mayor gestured at the infrared views of Earth on the monitors. "How many blooms show deterioration?"

Gerry glanced at the monitor. "I count . . . five. And it looks as if they've just seeded another, so that makes six. It's just that, you know . . ." He motioned at the screen. "It seems the phytosphere is catching on, getting an idea of what's happening . . . like I said it would."

"Gerry, please don't say that."

Gerry shook his head. "I'm just not sure yet. The hydrogen sulfide seems to be working in some blooms, and not in others. Omicron bloom, for instance. It's hardly made a dent."

The mayor's smooth face flushed. "That's not, like, the best news I've heard all day. Any way I can put a positive spin on it for Ira?"

He raised his brow, frustrated that the mayor should be looking at it this way. "I wouldn't say it's a complete bust, Malcolm. But the temperature relationships are complex." The mayor's face sank at this notion. "And I haven't quite figured them out." Hulke's face sank further, as if Gerry's inability to figure things out was just another breach in the confidence the mayor had placed in him.

"So there are . . . temperature relationships." The mayor didn't seem to like this at all. "Okay. Not what I was expecting, but if you could explain without getting too technical . . . so I have something to take back to Ira.''

Gerry collected his thoughts. "We should be getting an extremely cold infrared signature on the dead plant tissue, well into the darkest blues."

"But?" The mayor's pale eyes had now gone wide.

"Well . . . we *have* had a lot of blue, and all that tissue *is* disintegrating, but the disintegration in each bloom only reaches a certain point before it seizes up. It never gets beyond this green boundary here." Gerry pointed. "The green indicates that the plant material has actually grown inert. Not dead, just inert. There's no growth activity. It's like an oak tree in winter. It's still alive, but nothing's happening."

"So does that mean your brother's failed?"

Gerry shrugged. "There's been no regrowth in the affected areas. I wouldn't call that failure, but I wouldn't call it success either. Maybe what we're going to get is a shroud with a lot of holes in it. Which is better than a shroud with no holes at all."

"But if the U.S. keeps peppering the phytosphere with this hydrogen sulfide, and keeps starving the xenophyta . . . surely we'll get rid of it once and for all."

"I don't know. This freeze-up action happens faster each time. It might reach a point where the seeding will stall the minute it hits the phytosphere."

"But generally speaking, your brother's had at least some initial success."

"Given what I'm seeing here, I would say yes."

The mayor stared at the images on the monitors. "And what about . . . you know . . . your own research? Ira was asking about it."

"He was?"

"He hasn't *entirely* dismissed you, Gerry."

Gerry's eyebrows twitched upward. "That's just the shot in the arm I was looking for, Malcolm."

"He wanted to know about the . . . uh . . . anomalous band."

Hearing this, Gerry had to rethink his opinion of Ira. He motioned at the monitors. "You can see the band a lot better using infrared." He pointed. "It runs all the way from the north pole to the south pole. On the infrared scale, it fluctuates into yellow, even into orange near the equator, and that means it's generating a lot of heat. Heat means stress."

"Stress?"

"Whenever things are under great pressure, or great stress, they heat up. This heat band from north to south indicates that the phytosphere comes under global cyclical stress. I'm still trying to understand it."

"But it has nothing to do with your brother's poison?"

"No. It was there before my brother used the hydrogen sulfide. I'm working on some models to explain it. It's definitely not weather, like I first thought."

"And as for the hydrogen sulfide thing? Come on, Gerry. Let's try to be positive. Give me some good old Moon-spirited attitude."

Gerry shook his head. "Malcolm, science isn't a matter of positive or negative attitude. It's simply a matter of . . . careful observation. You don't want to cloud things up with any kind of attitude."

They brought Gerry a cot and he stayed at the observatory around the clock. All the good food was gone, and he ate emergency rations, what the Moon had on hand in case of war, famine, or political unrest on Earth: mostly soup packs, rice cakes, and a dozen different pill supplements.

Members of the committee drifted in and out to watch the monitors, and Gerry could tell from the tightness at the corners of their eyes that they were anxious, still rooting for his brother, but nervous because it seemed to be taking so long.

Mitch Bennett came in and made a show of checking over the equipment, but his eyes kept drifting to the monitors, his small lips pursing, his brow settling. He seemed angry at the shroud. He finally left after saying in a sullen tone, "It's like watching a piece of cheese ripen."

The mayor came and went in various states of

sobriety—and it wasn't funny, because Gerry knew what it was like to be a drunk—always smelling of booze, for the most part holding it together but then slipping up with a slurred word or two, running off to the observatory washroom for a quick nip, joking about what they were going to do when all the booze ran out, and finally staring at the main monitor as if it were an oracle.

"Do you think you're going to need a second *Smallmouth* still?" asked the mayor.

"Why? Is Ira changing his mind?"

"I'll talk to Ira. He's not . . . above fear."

When the mayor left, Gerry spoke to Glenda again, because that was one great thing about Neil's attempt: With the holes in the phytosphere, the lines of communication were open again.

"It seems to be stalling," she told him. "At least from what I can see in Old Hill."

"Any sign of Maynard?"

"No. But Buzz drove by again."

"I had some good times with Buzz. Except for Marblehill. Marblehill was a disaster."

"I wish he'd stop driving by. He came by last night. I heard his truck a mile away."

Ian came in a number of times and, surprisingly, he took only a few nips from his flask.

Gerry commented on it.

Ian motioned at the monitors. "All this . . . makes a man think. I always told myself I'd sober up by the end of it all. I'm cutting back as much as I can."

Stephanie came to visit him.

The minute she saw the monitors she said, "It's not working." And it was funny because Stephanie, nothing more than a showgirl, seemed to cut through the crap better than anybody else. "We've got to come up with something different fast."

He studied the monitors and realized Stephanie was right.

Each new seeding brought no more than a pinprick of deterioration, tiny points of stasis where the hydrogen sulfide was trying to gain a meager toehold. It was as if the phytosphere was now putting up its best guard against the attack.

He was with Stephanie when he first noticed a change around the existing holes. In infrared terms, it was manifested as a rim of yellow forming along the edges of the green, like the finger of God reaching out and breathing a new spring into the dormant foliage, yellow being an indicator of warmth, and therefore, of life.

His shoulders sank.

He showed Stephanie, and together they followed the growth for the next hour. He remembered the weeds in his Old Hill backyard, particularly the dandelions in spring; of how quickly his too-big lawn had been covered with a galaxy of ragged yellow stars, and how dozens of other green miscreants, genus unknown, had sprouted up between the patio stones and along the edges of the house. The phytosphere seemed vicious in its will to live. The yellow rims at the edges of the various holes seemed to pulsate as if with golden blood, and the holes themselves grew noticeably smaller. He took measurements, and electronically conveyed them to the mayor's office, Mitch's office, and even Ira's office.

The measurements spoke for themselves.

Attitude had nothing to do with it.

20

Neil's girls got up early at Homestead because they wanted to see the sunrise. Neil opened his eyes and watched them get ready at the sink. He would have smiled if the awful truth hadn't been revealed to him last night in a special drop from the Moon. *Dr. Gerald Thorndike has confirmed new growth in the phytosphere. Mechanism of defense: dormancy.* In other words, Neil had unleashed a toxic winter, and the xenophyta had survived by lapsing into a state of suspended animation.

And all the gunfire on the base last night. What had that been about?

He swung his feet out of the army cot he shared with Louise and glanced around their fairly large officers' barracks. He heard the rise and fall of jet engines on the tarmac—pilots gearing up for maneuvers. His head pounded. A hangover, but not an alcohol hangover—a stress hangover. Because what was he going to do now? Develop a virus? A plant disease? But how? He wasn't used to working like this, with scattered personnel and diminished resources. He was used to working with the full and generous backing of the United States government, and not in a place where *things were breaking down*.

And now Gerry.

Telling him he had failed.

"Let's see *you* do something, Ger," he mumbled under his breath.

"Huh?" said Louise.

"Are you going to get up and see the sunrise?" he asked.

This was their ritual now; sun worshippers, the lot of them.

"I'm thinking of painting the barracks. I'd like it yellow, Neil. See if you can convince Greg to get us some yellow paint."

"Isn't it enough he can feed us?"

She glanced at the girls. "Shall we let the girls go first?"

They hadn't had sex in a while.

"I have a few things to talk to Greg about."

"Yellow paint?"

He grinned. "Sure. Yellow paint."

They all got dressed and had their rations, and went outside in their shorts and T-shirts and sandals because even at this time of morning it was sweltering. It was glorious to see the sun slanting through the morass of melting green xenophyta. The entire parade ground was alive with light and shadow.

"There's Greg," he said.

"You're not telling me everything, are you?" said Louise.

He paused. "We're going to be fine."

"So can I come and talk to Greg with you?"

"I'd prefer if you didn't."

He moved off.

Colonel Gregory Bard was in uniform, but without his jacket. He was tall, and had pools of sweat soaking the armpits of his blue Air Force shirt. He was as skinny as everybody else. He cast a nervous glance over his shoulder as he approached Neil; that's what Neil remembered about Greg from all those years ago when they had been in the Air Force together, that he always seemed like a man who knew secrets, or who was involved in conspiracies up to his eyeballs. Greg's caginess dissolved as he watched the girls appreciate the sun. These girls. And Louise. In sunshine. His family. He was lucky to have them.

"So?" he said to Greg. "Is the place still standing?"

"It's still there."

"Any sign of damage?"

"Someone's broken in."

"They have?"

"But the place doesn't looked wrecked or anything," said Greg.

"So everything's okay? All the vehicles and so forth?"

"Everything looks fine, Neil."

"And you were able to land two choppers on the lawn okay?"

"That's quite a place. I had no idea you'd done so well for yourself. And right next to Chattahoochee. What a great location."

"And you've got some guys up there right now?"

"The best. Harmon, Earl, and Scott. You remember those guys? Then I got some young guys. Fernandes, Rostov, Douglas, Nabozniak, and Sinclair. All top-notch."

Neil gestured toward the west. "So those guys down at the other end of the base—"

Greg shook his head, a slow shifting of his chin from side to side as his eyes seemed to seek out an indeterminate spot on the tarmac. "Just some disgruntled airmen who think with their stomachs, not with their heads."

"How many are there?"

"Enough to make a nuisance of themselves."

"So, like a . . . a mutiny?"

"A mutiny? I wouldn't call it a mutiny. I would call it more a disgreement. About the way I've decided to ration the food. Especially now that we have a dwindling number of stores."

"But they have guns."

Greg squinted up at the sun. "And a few other things."

"Greg, I have to make sure my family is safe."

Greg looked away from the sun and focused on Neil. The change in attitude, though not profound, was signaled by a locking of his neck, a thrusting of his jaw, and a give-me-a-break narrowing of his eyes. "You don't have to worry about them, Neil. We've got a perimeter set up. And we're bleeding all the stores to this end. If those guys don't want to play by the rules, then it serves them right."

"Maybe you should just airlift me and my family out now."

Greg motioned up at the sky. "We have the second line to think of. I was speaking to Assistant Secretary of Defense Fonblanque personally about that. Once that's done—"

"Are they sending more troops to deal with this . . . this little base insurgency?"

"Insurgency? Come on, Neil."

"Whatever it is."

"A bunch of young cadets playing with guns who don't know any better. That's what it is. We'll have it mopped up in no time."

"Are you sure?"

"Neil, work on the virus thing. Let me handle everything else. There's no point in inventing problems for yourself when you've already got this big one to solve."

21

The shadow of the mending shroud closed in on Wake County, and to Glenda it was like a vise closing around her soul. Her forehead was moist with perspiration. She was wearing her lightest cotton dress, material so thin it hardly weighed an ounce, but the heat now seemed to have a physical presence, a touch that was soft but insidious, and the temperature quickly drained a person's energy.

She got up from bed and closed her hand around her cool rifle. Why didn't they just get it over with? The sheriff's brother drove by every couple of hours now, his rusted hulk of a vehicle bumping and rattling along the road like a mechanical ghost. She knew that they knew about the extra food, and she also knew that they were going to make a try, so why didn't they just do it? She listened, but heard no vehicle. Outside, a phantom green dusk settled over the dead, brown land. The quiet was like the breath of an old man expiring at Cedarvale in the middle of a sleepy afternoon.

She left her bedroom and stopped at Hanna's door. Hanna sat by the window, leaning into the waning light as if she were a plant starved for sunshine. She held a book in her hands, couldn't use the electronic reader, which she so often preferred for her school texts, but held an honest-to-God book, made out of honest-to-God paper; and it wasn't just any book, but one of Hanna's old books, a children's book. Hanna was holding it up to the remaining light with a far-off look in her eyes,

and she looked so stoned on the medication from Cedarvale that Glenda was worried about her, and wondered if she was abusing the medication as a way to
deaden her daily existence. When the medicine ran out,
what then? Would Hanna literally cough herself to
death? Would her body finally grow so weak from the
racking coughs and lack of food that she would slip into
a coma and die?

Day at a time, day at a time, day at a time—her mother's mantra came back with an urgent and panicked clarity. "Hanna?" she said.

Her daughter turned in the slow and lugubrious way
of a heroin addict riding the horse full speed. "Jake's
asleep. You know that, don't you?"

"What?"

"He was sleeping when I went for a pee."

"But it's only eight in the evening."

"He's been sleeping a lot."

Glenda hurried to the living room.

In the dim green light coming through the picture window she saw Jake sprawled on the sofa, his arm hanging
over the edge so that it touched the floor. The gun was
next to his hand, its barrel angled off toward the front
door, a box of bullets open beside it with a few car-
tridges, like scattered gold nuggets, on the floor. Yes,
sleeping all the time, fourteen to sixteen hours a day,
like the depressed old people at Cedarvale. Maybe she
should have raided the Cedarvale dispensary for some
happy pills as well.

She walked over and shook his arm. "Jake? Jake,
honey?"

His head shot quickly to one side, and he was insensible for a few seconds as he clutched wildly for the gun.

Once he had it, he sat up. "Are they here? Are they
here?"

"No, Jake, no. You fell asleep."

Jake cast an anxious glance out the window. "Is that
Buzz's truck I hear?"

She listened, her paranoia taking hold like a bad fever.

All she heard was the quiet. Not even any gunfire up in the hills anymore, as if they had all killed each other.

Jake got up and walked to the window. The fear came off him like sparks from a pinwheel—fear only a kid of twelve could feel. She walked to the window and joined him. She looked at the sky. The light of an August sunset seeped through the ragged hole in the green thing up there, and the edges of the hole, as it closed up, weren't so much green as turquoise, as if hailstones refracted the light. The road was empty. There was no sign of Maynard, Buzz, or Brennan—bastards, the lot of them.

"I'm going to one of the stashes to get some food," she said. "You need something to eat. Eat something, then go to bed."

"Which stash are you going to?"

"By the sycamores. Stash one."

"Can I go?"

"You've got to stay here. In case they come."

"You think they will?"

"They'd be fools to when it's light like this. We'd mow them down. But then Sheriff Fulton's always been a fool."

"I'll use the binoculars."

"Don't drop them this time."

"Mom, that was an accident."

"They're your father's good pair."

"When are you going to learn to trust me?"

She walked to the kitchen and out the back door.

All the dead things in the forest—animals that had starved—were rotting in this heat, and the whole county smelled like roadkill up close. She trotted over to the fence, painfully aware that any of Fulton's men could be taking a bead on her from up in the hills, and used the cover of the dead cedar hedge to make her way to the back.

She paused next to Leigh's shed and looked into the woods. With the light coming down in this eerie way, and the shadows gathering in the lifeless trunks, it didn't even look like Earth anymore, but like some weird and suffocated version of Earth.

She ventured more deeply into the woods. She came to stash one. She dug—and she dug and she dug until she had uncovered stash one. As she was hauling it out of the warm, dead earth, she heard the bump and rattle of Buzz Fulton's truck coming along the highway, but only for a moment before it died at the top of the hill, to the east of the house. Her heart jumped as if with booster cables and her shortness of breath worsened, and she listened and listened, and tried to hear the truck, but the silence, after the usual signature cacophony of his vehicle, was like a death writ. He wasn't passing by this time. He was stopping. Up at the top of the hill. And it couldn't be good, oh, no, it had to be bad, because if he was stopping at the top of the hill, it meant he had plans.

She shoved the stash into its hole.

She ran out of the woods into the yard, conscious of the thump of her sneakers against the dead grass. She entered through the back door, and locked it manually because the console didn't have power anymore.

The front door was open and, getting closer, she saw Jake standing on the slab of concrete they called the porch. He held the binoculars to his eyes and stared up the hill.

She stepped out onto the stoop beside him.

He took the binoculars away. "I think they're here, Mom. I think this might be the night."

"Did you make a head count?"

"Three for sure. But there could have been four."

"So you remember what I said?"

"That the old rules don't apply, and it's okay to kill if I have to."

"Just pretend it's one of your Handheld Sport games."

"Mom, it's a little scarier than that."

"I know . . . I know. Take up your position in the back. Don't come forward unless I give you the signal."

"I feel a little sick."

"Are you going to throw up?"

"I'm just really scared."

"Let's get ready."

They went into the house. Glenda walked to Hanna's room.

Hanna had now put her book aside and was looking out the window. "Is it them?"

"Buzz stopped up the hill. I think you and Jake should go to the woods, like we planned."

"I never liked Buzz. He was such an asshole at Marblehill. He actually came on to me."

"He did?"

"I never told you."

"But you were only twelve."

"Like I said, he's an asshole."

They left Hanna's room.

Jake and Hanna went to hide in the woods out back.

Glenda stayed alone in the house, on her knees at the front window, her rifle ready, scanning the highway, hoping Jake would give her a whistle if Maynard and his crew came from the back. She waited and waited, and slowly the hole in the sky got darker until finally it shone with the eternal blue of nighttime, a shade a hundred times darker than indigo, a ragged continent shiny with stars in the pitch-black of the shroud.

She crawled back to the coffee table and groped for her high-powered flashlight, glad Leigh had stashed away so many extra batteries. She struggled back to the window and looked out at the front lawn. It was now a shade brighter than it had been a moment before—and looking at that hole in the shroud, she saw that its edges were growing brighter as well.

After another fifteen minutes, a pale fingernail of Moon peeped out at her from behind the shroud, and she couldn't help thinking of Gerry.

When Sheriff Fulton finally came, he didn't show his face, but megaphoned from somewhere out in the dark.

"Glenda?" He waited for a response. "Glenda, we know you're in there. And we know you have food. Why don't you do the sensible thing and give it all up?"

She left the living room, went into the den, placed the flashlight on the high window ledge, turned it on, and shone it out at the front lawn. She left it there, beaming out into the dark, then retraced her steps through the dining room, then the kitchen, grabbed her second flashlight, moved quickly through the dining and living rooms to the other side of the house, and went into Jake's room.

She put the second flashlight on the window ledge and shone it out at the front lawn as well. Its beam intersected with the one coming from the den. She paused to measure the effect. A pale glow now lit the yard. Fulton would be a fool to come in from the front. Which meant he was going to come from the back. At least she didn't have to fight this war on two fronts. Not unless they shot out the flashlights, and she didn't think any of them were good enough marksmen for that.

She left Jake's room, feeling her way through the dark house until she got to the kitchen, carrying her rifle loosely in her right hand. She grabbed her extra purse from the top of the refrigerator, the one she kept all her rounds in now. She slung it over her shoulder and exited by the back door.

In the light of the Moon, she saw a ground-clinging mist creep over the lawn. She scanned the backyard. Her eyes strayed to the woods, and as the Moon clawed its way further out from behind the shroud, the poor dead things that used to be trees glowed as if from nuclear waste; not silver, not orange, but somewhere in between.

She leaned her rifle against the house. She heard Fulton's megaphoned voice from out front, like a nasal and electronic ghost moaning out of the darkness, his words now unintelligible because the house blocked the way. How long before he gave up trying to convince her?

She hurried to the fence that ran between her lot and Leigh's.

She got a ladder from the fence and carried it quietly to the back of the house. Made of Duratex, the ladder was light and easy to carry. She placed it against the mudroom, climbed to the top, put her rifle on the mudroom roof, dragged the ladder up, then leaned it against the side of the house so that it reached the top. Making sure the feet of the ladder straddled the mudroom peak securely, she climbed to the main roof.

She maneuvered around the low-pitched slopes with relative ease. She took up a position behind the satellite dish, and scanned the backyard. She had great lines of fire.

She got to her feet and moved to the front of the house.

The Moon was brighter now and she saw Buzz Fulton's truck parked at the top of the east hill, and two police cruisers further down.

She waited.

After several minutes she saw men crossing the highway to the east and disappearing into the yard of the house beyond Leigh's. Fear momentarily weakened her because up until now she had been hoping that they might never make a try for her food. She maneuvered back to her spot by the satellite dish and waited.

After about fifteen minutes, she saw two men at the back. They inspected the ground. Checking for buried food maybe? Then they came along the fence, crouched over. One of them was Maynard, the other Brennan. She had half a mind to let them break into the house and have their look around. When they found it empty, they might go home and never bother her again.

But then she decided it was best to end it once and for all.

"Maynard," she called, "I'd stop exactly where you are. One step further and you're going to have a bullet through your head."

The two men stopped.

"You're up on the roof?" called Fulton.

"Where's your brother?" she called. "Are there other men?"

"Glenda, why don't you come down from there and talk to us? We might as well try to be reasonable."

"Why don't you get off my property? You're trespassing."

"You know what we come for, Glenda," called Brennan. "We know you been hoarding. Just give us your food, and we'll be on our way. No one will get hurt."

"I don't think so, Brennan."

"Why don't you come down to the detachment office and join us?" said Fulton. "We've made quite a little place down there. I could protect you."

"For what price, Maynard?"

"Glenda . . . Glenda, I'm going to give you to the count of three to come down. I don't want to hurt you, and I don't want to hurt your kids. But I got to do what I got do. We're talking survival here, Glenda. You know how it is. Don't say I didn't give you fair warning. One . . ."

And suddenly it made complete sense to her, in the way anything can possibly make sense after such a long time in the dark.

"Two . . ."

Fulton was the enemy. The county's principal purveyor of death.

"Three . . ."

Yes, he was the heart and brains of the whole operation, and it was monstrous that he should have the county's women under his "protection," and it was up to her to stop all that. . . . *Now careful, Glenda, are you thinking straight? Have you taken all things into consideration? You're about to shoot a cop, and not just any cop. And yet . . . shoot him, and you shoot the whole works. Get rid of the head, and the body dies.* Yes, it made perfect sense to her, in a fear-crazed way.

"Glenda, you leave us no choice but to—"

And before he could say another word she targeted the sheriff's head—and it all came back to her, those weekends on the Smoky Hill River with her father, when the sun went down and the sky turned orange, and the partridges leaped into the sky. She took a bead on the sheriff's head with automatic reflexes and hands as steady as iron, and caressed the trigger so that the rifle fired by itself, adding her own bit of Armageddon to the Apocalypse, the shot rocketing through the air with a roar that echoed in the hills, the bullet hitting its mark as if foreordained.

She heard the sheriff grunt, and he went down like a cow in a slaughterhouse, just so much meat thumping against the poor, dead grass.

Brennan did an odd little jump, his legs splaying, his arms jerking, like he was on thin ice and had just heard a crack. Then he ran toward the back, and she had the oddest sensation that she was floating, because she suddenly felt invincible—but so worried, so terrified for her children, because Brennan was running toward the woods where they were hiding.

So she shot Brennan too, and she must have got him in the spine because his legs gave out from under him, and his handgun flew off toward the shed, a speck of darkness in the gathering moonlight. He dragged himself along with his hands, grunting and groaning, until she lost sight of him in the woods.

22

Gerry knew Kafis from Marblehill, but every time he saw the alien—and Kafis was here on the Moon with a contingent of five other aliens—he had to get used to the Tarsalan's appearance all over again, especially the bicephalic nature of his cranium. Under the alien's coarse, dark hair the impression of two separate casings was disconcertingly unmistakable.

Kafis's face was blue, the color of a robin's egg. The quality of his skin was like the quality of human flesh, with all the imperfections of pores, wrinkles, and blemishes.

His eyes were a little over twice human size, and were divided into sclera, iris, and pupil, like human eyes. His irises were amber, like Stephanie's were today, the color of a fine scotch whiskey, and his pupils, black like human pupils, were highly reactive, but not necessarily to light. The way the alien's pupils dilated and contracted reminded Gerry of the way a hummingbird dances around a bloom, in sudden shifts, so that when Malcolm Hulke burped after a particularly capacious gulp of synthi-beer, Kafis's pupils twitched open, then twitched closed, then twitched to the halfway point, the changes in aperture occurring with lightning quickness.

The alien's lips were delicate, a dark shade of blue. Kafis's teeth, though white, weren't really so much teeth as upper and lower semicircular serrated blades fitted along his gums like a mouth guard. Below his mouth was a delicate, pointed chin, impossibly small considering the size of the rest of his head.

As for his body, it was about the size of a Vietnamese man's, smallish and agile-looking.

And his hands . . . interesting . . . six digits—like those cats with six toes.

These particular Tarsalans spoke English. Physiologically, their tongues, mouth cavities, and larynxes were equipped for verbal language.

Kafis spoke English best of all—those summers at Marblehill with the Thorndike family had taught him well. And because he had learned most of his English from Neil, Gerry occasionally heard Neil's phrases in the alien's voice.

"It's a wisdom your negotiators should embrace," he was telling Hulke, who was halfway to getting drunk and arguing for the sake of arguing. "Think of it. As a species, you've been confined to this one system ever since you evolved from apes. What if something were to happen to this system? And something eventually will, of course. Your sun will, in a few billion years, go into its red-giant phase, and that will be the end of you. We've already talked to at least ten worlds, and they would be willing to welcome you as émigrés."

"I don't think you'll get many takers," said Hulke. "You may get a few screwballs."

"But then you might at least have a handful of humans on other worlds. The future of your race would be assured. And that's all we want as well. To plant some of our people on Earth. There's plenty of room on Earth, and my colleagues and I are at a loss to explain your intransigence."

"It's not *my* intransigence, Kafis. As far as intransigence goes, you'll have to talk to Earth."

"We would prefer you talk to Earth for us. It's been more than apparent these last nine years that our own negotiators aren't getting anywhere with them."

"Uh . . . Kafis . . . it's their ball of wax, not ours."

Kafis stared at the mayor as if he hadn't understood

a word. Then he rubbed his long, delicate, six-fingered hands together, and glanced at his five silent colleagues.

Kafis turned back to the mayor, and stared at Hulke for a long time, his eyes inscrutable. It really was hard to tell what he was thinking because it was like staring into the eyes of a cat or fish, especially because, characteristically, there wasn't much play of muscle around his eyes. But at last the alien seemed to dismiss the mayor. He focused on Gerry instead. Some of the muscles around the alien's small mouth twitched.

"Why do you attack us?"

Here it was, what Gerry had seen so often at Marblehill, the human mind confronting the alien mind, unable to traverse the gulf between.

Kafis continued.

"Why do you allow millions of your own people to die daily? We never meant this. Why do you set fire to your own house . . . then lock the door and stay inside? We came as your benefactors. We tried to teach you the way of things. But at last you made us force you to kneel, as we make our children kneel, even though it was the last thing we wanted. This you must understand: When the knee is on the floor, it's time to acknowledge that the lesson is learned. And this is the lesson we have tried to teach you. Life is worth living no matter what the cost. We mean to be your friends and help you any way we can. But you are like the bluntwog, who fights for the sake of fighting. The bluntwog doesn't understand the ways of harmony, or how the resolution of conflict should best be treated like a ceremony, something that must be performed so all sides can save face. We understand the nature of pride. But the true mark of a civilized being is humility. You show none. Instead of acknowledging our wisdom, you attack us. You force us to use the violence we abhor."

Gerry sat back and shook his head, feeling the gulf more than ever. "Earth has offered compromise after compromise, Kafis. In case you didn't know, compromise is a form of wisdom."

"But you attack us. You kill us. We have suffered ten thousand casualties."

There it was again, the unbridgeable chasm . . . and a certain inflexibility to the way Kafis thought about things, as if his way of thinking was *too* evolved, *too* hardwired, and *too* insufferably condescending. Put the phytosphere around the Earth and surely the humans will come to their senses and follow not human cultural norms, but Tarsalan cultural norms. Surely the humans will get down with humility on bended knee and acknowledge that the Tarsalans aren't their enemies but simply their teachers, wise ones who want only to welcome them into the Commonwealth of Worlds, to disperse the human race so that it can survive when the sun's red-giant phase at last comes. And if passive protest in the form of the phytosphere is needed as a teaching tool—a *cinerthax*—then surely the humans won't lock themselves in their own house and burn it down.

Kafis looked perplexed by the whole situation.

"Let me teach you a fundamental lesson about human beings, Kafis," said Gerry. "Push us, and we push back. No one's going to tell us what to do."

"Yes, but why push against reason and common sense? Do you not value your lives?"

"Of course we do. But we value freedom more."

"And we *offer* freedom. Freedom to live wherever you want on any of the habitable worlds. Wouldn't you like to see the Sungeely Falls on the planet Yravo from their two-mile summit? Wouldn't you like to see the ringed gas giants Osa and Meta so close in the sky of Hita that you can nearly touch them? And what about the diamond caves of Farostatar, where whole cities are built out of the precious gems? These are the wonders we offer. These are the freedoms that can be yours. Any of these planets would welcome you. And on any of these planets you would see a mix of races, species, and genera hailing from all parts of the local Milky Way. We offer you the galaxy, and in return, you fire your weapons at us so that we are forced to convert our peaceful shuttles into birds of prey, and shoot down your pilots like pesky insects. We now understand that the mothership is your next objective." Kafis sat back and his pupils twitched open to their fullest size. "And in that regard we have something we wish you to convey to your United Nations for us. We've tried to convey it to them ourselves, but so far they haven't acknowledged our overtures."

"Kafis . . . we've been told by Earth that they've abandoned any and all diplomatic initiatives." He thought of the most recent Earth drop, and how Earth planned to board the TMS and abscond with the phytosphere control device. "They're not even going to try with you anymore. They're going bluntwog on you."

Kafis continued right along, ignoring Gerry's interjection. "Please convey to them that should they actually succeed in damaging the mothership to the point where its life-support systems no longer function, we will then unilaterally claim as places of refuge those areas marked in the most recent U.N. counterproposal. Namely, the Kanem Region of Chad, the Arnhem Land Reserve in the Northern Territory of Australia, and the Chattahoochee National Forest in America's state of Georgia. We will secure these areas with military force and use their hinterlands as regions of supply, regardless of the cost to human life."

Gerry's face sank, and Kafis must have noticed it because his pupils shrank. In one of those brainstorms Gerry sometimes had, he realized he had made a breakthrough. He no longer wondered why Neil had such an easy time communicating with Kafis, and was pissed off at Neil for not telling him of this discovery sooner. If Gerry had discovered on his own that the whole key to understanding Tarsalans lay in the movement of their pupils, it would have been one of the first things he would have shared with his brother.

"You're on weak ground, Kafis. You obviously never expected us to respond with such overwhelming force, and now you're on the run. You can't go dictating."

"Nonetheless, we will stake these claims if life support on the mothership becomes unviable."

"Then let me give you some advice. You shouldn't molest any of the local population when you go down. Humans hate that more than anything in an invading alien. Especially in good ole Georgia. If you've got to take over, just take over nicely, and try to help everybody."

"Our survival will be our sole priority."

"So you understand after all?"

Kafis gave him a double take. "Understand what?"

"How this is about survival."

"Human, you exhaust me."

"You exhaust me too, Kafis."

Ian came to his room much later, just as he was going over the more recent views of the phytosphere, the ones with the toxin holes. Ian was like a caged animal and all he could do was pace in front of the twin beds, stopping occasionally to look at the dark lunar surface, or turning around and gazing briefly at the lamp, always with a look of bewilderment in his eyes. Gerry didn't know if Ian was here for a reason, or if he was here simply because he had to be somewhere. Sometimes Ian just . . . showed up. Was he drunk? Gerry didn't think so. He couldn't smell any booze.

Ian finally looked at Gerry. "This whole thing is spinning out of control."

The anxiety in his friend's voice was like the news the doctor gave you when you had a tumor. Gerry tried to rise to the occasion. He struggled to mount some semblance of courage. But he couldn't help remembering his wife's words: *If anybody gets too close to the house, that's it, Gerry, I'm not asking any questions.* And then there was Kafis, spinning out of control as well, his strange alien pupils twitching in fear as he considered the unviability of TMS life support. Gerry tried to show courage but, after a visit from the aliens, courage eluded him— the Tarsalans might go down to Earth; they might go to Georgia, which was right next door to North Carolina. And Glenda wasn't asking any questions.

"I thought we were going to beat it," said Ian, still pacing.

He didn't have to say more because his implication was clear—maybe they weren't going to beat it after all.

Then it was one non sequitur after another from Ian. "God, I've done some horrible things in my life." Just out of the blue, as if, with that thing knitting itself around the Earth, he had finally found it in his soul to feel remorse. It didn't matter that Gerry had no context; he understood it well, how the alcoholic could become a beast, how he could black out for hours at a time and have no memory of the abysmal things he had done. "Remember Maggie Madsen?" A pathetic chuckle, as if Maggie Madsen had been one of the bigger lost chances in his life.

"Ian, I thought we agreed we would never talk about Maggie again."

"Remember that night in the pool?"

"That was her idea, not mine. I had no idea she was going to come up to me that way."

"Yes, but you didn't do anything to stop her, buddy, even though you knew she was going out with me."

"You see what a bad thing alcohol can be?"

"If it was just that one night . . . but you stole her away from me."

"And I regret it. I told you that. That's why we don't talk about her."

"What ever happened to her? I wonder how she's making out down there in the dark."

"Last I heard, she'd married a car dealer in Norfolk."

"Really? She always struck me as the more adventurous type." Then came a whole sequence of, "What am I going to do, what am I going to do?"—the same six words uttered again and again, nonstop, a bizarre refrain wrapped in regret and anxiety. And still the pacing. Wearing out the rug. The clock moved, edging past midnight. Ian got more and more worked up, haunted by ghosts only he could see, driven—so much so that he finally punched the mirror, broke it, and drew blood.

"Jesus, Ian."

"Sorry, buddy."

Ian walked to the washroom and cleaned himself up. Gerry heard running water. He tried to concentrate on the stills of the phytosphere, but thought of the damned Tarsalans instead, coming all this way, reminding him of born-again Christians because they were all so smug, so sure of themselves, as if they had seen the Kingdom of Heaven. Ian came out of the washroom. He had a white towel wrapped around his fist. He radiated desperation.

"But there's still time, isn't there, buddy?"

"Time for what?"

Ian became distracted by his own thoughts. He went to the refrigerator, got a little booze bottle, twisted the cap off, sucked the contents into his mouth, but then spit the whole works out, not bothering to swallow, and uttered a string of obscenities, telling Gerry he had to *stop that stuff, stop that stuff, stop that stuff,* like a man with bipolar disorder in the manic phase.

"That's it, Gerry. I'm through with booze. I'm walking the straight and narrow from now on."

"Sit down for a while. I'll make some coffee."

Gerry played a role he knew well—the role of sponsor—remembering his own sponsor, Pat Turnshek, an old guy he'd met first at Bellwood, then at all the meetings afterward. When his own demons haunted him, Pat would make coffee, the magic elixir of A.A. meetings, the thing that made everything all right, even when everything was horribly wrong. So he made coffee, and soon it was dripping into the pot.

Ian sat in one of the chairs and rocked, as nervous as could be. "I always manage to say the wrong thing, don't I?" Another cryptic utterance, one Gerry couldn't immediately make sense of. "How did you do it, buddy? How did you marry such a nice wife?"

How his wife got into it, Gerry wasn't sure—Ian was all over the place.

He could have offered Ian the usual platitude, that he was lucky, but knew that it went far beyond luck, that it was his wife's compassion and forgiveness, and that she wasn't going to give up on him no matter how bad things got.

The test pilot motioned out the window. "I hate looking at it. It reminds me of all the terrible things I've done. I've got a lot to make up for, Gerry. I've got a whole list of bad things I've done to people. I've got to make things up in a hurry." He motioned out the window. "Before we run out of time."

Gerry stared at the coffeemaker. If they could all just drink enough coffee, maybe the phytosphere would disappear. Maybe the Tarsalans would go home. Maybe they would stay away from Georgia. And North Carolina. Ian started talking about the Tarsalans: how they creeped him out, how it wasn't natural for them to come all this way, and how sentient species were meant to stay on their own planets and make their own isolated homes surrounded by their own isolating light-years. And then it was back to Maggie Madsen again.

"In the pool, buddy. I couldn't believe it."

"Ian, I'm sorry about Maggie Madsen."

But Ian bluffed, saying, no, that was all right, we were just kids, we didn't know any better. "You're unlikely to do the same thing again, aren't you, buddy, steal a girlfriend out from under me?"

All Gerry could say was the same thing again. "Ian, I'm sorry."

They lapsed into morose silence after that.

They sipped coffee.

Gerry tried to bolster Ian's spirits by telling him it was never too late, and that Maggie Madsen wasn't the only woman in the world.

But all Ian could do was sit there and shake his head. "That green thing over the Earth—it gives me a whole new outlook."

23

Glenda stayed on the roof for close to a minute. Her heart pounded. Maynard didn't move. She thought of the ramifications. Cop killer. What difference did it make? The cops weren't cops anymore; they were just a band of desperate men in a land of kill or be killed. She didn't have to worry. There were no judges. No juries. No penal system at all. And the court was closed.

She at last got up from the roof. She descended the ladder, then shifted it, sliding it over the side of the mudroom eaves. She went down the rungs to the backyard, wondering if it was safe to whistle yet, or if any more men would come, or if she had killed the body by killing the head. The mist thickened and the moonlight brightened. She walked toward Fulton.

She knelt next to him, half believing that he might still be alive. But he was dead, lying on his stomach, his arms straight at his sides, his rifle under him, his finger twisted up under the trigger guard. Her hands started to shake.

"You prize-winning piece of shit," she said.

Tears flooded her eyes and she sobbed, a choking sound in the thick, stinky air of the dead woods out back.

"Mom?"

She turned.

The nightmare kept getting worse.

Buzz Fulton had a chokehold around her daughter's throat, and a gun pointed at her head. The two approached out of the woods. As they got closer, Buzz glanced at his brother.

In the gathering moonlight, Glenda saw a strange emotion play over the younger Fulton's face. His jaw protruded and the unshaven whiskers on his pale chin looked like a gunpowder tattoo. His eyes widened, then narrowed, then moistened, and for a few seconds he looked entirely unsure of the situation. He twisted his head to one side, as if he were wearing a too-tight necktie, then to the other side, and in the moonlight she saw a band of sweat glimmer down his left cheek like a silver ribbon.

Hanna was wheezing and wheezing, like a punctured bagpipe, and looking at her with wide, scared eyes.

"You killed him?" asked Buzz.

How to explain it to him? What lie would he possibly believe?

"Bullets started flying, Buzz, and I—"

"I heard only two bullets. And they both came from the same rifle. Yours. Poor Bren is dying back there. So don't go lying to me, Glenda."

She saw that the whole situation was at a bad dead end.

"I didn't want to, Buzz." And then she remembered what that guy in the supermarket had said to her during the Stedman's looting. "But it's every man for himself."

"Guess I'm going to have to shoot your daughter, then."

"Buzz, please . . ." She threw her weapon down, got to her knees, and clasped her hands in entreaty. "I was only trying to protect my children, like any good mother would. And if you've got to shoot someone, shoot me."

Buzz's lips stiffened in barely controlled anger. "Does that make sense to you, Glenda? That I should give you the easy way out and shoot you dead right now? While I've got to stay alive and suffer like this?" His voice was shaking now, and his eyes had clouded over with tears. "Doesn't it make better sense that I shoot your daughter so that you can suffer like I'm suffering?"

"Please don't shoot her, Buzz. I'll do anything. I swear

I'll do anything. I'll come and join the girls at headquarters if you want."

"I don't hold truck with what the boys are doing with those girls at headquarters."

"Then I can give you food, Buzz. We've got food. All kinds of it."

This stopped him. Then he said, "Why is it that people like you got food, and I don't have any?"

"I've got some hidden in the forest."

Buzz nodded, then grinned, even as tears thickened further in his eyes. "We knew you had it." He seemed to dwell on something for a few moments. He came out of his reverie with a businesslike squaring of his shoulders. "We might have a deal, Glenda. Get Maynard's flashlight. It's attached to his belt."

She knelt beside the dead sheriff and unclipped his police flashlight. Her hands shook so badly she could hardly manage the small task. She wondered if Jake was dead somewhere in the woods.

"You've got to promise that you won't kill us if I give you food."

"I promise." He flicked his head toward the woods and said, "Move."

She spoke to Hanna. "Honey, it's going to be all right. We'll just do what Buzz says and this will all be over."

"You listen to your mama, sweetheart. Uncle Buzz ain't going to hurt you." Buzz's slightly licentious tone reminded Glenda of how Buzz had come on to Hanna at Marblehill when she was twelve years old.

She walked ahead of them into the forest, hating to turn her back on the whole situation, cursing herself for being so stupid. She feared that at any moment she would hear a gunshot behind her, and that would be it; Hanna's short life would be over. She prayed to God, but she couldn't sense Him right now.

They walked to the end of the yard out past the shed. As she passed the shed and was heading toward the dead sycamores, she heard a noise—the slide of a foot along the dead grass behind the shed, the soft whisper of shoulders shifting inside a T-shirt—and, turning, saw

Jake emerge from the shadows, Leigh's pistol held up straight in both hands, just like she had taught him, his face so scared in the moonlight that his pale blue eyes bulged.

"You let my sister go or I'll blow your head off, Buzz."

Her first instinct was to curse him for being such a fool, and for now endangering his own life; but when Buzz jerked to a stop and flicked his head a fraction to the left, and his eyes narrowed with sudden tension, and fresh sweat popped out of his pores like water out of a newly divined well, she thought that, yes, she had to learn to trust Jake, and that she couldn't do this by herself, not in a world gone mad with hunger and darkness. She was going to have to count on her children.

"Easy there, son," said Buzz. "I can't believe your mama gave you a gun."

"Let my sister go or you're a dead man."

"Son, I guess it comes down to nerve. Who's got more of it? Me or you?"

Jake fired straight into the air, and Buzz's nerve crumbled.

"Let my sister go, or the next one's for you."

"Easy, boy, you don't want to have an accident."

He let Hanna go. Hanna hurried to Glenda. Glenda took her in her arms and stroked her hair.

"Now put the gun on the ground," said Jake.

"Jake, that's the only weapon I have. You don't want to leave a man defenseless with the shroud up there."

"I said, put the gun on the ground. I'm giving you a chance here, Buzz."

Buzz hesitated for close to five seconds, and in the light of the Moon Glenda saw the frantic thinking that was going on behind his eyes. Despite this scrutiny of his options, he at last put the gun down and stood up slowly.

"Now beat it," said Jake.

Buzz lifted both arms into the air and backed away. "It's okay, son, I'm on my way."

"Shoot him, Jake," said Hanna. "Don't let him get away."

"Don't you listen to your sister, Jake. Miss, I apologize for what I done to you."

"Jake, just shoot him. He's going to come back."

"Mom?"

"Let him go."

"But, Mom," said Hanna, "he's going to come back, I know he is."

"Buzz, I'm real sorry I had to kill your brother." And the tears came back because she really couldn't believe she had killed a cop.

"The Lord will make His judgment, ma'am."

"Shoot him, Jake!"

But Jake didn't shoot.

And Buzz finally disappeared into the dark woods.

Ten minutes later, as they were carrying food back to the house, they heard his truck out on the highway, its bump and rattle a sound that now terrified Glenda.

Back in the house, she foned Gerry, and he answered on the third ring.

"I wouldn't stay in the area," he said. "You don't know Buzz the way I do. He's a vindictive son of a bitch. When I was a regular at the Crossroads, there was barely a night that went by when he didn't get in a fight. Hanna's right. You should have killed him when you had the chance. Revenge is one of his main motivating principles. And now you've gone and killed his brother. In self-defense, admittedly, but that's something Buzz isn't going to understand."

"But where would we go?" asked Glenda.

"I'm told there's still limited cell-phone service in certain parts of the United States."

"We're getting partial service here, but it's a bit sketchy."

"See if you can phone Neil on his cell. Tell him what's happened. Maybe you can go down to Coral Cables. Do you have anywhere to recharge the car?"

"The nursing home pump is still working. At least the last time I was there."

She followed her husband's advice. She recharged her

cell phone by shining a flashlight at it for a few minutes, then tried Neil.

She tried throughout the night, but kept getting service interruption messages.

A little after midnight, service resumed and she was at last able to get through. It turned out he wasn't in Coral Gables at all. He was at an Air Force base, Homestead.

The change in Neil's voice took her by surprise. He usually spoke so confidently, as if he had the world in the palm of his hand. But now he sounded distracted. And more than distracted . . . what was the word? Yes . . . he sounded *diffuse,* as if all his energy and concentration had been scattered.

"I'm working on a new approach." But his words lacked confidence. She heard what sounded like gunfire in the background. "A virus. It actually works on a kind of interesting principle. It attacks the Tarsalan genetic component of the xenophyta directly, but . . . I . . . Jesus, Glenda, you shot a cop?"

And she explained to him how Maynard wasn't really a cop anymore but just a kind of feudal lord. Then she began to explain about Buzz.

"That idiot Gerry brought to Marblehill a few years back?" he asked.

"That's him." Then she explained that Buzz was a vindictive son of a bitch.

"Look . . ." Neil cut her off, as if the zany details of her war with the sheriff and his brother were beside the point. "I want you and the kids heading to Marblehill. One thing this whole exercise in futility has taught me . . . it's all about family. I've got some airmen stocking the place. And guarding it. We've got a bit of a situation down here at Homestead. And if this virus thing . . . if it doesn't pan out . . . me, Louise, and the girls will be heading up to Marblehill. I've got enough food up there to last a year. And I've got the place well stocked with medicine. . . . How's Hanna? How's she managing the heat?"

"She's getting bad, Neil."

She told him about the prescriptions she had taken from the nursing home, and that they weren't Hanna's regular prescriptions, and of how Hanna was buzzed most of the time and wheezing constantly.

"You remember Greg Bard?" asked Neil. "He was a friend of Ian Hamilton's. I think you met him at Melissa's christening."

"The Air Force colonel?"

"Right. He's getting things arranged for Marblehill."

"So there's going to be other families?"

"No. Just the airmen and us. Greg's a helluva guy. I'll make sure he knows about Hanna. What's she taking?"

Glenda gave him Hanna's prescriptions—her puffers and pills and so forth—and as he took the information down, she felt suddenly safe in a way she never did with Gerry. She could sense Neil's masterliness, and the overall command of his personality. Neil was going to pull it out of the fire for her. Neil was the alpha male, the king of the tribe, whereas Gerry had always been the quieter one.

"I'm going to have to drive manually," she said.

"That might pose a problem," he said.

"Why?"

"Because we're getting reports of widespread erosion. No plants holding things down. Greg says a lot of landslides everywhere, especially up in those mountains, and no road crews are going out for repairs. So you may have to feel your way along. Some roads are bound to be impassable."

"But one charge should do, right? It's not more than four hundred miles. And my car's got an upper limit of four hundred and fifty per charge."

"It depends on how far out of your way you have to go. Do you have a map? Like an old paper map? Or do you keep everything stored online? Because the satellite feeds can't provide maps to your car anymore."

"Gerry's got some old maps downstairs."

"He's still collecting maps?"

"Mainly old ocean maps. But I think he has some of the area."

"Take them, just in case. You might end up on back roads."

She had her kids pack in a hurry because she was afraid Buzz might return at any minute.

She tried to fone Gerry because she wanted to tell him where they were going, not Coral Gables but Marblehill, but she couldn't get through.

"I don't get it. I got through just a while ago. Now there's nothing. And the sky's still open."

"Mom," said Hanna, "things are breaking down everywhere. The shroud might be open, but do you think the people who run AT&T Interlunar are actually going to their jobs anymore? They're just trying to stay alive, like we are. This is the new Stone Age."

"Hey, it's the new Dark Age," said Jake, and laughed at his own joke.

She thought she might leave a note for Gerry, telling him where they were going, just in case he came back, and just in case their fones stopped working for good, but realized that if she left a note it might be a signpost to Buzz and he would follow them.

She and Hanna had a big fight about it.

"Mom, we have to leave a note."

"We can't leave a note."

"But if we don't leave a note, how's Dad going to know where we are? He thinks we're heading to Coral Gables."

"If we leave a note, Buzz will see it, and he'll come looking for us. He's been down to Marblehill before. He knows how to get there."

"Jake," said Hanna, "you should have shot him while you had the chance."

"You try shooting someone," said Jake morosely. "It's not as easy as it looks. It takes a lot of guts."

"Guts that you don't have."

"Mom, will you tell her to fuck off."

"Jake, do we have to use that kind of language?" asked Glenda.

Hanna frowned. "Shut up, Jake. Mom and I are having a serious discussion."

"We're not leaving a note, Hanna."

"Then how's he going to find us?"

"He'll figure it out. He's a pretty smart guy."

"You don't even want him to find us," said Hanna. "You're thinking this is your chance to finally get rid of him."

Glenda's anger flared and, in her worn-out state, she felt tears threatening. "How can you say that?"

"Because it's true."

"It's not true. We may have had some pretty rough fights—"

"You know what will happen to Dad if he can't find us? He'll die. He won't know where we are, he'll think we're dead, and he'll die of a broken heart."

"Hanna, listen to what I'm telling you. If we leave a note for Dad, Buzz will break in, see it, and come after us. I killed his brother. He's not going to forget that. It's not like I keyed his car, or egged his house, or butted in front of him at the bank. I *killed* his brother. I dropped Maynard in cold blood right in front of him. So I'm asking you, please. Don't leave a note. And don't try and sneak a note while we're getting ready. Just let me keep trying your father on the fone."

"That fone's a hunk of junk," said Jake. "You should have rented a better one."

"With whose money, Jake?"

"I'm leaving a note," said Hanna.

"No, you're not."

"We could leave a note with a clue in it," suggested Jake. "Something only Dad would understand. We wouldn't have to spell out that we were going to Marblehill."

"And what if he doesn't get the clue?" said Hanna. "You're such an idiot sometimes, Jake."

"Come on," said Glenda. "We're all tired. And we're frazzled. Let's just get to Marblehill. Don't you want to go there and see your cousins? Didn't you have fun there last summer and the summer before? And Uncle Neil is bound to have a fone, and a much better one than this. So let's just forget about the note. Let's pack, get in the car, and go to the nursing home so we can recharge. Before Buzz comes back."

She watched her daughter every step of the way. Hanna sullenly disassembled her clarinet—doctor-recommended for her asthma—in the light of one of the flashlights and put it into its case. She then packed some makeup, and a bag full of clothes, commenting on how Melissa and Ashley were going to make fun of her cheap, bargain-brand clothes, and finally finished by taking five puffs of her inhaler.

"Honey, don't overdo that stuff."

"Mom, fuck off."

Glenda didn't punish Hanna for saying this. She just went through the motions, and started packing.

Hanna broke down and cried, even though she was zoned out on her bronchodilator. She came into her mother's arms, and told her she was sorry for saying fuck off. But that didn't stop Glenda from checking Hanna's room one last time for a note, and checking it thoroughly.

She at last got into the car with her kids, like they were going on a summer vacation, and as she headed out on the road, she looked up at the sky. And saw that the Moon had finally disappeared behind the western edge of the shroud's toxic wound. She felt lonely then. She didn't know if she was ever going to see Old Hill again. She didn't know if she was going to see North Carolina.

But most of all, she didn't know if she was going to see Gerry again.

PART FOUR

24

Glenda saw the blaze a mile down the road, and knew that Cedarvale Nursing Home was burning.

The flames raged among the tall, dead trees, and they were thick and orange and capped with plumes of dark smoke. She was afraid the road to the underground garage might be blocked, that a recharge would be impossible, and that their plans for driving to Marblehill would come to nothing. But as she got closer she saw that only the Mercer and Dawes wings were on fire, and that the Hutchley wing, where the administrative offices, Palliative Care Department, and underground parking lot were, had yet to be touched.

She slowed the car as she came to the front gate. The smell of smoke scraped the inside of her nostrils. She saw a boy of ten or eleven run out from behind the security kiosk, his face smeared with dirt, his clothes caked with filth, so skinny and underfed that Glenda wondered how he had the strength to run. But run he did, along the front of the Hutchley wing and the Dawes wing, finally disappearing around the hulk of the burning Mercer wing.

Glenda glanced at Hanna, who sat in the front seat beside her, then over her shoulder at Jake, who was in the back with the handgun held loosely on his knee. "Stay alert."

"I know that guy," said Jake as he peered after the boy. "He goes to Talbot Public."

Not trusting her own eyes because she was forty now, she asked Jake, "Did he have a gun?"

"He had something in his belt," said Jake. "I couldn't see what it was. It looked like a stick."

"But you're sure it wasn't a gun."

"It looked like a stick."

She nodded. "We go in, we go out."

"I think his name is Buck," said Jake.

"Buck?" said Hanna.

"That's what I've heard other kids call him."

Glenda eased her foot off the brake and rolled into the complex. "I don't like this. Maybe we should come back later."

"Mom, let's keep going," said Hanna. "Let's get it over with."

"Buck, or whatever his name is, maybe ran off to alert the rest of those kids I was telling you about. The ones Whit was so worried about."

"So let's be fast," said Hanna. "In and out, like you said. And Jake, for Christ's sake, don't be afraid to shoot someone for a change."

"Mom, she's bugging me again."

"Hanna, please stop bugging your brother."

"I'm not bugging him. I'm just stating facts."

"Okay, I'll shoot someone. I guarantee it. And it just might be you."

"Let's calm down," said Glenda. "We go in, we get our charge, and we leave."

She eased past the security kiosk, veered left around the sign that said UNDERGROUND PARKING GARAGE—STAFF AND RESIDENT PARKING ONLY, and drove down the ramp, feeling the heat of the night even though the air conditioner was on full tilt. She ventured into the underground parking lot and followed the big white arrows. The place was dark. She was worried that the charger might be off-line, even though it operated independently from the main grid, but as she got to the second level she saw that, miracle of miracles, its indicator light was still flashing green, a welcome beacon, and that she could recharge her car after all.

"This place is spooky," said Hanna.

"Won't it be nice to go for a swim in Uncle Neil's pool?" Glenda said, trying to reassure her daughter. "I sure would like a good cooldown."

She pulled up to the generator.

Jake shifted in the back. "Mom, I'm going to stand over by that pillar to cover you."

"Jake, never shoot that thing if Hanna or I are in your way."

"Mom, I've thought a lot about using this gun. Just trust me."

The three Thorndikes got out of the car.

Jake took up his position behind the pillar.

Hanna coughed and wheezed in the close, thick air of the underground parking lot.

Glenda keyed in the sequence to the charging port, then went to the generator and entered her user name and password. The machine identified her, and itemized for her the output available—more than enough to fill her car. She took the generator's male hookup and inserted it into her car's female port, selected recharge, then hit enter. The generator hummed softly. Its computer linked up with her car's onboard software and, glancing at the dash, she saw the little blue bar move slowly forward.

The bar was halfway across when she heard a slow and steady whistle from behind Jake's pillar. She looked up. She saw the flicker of firelight at the other end of the garage, and in a moment several figures emerged, all carrying homemade torches. Those kids again. It finally dawned on her why these kids had set the Mercer and Dawes wings on fire—they wanted light. They couldn't live in the dark anymore.

She counted five altogether. They didn't walk. They swaggered the way kids swagger when they are acting tough. And in their toughness they neglected caution, and failed to consider that Jake might be standing behind the pillar with a gun.

When the boys finally reached Glenda and Hanna, a tall one in a denim jacket looked at them as if he had

lifted a rock and found bugs underneath. Then he turned
to another boy, the one they had seen run from behind
the security kiosk. "Buck, check the car."

Buck came forward.

Glenda reached into the front seat and lifted her rifle.
She didn't point it at Buck. She pointed it at Denim
Jacket, the leader, instead. She watched the three flanking boys lose their absurd expressions of toughness and
grow suddenly concerned that the lady with the car
should have such a big, mean-looking rifle.

"Yeah? And so?" said Denim Jacket, pulling the bottom of his jacket away to reveal a pistol shoved into his
pants. "Go ahead and shoot me, lady. We'll see who's
faster."

She looked more closely at Denim Jacket. Was he
high? In the light coming from the torches, his pupils
certainly looked small, and she wondered if, before
burning down the Mercer and Dawes wings, he had gotten into the dispensary.

"I don't want to hurt you," she said.

"Buck, check the car."

This time it didn't come to her in a blinding flash, like
it had with Fulton, that Denim Jacket was the evil one.
This time she found she couldn't pull the trigger, no
matter what, because Denim Jacket was just a kid, and
his parents were probably dead, and starvation was
bound to kill him by Thanksgiving. She let Buck come
ahead, and Buck inspected the car, then backed away
and looked at Denim Jacket with wide eyes. He said, in
a voice that hadn't yet changed, "They got food."

Denim Jacket pulled out his pistol and pointed it at
Glenda's head. He said, with a crooked smile, "What
now, lady?"

She knew he was acting tough because he understood
the new politics well, and that he couldn't act weak, not
in front of his friends, or they would tear him to pieces.
She was afraid of Denim Jacket, yet felt motherly toward
him as well. His brown hair was a mess, matted with the
grease hair develops after it hasn't been washed in a
while. He was pale. His eyes, she saw, were blue, like

the surf at Nag's Head, and the freckles spattered across his nose were like specks of chocolate. He had a green armband that looked as if it were made of ripped surgical scrubs, and she saw that the other boys wore armbands as well—they were wearing colors as though they were in a gang.

Denim Jacket looked like he was in grade nine, a year or so younger than Hanna, and he spoke with the accent of the hills. He was old North Carolina, as tough as they come, but scared . . . frantically scared, despite his show of callous indifference to the whole situation.

"Where's your mama?" asked Glenda.

A small paroxysm of emotion quivered over his face, and she likened him to a broken pot that had been glued back together, only the glue hadn't set yet.

"Where's yours?" As smart-ass remarks went, this was fairly lame, and she could see that he was having a difficult time holding it together.

"Dead," she said.

"Dead how?"

"Diabetes."

Denim Jacket shrugged. "Big deal."

"Why don't we share some of this food with you?"

"A guardsman killed my own ma. Happened last month."

And then a deafening roar exploded from behind the pillar where Jake was hiding, and Denim Jacket's face seemed to bend toward the center, even as his lips formed a perfect O, his eyes squinted in pain, and a fine spray of red erupted from his temple. His arm went down, the gun fell from his hand, and he crumpled to the concrete floor.

The other boys dropped their crude torches and scattered; for a second she thought it was just boys running away from their own mischief, like they had egged a house, or let the air out of someone's tires, or left a burning bag of dog shit on somebody's doorstep, because they ran like all boys run, flat out, and with the pump and effort of crazed terror. Glenda thought all this in a split second but then remembered it wasn't boys playing mischief anymore—it was another sequence, another beat, another slice of goddamned life from the end of the world. She had killed a cop, and now her son had killed a child. Kids killing kids. That's when you knew the Apocalypse had truly arrived.

Jake ventured from his pillar, and he looked scared and proud at the same time, and not at all like her son, but like a boy she didn't even know. He was breathing hard, his chest rising and falling under his T-shirt, and he walked toward them with an odd lurch, as if the strength had disappeared from his legs. The torches lay scattered around Denim Jacket, casting wisps of black smoke, and Denim Jacket sprawled there, bleeding profusely from the head, the blood spreading and spreading until it finally reached the drain next to the generator and started trickling down.

"I told you I could shoot someone," said Jake, looking at his sister.

Glenda could tell that Jake didn't fully understand what he had done.

As for Hanna, she had gone catatonic and was just standing there with her limp hair in front of her face, trying to manage her wheeze while she stared with sightless eyes at the blood trickling down the drain.

Glenda looked at her son and saw he wanted her to say something, to give approval, but every muscle in her body was rigid, and it was like her mind was frozen.

She heard the kids yelling to each other on the next level, some spontaneous communication, perhaps a warning, but it was too echoey down here, and she couldn't make out the precise words.

"Mom?" said Jake.

She nodded, but it was a dull and distracted nod.

"Mom, he had a gun pointed right at you."

"I know."

Jake broke down and cried.

She went to him, and took him in her arms like the child he was. And even when the generator clicked off because her car was full, she kept holding him because he couldn't seem to get his sobbing under control. He didn't cry often these days; she couldn't remember the last time he had cried. But he was crying now. She heard his voice crack, and realized his voice was changing.

"Let's get in," she said. "We're full."

"Mom, are you happy I killed him?"

And in a voice that was as dead as Denim Jacket, she said, "Yes, Jake, I'm happy you killed him."

She lifted Denim Jacket's gun and brought it into the car with her.

They drove up to the ground-floor level and out to the gate. Cedarvale continued to burn. Where was Whit? And the remaining residents? Were they all dead now? Had Whit made it to Detroit?

She took some food out—four cans of Irish stew— stacked them on the curb next to the security kiosk, put Denim Jacket's gun on top, and then drove off into the darkness. She wasn't going to leave Buck and the others without a gun.

25

At Homestead, Neil studied the new downloads from the Department of Defense with misgiving. Only so many launch vehicles left, and according to his virus specs, dispersion would fall short by twenty-five percent if he didn't come up with a solution. Secretary of Defense Sidower was indeed correct in his bleak assessment—except for what they had in the United States, and in U.S. bases abroad, launch infrastructure worldwide, particularly in terms of personnel, had been degraded to the point of zero capability.

Was there a solution?

He entered the parameters again, just in case he had made a mistake—lift requirements versus existing launch capabilities—and came up with the same dead-end numbers. But then he widened the data pool, and entered the parameters through a games-theory program Kafis had given him one summer at Marblehill, something the Pentagon computer geeks didn't have, just to see what would happen. Outside, on the air base, the last of the sun was slowly disappearing.

"Analyze," he told his waferscreen.

Sixty seconds later his waferscreen gave him an answer he hadn't been expecting—the Moon.

He scrutinized the data. It turned out that AviOrbit had dozens of interlunar shuttles crated in various warehouses, some out of service for decades, but all possessing, to varying degrees, launch potential. His waferscreen told him that if these shuttles were refurbished, they could be transformed into crude missiles.

He sat back, glad that the Tarsalan software had taken into account this phantom resource. Was it possible, then? Could he win this chess game after all?

He entered further parameters about the virus itself. Because it was a virus, it could be grown and cultured in a lab. Unlike the toxin, it didn't need an existing chemical production infrastructure. Checking lunar inventory, he saw that the Moon in fact had the basic building blocks for his virus, and could manufacture it in significant quantities. They even had Tarsalan blood in cold storage—there for emergency purposes should the Tarsalans ever need the Moon in a medical capacity—and could therefore also devise the Tarsalan-specific virions.

He breathed a sigh of relief. It could be done. And if it meant he had to pull another Luke Langstrom on the Moon, then that's what he would do. Co-opt the Moon a second time. And truth be told, he was curious. His brother had come up with the flagella thing. But had he come up with anything since? It would be interesting to see exactly what his brother was doing.

He lifted his phone—*the* phone—and entered a page. He wondered how long it would take the secretary of defense to get back to him.

When a firefight erupted between the opposing factions an hour later, the secretary still hadn't gotten back to him. The hole in the sky above the southeastern United States had now closed up entirely, and it was pelting rain vehemently.

The firefight, as usual, was at the other end of the base, but Neil and his family still followed their established protocol. Neil got on the floor. The girls crawled under their cots.

Louise didn't follow the protocol this time. She kept rolling her paint roller, spreading yellow paint over the walls, as if she were sick of firefights.

"Louise, get on the floor."

She continued to paint.

"Mom, a stray bullet could reach here," warned Ashley. "Or the soldiers might come."

"Sweetie, it's all right. Colonel Bard never lets them get close to us. So let's just continue with our lives. I'm not going to let them bother us anymore. And I'm almost finished with this painting. I want to get it done. What do you think of the color? I think it really brightens up the place."

Neil stared at his wife as she went back to painting. He heard more gunfire, but it was so distant he thought that maybe she was right—Colonel Bard would keep the breakaway airmen at the other end of the base forever. As he watched his wife work, he had to wonder if this frantic little woman who was painting the army barracks a sunny shade of autumn gold had become unhinged.

He got up from his hiding spot on the floor and lifted a paintbrush. He poured some paint into an empty ration container, walked to the window, and started painting the window frame.

"Dad, do you think that's wise?" asked Melissa.

"Your mom's right." He was feeling slightly unhinged himself. "I'm getting sick of hiding on the floor."

He dipped his paintbrush into the container, even as he heard the *rat-tat-tat* of machine-gun fire nearby. The old, bold confidence was gone, despite the prospect of getting the Moon's help. He couldn't help thinking of Kafis. Especially when Kafis's pupils dilated to the halfway point. The halfway point always meant that Kafis thought Neil had missed something important.

"Dad?" called Melissa.

What did he even care about Kafis? He was going to beat Kafis. The virus module had backups to its backups. It had failsafes to its failsafes. He had thought it through again and again. He couldn't have missed a single thing. And if they got the Moon on board . . .

"Dad!" Melissa's voice penetrated the racket outside. "Yes?"

"Your phone."

He stiffened. He listened. His phone. How could he

have missed something like that? He was only fifty-two. Was his hearing getting that bad?

He put the paintbrush in the ration container, walked over to the table, and lifted his phone, his precious link to the secretary of defense. Only it wasn't Sidower—it was Deputy Secretary of Defense Leanna Fonblanque.

"Where's Joe?" he asked.

"We've moved the entire government to the 937 facility in New Mexico."

Neil took a moment, intellectually and emotionally, to assimilate this. "And you didn't take me and my family?"

"Were you notified?"

"No."

"Then you're not on the list." The deputy secretary sighed. "937 is a long-term facility."

"You don't have to explain what it is. I helped develop it."

"Then you understand that theoretical science won't be a number-one priority when we reemerge. Technical and infrastructure support will be. I'm sorry, Dr. Thorndike."

At that moment he felt betrayed by his government, and almost didn't tell her about the Moon's hidden launch capability. Fuck it. He had his own 937 in Marblehill. He didn't need the president's twenty square miles of underground bunker in New Mexico.

"So are you in touch with Joe, then? And the president?"

"I am."

"And they've left you in charge of this . . . this effort I'm making? Because I've come up with something they might be interested in."

Fonblanque paused, and he read a half-dozen things in that pause, chief of which was pity. "I understand you have problems at Homestead. A breakaway faction?"

"Colonel Bard is containing it."

"Good."

"Are we getting closer to a full-scale assault on the TMS?" he asked.

"The Pentagon's plans are proceeding apace, Dr. Thorndike. That's all I'm authorized to tell you."

This, then, was another rebuff. He pictured the deputy secretary somewhere in her own safe house, in her sixties but sporting every cosmetic enhancement and procedure in the book so that she looked closer to thirty, helicopter ready outside for the moment she thought she had to go to 937.

"You tell the president everything's fine," he said. "I'm firmly in control of the situation. And I have a great idea. Something that will improve the dispersion odds of the virus greatly."

"Is that gunfire I hear?"

"I've come up with a solution for the launch shortage."

"Dr. Thorndike, we're putting most of our effort into the TMS effort. So don't worry too much."

Another revelation. They didn't care about the virus anymore. The second line was on the back burner. They were making other plans. Plans to wrest control of the on-off switch from the Tarsalans.

"I guarantee the virus is going to work." The old, bold confidence was a brittle thing at best. "But we need launch capability."

"We've taken some of our older units out of mothballs. They're being refurbished as we speak."

She gave him the number, and of course it wasn't nearly enough.

"I've run models," he said. "Using Tarsalan gamestheory software. The Moon—or AviOrbit, at least—has all kinds of old shuttles in storage. They can easily be converted into crude missiles."

The assistant secretary paused. "I'm listening." And he realized from the tone of her voice that he had her on board again, that he had them all on board, and that he had come up with another great idea.

"They've got over seven hundred crated away in various warehouses. Some are nearly a century old, but others are only ten or twenty years old."

She paused again. "You signed off against the Moon.

I have the document right here. Lunar interference represents a category-eight risk. You've written it right here. How are they going to react?"

He hated the taste of crow. "Nectaris is always asking for handouts. And this mayor they have . . . he won't take much persuading if you make him understand it will be to his advantage. As for AviOrbit, promise them anything. Even subsidies. We have to hit the Tarsalans hard, and hit them fast. Our dispersion area has to be as wide as possible. We have to quickly reach the saturation point before the xenophyta's natural defense system responds. Let's see if we can get the Moon on board a second time. They've already given us Luke Langstrom. Maybe they'll give us everything. Including some updates on what my brother is doing. Maybe he's come up with something else besides this flagella thing. It could all turn into something useful."

The deputy secretary admitted it sounded promising. "I don't think anybody considered the Moon as a launch resource, Dr. Thorndike. Excellent work."

Here it was again, the primary theme of his life—people in power telling him he had done good.

Yet when he finally ended his call to the assistant secretary, he was anxious. The rain beat against the windows. Was he getting anywhere closer to solving the puzzle of the shroud? The gunfire abated and the girls crawled out from under their cots. And would the virus work on a mass scale, and not fizzle the way the hydrogen sulfide had?

Where was his confidence? He had to tell himself that the virus would work. That it was going to turn the xenophyta into mush from the inside out, so that it would rain from the sky like Oobleck. Yes. Oobleck. The king said he was sorry, and the Oobleck stopped. Simple. The whole viral thrust was meant to be simple. And simple was best.

Simple was the only way he could make sure he didn't miss anything.

26

What Gerry didn't like about it was how it felt like an intervention, the kind his wife, his brother, and his brother's wife had staged before throwing him into Bellwood two years ago.

He glanced at Ian, and could tell Ian knew nothing about it. Then at Ira, and what was Ira doing here, anyway, because Ira never came to these things? Then at Mitch, who stared at his hands like a Judas.

But unlike his first intervention, where everything good in the world had materialized afterward, and he had finally found the peace he had always been looking for, and, wonder of wonders, had found it without the bottle, this intervention had all the hallmarks of a cancer and felt like it was leaching the life out of him.

"But what about that first drop they sent?" he said. "They were so hard-assed. It was like a slap in the face. Telling us to butt out because they thought we would blow it. And my damn brother signing off on it because he thinks he's king of the world."

Hulke looked away. Gerry could tell the mayor had mixed feelings about the whole thing. "Well, Ger, they sent us the blueprint for the virus, and Luke's taken a look at it, and Luke seems to think it's . . . how can I put this? . . . a kosher little bug and, unlike the toxin, something we can grow up here."

"I thought Luke wasn't part of our effort anymore."

The mayor looked away. "We've kind of been using him all along. On a consulting basis . . . and keeping it hush-hush . . . because you seemed a little miffed at him when he broke camp with us."

Gerry shook his head. "I wasn't miffed at him. I welcome his input. I was mad at the toxin. I knew it wasn't going to work. And I was right. These are the Tarsalans. They're going to think of all the obvious things. And now Neil wants to try a virus? A virus won't work for the exact same reason."

"No, no. . . . Luke said it will. He said it will beat the crap out of the thing. . . . Maybe not in those exact words . . ." The door to the mayor's office slid open. "And . . . well, well, well . . . speak of the devil. . . . Luke, we were just—"

"Sorry I'm late," said Dr. Langstrom, coming through the door.

So. Here it was. The last nail. Why did things always arrange themselves this way in his life? Same thing at NCSU. Thought his job was safe, had no idea of the political intrigue brewing behind his back, and bang, we're sorry, Dr. Thorndike, but the Ocean Sciences Department is in a precarious position right now, and yes, you've really bounced back since your unfortunate stay at Bellwood, but we're looking at a serious lack of funding at the present time . . . and here it was all over again. Poor old Ger, only wanting to help, doing his damnedest to figure out Kafis's little puzzle, and then having the rug pulled out from under him, and Langstrom bouncing through the door as if he belonged here more than Gerry did.

"Hello, Luke," he said, trying to stop the frost in his voice.

The Martian scientist nodded deferentially. "Gerry."

The mayor tried to alleviate the tension with some blustering hospitality. "Wish I had a plate of bonbons, or something, Luke, because I know you like your sweets . . . but we're getting . . . uh . . . drastically low in the supply side of things, and we . . . you know . . . got a little hoarding going on . . . so I guess all I can give you . . ."

"Yes, crudités. Moon-grown?"

"We grow a fine carrot."

"And the dip?"

"Uh . . . synthetic. But real low-cal. In fact, zero-cal."

"You're not insulted if I pass?"

"Me, insulted? No, of course not. Have a seat. There's a spot beside Ira. You know Ira, don't you?"

"Yes, we've met."

"Hi, Luke."

"Hello, Ira."

"We were just telling Ger, here . . . about Dr. Thorndike's virus."

And this rankled Gerry as well, because he was "Ger" now, nothing else, while his brother was still Dr. Thorndike. He watched Luke take his spot beside Ira.

Gerry glanced at Ira, a man in his early sixties with an odd birthmark on his right hand, a narrow face, intense blue eyes, a receding hairline, and an obvious Ashkenazi contour to his nose. He had a benign but nearly frozen grin on his face. What was Ira getting out of all this? What kind of tariff concessions had the U.S. government made to the lunar contingent of AviOrbit?

"I've developed a few vials of the virus according to Dr. Thorndike's blueprint," said Luke. "Lothar Hydroponics had the base tobacco mosaic virus on file. The Tarsalan components came from the Aldrin Health Sciences Center. The cross-species enzymes and catalysts were easy to synthesize using basic laboratory techniques. The beauty of this thing, Gerry, is that unlike the toxin, we can grow it here on the Moon. Kudos to your brother. We mount multiple warheads of the stuff on some of the old interlunar junk Ira has hanging around and we go in with a coordinated attack."

The unfairness of the situation struck him afresh. "Wait a minute. Ira can give my brother launch vehicles but he can't give me another *Smallmouth*?"

Ira's grin transformed into a hard-faced frown. "It's not that we can't give you another *Smallmouth*, Gerry, it's just that we don't see the point. Mitch and I have talked about this, and we've basically concluded that your . . . research . . . Pardon me if I'm blunt, but your research is going nowhere." He lifted his palms. "These flagella, for instance. Yes, the first *Smallmouth* has shown us that when they're in the sphere, they're active, and that they link each xenophyta organism to the next, but so what? And this expensive infrared equipment we've given you? What have you done with it? You've shown us some pretty colors and told us that the phytosphere has different temperatures in different places, and that there might be a cyclical weather system in it . . . but really, what have you given us in terms of a concrete scientific return, or even a first step toward a working solution?"

Gerry's anger flared. "Yes, but this cyclical weather system . . . I'm beginning to think it's more than just a weather system—it's a definite stress band. Did you read my report on it?"

"You mean you've finally written a report?"

Gerry frowned but pushed on. "The pattern's too regular to be a weather system. If we can figure out what's causing it, we could be one step closer to a solution. I'm hypothesizing that the stress band could be part of the phytosphere's operating system."

"*Could* be," said Ira, now sounding tougher. "That's all I hear from you, Gerry. I've been an executive for thirty-one years, and I've worked with all kinds of people. I've hired people, and I've fired people. And the people I fire most are the ones who always say could be, might be, or maybe. Gerry, you don't know how to get things done. Not like your brother does."

"As far as I can see, my brother hasn't accomplished a thing except spend a lot of money. All I'm asking for is one more *Smallmouth*. Let's go into the phytosphere and follow the stress band. Let's find out what it is. It might reveal the exact piece of information we need. We could have the answer in as little as seventy-two hours."

"I'm sorry, Gerry, but I have to put what resources I have into retooling these old Earth-Lunar shuttles."

"But the virus isn't going to work. You don't think the Tarsalans haven't engineered an immune system into the phytosphere?"

"Gerry," said Luke. "That's the beauty of this virus your brother's designed. It *attacks* the immune system. The Tarsalan genetic component. And it's going to cripple that component first and then spread out using the omniphage I've created. This omniphage of mine is quickly turning into the workhorse of the whole project. The only way the Tarsalans can respond is to preemptively vaccinate the entire shroud, and hope that the necessary antibodies develop in time. And they can't. It's impossible. I've tested your brother's virus. It's a hundred percent effective."

"You've tested it on *our* samples?"

Luke shrugged. "Where else would I get samples?"

"Yes, but you didn't kill them all, did you?"

"I wouldn't do that. In fact, I'm culturing a new supply."

The rawhide hat moved ominously into view. "Don't you realize what you're doing?" said Ian. "You're undercutting the only man who's going to save the situation."

"Give me another *Smallmouth,*" pleaded Gerry, "Let's take an in-depth look at the stress band."

The mayor interjected. "Ger, we've sent your research to . . . you know . . . to your brother's team . . . just so that they can take a look at it. I think that's all we really have to do. There's your in-depth look, so you have nothing to worry about."

Now he felt doubly betrayed. "Without my authorization?"

"We just want them to double-check its validity."

His face settled. "It's valid, Malcolm. It's predicated on strict observation, not on wishful thinking."

"We're wasting a lot of time here," said Ira. "We should be focusing on refurbishing our launch vehicles and developing a stockpile of virus." Ira squared his shoulders and turned to Gerry. "Gerry, you're off the project. That's what we're really here to talk about. That's why I'm here. Thanks for all your help, but it hasn't worked out. We'll let you know if we need you on a consulting basis."

Gerry's eyes widened. Yes, an intervention. Or a repeat of NCSU. "So I'm fired?"

The mayor jumped in. "No, no, you're not fired, Gerry. Go back to Alleyne-Parma and work your butt off. Keep making those observations. Write it all down. Give us another damn bargaining chip we can use with Earth. It's just that . . . as for the overall direction . . . I think we better go with your brother's plan."

"So, in other words, Neil's in charge now?"

"We're going to help Earth give it this one last shot," said Ira.

"Mitch . . . I thought you were with me."

Mitch looked up. "Gerry, you haven't even reached the drawing-board stage of a solution. What do you want me to say?"

"I want you to say you'll give me another *Smallmouth*. If you give me a chance to get inside the phytosphere one more time, I'm sure I'll figure out what's causing the stress band. And once I do that—"

"Once you do that, Gerry, then what?" said Ira. "Don't you see that we're running out of time? The situation is critical on Earth. The average human takes anywhere from thirty to seventy-five days to starve to death, and we're well over the seventy-five-day threshold now. The number of survivors is going to be considerably beyond the right side of the decimal point in terms of percentages. And another *Smallmouth* isn't going to help any of that. So do what Malcolm says. Go play at Alleyne-Parma, but leave the real work to us."

His feelings were hurt, his ego bruised, and he felt like he needed a drink badly. But as Gerry took the train to the observatory an hour later, he still held a solid belief in himself flickering deep within his soul, and he knew that his brand of question-driven science, so completely devoid of ambition and conceit, would at last solve the puzzle of the phytosphere.

He got off the train and took the moving sidewalk through a pressurized polycarbonate surface corridor. The observatory loomed before him, a bubble, catching

the sun's light and reflecting it with diamond-bright intensity. He glanced at the black sky. Somewhere up
there, AviOrbit technicians took the old Earth-Moon
shuttles out of storage and turned them into missiles.
What would the Tarsalans do to the Commonwealth of
Lunar Colonies when they learned the Moon had partici-
pated in the launch? He tried not to think about it.

He used his special pass to gain access to the closed-
down tourist attraction, and shuffled along the polished
floor of the big circular corridor until he came to the
entrance to the viewing area.

As much as he tried not to think about it, he couldn't
get it out of his mind. Somewhere back in Nectaris, lab
workers cultured samples of the virus and piggybacked
them onto Luke Langstrom's omniphages. He stopped.
The omniphages. If it was a eureka moment, it was an
unenjoyable one. Because didn't the Tarsalans already
have experience with Luke Langstrom's omniphage?
They now probably understood the omniphage better
than Luke did. He sure hoped his brother had considered that strategic stumbling point.

He settled himself by Heaven's Eye and took fifteen
minutes to get the apparatus up and running.

He was just sitting down to observe when he heard a
distant rapping from out in the corridor. He thought it
might be Ian at the observatory door, strange new Ian,
the sober Ian who wanted to walk the straight and narrow. He bounce-shuffled out into the corridor, followed
its curve around to the public doors, and saw that it
wasn't Ian, but Stephanie, standing at the top of the
stairs wearing her silver, orange, and magenta jumpsuit.
She reminded him of a Day-Glo kitten who had followed
him home. He swiped his access pass on the inside scan-
ners and the doors opened.

He presented himself with his palms upward. "Behold,
poor Caesar."

"What? Oh. Right. Cute. A little weird, but . . ."

And then she just stood there looking at him as if he
were the biggest nerd in the world.

He moved awkwardly aside. "Come in . . . come in."

And he swept his hand toward the interior of the observatory like a ringmaster presenting the next circus act. "I talk like that sometimes."

"I noticed." She arched a brow. "But then I notice a lot of things about you. For one thing, I notice that you let people push you around."

The accusation struck him as uncharacteristically harsh of Stephanie. Yet it seemed pointless to defend himself, so he just tried to elaborate on the circumstances. "Ira was their point man. And he holds the purse strings."

"So?"

"He and I come from two different mind-sets."

"So?"

"So he's not going to listen to me when he can listen to my brother."

"I used to let people push me around all the time, but not anymore."

"I haven't given up, Stephanie."

"I know you haven't. I just wanted to come here to make sure of that."

"I can't give up."

"I know."

"And in a day or two, I'm going to bug them again about a second *Smallmouth*."

"Let's go look at Earth."

"Yes, the many-storied globe."

"Uh . . . right."

They walked down the corridor toward the observatory, past the ticket booth, the concession stand, and the public washrooms. She slipped her hand through his arm, and it felt good, reminded him of his wife, and he took support from it, even though she was young enough to be his daughter.

"I haven't seen Gwen around," he said. "What happened to her?"

"She's gone back home to Copernicus, now that all the shows have closed."

"Oh. She's from Copernicus. And what about you? What about your mother and father?"

"I never met my father, and I don't get along with my mother. I'm making it on my own."

"You don't have a boyfriend?"

"I do."

"You do? Who?"

"You."

"Steph . . . I wouldn't think of me as your—"

"A boyfriend can be many things. One of the things he can be is married. Another thing he can be is alone. And you're really alone, Gerry. You need me. You might not know it, but you do. And that doesn't necessarily mean there has to be anything physical."

He nodded. She was young, a trifle overdone in her expressions, but he appreciated her sentiment anyway.

"You're a sweet man," she said.

"Thanks."

"No, I really mean it. And you're awfully smart."

"Thanks. You're full of compliments tonight."

"I'm just trying to soften the blow."

His eyes narrowed. "Soften what blow?"

"The blow you're going to feel when I point out the obvious to you. I was hoping you were going to get it by yourself, and I wasn't going to have to say anything because I didn't want to bruise your ego, considering how bruised it's been already, but now I realize that we can't wait any longer."

He stopped. "Can't wait any longer for what?"

He was starting to feel more like an idiot every second.

"Let's just get to the observatory, and I'll show you."

"Something about the phytosphere?"

"Like I say, you're awfully smart."

His face warmed. Had he really missed something? What could he have missed?

In the observatory she presented the monitors like a showgirl, with a jutting of her hip and a *c'est voilè* posturing of her hands, as if the monitors were the prize behind Door Number 3.

He didn't get it. "I'm sorry?"

"Turn on the accelerated infrared footage."

He did as she said. "It's on."

"Take a close look and tell me what you see."

He saw the same thing he always saw, the stress band from north to south. "Okay . . . Okay, what am I missing?"

He was afraid she was going to disappoint him with something that had absolutely no relevance.

"You're sure you won't be upset? I know the male ego is . . ."

He looked more closely at the screens. "Steph, if you can offer some fresh perspective . . . something I've been missing. . . ."

"Look closely at the archival screen, Gerry. Tell me what you see. You won't get mad because a showgirl figured this out, will you?"

"Of course not."

"Just take a look and see if you can puzzle it out."

"What am I supposed to see?" he said.

"Isn't it obvious?"

"On the archival screen?"

"Yes, that screen."

"I see the same thing I always see. The stress band."

"Speed it up some more," she said.

He sped the whole thing up, splicing three weeks into a four-minute segment.

"So?" said Stephanie.

He bowed. "Master, I admit my profound ignorance."

"Gerry, you're a goddamned ocean scientist."

It was one of those sublime moments of humiliation, when a girl of twenty-two who had no scientific background and just went around *feeling* her way through life, not analyzing it, could outguess him in the overall pattern of a natural phenomenon. Despite the humiliation, he could have kissed her.

"I see tides."

"Exactly."

"It's gravity."

"Yes!"

The more he looked at the patterns, the more it became clear to him—he was seeing tides. Tides in the actual phytosphere itself, with the tidal pattern affected by the underlying weather systems, so that the stress band wasn't a precise thing, but more a ragged line stretching from north to south poles. No wonder he had been confused. Moon tides. And with this realization, the dominoes fell into place—why the flagella behaved one way when they were in orbit around the Earth, and why, when in the lab, with no cohesive center of gravity, they fell apart. Gravity, acting as an anchor, triggered the flagella to cling. Take that gravity away, and the trigger was gone.

"Do you want to have sex now?" said Stephanie. "You've kind of got this glow about you. I'm sure your wife would understand."

"Stephanie, we just had something better than sex. We had a meeting of the minds."

She looked doubtful. "If you say so."

"And you might have saved Earth."

Her voice became giddy. "Really?"

"Yes."

He had a sudden vision of a solution so vast, so unexpected, yet so simple, so predicated on the basic laws of physics, that he wondered if Kafis, in the twin-brained complexity of his mind, would suspect such a blunt and obvious attempt.

But first he had to prove his theory.

And for that, he had to get Ira back on board.

Not for a second *Smallmouth*.

No, he had much bigger plans now.

27

She drove through the night, and what a night—*the* night, the one that would never end. The rain came down hard, blurring the windshield. She hunched over the steering wheel so strenuously that her shoulders ached. Hers was the only car on Route 64, and Georgia was still hundreds of miles away. She knew the mountains were coming soon, and was afraid to go into them because, what with all this rain and no grass or other plants holding anything in place, she was worried about washouts.

The emptiness of the highway frightened her. She and her children were targets because they had food in the car. She didn't want to stop, was afraid to stop, but sensed Jake growing antsy in the back.

She looked ahead and saw a town. "What'd you say this town was?" she asked Hanna.

Hanna turned on the flashlight and looked at the map again. "Dunstan."

"Jake, do you have to go for a pee?"

"Yeah."

"Okay, we'll stop here."

She eased her foot on the brake and pulled over to the shoulder. Jake got out, walked to the ditch, and peed. The air coming through the open door was damp, and it made her skin sticky.

Lightning flashed and she saw the outlines of the town, its downtown section like an overgrown prop for a train set, none of its lights burning, the buildings looking carved out of cardboard, lifeless, without any soul.

She glanced in her rearview mirror and saw head-lights, and knew it was probably nothing, just another hapless traveler driving from nowhere to nowhere, but couldn't help feeling paranoid, especially when they had food in the car and everybody was fighting for what lit-tle remained.

She leaned over the backseat. "Jake, honey, are you nearly done? There's a car coming."

Jake zipped up and got back in the vehicle. She put it in gear, hoping that the person behind wouldn't see her parking lights. She wished there was some way to turn them off, but they stayed on all the time.

She ventured into town. The lone traffic light, as dead as everything else, was dark like the dark windows around her, and swayed in the wind. Lightning flashed again. Her plan was to keep going, travel west along 64, but at the last second she swung left onto the town's secondary road, Vine Street. She wanted to hide from whoever was behind them. Her blood drummed past her ears. She looked around for someplace to hide, and in the next lightning flash saw a church; and, no, she wasn't religious, but the church seemed like a beacon, and all the knee–jerk responses she'd been taught in Sunday school came back: how a church, any church, was a sanc-tuary, and how the good Lord would protect. She swerved into the small lot in front.

Only thing was, the church was still fairly close to Main Street, and she didn't feel safe sitting in the car like this. It might be better if she and the kids . . .

"Kids, get out. We'll go up to the church porch until this guy passes."

"Mom, why are you so worried?" asked Hanna.

"Because we've got food. Do you want a repeat of Cedarvale?"

They all got out of the car, climbed the broken con-crete steps to the church lawn, hurried up the walk to the church porch, and huddled under its roof. Glenda got on her knees behind the railing. She wondered how her world could have changed so much, so that she would feel the need to hide from anybody who happened along the highway. She felt vulnerable, and miserable, and as if she still had far to go before she reached Marblehill.

She listened for the car and thought she heard it coming through the rain, the tires ripping against the wet pavement, but it was just the sound of the rain itself, a steady hiss, fluctuating in pitch. For the longest time the car didn't come, and she thought it might have turned onto a side road, that perhaps it was a local farmer going back to his farmhouse; but then she heard the vehicle, and over this uneven section of 64 it made a bump and rattle she recognized only too well. She felt both hot and cold, and her body automatically tried to adjust with a sharp intake of air; but once the air was inside, she couldn't let it go, as if, with this new emergency, this terrible threat, her lungs had suddenly seized up.

Her mind froze as well, and it wasn't until a few seconds later that she began to put it all together: why Buzz was here, how he was here, the reason behind this I-shot-the-sheriff-but-did-not-shoot-the-deputy scenario. The truck passed the intersection at Main, not more than a quarter block away. There could be no mistaking the geriatric jalopy. She was sure the truck might turn onto Vine, but it kept going. Her shoulders remained tight, and she gripped the edge of the porch railing as if she never wanted to let it go. At last she found herself exhaling. Lightning flashed yet again. She caught a glimpse of the truck climbing the road into the mountains, a quarter mile distant.

She turned to her daughter. "I told you not to leave a note." Her tone was icy, and she didn't mean to speak so harshly to her daughter but couldn't help it.

"I didn't leave a note."

"Then why is Buzz following us? I told you this would happen."

"Mom, I didn't leave a note. How could I leave a note? You were hovering over me like a vulture."

"I left a note," said Jake, defiance in his voice.

She turned. She barely discerned the outlines of Jake's face in the dark. "Didn't you hear what I was telling Hanna?"

"Mom, I wasn't going to have Dad come home and not know where we were."

"Yes, but I said I was going to keep foning him."

"Don't worry. I didn't say Marblehill. I used a clue. Like I said we should."

Her lips pursed, her eyes momentarily moistened, and she felt an odd mixture of sympathy and pity for her son; he was, after all, only twelve, and was bound to do childlike things. He couldn't reason the situation through the way an adult could, and really, when it came right down to it, how could you control your kids in a circumstance like this? A clue. Like it was a game.

"And what did you put in your clue?" she said, hoping for the best.

"I said we were going to Chattahoochee. I didn't mention anything about Marblehill."

Her exasperation jumped a notch. "Yes, but Buzz knows Marblehill is in Chattahoochee. A clue like that . . . it's not really a clue at all."

And of course kids might think they were outsmarting adults, but they rarely did.

"Hanna said I should make sure it was a clue Dad would get."

Now he was blaming Hanna, another kid thing to do. She wanted to trust him, but how could she ultimately trust a twelve-year-old?

Jake tried to stick up for himself some more. "It's a good thing I had to take a pee, otherwise he'd have caught us for sure. Now he's never going to find us."

"Yes, but he doesn't have to find us. There's only one road into Marblehill, and if he doesn't find us now, he'll be waiting for us once we get there."

Hanna interrupted her. "Mom, there's a big dog out by the car."

She turned. The lightning flashed. She saw the dog. Just a glimpse of it; a large white mastiff, what she would have called a British bulldog, only she didn't know breeds that well. The dog was huge, and so skinny she could see its ribs sticking out from under its fur. The ribs scared her, because she had never seen a dog so emaciated before, and when dogs got that thin, that starved, with no owners or masters around, it meant trouble. She didn't forget Buzz, not entirely, because Buzz was definitely a big problem, something they would have to face, like a hurricane brewing out in the Atlantic that was going to get here sooner or later. But for the moment she shoved Buzz to the back of her mind and concentrated on the dog. Not only the white dog, but also another dog that was now coming up the street. This was a big dog too, but it was a dark one, and in the next lightning flash, she saw that it had some Rottweiler in it.

Jake suddenly got up and extended his hand. "Here, boy."

She pulled him back. "Jake, what are you doing?"

"I want to see if he's friendly."

"He might have gone wild. Look at him. And now there's two."

"Mom, why can't we have a dog?" he asked.

"You know why. Because of Hanna's asthma."

"Maybe when Hanna goes to college."

As if the future were still the same, and not vastly altered. In the next lightning flash she saw both dogs looking up at the church, sniffing the air. Then they started nosing around the car. It was so dark she could hardly see. She hoped that by the next flash they would be gone. This wasn't right, dogs in the pouring rain like this, alone, at night, without masters, their ribs like the bars on a jail cell.

They slavered around her car, as if, even through all that metal, they could smell the vacu-paks of Chinese noodles and cans of Irish stew.

Another dog came along. She was relieved to see that it was a lot smaller, one of those Jack something terriers, and she thought this dog would just sniff the car with the others. And it did for a while, but then came trotting up the steps, and it didn't even look like a dog anymore but more like some creature from the depths of Hell, because all its fur was plastered to its skinny body and its ribs were like the fingers on a corpse, and when it barked, it wasn't so much a bark as a shriek, the oddest and most unnerving thing she had ever heard, as though the animal were possessed.

The bark acted like a siren call to the other two animals. They stopped sniffing the car and came up the steps. The bulldog's chin was up and his jaw was forward, and he looked like a prizewinning fighter ready to jump into the ring and tear someone to pieces. She didn't feel safe up here on the church steps anymore. Hadn't she read about this somewhere, dogs going wild, turning feral, packing, cooperating in order to get their gullets filled with whatever fresh meat they could find? And it was like she could sense they were feral because she herself had gone feral. The darkness had changed her into something that was dangerous: a cop killer. So what had it done to these dogs? Their owners had obviously abandoned them. She knew it was happening all over the country: pets getting abandoned. But what actually happened to animals when they were forced to live in darkness all the time, and when they had no choice but to subsist on food that didn't come out of a can but had to be found or killed?

The Jack something terrier shrieked again. The shrieking acted like amphetamines on the bulldog. It shifted and pranced over the churchyard, like it was slowly working itself up. Meanwhile, the big, dark dog growled, an unearthly sound, and in the next lightning flash she saw its face, like one of those African masks, murder sketching its way across its emaciated features. She felt compelled to get back to the relative safety of the car.

"Jake, do you have your safety off?"

His hand roved to the butt of his gun, and he nodded. The air was filled with the smell of dog saliva. The proximity of the animals set Hanna's lungs off. She wheezed, and after a moment she coughed. The coughing must have enraged the bulldog because it charged the church steps, making a feint all the way to the bottom, then turning away and going back to the yard.

"Okay . . . walk slowly to the car. Hanna, stay between Jake and I." She pumped a round into her rifle. "Don't make any sudden moves."

But it was no good and she knew it, because the second they rose from the church porch, the dogs went wild, growling and barking and working themselves into a frenzy. She thought she and her children would be trapped here, and that Buzz might come back, and that they would wind up in a gunfight with the sheriff's brother. So she tried the church door, but it was locked. They had no choice. They had to go to the car.

She and her kids went down the steps, and it was indeed no good, because the little dog came right up to her and tried to nip her heels. She kicked it out of the way, and that's when the bulldog tried to get around in back of Jake and rip a chunk out of his thigh, and as much as she liked dogs, and would have owned one if Hanna hadn't had asthma, she knew she had no choice. She fired at the bulldog, clipping its haunches. It went squealing away, at first not knowing if it had been crippled or not, but then falling over and trying to drag itself through the muddy churchyard with its front paws. The way the white mastiff acted was a horrible reminder of Brennan Little.

The other two dogs bolted.

But the bulldog . . .

Goddamn that bulldog. Her eyes flooded with tears. The thing yelped in exquisite agony. It tried to crawl away, but it couldn't move. She remembered a dog up the street from her childhood home in Kansas, and how friendly she had been with it. . . . She was really a dog person. But now she had to put this one down, and it was breaking her heart.

She walked across the churchyard and got it over with.

Once in the car, they headed up the mountain; and while she had gotten her tears under control, she still felt so blue about the dog that she wondered if she would ever feel unblue again. Jake reached forward and patted her shoulder.

Hanna, meanwhile, was wheezing and wheezing. "Mom, I've got to have some."

"Sweetie, it's not time yet. And it's dangerous if you take too much. You know what Dr. Saleh says."

"Mom, I've been taking a few extra hits every now and again, and it hasn't killed me."

"It's only been making you high," said Jake.

"Jake, you don't know what you're talking about, so just shut up."

"Kids at my school use puffers to get high," said Jake.

"That's because kids at your school are stupid, just like you. Mom, can I have some?"

She didn't want to fight it. She was too upset about the dog. "Does your heart feel funny at all?"

"No, not at all."

"Jake . . . dig it out. One puff, Hanna. We're running out."

"I'm going to need at least three."

"Three? Have you been taking three all along?"

"Mom, I know what I need. This nursing home stuff isn't as good as the usual stuff."

"Yes, but you're supposed to take only two puffs."

"I'm nearly seventeen. I think I can look after myself."

Jake handed the puffer forward. Hanna lifted it to her mouth like an old pro. She pressed the mouthpiece between her lips, squeezed the plunger, and inhaled. Glenda heard a little burst, but it was weak, and she was indeed afraid that they were running out. Hanna squeezed again, and this time nothing happened. Her daughter pulled the bronchodilator away and looked at it as if it were a criminal. Then she tried again, but again got nothing. She pulled it away from her lips a second time.

"It's empty, Mom. These nursing home ones are no good."

"But that's the last one we have. It's supposed to last us to Marblehill."

Like the drama queen she sometimes was, Hanna flung the empty inhaler over her shoulder into the backseat with the carelessness of Henry VIII tossing away a chicken bone. "Great. What am I going to do now?"

Glenda could have argued with Hanna, underlining for her daughter the foolhardiness of what she had done, especially with the overdosing. But where would it get her? Instead, she simply contemplated their grim, drugless situation. They weren't a quarter of the way to Marblehill, and Hanna was out of inhaler. The wheezing would start. The coughing would start. And it wouldn't let up. And her daughter would weaken. And to be weakened in the new Stone Age was more dangerous than overdosing with Alupent. So she didn't rant the way she might have in normal circumstances, but let it go, hoping that somehow, up the highway, they might find an abandoned pharmacy, and that in that pharmacy they might conceivably search out some medicine that Hanna could use.

She gripped the wheel and peered out the windshield, racking her brains for a solution, but the only fix she came up with was getting to Marblehill as soon as she could, where Neil was stockpiling medicine for the long haul.

She glanced up the hillside and saw that her brother-in-law was right: erosion had become a big problem. All the small plants on the forest floor had died a long time ago. Root systems had rotted in the ground, and that's why the ground had that stinky smell so much of the time. But now the rain was washing everything away, and she saw that many of the dead trees had toppled one against the other, so that the forest looked like a crowd of drunks, all leaning trunk to trunk for support.

And what was this up here? She eased her foot on the brake. Damn. Part of the road had cracked away into the gully below. She stopped. Mud from the hill had washed over the road, but it wasn't deep, and she could easily get through. What bothered her were the big cracks and how a giant slab of asphalt curved over the hill like a macadamized waterfall.

"I'm going to take the car across this section myself," she said. "You guys get out and walk."

They grumbled a bit—kids always grumbled about having to walk—but at last they left the car and trudged down the highway, getting drenched to their skin in the rain. She put the car in gear and proceeded, thinking to herself, *day at a time, day at a time, day at a time*—and the road held, felt solid under the car, and after a few minutes she made it across the cracked section, the highway became whole again, and the kids got in.

Hanna's eyes had that glassy look they always had after a hit of Alupent. Glenda gave Jake a glance. Jake was looking at Glenda as if he were curious about what she was going to do next. And she realized that they were all getting to know each other in an entirely unexpected way, and that they weren't just a family anymore, but survivors, and that the issues were no longer those of getting to school on time or finishing homework or trying to get more hours at the nursing home, but of simply trying to stay alive.

Jake said, "Mom, I'm sorry about the note. I just thought . . ."

She continued along the highway. "What's done is done. And maybe he didn't even see the note. Maybe he just guessed. He knows we go to Marblehill from time to time. And he knows we're broke and can't go anywhere else for a holiday. I mean . . . where else would we go? So . . . maybe it's not your fault."

"It's just that I didn't want Dad to die of a broken heart." He could hardly get the words out because he was all choked up.

"It's okay, Jake. Don't worry about it. We've got the rifle. We've got the gun. We should be okay."

They had gotten no more than another mile when she saw what she at first thought was some kind of optical trick sneaking in from her left field of vision, changing the monotonous look of the highway so that the road appeared to be bending in an odd way, out toward the valley. But then she had to ask herself, was it the movement of the car toward the trees, or of the trees toward the car? Because the trees really looked like they were shifting, and she suddenly remembered a line from grade ten English class, "Till Birnam wood remove to Dunsinane," because the forest honestly looked as if it were moving. The apparition was so strange, so unexpected, that she felt momentarily dizzy. Then all the bits of visual information collected into a coherent whole, and she realized she was seeing a landslide, like a freight train filled with upright trees rolling down the mountainside at fifteen miles per hour, not in a great rush, but indomitable and massive, the whole dead forest skiing downhill *en masse*.

"Holy shit!" said Jake. "A landslide!"

She slammed the brakes and the car jerked to a halt. Her body was now rigid and her heart pounded, and panic overcame her like a tsunami. She put the car in reverse and backed up, nearly swerving over the edge—God, she wasn't good at driving in reverse. She slowed right down, because she thought that maybe her reverse driving might kill them. Yet she was desperately fearful that the landslide would spread. Would the mountain suddenly flatten like a mound of strawberry jam? No. This section held, and at last she brought the car to a stop, and they watched the landslide from a safe distance.

It wasn't until the landslide petered out that she thought of practicalities. How were they going to get around it? Would they have to take a detour?

She took a nervous breath. "Hanna, let's see the map."

Hanna dug out the map. The thing was at least twenty-five years old, and falling apart. Glenda had a look. She studied the various highways and side roads. Yes, a considerable detour. How could they do that, and get all the way to Marblehill on their remaining charge without having to walk part of the way? And how could they possibly walk when Hanna had run out of medicine and wouldn't have the breath for it?

"If we don't find a way around this," she said, "we'll have to go back to Dunstan and take 74 to Charlotte." She peered up the road. "I'm wondering if we can get around on the right shoulder." Was it worth it? Could they take that risk? "There's a little ledge along there." She turned to her kids. "What do you think?"

Hanna and Jake inspected the ledge.

"Are you insane, Mom?" asked Hanna.

Glenda stared at the huge, muddy impasse. Which was the greater risk? Trying to get by on the right shoulder or going back and having to walk in the dead, dark countryside around Marblehill, the place where Buzz was most likely to ambush them? She thought the road was at least worth investigating.

"We should see how extensive the landslide is," said Glenda. "If it's a mile wide, we'll turn back. If it's just a little ways . . . because if we have to take 74 to Charlotte, we're not going to make it all the way to Marblehill on this one charge. We'll have to walk partway."

"Maybe we'll find some place to charge further along," said Jake.

"I don't think so," she said. "Everything's closed in Wake County. I think it's the same everywhere." She had a look at the ledge a second time. "You guys stay here."

"I'll come with you," said Jake. She could tell he was trying to make up for leaving the note back at the house.

"Jake, don't desert me," said Hanna.

"I'm going with Mom," said Jake. "You'll be okay in the car." Jake reached over the seat and patted his sister's shoulder. "Just sit back and relax. It shouldn't take long."

"Mom, make him stay here."

"Give her the gun, Jake. Just in case."

"Mom, that's my gun. She doesn't know how to use it."

"She says I get the gun, Jake. Hand it over."

Jake reluctantly gave her the gun. "Just don't point it at us. You've got to think safety first with a firearm."

"We'll be back in five or ten minutes," said Glenda.

Glenda and Jake got out of the car. The rain soaked their clothes instantly.

As they got closer to the landslide, it reminded her of a sleeping monster. Dead and broken conifers stuck out of its muddy back like giant quills. Yet, by its own momentum, and by the constant erosion of the rain, debris had caved away from the leading edge of the landslide and left a narrow passage along the outside shoulder of the road—a ledge perhaps wide enough for her car?

She looked up the mountainside. God, there was really nothing holding it in place anymore. As they made their way into the narrow passageway along the right side of the road, she felt like the sleeping monster might suddenly open its maw and devour them. To the left, rain ran in rivulets over the broken-away part. She pointed her flashlight at the rivulets, holding her rifle in her other hand. The water was brown and muddy.

She shone her flashlight further afield. "I think it ends up here. We might make it."

"Except it's all caved in up here."

"Just a bit. Maybe the car can get through."

"Not without getting stuck in that mud."

"Let's have a look."

She climbed the caved-in section, her feet sinking up to her ankles in mud.

As she got close to the other side of the caved-in section, she saw the headlights of a parked vehicle beyond the furthest extent of the landslide. She turned her flashlight off and got to her knees, because even though she couldn't immediately confirm who it was, she knew it had to be Buzz—Buzz, maybe coming back down the mountain because he had reached a different impasse further up, and was now being thwarted again by this new obstacle. Jake got to his knees beside her.

For several seconds she couldn't move, couldn't even look. She was caught in the grip of her own survival instinct, keeping down in all the sopping mud where Buzz couldn't see her. But then it dawned on her. She had an opportunity here. She had her rifle. And it wouldn't be like killing that dog, because she could kill

Buzz easily. All that hurt he had brought into their home. Always coming around with a twelve-pack or a fifth of Jack. Driving a wedge between Gerry and the rest of the family so that sometimes she would go to her bedroom while they were out on the front porch drinking and weep until she couldn't weep any more. *I shot the sheriff but I did not shoot the deputy.* Well . . . now was the time. She steeled her nerve.

She got up on one knee and readied her rifle. And to think, he had made a pass at Hanna while at Marblehill.

In a moment she saw a figure appear in the glow of the headlights. Through the blur of the rain, the figure resolved into Buzz Fulton. She took aim, exhaled, squeezed the trigger, and fired—but fired just as some mud shifted from under her knee. It wasn't much, but still enough to make her miss.

Buzz ducked and circled back to his truck in a crouched position. She pumped another round into the chamber and fired at his windshield. If she couldn't get the man, she would get his truck, damage it as much as she could so he would have a hard time following them. But before she could fire through the front grille, Buzz started firing back. A bullet rocketed through the air toward them and thudded into the mud not five yards away, making a small, lugubrious splash.

"You sons of bitches!" he called.

Then he pumped round after round in their general direction.

As much as she would have liked to shoot Buzz's truck to pieces, Glenda knew her only option was to retreat, especially because she had her child with her, and also because she was starting to fear that all the gunfire might trigger the mountain into another mudslide.

"Jake, back to the car."

Jake ran—fast but clumsy in the thick mud, and looking as if he were ready to hit the dirt at a second's notice.

Glenda fired one more round at the truck, then ran as well. She slipped and fell, scraping her knee badly on a small part of road that was clear of mud, but got up and continued, blinking through the torrential rain, wondering when more of the mountain would topple into the valley. Jake ran ahead of her, finally leaving the mud behind and dashing along the ledge until he came to the car. She, too, came to the ledge. Great clumps of mud fell from her shoes.

Jake dove into the backseat.

Glenda reached the car, pushed the rifle over Hanna's knees, got into the driver's seat, put the car in gear, swung round, and headed down the highway, not caring if they ended up walking part of the way to Marblehill.

Anything was better than being shot at by Buzz on this mountain.

28

Two days after the virus launch, Neil stared up at the sky from the Homestead parade ground as if it were his own personal masterpiece. Light. Once again. He could have cried for joy. Not the big gaping holes of the first attempt. No. Just these big brown blotches that were like onionskin. Like looking through a thousand blurry skylights—translucent apertures that let the beautiful glow of the afternoon sun in.

Louise stood next to him, clutching his hand. Ashley and Melissa stood next to Louise. Morgan . . . Morgan played out in the huge puddles dotting the parade ground.

The silence, after so many days of gunfire, was unreal. It was like Christmas Day on the Eastern Front.

But where the hell was Greg?

He thought he should ask Morgan to get out of the puddle, but she looked happy playing in all that mud.

Louise squeezed his hand and glanced toward the other end of the base. "Maybe they'll stop."

"Maybe they will." He motioned at the sky. "The Moon is going to launch in the next couple of days."

"I knew you could do it."

He took a few steps out into the yard, where he got a wide view of the runways beyond the parade ground. All the grass was dead. A lot of it had been washed away in the rain. In the brown light coming from the sky, the horizon reminded him of the brown sky he had seen on Mars when he had been a visiting professor there years ago. God, it looked . . . *otherworldly* out on that runway—like the surface of one of the moons or inner planets, with nothing living, nothing able to live, just a horrifying wasteland.

He heard a lone gunshot from the direction of Homestead's main gate. They all froze. Christmas Day on the Eastern Front was over.

"Kids, go inside," he said.

"Dad, I want to stay out here," called Morgan.

"Morgan, don't argue with Daddy," said Louise.

With a sharpness he didn't mean, he said, "All right, Morgan. Out of the puddle. You're ten years old. You shouldn't be playing in puddles."

"But, Daddy, it's fun."

"Morgan, right now."

She got out of the puddle and came toward the barracks.

He turned to Louise. "What are we going to do with that kid?"

He and Louise got the girls inside.

He heard a few more gunshots from the opposite side of the base, but it wasn't amounting to much. He glanced around the barracks and felt cramped, at odds with his family.

Once they were settled inside, he lifted his cell and tried his sister-in-law, Glenda.

It took him a while, but he finally got through.

"Where are you?" he asked.

"Just west of Charlotte."

"You should have been at Marblehill by now. Lenny called me an hour ago. He was expecting you a couple days ago. What happened?"

"It's tougher than you think." Then a pause. "I see light. Are we going to be okay?"

"We launched forty-eight hours ago. The Moon is going to launch on Tuesday."

"The Moon is?" She sounded suddenly breathless. "So you've been talking to Gerry?"

He glanced at Louise. "Not directly."

"But they're helping you?"

"Luke Langstrom's in charge now. I don't know how that came about. But he's been . . . cooperative."

"You mean Gerry's not running things anymore?"

"I don't think so." He sighed. That was the thing with Gerry. He always thought he was going places, but he never was. "I don't think he's officially *off* the team. I think he's still doing things for them. But more on a consulting basis." The signal hissed for a few seconds, and that was fine because it gave him a chance to change the subject. "So you're west of Charlotte? You sound a little shaken."

"Where do you want me to begin?"

"Are you okay?

"We ran into a landslide west of Dunstan, and had to turn around. We had to detour along 74. Plus we have Buzz Fulton following us."

She told him of her unnerving encounter with Buzz Fulton up on the mountain.

"Have you seen him since the landslide?"

"No. But he knows we're on our way to Marblehill." Glenda told Neil about Jake's note. "Then we got taken prisoner in Charlotte. This . . . gang, or . . . I don't know—they were all in National Guard uniforms. They held us for a few days, and tried to find out where we were going, but I didn't tell them. They weren't all that bad, really. I gave them a story about Hanna's asthma. I said I was trying to get to this clinic in Spartanburg. Then this morning, when they saw light in the sky, the good ones decided to let us go."

"Did they give you a charge for your car? Because, with that detour . . ."

"You're kidding, aren't you? They took all our food. And our rifle. But we still have a handgun. We managed to hide it from them."

"How many rounds left?"

"Twenty-seven."

"Without an extra charge, you may have to walk part of the way. You realize that, don't you?"

"I've been thinking of nothing else."

"I'll phone Lenny and let him know you might be coming on foot. Do you have a flashlight?"

"Yes."

"And is the battery good?"

"So far. But we've used it a lot."

"Try to conserve it," he advised. "When you get near the gate, flash it three times. These airmen . . . they've got the place stocked to the gills with military weapons, and they've got orders to keep intruders out."

"So, three times," she said. "Hang on, hang on . . . there's something on the road ahead. Let me give you to Hanna for a sec."

He heard the phone shift hands.

"Uncle Neil?"

"Hi, sweetie. How are you doing?"

"Can we go swimming at Marblehill?"

"You can do anything you like. Is Jake doing okay?"

"He's sleeping. We got captured by these National Guard guys."

"Your mom was saying."

"But they let us go."

"Were you scared?"

"For a while I was. But then I saw that they weren't really so bad. One of them had a guitar."

"Is that right?"

"But he wouldn't let me try it. He said it belonged to his dad."

"Oh."

"Okay . . . okay . . . here's my mom. She wants to talk to you again."

He heard the phone shift hands a second time.

"Is everybody doing okay down there?" asked Glenda.

"Colonel Bard had to reduce our rations."

"You sound a little on edge, Neil."

"Glenda, the reason I called . . . and this is strictly hush-hush, and I don't know whether you want to tell the kids or not. But the reason I called is to tell you that the United States and its allies are going to move against the TMS any day now. And early this morning I was informed by the assistant secretary of defense that if the TMS becomes unviable, the Tarsalans have vowed to take control of those planetside areas offered in the last U.N. counterproposal. That includes the Chattahoochee National Forest. So you have to be careful of your approach."

She was silent for several seconds. "So . . . when you say take control . . ."

"It's going to be hostile."

Again, a pause. "Do you think they'll get anywhere near Marblehill?"

"If they do, they're going to get a lot more than they bargained for."

The next day, perforations developed in the shroud's brown freckling, and unimpeded sunlight reached the Earth's surface. The mood at Homestead was buoyant. Neil couldn't have been happier. All morning and into the afternoon he didn't hear a single gunshot. The ceasefire lasted all night, and when morning came there was an actual dawn, diffuse and brown, with a light so fragile and amber that it reminded him of atmospheric varnish.

All that day, peace reigned. He spent much of the afternoon looking at his book. It was an art book, with full-color plates, and its title was *The Impressionists*. The Impressionists, he decided as he gazed at a particularly evocative painting by Mary Cassatt, were the great painters of light, from the great age of light, before this current age of darkness. This painting by Cassatt was called *A Reader in the Garden,* and as a study in sunlight, it had a great emotional impact on Neil in his current strained circumstances.

He turned the book around and showed his wife. "You know what the caption says? It says, 'In fresh bright light, in the middle of a flower garden, a woman sits reading.' Look how she just takes it for granted. Not only the sunlight, but the flowers. Look at the light in this painting. Look at the shadow. And then look outside.

Melissa got up, came over, and put her arm around him. "By next summer we'll be back home. I'll help you put cocoa shells on the garden. We'll have flowers just like hers."

He patted her hand, and realized it wasn't a girl's hand anymore, but a woman's.

For the rest of the afternoon and evening he looked at his book. In the title of every work, sunlight was implicit. *Regatta at Argenteuil. Countryside with Haystacks. Village Along the Seine.* He concentrated for a long time on Alfred Sisley's *Village Along the Seine.* He read the caption. "One feels the pleasure of the painter in the sun-dappled trees in the foreground and the clear light on the houses on the other side of the river." Painted in 1872. He wanted to be on the banks of the sunlit Seine in 1872, right there with Alfred Sisley as he painted his sun-dappled trees and clear-lighted houses.

"When this is all over, I'm going to retire."

He woke up in the small hours of the morning drenched in a fearful sweat. A dream. A stupid dream. The Cameron Chess Study. He and Kafis playing chess. Kafis's pupils shrinking to their midpoint in that sneaky and aggressive way they had as he checkmated Neil. Checkmate. The word echoed in his mind.

But then he realized that at exactly this moment—and he confirmed it with a quick glance at his cordless alarm clock—the Moon was launching.

"Checkmate, Kafis," he said into the dark that he had grown to hate.

He expected to see even more brown spots over the next couple of days—the Moon launches burning through the phytosphere the same way a lit cigarette burned through upholstery—but new spots didn't appear. He sat in the parade ground for most of the afternoon and looked up at the sky with a pair of enhanced binoculars, military ones equipped for infrared, hoping to see some telltale activity. Not only did he fail to spot any new lesions, but the existing ones seemed to be stagnating in their growth.

He had his dwindling scientific staff keep an eye on the phytosphere for the rest of the day—many of his people had abandoned their posts, finding the growing instability at Homestead too nerve-wracking.

When the sun went down, a young Air Force technician said that there was no significant growth in the virus lesions, and that, in fact, some of them were scabbing over with what seemed on the spectrometer to be a form of carbon sheeting.

Neil had a look at the readouts, and after scrupulous analysis he realized, with a sickening sense of dread, that instead of the targeted Tarsalan DNA component responding in defense to the insult of his virus, it was actually the xenophyta carapace component that was responding, capturing and encapsulating the virus during its lytic phase, trapping the reproducing viruses in little cages of superhard material, and at the same time neutralizing the omniphages. Was this his endgame, then?

He told Colonel Greg Bard about it an hour later.

"It's like when a computer gets a virus. If the computer can't delete it, it quarantines it. The carapace, or at least extraneous calcifications of carapace material, are surrounding and encapsulating the virus, effectively jailing it so it can't spread." He shook his head, nonplussed by his own blindness. "I didn't see it coming, Greg. I was so focused on defeating and confusing the defense component, I didn't consider the possibility that the carapace element might pick up the slack. And now I think we're screwed."

The new offensive came an hour after that. He didn't know how the opposing side got a tank, but he heard it at the other end of the base: the hum of its fusion-cell-powered engine, the creak of its tracks, and the nearly inaudible rumble of its massive weight getting closer and closer. He packed up what he could, had the girls throw clothes into bags, and as gunfire erupted in the stale brown dusk of the slowly closing virus holes, he and his family ran the two hundred yards to the Officers' Club.

Airmen sandbagged the Officers' Club.

Neil and his family entered and turned left. Emergency lights lit the corridors. His girls did exactly what they were supposed to, just like in the drills. Some airmen clutching rifles, led by Colonel Greg Bard, emerged from a ready room and ran down the corridor toward them, dark blue helmets on their heads, light-gathering goggles over their eyes, tramping down the hall in sync, grim-faced and intent.

Bard stopped and gave them a smile. "Hi, girls."

The girls gave him halfhearted and frightened hellos.

Then Greg turned to Neil and offered an apologetic shrug. "Looks like they're . . . you know."

"Is it bad?"

"We knew it was coming."

Something in the way Greg said this made Neil's stomach roll in fear. "But you're sure you can stop them."

Greg looked away. "I don't know where they got that tank." He seemed distracted for a few seconds but then his attention focused. "And actually . . . I was coming over. I want to give you these." Greg took out two aerosol spray cans. Neil instantly recognized them as the spray they used to disable Tarsalan flying surveillance macrogens, a defense-department-contract product that had been in limited use in sensitive areas for the last several years, and had recently become commercially available. "Lenny's telling me they need some up at Marblehill."

The implication of this overwhelmed Neil. "Why would they need some up at Marblehill?"

"Because it's happened, Neil. Last night at about two in the morning."

Neil felt his forehead growing moist. He took the two cans and stuffed them into his bag. "And the . . . the TMS?"

"A write-off."

The implications deepened like water in a well from which he couldn't escape. "And the phytosphere control device?"

"They haven't told me one way or the other."

"And the Tarsalans?"

"A lot are coming down. Lenny says they've had at least three confirmed landings in Chattahoochee. That's why they're going to need some of this spray stuff. Though he thinks a few macrogens might have already penetrated Marblehill."

Neil shook his head. "I . . . don't know what to say."

"Lenny's on his way."

Neil's heart thumped in sudden overdrive. "Really? Right now?"

Greg gave his head a little nod, looking bewildered by the situation. "It's high noon in Dodge, Neil." He put his hand on Neil's shoulder. "The helipad is just behind the swimming pool. There's an emergency exit back there."

"And we should be okay in the pool area, waiting for him?"

"It's the safest place in the club. We're done with the second line, aren't we? We gave it our best shot."

"Is he going to get here before—"

"Like I said, I don't know where they got that tank."

"What about calling in an air strike?"

"The risk of collateral casualties would be too high."

He nodded, deferring to Greg's experience. "I guess we'll see you when the helicopter gets here."

"I hope so."

Greg went his way, and Neil and his family went theirs.

They turned left down another corridor, and in the middle of this corridor, doors led out into a courtyard where Neil saw crates and crates of ready-to-eat rations stacked on skids—this was where they were keeping the food. He continued along past a gymnasium, sweating in the wild heat, slowly coming to the realization that he had indeed played his endgame, and that it had failed.

They pushed through some double doors, and now the corridor smelled of chlorine. He understood what Greg meant, that the pool had to be the safest place in the whole complex because it was right in the middle of it all. They went in through the men's changing room, where the air was damp, and heavy with the scents of B.O., deodorant, and cleanser.

"Careful, it's slippery here," he said.

"I can hardly see," said Louise.

"Let me open this door."

He opened the door to the pool area.

The windows—high, narrow ones—let in a ghostly brown light, probably the last natural light they would see for a long time. Louise and the girls filed through.

The pool was large. At the far end he saw a diving board, as well as a series of diving platforms. He saw some orange life rings with the word "Homestead" stenciled in black on each. It was just an ordinary institutional swimming pool, but for some reason it had a profound effect on Neil. In this age of the phytosphere, he saw it with new perspective, and the pool struck him as a museum exhibit from a time gone by. Swimming for pleasure. Swimming for recreation. Even swimming for exercise. Those were things of the past. He remembered his father's swimming pool in suburban Illinois. Remembered himself, Gerry, Ian, and Greg horsing around in it, playing Marco Polo.

"Let's set up by the diving board," he said.

"Can we go swimming?" asked Morgan.

"We have to listen for the helicopter, sweetie. And we should be . . . ready. For anything."

Yes, ready. They were stuck here. Until—and if—Lenny came in the helicopter. And once they got in the helicopter, then what? How long could they last at Marblehill? And could he trust Lenny and the rest of the airmen not to mutiny against them? What if the airmen turned against his family?

He looked up at the windows, hearing gunfire far to the west of the Officers' Club.

How long before the goddamn dark came back?

He was just thinking he might take out his book again, try to lose himself in Monet's water lilies, when his phone rang. *The* phone. He reached in his bag, pulled it out, engaged it, and pressed it to his ear.

"Not too good," he said, when Fonblanque asked him how things were going at Homestead.

And then he told her they were abandoning the base, and how he had devised his own 937 at Marblehill—rubbing it in because he didn't need them, the whole Oval Office crowd—he could survive on his own.

When she asked him about the virus, he had to tell her the truth.

"It looks as if the *carapace* responded. I've theorized that carapace material has jailed or quarantined the lytic-phase virus. There's no way the virions can spread."

"Is there anything else you can do?"

He didn't like the desperation he heard in her voice, as it allowed him to guess what had happened to the phytosphere control device. And he didn't like how she naturally assumed they were still all part of the same team. It galled him. She obviously wanted him to work miracles. But the infrastructure was gone. The resources were practically nonexistent. His shoulders settled and a great bitterness overcame him.

"Given what I have to work with, I don't think so."

"And you've had a look at your brother's stuff?"

"It's all garbage, Leanna. There's something about a stress band, but it's . . . useless observation."

"So you have nothing encouraging I can pass on to the secretary or the president? Because the TMS offensive didn't go exactly as planned."

A thin layer of perspiration came to his forehead. Outside, the gunfire was getting closer. "So I heard."

"From who?"

He hesitated, then decided it didn't matter. "Colonel Bard."

"We were hoping to secure the Tarsalan phytosphere control mechanism."

"And?" But he already knew what she was going to say.

"Our orbiting mines were effective beyond our expectations. The control mechanism has been damaged and is no longer operational. We now have no effective means of turning off the phytosphere from their end."

Neil's shoulders sagged further. The absolute idiots. "If there's no way to shut it off, it's just going to grow and grow. You know that, don't you? To be honest with you, Leanna, it could turn into a real . . . doomsday scenario. I mean, if it's gone—have your troops confirmed that the control system has in fact been destroyed?"

"Damage reports are still coming in. Our technicians are looking at it. The growing consensus is that it's beyond repair."

He cast around for possible solutions. "What about Tarsalan survivors? Maybe they can help us develop a new one."

"There haven't been many survivors."

He exhaled, and for the longest time he left his lungs empty, as if there were no point in breathing anymore. But at last he took a deep breath and sighed. "How many Tarsalans killed?"

"Confirmed or expected?"

"Confirmed."

"Over twenty thousand. But it could rise as high as thirty. As for our own troops, only seven hundred."

He took another deep breath, fighting to get his anxiety under control. "Did they think we were bluffing?"

"I don't know what they thought. I'm surprised we destroyed the TMS as easily as we did. I don't think they were expecting such a strong military response. The alien mind-set . . . it's a hard thing to second-guess."

"What about refugees?"

"Our Maxwell fighters have orders to escort as many to Earth as they can. But some of our pilots have been engaged."

"Are any Tarsalans getting through to the reserve areas listed in the U.N.'s last counterproposal?"

"We believe so."

"What about Chattahoochee National Forest?"

"We have three civilian reports of alien landings in and around Chattahoochee, and dozens of reports of landings throughout the southeastern United States. It seems the Tarsalans have already engaged several units, and my analysts tell me the fighting is expected to worsen in the coming days."

Darkness came an hour later. The fighting drew closer. His daughters looked up at the narrow windows, their faces apprehensive. He heard men yelling outside. And then he felt vibrations through the tile floor.

A second later he heard the squeaking of tank treads, then a wild cracking from the squash courts. Dust floated down from the windowsills as it was shaken loose. The water in the pool vibrated. And at last the wall that separated the pool from the squash courts bent toward them, the bricks coming apart as if they were made of marshmallows, then collapsing; first just a hole ten feet up as the tank's main cannon came through, then a wide area below as the front part of the tank shouldered its way in.

The roar echoed through the pool area. The girls cried out and, instinctively, Neil grabbed Louise and shoved her to the floor. The tank came forward and ground its way right into the shallow end of the pool, the hot metal of its engine compartment hissing and steaming, its turret swiveling away from them toward the dressing rooms.

Several enemy airmen came in behind the tank.

The tank pivoted on its right track, turned toward the dressing rooms, then proceeded forward, its treads catching the far lip of the shallow end and pulling the armored vehicle out of the water. The tank then plowed right into the wall and continued on through the dressing rooms, eating through the Officers' Club the way a termite eats through wood. Gunfire erupted from the direction of the dressing rooms, and bullets rocketed into the pool area. The enemy airmen took up positions on either side of the pool. The airmen saw them but seemed to realize they were noncombatants, and left them alone.

Neil gathered his family and got them on their stomachs behind the diving tower. He glanced at Morgan. The corners of the young girl's lips were drawn so that he could see her bottom teeth, and she looked determined to bolt regardless of the danger. Ashley was breathing fast and looking as white as paper. Louise stared at her own clenched fists as if she didn't want to see what was going on.

Melissa was looking at the windows high on the wall behind them. He saw in her eyes some of his own bold confidence. "Dad, I think I hear the helicopter."

A moment later, he heard it himself, the *blup-blup-blup-blup* of the rotor chopping the air, Lenny getting closer and closer, even as *things broke down* at Homestead. He saw the emergency exit at the back. And while he knew it was a risk to get up from their cover behind the diving platform, he realized the situation was getting worse as the opposing sides fought for control of the food supply in the courtyard.

"All right, listen to me!" He pointed. "On my count, we run for the door!"

"Dad, what if it's locked?" asked Melissa.

She had a point.

"I'm going to check it. When I wave you over, run like hell."

He crawled on his stomach across the tiles to the door. He reached up, pressed the panic bar, and the door opened. He heard the helicopter even louder now. Florida smelled like rotten hay. More bullets rocketed into the pool area. He waved his family over.

Louise and the girls ran in his direction. But then Morgan slipped on the tiles. She went down, clutching her ankle, and started crying.

"Go on, go on!" he told the others.

"Get her!" cried Louise.

"Just go!"

They went out, and he returned to rescue Morgan.

He gripped her by her shirt and dragged her across the tiles like a hundred-pound sack of potatoes.

As he reached the door, a deafening boom resounded throughout the pool area—the tank firing its cannon somewhere beyond the ruins of the dressing rooms.

The air was now choked with dust. He pulled Morgan out the door, and the heat of the Florida night, supercharged because of the phytosphere's heat-trapping ability, settled over him like an electric blanket on high.

The helicopter came two minutes later, its landing lights bright in the darkness. He squinted in the dust the rotor kicked up. The helicopter's side door slid back and he saw a fully armed airman kneeling there, ready to help him. But where was Greg? The airman waved them over.

"Let's go!" Neil shouted to his family.

They ran to the helicopter.

The airman said, "Dr. Thorndike?"

"Are you Lenny?"

"Get in."

"What about Colonel Bard?"

"He's not with you?"

"No."

"Then we're going to have to leave without him. This area's too hot. Get in."

So. That's how it would be.

He lifted Morgan into the helicopter, and helped Louise in as well. Lenny gave both Melissa and Ashley a hand up.

Neil stood there with his hands against the helicopter. And now it really did feel like failure. Because not only had he failed the whole world, he had failed his friend. He climbed into the helicopter. His wife was staring at him. Louise knew exactly what he was feeling. She reached out and touched him. He tried to give her a reassuring smile, but it simply wasn't in him.

Lenny lifted his finger into the air and twirled it a few times. The pilot worked the manuals and the helicopter rose.

As it climbed higher and higher, Neil got a better view of the Officers' Club. An intense firefight raged in the courtyard. He saw muzzle flashes and tracer bullets. Someone had set the food on fire, and in the light of this fire he saw the tank. One man stood off to the side. This man X-ed his arms toward the helicopter, and Neil thought he must be Greg Bard. But before he could get a better look, Lenny slid the door shut and the helicopter banked, then nosed north toward Marblehill.

29

Kafis came once more to the Moon, this time with dire news.

The alien phrased it to the gathered members of the committee the way he phrased everything, as if he were a Buddhist monk talking to his disciples. Gerry stared at Kafis in growing alarm. The Tarsalan spoke of the loss of the phytosphere control device in terms of games theory, and said that they had used a Tarsalan mathematical method of decision-making when choosing the phytosphere as one of their teaching tools. Unfortunately they had never factored into the computational framework the notion that humans might inadvertently destroy the device with a surfeit of firepower.

"So it's gone?" asked Gerry, speaking out of turn because technically he was just an observer now.

"It's degraded to the point where it can't be used in either augmenting or dissipating the phytosphere. Left on its own, the phytosphere will continue to grow."

Malcolm Hulke rephrased. "So you have no way of turning it off?"

"Your people have robbed us of this option, yes. As a teaching tool, it has failed. We take our failure with humility. And we express our deepest apologies to the people of Earth."

Gerry stared at Kafis in wonderment. "You destroy a whole world and the only thing you have to offer is an apology?"

"It is you who have chosen to destroy yourselves. We

could have lived in peace. These principles of property you hold so dear . . . so that you think you can say who owns what, and who can come to your world and who must stay away . . . this is an erroneous path you have followed."

"Fathead is speaking bullshit," said Ian Hamilton. Kafis's pupils opened a notch as he regarded the test pilot. "It's our planet. We get to say who's welcome."

"Yes, but is Earth rightfully yours? Is it rightfully anybody's? There are thousands of species on your planet. How can you say it belongs to just humans?"

"There are over twelve billion people on Earth," said Gerry. He couldn't help thinking of his wife and children. "And now they're all going to die."

"Gerald, you are understandably angry. But you must accept it. The bright blue jewel you call your home is lost. The control mechanism for the phytosphere is gone. There is nothing we can do for you."

"You can help us build a new control device, Kafis. Here on the Moon."

"We've made a complete inventory of the Moon's technological resources. Even if I were to reveal to you the methods involved, you wouldn't have the materials."

"It's gravity, isn't it?" said Gerry.

This stopped Kafis. "Human, you always surprise me."

"Am I right?"

"You must claw your own way to wisdom, my son. The Earth is not my concern anymore. I'm here to negotiate with the Moon."

"Gravity?" said Ira.

"You want to negotiate with the Moon?" said Hulke.

Kafis turned to the mayor. His pupils widened to their fullest. Gerry wasn't sure what this was supposed to mean, but guessed that Kafis was now going to try to manipulate Hulke.

"What's this about gravity?" said Ira. "This is the first I've heard about gravity."

He glanced at Ira. Did the man actually care about the Earth after all?

"Because of the actions of a few misguided men on

Earth," said Kafis, "the Moon now finds itself in a precarious position. So does the mothership."

"The phytosphere is reactive to gravity," Gerry told Ira. "I sent the report to your office this morning. You haven't read it?"

Ira frowned. "Everything is reactive to gravity. Jesus, Gerry, tell us something we don't know."

The rebuke stung Gerry. And maybe Ira was right. Everything *was* reactive to gravity. What was he going to do about it? Especially in relation to the phytosphere?

"Gerry," said Hulke. "If you don't mind, Kafis has raised a . . . a point of some pressing concern for the Moon. Go ahead, Kafis."

Kafis continued. "We find ourselves thrown together in this . . . this lifeboat you call your Moon. Look beyond your office window. You see fifteen of our craft. In each of them are a dozen of my people. They are refugees. We ask you for refuge on the Moon."

"Kafis . . . that's not going to fly so well with the general populace. Especially because we're running out of food. We've got our hydroponics facilities going full steam to augment things, but it's hardly enough to feed . . . a couple of hundred extra hostiles. People are going around hungry all the time. When the reserve runs out, it's going to be slow starvation, with just enough coming in from the hydro facilities to make us think we might hang on for another year or two before . . . before we're overwhelmed by it all. I'm sorry. We can't take you. Politically, it's not possible. And the Earth would have a bird."

"Ah . . . but we don't come expecting to get something for nothing. We have always offered something in return. Not only in our negotiations with Earth, but now also in our negotiations with you. Yes, we are refugees, but we are also scientists and technicians and inventors, and we have a long history of turning uninhabitable rocks into oases. We have the means to double, triple, and even quadruple your food supply. And you need never worry about your air or water again. Humankind can find its new homeworld here on this Moon. This barren rock can now be the cradle of your civilization. Our technology can easily achieve this, if you'll only let us live here as refugees."

Hulke glanced around the room. His eyes glowed with euphoric seriousness. Gerry felt the mayor was losing sight of the essential emergency.

He pressed the point. "What about Earth? What about the millions of people who are dying down there?"

Hulke turned to him. "Gerry . . . I hate to be obvious about this, but maybe we should concentrate on saving what we can. I'm really sorry about your family. I'm sorry about everybody on Earth. But the toxin thing has failed, and the virus thing has failed, and I guess you were right about both of them; kudos to you. Now Kafis is telling us that U.S. forces have destroyed the Tarsalan phytosphere control mechanism, and that there's nothing they can do because they don't have the resources to build another. Kafis is trying to help us here on the Moon, now that he can't help Earth. And as mayor of Nectaris, I have to think of lunar lives first."

"Kafis, tell us how to build one of these control devices," said Gerry.

"Gerald, the technology involved is so beyond the scope of your understanding—and the Moon's resources—that it's simply not possible. I come here to offer you what *is* possible." And here he went into an elaborate discussion of turning the Moon into the cradle of humanity, of how he and his experts had tallied every nut and bolt on the Moon, and calculated down to the last gram its every natural resource, had assessed all the scientific and technical talent on the Moon, and had come to the conclusion that if they used absolutely everything available to them they could make the Moon self-sustaining. "Especially if AviOrbit hands over its assets."

"Now just hang on there," said Ira.

"That includes your manufacturing facilities, in-service spacecraft, and all singularity drives—including the current models set for delivery to the Federated Martian Colonies Transit Collective."

"Hey, you can't take those. That's our biggest order to date."

"Those drives will be needed to harvest comets in the short term. I believe the drives have a service life of five years. By that time we'll have built our own drives for you."

"Yes, but I haven't the authority to sign things over to you."

"And whose authority do you need?"

"Head office in San Diego."

"AviOrbit, as an entity on Earth, no longer exists." Kafis paused, and his pupils shrank. "Ira . . . my friend . . . we must think in terms of a . . . a new beginning. We are sitting around this table . . . and we are making history. The Tarsalans—those of us who remain—offer you heart-felt assistance and a disciplined plan."

Kafis continued with a more detailed discussion of how the Moon could sustain itself indefinitely. Gerry hardly caught any of it. All he could think of was his family. Of what they were facing. No matter how lucky and careful they were, the food was going to run out. He glanced at Stephanie.

Stephanie leaned over. "Kafis is hiding something."

"Let's get out of here," he said. "I can tell we're not wanted."

He and Stephanie got up and moved toward the doors.

"Gerry?" said the mayor.

"You'll go down in history, Malcolm, but not the way you think."

Gerry and Stephanie left the room and walked down the corridor.

He took out his fone as he came to the Council Chamber and tried to contact Glenda, but all he got was the AT&T Interlunar message. Tears came to his eyes and he quickly wiped them away with the back of his arm.

Stephanie put her hand on his shoulder. "I'm sorry, Gerry."

"There's got to be something I can do."

"What do you think the people on Earth would do to Kafis if they ever got their hands on him? He's playing the only card he can. Staying alive until reinforcements arrive."

"Reinforcements?"

"Don't they live a long time?"

"Two hundred and fifty years."

"So he can spend forty on the Moon. That's how long it'll take for reinforcements to get here. I'm sure they've already sent their Mayday."

He shook his head. "And they say they're not warlike."

"So when reinforcements arrive, they open the shroud, get rid of it, and go down and resuscitate Earth. It'll be theirs for the taking. We'll be supplanted in our own solar system. That's why he got so cagey when you started talking about the gravity thing. And when he told you he was impressed, he was just throwing it in your face. I'm sure he could easily build another phytosphere control device if he wanted to."

Down the corridor he heard the door to the mayor's office open and close.

A moment later, Mitch Bennett came toward them. The small engineer cast a nervous glance over his shoulder, as if fearing someone was following him.

When he reached them he said, "The gravity thing. I read your report."

At that moment, Gerry knew he had an ally. "It's my working theory. Only I have no way of proving it."

Mitch once more glanced anxiously over his shoulder. "I think I have a way . . . of helping you."

Gerry studied the engineer. "How?"

"Ira would fire me if he knew I was talking to you like this."

"Ira's a jerk," said Stephanie.

"We have these old singularity prototypes," said Mitch. "They produce gravity as a by-product. These prototypes are small. You could run some simulations to see what gravity does on a small scale to the xeno-

phyta, like you've written in your report. I know some
of the guys in Copernicus, where we have them stored."

"And why do you want to help him?" asked
Stephanie.

His face settled. "Because I'm on a five-year contract
here, and my family's . . . on Earth. My partner."

Stephanie's lips pursed in sympathy. "You never
told us."

"I prefer . . . to keep my personal life to myself. Ira's
a bit of a dinosaur."

Gerry considered the possibilities. "Could we simulate
the Earth-Moon system?"

Mitch's eyes widened. "You want two fields?"

"If we're going to get a true understanding of what's
going on . . . of what Kafis is hiding from us . . ."

Mitch's lips twisted to one side as he glanced over the
railing into the Council Chamber. His chin came forward
and his eyebrows rose, and he nodded distractedly.
"It's possible."

"And how soon can it be arranged?"

Mitch considered. "If I have the guys get started on
it right away . . . maybe by tomorrow."

"I need to get the samples. They took my card away."

"Don't worry about samples. I'll bring those. You just
bring your mind, Gerry. We're nothing but a bunch of
engineers. We need someone telling us what to do."

The next day, in Copernicus, Gerry stood with Stephanie in the control booth behind Mitch and two other
technicians. Out in the control area—a pressurized warehouse space about a thousand yards square—two platforms stood ready, each capable of generating its own
singularity and gravitational field, a speck of laboratory-
created black hole, as Mitch called it.

The first and bigger generating platform stood anchored
in the center of the control area, while the second had
wheels and was set to travel around the main platform,
much the way the Moon revolved around the Earth. Infrared cameras—dismantled and reconfigured from the
Alleyne-Parma cameras—hung from overhead scaffold-

ing, ready to record the results. The wheeled platform—Platform 2, as the engineers called it—ran on rails.

Gerry tapped his chin a few times. "Is there any way we can take Platform 2 off its rails?" he asked Mitch.

A knit came to Mitch's brow. "Why would you want to do that?"

"Because I want the option of increasing its gravitational pull. The closer it gets to Platform 1, the stronger its gravitational pull against Platform 1 will be."

"Oh, you don't have to worry about that," said Mitch. "We can control the g-force artificially from here. But why would you want to increase gravitational pull?"

Gerry didn't immediately answer. "You've got both platforms geared to their scale strengths?"

"Yes."

"Then let's give it a shot."

Mitch spoke into a microphone. "Sal? Kev? You can take the xenophyta into the control area."

Two junior technicians emerged from doorways leading into the warehouse, pushing big carts loaded with lab coolers. They maneuvered these carts as far as Platform 2's rails, then lifted a total of eight coolers over, placed them equidistant in a circle around Platform 1, and bolted them into place. They unclasped the lids from each.

Gerry glanced up at the regular camera monitors and got a top view of the nearest cooler. How harmless the living xenophyta looked. Nothing but a box of green sludge. And yet this sludge was killing millions on Earth.

Sal and Kev left the control area.

Mitch and the other engineers charged up the first singularity.

At first nothing happened, and Gerry thought his gravity theory was a bust. But, after a minute, an emerald mist rose from each cooler, and this emerald mist stitched itself in a perfect sphere around Platform 1's singularity. As the minutes ticked by, the emerald mist thickened, until finally it was so dark it was almost black. The infrared cameras showed a warming of the entire sphere, with parts of it edging into yellow. The xenophyta maintained the same scale distance from the singularity that the phytosphere did from Earth.

At this point, technicians engaged Platform 2. It circled around Platform 1, simulating the movement of the Moon around the Earth. As the final xenophyta in the coolers drifted up and joined the rest of the miniphytosphere, the technicians keyed in the necessary sequence and soon the secondary singularity exerted a gravitational pull in scale relation to the Moon's.

According to the infrared cameras, a stress band developed immediately, an amorphous bar of heat that traveled from the north to the south pole, and went around and around with the revolutions of the Moon. Tides proven. The phytosphere began to slowly counterrotate. This counterrotation was centrifugally strong enough to keep the model phytosphere in place, while the pull of Platform 1's gravity kept the whole thing tethered. Gerry realized that the phytosphere was a delicate thing, as nuanced as an egg.

"Could we send in the probe?" he said.

Mitch leaned into the microphone. "Kev, do you want to introduce the probe?"

Kev emerged from one of the doors. This time he was safety-belted to a long nylon strap. As he got closer to the singularity, he had to dig his heels in against the artificial gravitational pull. Even inside the control booth, Gerry felt a slight tug toward the observation window.

Kev carried a Styrofoam ball the size of a softball. He waited for the Moon to pass, stepped over the rails, and approached the Earth. The whole primitive setup reminded Gerry of all the cheap, underfunded research projects he had ever been involved in. Kev unlatched his tether so the Moon wouldn't crash into it, crawled to a ring anchored into the concrete floor, attached himself with a smaller tether, and stood up, a man in a white hazmat suit standing before a large green sphere that was like a boiling and shifting ball of algae.

Kev tossed the Styrofoam ball into the phytosphere and the gravity pulled it in. A string was attached to the ball, as they didn't want the ball crashing directly into the singularity, but rather for it to hover inside the phytosphere. Various instruments were embedded in the Styrofoam ball, including a microscopy camera. Here was *Smallmouth 2,* thought Gerry, not without some chagrin: a Styrofoam ball and a piece of string. Yet he was used to this kind of thing, working with everyday household objects and coming up with at least some kind of scientific result. In the cash-strapped Department of Ocean Sciences at NCSU, that's the way he had done things.

Kev now looked like he was flying a kite, only the kite was a giant green sphere about twelve yards in diameter.

Gerry went over to the microscopy screen. "Let's see what we've got."

Stephanie and Mitch crowded behind him as he took a seat.

Gerry pointed. "Just as I suspected. The flagella have grown active, like they do in the real phytosphere." He double-checked a readout screen, which had graphs to measure and tabulate a number of phenomena. "You can see that the cellular electrical activity within the flagella has increased tenfold. In other words, they're flexing their muscles and joining up with each other. And look at this. They're actually producing the scaling material for the carapace. Probably not at the same rate they actually do in the phytosphere, because we haven't provided this sample with any water or light, but I think we can safely conclude that gravity is definitely the trigger. Without gravity the xenophyta more or less remain in a state of stasis. Add gravity, and it's like rain has come to the desert. Everything starts to grow."

"So how's this solve our problem?" said Mitch. "How can we possibly take the gravity away and put the phytosphere in stasis mode? We would have to take the whole Earth away in order to stop the gravity trigger."

Stephanie put her hand on Gerry's shoulder, as if preparing him for the blow of what was looking like another impasse.

"We don't have to take it away," he said. "We don't

even have to worry about the Earth. It's the Moon we have to concern ourselves with. The Moon creates the stress band, and that's the key to solving this whole problem. We just have to fool around with it. What happens when the stress band passes over the flagella? I always knew there had to be a connection between the two. You see how there's an excess of electrical activity in the flagella? And look at this statistic. About two percent of the flagella are shorting out completely and not coming back online after the stress band passes. The other ninety-eight percent all seem to experience some kind of seizure activity before going back to their usual profile. Because the stress band isn't strong or constant enough, it gives the small percentage of destroyed flagella a chance to regenerate. If it *were* strong enough . . ."

Mitch looked more closely at the readouts. "Gerry, I think you're onto something."

"Let's increase the Moon's gravitational field. I want to see if we can increase the short-out rate by upping the pressure of the stress band. In fact, I want to increase the gravity until we get a hundred percent short-out rate. Let's kill all those damn things if we can."

"Gerry . . . are we working toward a model here? Because how the hell do you expect to increase the Moon's gravity in real life?"

"I expect to do it on a shoestring budget, like I do everything else."

Mitch hesitated, but finally gave his technicians a nod.

The technicians keyed in the necessary commands to increase Platform 2's gravitational field.

As the strength of the gravity increased, Gerry watched the readouts carefully, making sure all of them were recorded, particularly the short-out rate. The short-out rate in the flagella increased from two percent to five, and then ten percent, even as the temperature of the stress band rose dramatically. As the short-out rate reached fifteen, then twenty percent, the color of the small phytosphere changed, becoming a light green. Its entire surface quivered. The short-out rate jumped exponentially to forty percent, then to eighty percent, as the mock-up Moon exerted an ever stronger pull on the scale-model Earth.

At last the whole phytosphere crumpled.

As the stress band passed around it one more time, it exploded in a sloppy and gelatinous splash, like a water balloon filled with mint jelly.

Kev was left standing there in a hazmat suit covered with green slime. *Smallmouth 2* hovered up near the singularity.

"Okay, you can cut the fields," said Gerry.

Mitch had his technicians do so.

There was a feeling in the room of fundamental and groundbreaking discovery. As the fields hummed down to silence and Platform 2 rolled to a stop, everyone stared at the splattered control area. Gerry looked at the readouts again. Theoretically, it was possible. But how? And with what resources? The Styrofoam ball plopped to the floor.

He glanced at Mitch. Mitch was looking at him in . . . *amazement*.

Yes, theoretically, it was possible.

If only he could figure out how.

PART FIVE

30

Darkness was her world, and her car was her life.

At last they reached Georgia. Glenda couldn't believe how long it was taking them to travel the four hundred miles from Raleigh to Marblehill. She was anxious because her charge was getting lower and lower, and Hanna's coughing was getting worse and worse. They were well up in the mountains and, luckily, there hadn't been any more road washouts or landslides. The rain had stopped, and the hills were holding. What bothered her were the immense fog banks—fog so thick it was like cheese, with a stench like rotten algae.

She took 441 south through Clayton, Tallulah Falls, and Turnerville, glad to reach Turnerville because the hills and valleys weren't so big, and the road didn't wind so much. Also, there was some farmland, not the chilling and grotesque dead forest all the time, which was really starting to frazzle her. But she was also unnerved to reach Turnerville because Turnerville was where they really had to start looking out for Buzz.

Though it was ten o'clock in the morning, the sky was black. The only light came from her headlights. They pierced the misty gloom like twin swords.

Ten miles later, they came to Clarkesville. She veered onto 17. The charge needle was on empty. Yet Clarkesville was a heady milestone to Glenda, the last town they passed before they reached Marblehill. She remembered the road now, and didn't need Gerry's old map. Seventeen twisted north to 75, at which point she turned left on 75 and headed west again on an old black-top highway that looked as if it had been abandoned by road crews years ago.

She was no more than a mile along 75 when a cloud of flies enveloped the car. She slowed right down because she couldn't see through the flies. They landed on her windshield and didn't blow off. This made seeing difficult. She turned on her windshield wipers and brushed them away. But too late. She bashed into some-thing, and the car lurched to a halt. Her kids jerked forward in their seat belts. The pressure of Hanna's seat belt against the girl's chest made her cough again, and it was a miserable, exhausted cough.

"Jake, give me the handgun," said Glenda.

"What'd we hit?"

"I don't know. I can't see a thing. These damn flies."

Jake handed the gun to her, and she got out of the car.

She shut the door so the flies wouldn't get in, and walked around to the front. The flies immediately got in her hair, eyes, and ears. She brushed them away as best she could, but there were so many that she made only a halfhearted effort, and then resigned herself to suffering through them.

She shone the flashlight on the road and saw that she had run into a dead horse. The horse looked as if it had been shot through the head. Who would shoot a horse through the head? The animal was horribly emaciated, and starting to putrefy.

Shining her flashlight further up the road, she saw three other dead horses blocking the way at various dis-tances. At last, far ahead, she saw a truck with a horse trailer, the trailer jackknifed across the road. She cast her flashlight along the shoulder and wasn't sure if she would have enough room to get by.

She approached the truck slowly, walking through this bizarre scene of equine mayhem with an overwhelming sense of apprehension. The other three horses looked as if they had also been pulled out of the trailer and shot. The flies got thicker, and the stench was horrendous.

This was what she hated about her new world, how every so often a scene from Hell would arise, and there would never be any emergency crews to clear it away, only the terrifying effects of nature on dead flesh. She lifted the handgun and walked closer to the cab.

As she rounded the front of the horse trailer and came to the pickup truck, she peered in through the driver's door and saw a man slumped forward against the steering wheel, a bloodstain shaped like a spider tattooing the side of his head. The dashboard lights were on, and the computer screen was telling her that while the engine might be off, the electrical was still on, and draining the charge at a rate of two percent per hour. Glenda had a wild hope that they might use this truck to get the rest of the way to Marblehill. Her hopes were further bolstered when she leaned over and looked at the charge gauge—it was a quarter full. Here, at the scene of this odd horse slaughter, they might find salvation.

But then she heard a noise from down the road. Her head swung in the direction of the sound. For a few seconds the noise disappeared, but then it came back stronger. Buzz. Like a hurricane coming in from the Atlantic, bound to get here sooner or later. Why couldn't she be lucky every now and again, the way Neil and Louise were? Why couldn't things go her way just once?

She took one more longing glance at the charge gauge in the truck, then ran back to her car. There was no time to make the switch.

Jake was up on his knees on the backseat, peering out the rear window. Hanna coughed and coughed, so miserable that she was in tears. Glenda handed the gun to Jake.

"I can't see him yet, Mom."

"He's back there. The road climbs and dips."

She got in, put the car in gear, and the dashboard immediately flashed a warning telling her she'd better charge up now or risk getting stranded. She had no choice but to ignore it. She leaned forward so she could get a better view through the windshield, eased her foot off the brake, backed up a bit, and maneuvered first around the dead horses, then the trailer, and finally the truck. Once past the truck she accelerated.

She looked in her rearview mirror and saw Buzz braking at the horse massacre site. He came to a stop, got out of his truck, and went to investigate the animals. He left his headlights on and was silhouetted in their glow.

He must have seen them because he lifted his rifle and shot toward them. The back window smashed.

"Jake, get down!

Jake was already down, but he lifted the gun and fired blindly a few times out the smashed back window. She glanced in the rearview mirror again and saw Buzz running back to his truck for shelter. Then she just concentrated on getting as far ahead of him as she could.

As the road dipped down into a gully, she saw a track leading through a fence off to her left. With her charge light blinking, she knew she didn't have more than a mile or two left. She swung left onto the track, where she saw a stand of dead trees up ahead, her headlights illuminating their gray trunks. She felt like she was in an airplane, and that the engine had just given out and she was now gliding. She wanted to turn her headlights off because she was sure Buzz would see them in the dark; at the same time, she was afraid she might crash into a tree if she turned them off. So she kept them on . . . until they failed all on their own.

She swung off the track and crashed into the dead bushes, hoping to hide the car with this last desperate maneuver before her final charge ran out. Junker that it was, the car behaved abysmally, and she found herself in a small creek once the twenty-second ordeal was at an end.

"Get out of the car!" she cried.

"Where are we going?" asked Hanna.

"As far away from here as we can."

"She's spent?" said Jake.

"She's spent."

He peered over at the dashboard as if he didn't believe her, but finally nodded in a way that was far too grown-up.

They got out of the car and she was immediately surprised by how slippery the ground was, how it seemed to seethe underfoot with a rottenness all its own, and how it sent up a smell, not quite like a dead rat festering behind a baseboard but still carrying the sweetness of putrefaction.

They struggled down the creek bank. At last they reached the edge and waded into the water—the creek seemed to be the clearest path anywhere. The sound of Buzz's pickup got closer and closer.

She started to cry. Who was meant to take this? One of Satan's agents was following her through Armageddon. That was more than any housewife and part-time nursing-home attendant should be expected to take. She didn't even have her car anymore.

"Keep going straight up," she said.

"Mom, the bottom's slippery," said Hanna.

"Just stay along the side."

She glanced back toward the road and saw Buzz's truck coming along the crumbling blacktop, bumping and rattling as it took the potholes, pink haloes forming around his headlights in the mist rising from the ground. As he reached the track, he slowed down.

She turned around. "I can't see a thing."

"Mom, let's climb up here," said Jake.

She peered into the blackness and perceived some dead brambles in the stray glow coming from Buzz's headlights.

"Okay."

"Mom, I'm going to shoot him."

"You can't shoot long-range with a handgun."

"If he gets anywhere close, I'm going to shoot him."

"And what will you to do if you miss? He's got a rifle. A rifle's more accurate than a handgun. Hanna, are you all right?"

"I can't breathe."

"Come up here. There's some logs we can hide behind."

They all climbed up onto the bank. She reached the logs. They looked like lengths of cow fence that had never been used and, to her surprise, they were dry. After all the rain, things were drying out again in the intense heat.

"Let's get behind here."

She got behind the logs. Jake settled in beside her. Glenda took Hanna's arm and guided her. Hanna started coughing again.

"Hanna, just try to keep them down for the next little while."

"Mom, I can't . . ." She couldn't finish her sentence because she started coughing again.

Jake gave his mother a glance.

Glenda shrugged. "Sweetie, just try."

Jake took off his T-shirt, scrunched it up, and handed it to his sister. "Cough into this, Hanna. See if you can muffle them a bit."

Hanna nodded woefully, took her brother's T-shirt, and pressed it to her face. She struggled valiantly, managing to keep the explosions to a minimum, stopping the ragged, barking coughs that had plagued her ever since her medicine had run out, but Glenda wondered if it would be enough, especially in the dead quiet of the countryside. At least they were by a creek, and the current made a bit of noise—maybe enough to cover the sound of Hanna coughing.

Buzz turned off the road and came along the track, driving slowly, no more than two or three miles per hour. As he approached, he shone a flashlight out the driver's-side window. Its beam was powerful, fully charged, and cut through the misty air with silvery precision, catching like bright flecks the flies that spun and whirled above the dead grass. Glenda wondered how Buzz was keeping his engine charged, but then remembered that his vehicle had a gasoline backup system. At last, his flashlight beam found her tire tracks, then the back of her car. It was funny yet awful to see the family car half in the creek like that. Buzz turned off the track and drove toward her car through the field. Hanna coughed and coughed into Jake's T-shirt, muting the noise. Glenda rubbed her back, trying to comfort her.

Jake peered over the logs, then started reloading the handgun.

Glenda tried to get her crying under control, but she was scared and her heart was filled with a great sorrow, not only for herself and her children, but for the man who was trying to hunt them down. How Buzz must have loved his brother. She regretted killing Maynard. Never wanted to. But what choice had he given her?

Buzz drove about halfway to the car and stopped. He got out of his truck and crouched behind the front fender for a long time, his rifle poised over the vehicle. Jake finished reloading the gun.

At last Buzz called out. "Glenda?" He obviously thought they were still in the car.

Jake's hand tightened around the gun. Glenda reached over and rested her hand on his arm. Hanna continued her muffled coughing.

"Kids?" said Buzz.

Buzz waited another minute before he finally ran crouched over to the creek and took a position on his stomach ten yards upstream from her car. He crawled into a small hollow and disappeared from view for the next minute.

Hanna continued to cough, muffling it well. Still, could Buzz hear that? And just where the hell was he? She couldn't see him anywhere.

But then he sprang up on one knee, reminding her of a gopher coming out of its hole, and shot at her car, expertly pulling the bolt back after each round, expelling the spent cartridge, loading another one into the chamber, and squeezing the trigger so that he got off a shot every second or so—seven in all, emptying his magazine into the vehicle. He shot with vengeful intensity, his heated emotion guiding his actions. Each muzzle flash was a tongue of white flame. The reports echoed in the hills, and the sound of bullets clanking into her poor old car dried up Glenda's tears immediately.

Her fear was now as cold and numbing as an anesthetic. Six simple words drifted through her mind: *This guy wants to kill us.* They were obvious words, and framed a fact she already knew, but until now they had been something only her mind had acknowledged, not her body. Now they filled her every blood vessel, every sinew, every bone with fear. Her physiological terror made her break into a sweat. She wanted to run, but checked the urge because to run now would only alert Buzz to their location. She swallowed and swallowed, but there seemed to be a hard clot of dryness in her throat that stopped her from swallowing with any degree of success. Hanna ceased coughing, as if the coughs had been scared right out of her. Jake was still on his knees with the gun poised over the pile of old logs.

Buzz meanwhile went back to the ground, and in the peripheral glow of his truck's headlights, Glenda saw him reloading, thumbing one cartridge after another into his magazine.

At last he got back up.

"Glenda?" he called.

He stared at the car a moment more, then scanned the surrounding countryside. Now even Buzz looked scared.

"Glenda, why don't you just give up? You know I'm going to get you sooner or later. I know you're on your way to Marblehill. If you come out now, I'll spare your children."

Hanna started coughing again, but she once more muffled it with Jake's T-shirt, forcing herself to halt the loud, barking explosions and making do with smaller, less percussive ones.

Buzz bolted for the car, dropping to his knees as he reached the driver's door, then looked all around the countryside again. After another minute, he stood up and looked inside the car. He shone his flashlight in through the windows, first in the front, then in the back. At last he got to his feet and kicked the car as if he were angry at it, then kicked it again, and finally swore.

He opened the back door and started going through their stuff.

"Mom, I think I can get him," whispered Jake.

"Jake, not from this distance. Not with a handgun. And what's he wearing? Looks like some kind of . . . flak jacket."

It was hard to tell from this distance, in the dark and from behind all these bushes, but the more she looked, the more she grew convinced that he was wearing a bullet-resistant vest. It would make sense, his brother being a cop and all.

Buzz rummaged through the back, dimly illuminated by his truck's headlights, pulled out Hanna's clothes bag, and tossed it into the creek. He found the map, folded it, and tucked it into one of his vest pockets. Then he stood up and looked over the roof. He seemed to stare right at them.

Jake squirmed. "Mom?"

"No, Jake," she whispered.

Hanna coughed and coughed, and it built and built, and finally she had one of her loud, racking coughs. Buzz immediately lifted his rifle and fired in the direction of the cough. The three Thorndikes sank right to the ground. Hanna continued to cough, struggling and struggling, but she simply couldn't keep them down.

"I hear you," called Buzz. "Why don't you just come out and get it over with? You got to pay for what you did, Glenda. So why prolong the agony? Why make your kids suffer like this?"

"Mom, I'm going to kill him."

And before she could stop him, Jake was standing up and blasting away with the handgun. She grabbed his pant leg and tugged him, but he continued to blast away, and she hoped—God, how she hoped—that he would get Buzz with a good head shot that would take him down once and for all.

She gripped the top log and pulled herself up. Buzz ran wildly back to his vehicle, so spooked by Jake's fusillade of bullets that he didn't have the good sense to take cover behind her own car, but bolted toward his junky old truck like a deer in hunting season instead. Jake

fired and fired, but he was just wasting bullets. At last
the gun was empty, and he ducked back down and fumbled in his pocket for more rounds.

"We're going this way," said Glenda, and grabbed
them both by their sleeves.

They headed away from the logs and felt their way
over the rough, uneven land. She kept glancing behind
to see if Buzz would follow them, or fire at them, but
all she saw was his truck now, with its headlights piercing
the gloom. She had the flashlight, but she didn't dare
turn it on. The land rose through trees that were no
more than a few feet taller than she was, Christmas
trees, only all the needles had fallen off. A ridge curved
upward to the right. She glanced over her shoulder again
and saw Buzz emerge from behind his truck. He leveled
his rifle across the front of his truck and shot in the
direction of the logs.

"Just keep going," she said. "Climb the ridge. We'll
circle back to the road in a little while."

"Mom . . . we've got to figure out some way to ambush him," said Jake.

"Let's just make for Marblehill. Once we get to Marblehill, we'll be safe."

This was her credo now. Get to Marblehill. Only she
wasn't sure she believed it anymore. Was anywhere
safe? Could she and her family trust the airmen there?
And what about the Tarsalans? Wouldn't some of them
be landing in Chattahoochee once the TMS was destroyed? Maybe the TMS was already destroyed. *We'll
be safe, we'll be safe, we'll be safe.* But was that possible?
Tears came back to her eyes.

As she finally reached the top of the ridge, she looked
down at her car. Buzz now poured gasoline into its interior. In a moment, there was light. Lots of it. Her whole
car was engulfed. She stared at the light, even as her
feet trudged forward. It was indeed the second Stone
Age, she decided. Because, like a cavewoman, she found
any fire, even the one that was taking her car away from
her, mesmerizing.

31

Gerry called a meeting in Section A of the H. G. Wells Ballroom two days later.

He had Ian and Stephanie at the door checking everybody who came in. Nectarians filed in by ones and twos, and they all had special invitations in their hands—not just anybody could come. Many had donated to Hulke's campaign for reelection. Some were union leaders. Others had highly placed managerial positions at the various hotels and casinos. Some owned cannabis bars. A large contingent of showgirls came. In short, invited to the meeting was a broad cross-section of Lunarian society, representative of Hulke's core constituency; people whose mere presence would put pressure on the mayor.

Hulke arrived somewhere in the middle of it, peering around, trying his best to look at ease. He walked up the aisle with his usual mellow gait, but his face was red, his shoulders riding higher on his body than they usually did. He looked as if he had been outdanced at a dancing competition.

He came to the platform. "Gerry . . . I hope you don't mind if I'm skeptical about this."

"Kafis is lying."

"Not about turning this place into a self-sustaining paradise. We had a meeting this morning. He showed me the plans."

"We can save Earth."

"I don't think so."

He decided that Hulke needed forgiveness. "I'm glad you're here anyway."

"You're not going to change our minds, Ger."

"Look, here comes Luke."

Luke Langstrom shuffled up the aisle.

When he finally reached them, Luke gave Gerry a bow. "I admire your persistence."

"Thanks for coming, Luke."

"Wouldn't miss it for the world."

The mayor and Luke drifted off and took seats on the brown, stackable chairs.

Gerry kept his eye on Hulke. Hulke watched the door. The mayor saw more and more of his campaign supporters and contributors come in. It was as if Hulke could sense the noose tightening, just what Gerry needed. At last Hulke got so nervous that he came back up to the front.

"Gerry, you've invited some extremely . . . influential people."

"What I have to say tonight involves everybody on the Moon."

"Where did you find these names?"

He shrugged. "Stephanie helped me."

Hulke frowned. "A lot of these people . . ." He gestured out at the ballroom. "They're coming out of respect. Because you're an Earthman. I don't want you to get your hopes up."

"How would you like to go down in history as the man who saved Earth?

"Considering I'm going down in history as the man who save the Moon—"

"It's not enough, Malcolm."

"Gerry, I'm not your enemy. I have to be practical."

"I know who my enemy is. Do you see any Tarsalans around?"

"No.

"Look, there's Ira. Christ, he looks pissed."

Hulke turned around and spotted Ira. "I better head him off at the pass."

Hulke left.

The mayor and Ira met halfway up the aisle and exchanged some words.

Mitch, who was sitting behind the table on the platform, shifted nervously.

At the back, Ian and Stephanie closed the doors. Ian started spraying a spray can of the commercially available debugging aerosol into the air. Some people glanced at him, curious about what he was doing. Others seemed to know. One thing Gerry knew for sure: The Tarsalans had to have macrogenic airborne surveillance units in the room. And, in fact, a moment later the charged particles from the spray can attached themselves to the various flying listening devices, making them glow as if with a phosphorescent dust. Like ice crusting on the wings of aircraft, the areosol finally brought the devices, one by one, to the floor.

Ira left the mayor, came to the platform, and in the midst of a dozen miniature crash landings had a few hot, quiet words with Mitch.

Gerry walked over to lend Mitch support. The small, unassuming technician was really the hero in all this.

But then Ira swung on Gerry unexpectedly. "Do you have any idea how unstable those early prototypes are?"

Gerry glanced at Mitch. "You told him?"

Mitch looked as if he were hanging by thumbscrews. "He's my boss."

Ira had gone red in the face. "You could have gotten everybody killed at Copernicus. And why did you have to initiate the fields in the first place? Those two units were put on ice for a good reason."

"Ira, sit down. Don't go blaming Mitch. I'm the one behind it all. If there are any charges to be laid, or bills to be paid, I'm your man. I'm not entirely unfamiliar with sitting in jail. And I'm so far in debt already, a little more's not going to hurt."

"Why isn't Kafis here?"

"Because I didn't invite him."

"I think Kafis should be included in any official meetings."

"In case you haven't noticed, this isn't official. This is just Gerry shooting the breeze."

"Which is what you've been doing all along."

Ira walked away in a huff and took his seat.

Ian continued to spray the aerosol into the air. Stephanie, meanwhile, switched off the lights. As the last remaining bugs crash-landed on the red carpet, they luminesced like daubs of neon paint. Gerry walked to the microphone and pointed to the bugs.

"You see those?" he said. "The Tarsalans are recording everything that's going on right now. Let's get rid of their bugs. This meeting is for humans only. If those nearest the surveillance units could please step on them?"

He watched various audience members step on the macrogenic listening devices.

"This whole demonstration serves a twofold purpose," he said. "Number one: We're getting rid of their bugs. Number two: No matter what some people might say, we're still at war with the Tarsalans. And we have to be careful because now we have some of them on the Moon, two hundred, in ships out in the Alleyne Crater. And they're offering us a deal. They say they'll make the Moon a self-sustaining home for us. In return we must let them live here as refugees. They say they've inventoried every screw, nut, and bolt on the Moon, and that if we're careful, we can maintain independent life support here indefinitely. They tell us that Earth is lost and that, during the attack on the TMS, the phytosphere control device was destroyed by U.S. troops. They tell us that there is nothing to be done for Earth. And after spending the last forty-eight hours studying the inventory on the Moon for myself, I have to agree with them—we don't have the materials to fix the situation on Earth. Indeed, the engineering materials needed to destroy the phytosphere are considerable, and they are not on the Moon, yet, paradoxically, not out of our reach either."

He glanced around to see what effect this statement had on everybody; at least they were all listening.

"But before we get into a discussion of just what the engineering necessities might be, we should take a look

at what exactly we have to do to destroy the phytosphere. Because that's what this meeting is all about."

The mayor stood up. "Uh . . . Gerry, my man . . . with
all due respect, the Moon cannot at this time embark on
a project to destroy the . . . uh . . . phytosphere."

"And that's why I'm glad you're here, Malcolm. Because I think there should be some political discussion.
I see several council members here . . . and even some
members of the media . . . and is that Richard Glamna
from the LBC I see? And I guess the political question
of the hour—and I'm sure the one that's on everybody's
mind, and the one people are going to take to their
graves with them if they don't answer it morally—is how
do we live with the deaths of twelve billion people on
our consciences without even *trying* to help them? Because it *is* possible to help them. There is a way we
can save the Earth." He felt mildly buoyed by his own
statements, and thought this was what Neil must feel
like a lot of the time, making bold proclamations like
this. "If we start working now, we can destroy the phytosphere in as little as four weeks."

And here he outlined in layman's terms all the research he had done since the middle of June: his work
on the flagella, on gravity, on how gravity affected the
flagella—and it was like he was in Jarrell Hall again,
because every time he gave a lecture, he understood his
material better; and it all made perfect sense to him.
The flagella acted not only as connecting limbs, but also
as a kind of brain stem that looked after the lower func-
tions, those basic muscular and hormonal roles that
made the phytosphere behave the way it did. He thought
of the simple physics of a force activating the triggering
system: the carefully calibrated dance of gravity between
the Earth and the Moon. And it was fortuitous that he
was an ocean scientist, and that there should be tides
involved, and that it was the tides in the phytosphere
that had finally tipped him off to the whole system. As
he explained more and more background, the room grew
silent and an atmosphere of belief seemed to ferment in
the air, the genesis of comprehension, and a faith that

this thing—this magnificent but terrifying darkness of the Tarsalans—could at last be defeated.

He showed the tape from Copernicus—poor Kev floating the ridiculous *Smallmouth 2* up into the laboratory-created phytosphere, the orbiting Platform 2, the stress band, and the whole shroud disintegrating when the gravitational pressure became too great.

Then he went through for them the exact measurements he had taken, particularly how much they had to increase the Moon's gravity—how forceful they had to make the stress band—just what they had to do to the phytospheric tides in order to break the whole thing apart.

"What many of you don't know is that at one time the Moon was a lot closer to Earth. Geological evidence suggests much higher tides a million years ago. Why were the tides higher? As a hydrographer, I've made an in-depth study of this phenomenon. The tides were higher because the Moon's gravitational pull was stronger. The Moon's gravitational pull was stronger because it was that much closer back then. I believe the Tarsalan phytosphere control device is a gravitational field apparatus. They have a technological culture that is over a million years old. Follow the natural history of the two technological cultures we know, us and the Tarsalans, and you see we learn to control, one by one, the forces that surround us. Fire, wind, electromagnetism, fission, fusion, solar . . . and in the singularity drive, humankind is now taking its first small steps at controlling gravity. A million years from now, controlling gravity will be child's play for us, just as it is for the Tarsalans. Have you ever wondered why the TMS doesn't spin; why it doesn't employ that particularly primitive technique for establishing artificial gravity? What about the thousands of other, smaller Tarsalan craft? Same thing. They don't need to spin because the Tarsalans have devised a more advanced way of controlling this fundamental force."

Ira interrupted him. "In other words, you're telling us something we already know, that Tarsalan engineering capability is far more advanced than ours. Gerry, they've taken our inventory. Say you're right, and a gravitational device of some sort is what controls the phytosphere. Say in fact that the phytosphere control device U.S. Forces destroyed actually operated on gravitational principles. Don't you think the Tarsalans would build a new one and save the Earth if they had the materials in inventory? I have an idea of what it takes to create an artificial gravitational field. Each time we burn one of our singularity drives, we get a gravitational field as a side effect. We're talking cutting-edge physics here. And to make a gravitational field strong enough to destroy the phytosphere, you would need laboratory resources so vast that I don't think they could be developed by us *or* by the Tarsalans in the remaining time Earth has left. You give us a timetable of four weeks. Gerry . . . that's just too much to believe. Especially when so far you've given us nothing."

"I've got the timetable right here, Ira. You can take a look for yourself."

"But how do you expect to develop and implement an artificial gravitational field on such a gargantuan scale when we have such minimal resources on the Moon? If you combined every singularity drive we have, you wouldn't even reach one one-thousandth of the power you would need for something like this. No offense, Gerry, but I think this meeting is adjourned."

"I never said I was going to develop and implement an artificial gravitational field."

"Then why are we here, and where is this going?"

"If you'll let me discuss the physics of the thing . . ." He motioned at all his measurements.

Ira threw up his hands. "Be my guest. You're the *scientist*." He loaded the word with derision.

"Going back to what I was saying about the Moon— a million years ago it was a lot closer to Earth, and its gravitational pull was that much stronger." He looked around at his audience—showgirls, movers and shakers, cannabis bar owners, small-time councilors, pimps, and prostitutes—and he knew they all had mothers and fathers, perhaps brothers and sisters, and even children. A great emotion swelled in his chest as he thought of Glenda, Hanna, and Jake. "I don't need anything like a complex Tarsalan gravitational device. I just need simple physics. And simple physics tells me that we can save the Earth. It tells me that it's our duty and responsibility to save our suffering fellow human beings on Earth. And as for the engineering miracles involved? They're not miracles at all. The math is so perfectly juvenile that even a child can understand it."

He leaned forward over the lectern. "I need a mass of sufficient size to act upon the Moon, a force that will push the Moon, in the short term, two thousand miles closer to the Earth. This repositioning of the Moon will exert the necessary gravitational force to destroy the phytosphere. To get that result, I require a planetoid-sized body roughly twelve miles across striking the Moon at approximately a hundred miles per second. This will degrade the Moon's orbit the necessary distance, and thereby increase its gravitational pull enough to fracture and destroy the phytosphere.

He lifted his hands because he saw Ira rising with what looked like a million objections.

"Ira, please . . . stop."

"What happens to the Moon when this planetoid-sized body strikes it at a hundred miles per second? I mean . . . Ger . . . why don't you just hand out loaded revolvers and we can get it over with?"

"If the Moon had an atmosphere, Ira . . . if the Moon had oceans . . . but it doesn't. It's just a rock. Fire a bullet at a big rock and see what happens. Not much. Mitch and I have done the calculations. If a body this size were to hit the Earth, you're right, it would be a planet killer. But not so on the Moon. The Moon is designed to take hits. It's been taking hits nonstop for the last four billion years. A body this size strikes the Moon, and yes, I admit, it will hit the surface with a force of nineteen million megatons, create a peak-ring crater two hundred and twenty-five miles across and six miles deep, and generally shake up the Moon. But it won't be a planet killer. Everybody will survive. And there'll be minimal damage to the Moon's infrastructure."

"Why should we believe you?" asked Ira. "And how are you going to pull it off?"

Gerry turned to Mitch. "Mitch?"

Mitch nodded and got up. "Uh . . . Ira . . . it's possible. And it's feasible with the . . . the inventory AviOrbit has on hand. We take the FMC Transit Collective drives and we boom them—like a big log boom. We take them out to the asteroid belt. We already have our . . . designated body. Gaspra, if you want to know, as it more or less coincides with our dimensional requirements. I'm really sorry, Ira, for going behind your back like this."

"You're not going to use the FMC Transit Collective drives."

Mitch kept going, despite being cowed. "We boom these drives together and we take them out to the . . . asteroid belt. I know . . . I know . . . pretty wild . . . but, you know, I've gone over all the math . . . and actually I've had some of the telemetry guys . . . and we boom them to one of our freighters . . . we were thinking the *Prometheus,* because she's just been freshly serviced and fueled, and she's ready to go . . ."

Mitch continued to outline the whole scheme in a quavering voice: how they would fly the *Prometheus* to the asteroid Gaspra because Gaspra was ideally located in relation to the Moon at this point in its orbit; how they would then anchor the *Prometheus* to the "front" of the asteroid, then drill the five FMC Transit Collective Drives into the body of the asteroid and lay in a collision course for the Moon; explained that the crew would consist of himself as engineering specialist, Gerry as science specialist, and Ian Hamilton as pilot; and how, at the last moment, as Gaspra came within striking distance, the crew would eject in a special survival pod.

"And what's beautiful about the math is that it allows for a certain margin of error, especially in terms of our angle of descent, and in the way the strike zone doesn't have to be a hundred percent accurate but just what

Gerry is calling a generalized region of effectiveness . . .
so, as Gerry says, the math is, well, juvenile." He quickly
added, "Don't take that in any insulting way."

Ian Hamilton got so fed up with Mitch's apologetic
tone that he bounded down the aisle of the H. G. Wells
Ballroom and leaped to the platform in the Moon's
weak gravity.

"Goddamn it, Ira, you're fired. You're fired, you're
fired, you're fired. We're going to take those damn FMC
drives, we're going to bolt them into Gaspra, and we're
going to ram Gaspra down the Moon's goddamn
throat." He spoke with the fervency of a man who was
desperately trying to redeem himself, who was trying to
make up for all the bad things he had done in his life.
"And the three of us up here are the only ones who
have guts enough to do it. I mean . . . where are your
balls? Do you really want to go for this Tarsalan deal?
You really want to trust those fatheads after what they
did to the Earth? Tell 'em, Ger. Tell 'em that they're
nothing but a bunch of goddamn liars."

Gerry stared at the crowd of Lunarians. Fathers,
brothers, sisters, mothers, wives, daughters, children—
every one of them. "We could indeed take the Tarsalan
deal," he began. "The Tarsalans could rig the Moon so
that it would indeed become a self-sustaining outpost for
the next thousand years. But make no mistake. It would
be *their* outpost, not ours. And in forty years a backup
force from their homeworld would arrive, and they
would use a new gravitational device to dismantle the
shroud, and they would then, at last, immigrate to Earth,
just like they've always wanted. Only there would be no
human survivors left down there anymore, and Earth
would be theirs for the taking. Is that what you want?
For the Tarsalans to come in and take over? Kafis isn't
dumb. He's got two brains. He has a million years of
technological culture behind him. That's why I didn't
invite him to this meeting. That's why I had Ian spray
the whole room for bugs. Because Kafis knows it's possible. He realizes there's a way we can save ourselves. But
is he letting on?"

He stopped, once again thinking of his wife and kids.

"Please, I'm asking you . . . we've got this chance. We can do it. Mitch and I have gone over the mission specs again and again. It will work. Do we tie our destiny forever with the Tarsalans? Do we let them control us? Or do we take control of our own fate? There are those of you out there who I know have people on Earth." He ventured to his own thoughts of a moment ago. "You have fathers, brothers, sisters, mothers, wives, and daughters. You have husbands. Are you just going to abandon them? Are we going to desert our brothers and sisters on Earth? Do you want that on your conscience? I know I don't. So let's do what Ian says. Let's take this chance, and do what's right. Not what's safest for ourselves, but what's *right* and decent for all of humankind."

32

Neil, sitting next to the helicopter door, banged his head as the aircraft shifted suddenly—and from that moment, his left contact lens wouldn't work, no matter how many times he tapped his left temple.

In the wake of his great failure, nothing seemed to make sense anymore. His life became little more than a series of disconnects, and it became a lot worse when Lenny swerved to avoid incoming fire.

Morgan cried the whole way. Lenny kept glancing at her, as if he wished she'd shut up. And while the two other airmen *seemed* miffed about the whole rescue operation, Neil couldn't really tell, because he couldn't see them that well anymore, not with one eye in focus and the other eye out of focus.

At one point Lenny tried to tell him something, but the helicopter was too loud, there were only enough headsets for the three airmen, and, try as Neil might, he couldn't make out a word Lenny was saying.

He asked one of the airmen, Douglas, what was happening, and Douglas had to shout to be heard. All he said was that they were being engaged—sporadically— then added that it was amazing what those fatheads could do in the way of weapons, given a minimum of materials.

Neil just smiled; and this was the other thing that bothered him—the smile on his face, the one he couldn't seem to shake. It was an apologetic grimace, a bewildered one, like the smile of a man in the first stages of

Alzheimer's, fighting to remain polite even though his life was in flames. He couldn't look at Douglas. As if he had failed Douglas in some way.

And then there came another disconnect. He zoned out. He didn't know where he went. It was another big blank. Until the third airman, Fernandes, swung the big side door open and started firing his fifty-caliber machine gun at the ground. His children cowered. His wife looked catatonic. And the repeated muzzle flashes from the big gun lit up Fernandes's face as if with a strobe, so that Neil saw the light-collecting goggles over Fernandes's eyes, and the way the sweat dripped down his cheeks and off his chin, as if manning the big gun was hard work, like operating a jackhammer. Fernandes didn't look particularly worried that he was in the middle of combat, though occasionally the corners of his lips twitched downward, as if involuntary spasms of the face were necessary to work the big machine gun.

Louise said something to Neil, but she had such a soft, delicate voice that she couldn't make herself heard, so he just nodded . . . and then . . . and then . . .

Another disconnect.

They were on Marblehill's big front lawn, and he had the distinct sense, as Lenny helped him out of the helicopter, that he had crossed over into another era, and that he was now in an age where only bad things happened, so different from the previous age of smiling good fortune. He was sure he heard Lenny say, "Your girls will have to learn how to shoot, of course." And then he said something about tactical advantage and strategic value, words Neil didn't understand because he had that smile on his face again, and when he had that smile on his face the whole world became opaque.

He caught sight of Marblehill. Huge bullet holes pocked its stone facade. Were they bullet holes? No. The Tarsalans didn't use bullets. How did the translating device put it? Vibration modules? VMs for short? Was that it? A weapon that did its damage by shaking materials beyond the point of their molecular-cohesion tolerances? Yes. It was coming back to him. Those long talks he had had with Kafis by the pool. He glanced toward his pool, the deep end visible behind the west wing of his house, but could barely make out the diving board in the glow coming from the helicopter. Then the helicopter shut down, the lights went out, and another airman, Sinclair, came from behind one of the stone pillars of the drive-through portico with a flashlight and waved them in.

"So?" said Lenny when they reached the portico.

"Nothing," said Sinclair.

"We need food," said Louise.

Sinclair gave her a look, and it wasn't a nice look; it was a look that said, why are you here, what good are you—you're nothing but extra baggage.

Lenny, on the other hand, was polite, and it was, *Mrs. Thorndike, if you could please step inside, and yes, Mrs. Thorndike, that is coffee you're smelling, and yes, we have coffee, real coffee, and we'd be glad to get you a cup, and I hope you know how to make good coffee, because we buried Nabozniak yesterday, and it's too bad because Nabozniak was a whiz in the kitchen. Not only that, he knew how to crunch his own rounds—we've got a round-making kit, and maybe we can teach Morgan to make rounds, turn her into a real combat asset, because what we've got here, Mrs. Thorndike, is a bona fide alien invasion—they started coming down last night, and they sent some bugs in, and gosh we're glad you brought the spray because we really need it, we should have thought of spray in the initial planning stages, but it's too late, and they know we have food in here, yes, that's right, they eat human food, they're like us in a lot of ways . . .* and it was as if Louise was hypnotized by everything Lenny was telling her. Yet it all sounded familiar to Neil, as if he had dreamed about this alien invasion long ago, and this was nothing but a peculiarly frightening summation of the whole thing.

And . . . disconnect again . . . because it was late, it was early, but it was neither late nor early because these two qualifiers didn't apply anymore. It was dark—the only qualifier. As a result of his two miserable failures, it was dark all the time now. They sat in the second-floor games room—five remaining airmen, his three daughters, himself, and his wife; and they had the gas generator hooked up so that they could have some electrical lights, and he heard the generator humming at the back of the house. Lenny was giving them all a lecture on how to use the airman weapon of choice, the Montclair Repeater, a nasty little submachine gun about the size of an umbrella.

"The rounds are more like darts, but they explode on impact. The thing you have to remember about Tarsalans is that they don't kill as easy as we do. Rib cage like a rhino. That's why an exploding round is an advantage."

He disassembled the weapon, reassembled it, snapped the banana clip in place, then said, "Four hundred rounds a clip. Ingenious."

He passed it around. Neil could hardly believe his girls were handling one of the most vicious military weapons ever devised, that it had actually come to this; his precocious, bright, pampered, pretty, and innocent daughters being forced to protect themselves from alien invaders with military-style firearms. When it came his turn to try, he smiled his idiotic smile, and briefly—ever so briefly—broke into tears. He caught Fernandes and Rostov looking at him. Neil handed the weapon to Morgan. A bloody Montclair Repeater in Morgan's hands when she couldn't even read.

"When you're not engaged, hold the barrel pointed toward the ceiling, hon," Lenny reminded Morgan.

The gun went to Ashley, then Melissa. Neil remembered this from the Air Force. Standard weapons training. But what he didn't remember was little girls with guns.

Melissa went first, walking to the window with a strange fire in her eyes, pointing the Montclair out the casement, and shooting out into the grounds. Melissa, the oldest, was like him, ready to try new things, embracing this harsh new world as the status quo, accepting it readily.

Then it was Ashley's turn, and Ashley was petulant about it, rolling her eyes a time or two as she took the weapon and walked to the window. She fired the Montclair without even looking. An involuntary squeal escaped from her lips as the weapon jumped in her hands.

"You've got to grip it, kitten, if you want to stop that recoil," was all Lenny had to say.

And finally it was Morgan's turn. Neil was hardpressed not to intervene, because this was just a tenyear-old girl after all, but what if it came down to just Morgan at the end of it all—just her, and a handful of aliens trying to harvest the countryside without due regard for human life? So he gave her a chance. And she did okay with it, seeming to understand with a profundity that apparently escaped the other two just why Lenny was asking her to shoot the weapon in the first place.

And then . . . another horrible disconnect. Where he just sat there with Rostov on guard duty, with headsets on, listening through the various microphone plants in the forest beyond the perimeter, hearing crunches and cracks, and the trees settling bit by bit into decrepitude. Hearing the wind blow through the once magnificent Chattahoochee National Forest. Occasionally going to the back to check on Louise and Melissa, who scanned the grounds to the rear through light-gathering goggles. Bits and pieces of the long, perpetual night of the shroud gluing themselves together out of one disconnect after another, until finally Lenny told him how the senior airmen on their little staff, Harmon, Earl, and Scott—Neil's old friends, Greg's old friends—had fought brilliantly, but had finally succumbed to the Vibration Modules, the VMs, those insidious Tarsalan weapons they had all grown to fear so much.

"Buried them out by the pool. I hope you don't mind."

And in Lenny's voice he heard a letting go of hope.

Later, near the end of his shift with Rostov, Lenny came to the front and asked, "What went wrong?"

So Neil became Dr. Thorndike again, and tried to explain some of it to Lenny, how with the hydrogen sulfide, the xenophyta had gone into a state of suspended animation; and how, with the virus, the carapace had surprised everyone by jailing the virus during its lytic phase. Lenny stared but said nothing. And in that stare, Neil saw doubt and, aggravatingly, some Monday-morning quarterbacking, as if Lenny thought Neil should have figured out the pitfalls ahead of time.

After that, he slept for a while—at least as much as he ever slept in this perpetual night—a light doze that never released him into the sweet oblivion he craved so much.

Fernandes came for him three hours later. "We've got a full alert, sir."

Neil took up a position with Louise and Morgan in his study on the second floor. The only light came from the control panel of the communications equipment, but it was enough so that he could see their faces—and their faces were tired and thin and, most of all, fearful.

He lifted the light-gathering goggles and strapped them to his eyes, then raised himself to the windowsill and looked out at the grounds.

He could see them. Yes. Sketched in the ghostly green of the goggles's light-gathering properties.

Aliens.

Inoculated and biologically adapted to live here, the first Tarsalan immigrants, maybe surprised that they were now soldiers, perhaps baffled by human intransigence, and certainly distressed, the way they all were. The goggles magnified. He saw them clearly, five altogether, their huge, bicephalic heads covered with shaggy black hair that reminded him of a bison's pelt, visible among the dead yew trees.

He saw a small burst of light from the right, out beyond the six-car garage, like sparks from a welder's torch. The sparks rose toward the mansion, and as they got closer to Marblehill they drew apart, and pulsated, like the flickering radiance of a pulsar. Chatter drifted up from the radio on the floor. Lenny's voice, the voice of command, but also the voice of desperation. Through the goggles Neil watched the Tarsalans shift to the left, where they took cover behind the stone wall. Then the tattoo of Montclair Repeater fire erupted from the house, with every fifth round a tracer. Louise and Morgan looked at him. He gave them a nod, and they tentatively rose to the window and, with shaking hands, pulled their triggers.

He did the same.

The whole thing seemed surreal. Especially watching Louise shoot her Montclair. She was a housewife, for God's sake, not a combat soldier. And Morgan was a ten-year-old grade-five student with Attention Deficit Disorder who had to take medicine just so she could concentrate. And he was a fifty-two-year-old physicist and biologist, a university professor with a spreading paunch and a taste for fine wines. Yet now he was blasting away, praying that the VMs wouldn't get anywhere near him. Their light shifted against the ceiling, making green and blue squares, like geometrical ghosts. As they got closer, they began to whine and shriek. They floated with a not particularly urgent velocity toward his study on the second floor, and he shot at them, and they were easy to blast out of the air, but there were just so many of them, as if the Tarsalans believed that the basis for all successful technology was redundancy to the Nth degree.

How it happened he wasn't sure, because he was too busy shooting out the window, too much in the grip of his own frantic combat mania, shooting but not even looking where he was shooting. Yet . . . yet the next disconnect was framed in the context of Morgan screaming at him, tugging at his sleeve, pointing at Louise, who was lying on her back on the handwoven Moroccan rug, quivering in the oddest way. At first he thought she was having a seizure, but she was quivering so fast she actually looked blurred around the edges. When he placed his hand against her chest it was like placing his hand on the hood of a car, because his hand vibrated the same way. He saw a tiny, bloodless hole on her neck. Her eyes were half closed, and she didn't seem to be in any particular pain.

But then she got a nosebleed.

And shortly after her nose bled, she died.

He didn't immediately feel the overwhelming grief he knew he would later feel. He just felt . . . disappointed. Disappointed that all the plans they had made for their sunset years were coming to nothing.

"Is she all right?" Morgan kept asking.

"No, sweetie," he said. "She's not all right. She's dead."

He said the words slowly because he felt he always had to say things slowly for Morgan, just to make sure she understood.

Morgan was not, as Lenny might have said, a combat asset after that, because she simply clung to her mother, crying and crying, occasionally trying to wake her mother up as if she still didn't understand that Louise was dead.

His initial disappointment faded, and was replaced by a . . . a knowledge and certainty that he had nothing left to live for, except . . . except as Louise's avenger.

He lifted Louise's Montclair from the floor and checked the little electronic monitor on the side. Two hundred seventy-two rounds left. His own weapon had 234 left. Armed with two weapons, one in each hand, their butts pressed against his biceps, he stood up like a thriller-action hero, heedless of whether any more VMs were coming, and fired away. Through his light-gathering goggles, he saw the alien bastards moving through the dead forest and, in the nanoseconds it took him to squeeze both triggers, he had a memory of Louise out there in the woods picking wildflowers; because that's what she did when she came here, picked wildflowers, put them in a vase, and tried, with varying degrees of success, to paint them with watercolors.

Every fifth round was a tracer, and the ammo arced over the grounds like hot little hornets in the light-gathering lenses of his goggles. He killed one of the alien bastards, and then another, and finally a third, and saw the remaining two scatter into the woods, their bodies like human bodies, but the proportions different so that the arms were too long and the legs too short; yes, alien bodies, human parodies, and they all deserved to die now that they had taken away his sweet Louise.

He fired until he stopped feeling the kick from his weapons. And shortly after that he realized it was extremely quiet. He looked down at Louise. Morgan wasn't there anymore. He took a deep breath. What was he going to do now? *We're going to be all right. People with money are going to weather this thing just fine.* His words came back to haunt him. Was it a character flaw, the hubris he had felt all his life? So that he had even believed he was immune to the Apocalypse?

He dropped the Montclairs to the floor. Their barrels smoked. He was hot. Drenched in sweat. He collapsed to his knees. His eyes moistened, yet the guttural howl that tried to escape from his throat simply wouldn't come, especially not now, not when Morgan came back into the room with the other girls. He knew he had to keep it in, make his girls understand in a calm, reasonable way that things like this happened in the Apocalypse; children lost parents and parents lost children.

Ashley came to him. Melissa came to him. And Melissa was still clutching her Montclair, as if she had forgotten she had it in her hand. They cried, but they didn't wail—the Thorndike family wasn't given to excessive displays of emotion—but in their quiet sobs he felt an especially keen agony, something that seemed to grab all his internal organs and drag them downward. Here was the family, what was left of it, the two older girls clinging to him while Morgan fussed around Louise like the strange child she was, trying to wake Louise up.

"Morgan, come here."

When Morgan came to him, he clung to her tightly, because Louise had always been so worried about Morgan, and Morgan always needed a lot of support, and yet it was now Morgan, a ten-year-old girl, who stroked his hair, even as his own tears came faster, and said to him, "It's okay, Daddy. It's okay." She showed a strength that surprised him. Portrait of a family in great grief. With only the father left now. And that was the worst of all possible situations because he wasn't sure he knew how to be a father. He had always been a professor and a scientist, too focused on his career, and hadn't even really watched his kids grow up.

He heard combat boots coming along the hall. He looked up. Lenny stared at him in the light coming from the communications apparatus. Lenny had a scratch on his face, not a deep one, but still angry and red. The airman glanced at Louise, then back at Neil.

Neil said, "Sorry. I tried."

And Lenny responded by saying, "They got Douglas and Sinclair."

"How long before they try again?"

"Who knows?"

"There's a cave," he volunteered. "Did you find the cave? It's all limestone along this ridge."

Lenny's eyes narrowed. "Like for a fallback position?"

"The VMs will have a tough time."

"What about your sister-in-law? If we go up there . . ."

And thinking of Glenda, he felt a great comfort. "She'll figure it out. But maybe we should . . . maybe I should show you where this cave is . . ."

He lost sight of that particular objective over the coming days.

They buried Louise. Out by the pool next to the others. They wrapped her in a sheet, and put some photographs of the kids in with her, and also one of her watercolors, and Lenny said something about her even though he didn't know her, the usual things: good mother, good wife, all-around decent person, and, goddamn it, they would make the Tarsalans pay for this. This last bit came in a sudden outburst that shook Lenny's body from head to toe.

What was so strange about it was the heat, over a hundred and ten degrees, as if after triggering a short nuclear winter the phytosphere was now rebounding with a long and lethal summer, true to his prediction, even though they were well into October now.

And when Fernandes and Rostov broke the earth, it was like dust, as moistureless as talc, so that it blew away into the tinder-dry forest in little brown puffs, like so many fleeing ghosts.

33

Gerry stood next to the comlink in the mayor's office. Around him were Ian, Mitch, Ira, Stephanie, and the mayor's assistant, Damian. Hulke sat in front of the comlink, his face masked in his usual self-immolating grin. On the monitor Gerry saw Kafis's face and, in the background, he caught a glimpse of another Tarsalan, this one checking something on another screen. It was this other Tarsalan that bothered Gerry. What was he doing? What was he checking? Was it game over for their little conspiracy, even before it had properly begun?

"Council has voted to accept your . . . uh . . . solution," said Hulke, with not even the slightest quaver in his voice, as if his nerve had been hardened by years at the blackjack table. "We would like to invite you and your entire delegation to a celebration dinner in the Nectaris Council Chamber tonight at eight. My advisors and I think our new partnership should be marked in a special way, and so we're bringing out of stores the finest cuisine still left in our inventory—I should tell you, Kafis, that the cuisine on the Moon is world-renowned. We of course expect you to make a speech, and I myself will make a speech as well."

"You've taken an excellent first positive step, Mayor. My delegation will be eager to meet with your people. The Moon has turned a new page in its history."

"I couldn't agree with you more, Kafis."

The communication ended. The mayor turned to Gerry. "How was that?"

"What was that other one doing in the background?"

"I imagine he was there to stop me from reading Kafis too easily. It's an old poker trick. Always have people in the background for distraction purposes. That's why I had Damian right next me."

"What do we do now?"

"We let the caterers get to work."

An hour later, Gerry, Stephanie, and Ian stood by the railing above the Council Chamber. Dining tables had been moved in, and caterers in white shirts, black pants, and black bow ties scurried around arranging artificial gardenias as centerpieces. Ian stood apart from Gerry and Stephanie, but kept glancing at Stephanie, lifting his chin from time to time and clenching his jaw, peering at her as if she were the strangest woman he had ever seen.

"I hope this works," said Gerry.

Stephanie put her hand on his shoulder. "They'll be arriving in an hour. Why don't we get dressed?"

Gerry went back to his hotel room, put on a white blazer, a purple T-shirt with the NCSU logo, and his pair of baggy corduroys, the most stylish clothes he had brought to the Moon. He then went back to the Council Chamber. Drinks were served. People and Tarsalans sat. Speeches were made. And one by one, over the next half hour, humans inconspicuously left the hall. Some brave souls, equipped with hidden breathers, stayed, as a complete disappearance of all humans would make the Tarsalans suspicious. But at last, the big pressure doors closed, and oxygen thinned gradually, and at first the Tarsalans were none the wiser. But when they finally figured out what was going on, it was too late; they couldn't get out. They upbraided the humans who had remained inside the Council Chamber, but by this time those humans had strapped breathers to their faces and barricaded themselves behind some tables. In any case, there was nothing the Tarsalans could do to harm the brave humans, because they were too oxygen-deprived to do much of anything. Gerry watched everything on a monitor. He felt guilty. He didn't like to trick people. Or Tarsalans. At one point, Kafis loosened his collar, as if that would help. Gerry found the gesture pathetic, and wanted to assist Kafis in some way.

When ninety percent of the Tarsalans were subdued, oxygen was slowly pumped back into the Council Chamber—but it was combined with halothane, an inhalational anesthetic brought over from the Aldrin Health Sciences Center. Those not yet knocked out were rendered unconscious in a matter of seconds. Nectaris Security moved in, faces masked with breathers, and cuffed every member of the Tarsalan delegation, then began moving them to detention. Gerry sighed. As much as he hated lying, he was relieved by how smoothly the whole operation had gone.

Gerry lived in his Computer Assisted Pressure Suit for the next three days, cramming a month's worth of training into the space of seventy-two hours, thanks to AviOrbit's ingenious CAPS software.

He was out on the Moon's surface with Ian and Mitch, and they were anchoring a singularity drive mock-up to the ground. His boots bit into the surface with bear trap–like crampons—what he would have to wear when he walked around in the negligible gravity of Gaspra.

He fired a T-bolt through a brace with his pneumatic drill, the gray dirt puffed beneath him. The T-bolt, easily the size of his arm, penetrated the surface and latched the mock-up to the Moon, even as his monitor told him his crampons had increased their pounds per square inch tenfold—what they would have to do if he wanted to stop his pneumatic drill from shooting him off the surface of Gaspra, where the escape velocity was no more than a few scant miles per hour.

"Anchor seven secure," he said.

"Say it with more enthusiasm, buddy. We're going to the asteroid belt."

"I feel like a Roman senator on the Ides of March."

"Why does he talk like that, Ian?" said Mitch, who was getting ready with anchor eight.

"Bud, they got what was coming to them," said Ian.

"I don't like how we had to lie to them. What are all these other worlds going to think of us once they find out what we did?"

"That Malcolm . . . he's a Fast Eddie, isn't he?" said Ian.

"I'm ready to secure anchor eight," said Mitch.

"Go ahead, little guy."

"They're going to think we're monsters," said Gerry.

Another voice cut through their suit radios: Ira, speaking from control. "Could we cut the crap? We're on a tight schedule."

"Relax, Ira," said Ian. "The CAPS will babysit us through the whole thing. You've taken the magic and mystery out of suicide missions."

"They walked right into it, didn't they?" said Gerry.

"Hulke's got a superb poker face," admitted Ian.

"Yes, but the Tarsalans are supposed to be smart."

"The Tarsalans were desperate. They wanted to believe what they wanted to believe."

Gerry shook his head. "In other words, they still haven't figured out that we're willing to risk our own survival for the sake of our principles."

"You think they would have learned that by now. It's been nine years."

"We should offer them a concession," said Gerry.

Ira's voice came over the radio: "Like you said, Ger, they walked right into it. It serves them right. And let's remember who's idea it was to depressurize the Council Chamber in the first place."

"We don't have any weapons on the Moon. What else was I supposed to do?"

"And the halothane was a nice touch," Mitch piped in.

"And the way Kafis loosened his collar," said Ira. "I haven't had a good laugh like that in a long time. You know what? I found it inspiring. To see a couple hundred Tarsalans all unconscious like that. It gave me . . . I don't know . . . a secure feeling."

"I feel sorry for them," said Gerry. "They're so far

from home. They're obviously terrified. And now we've locked them all away."

"No one's going to run interference on our damn mission," said Ira.

A burst of dust came from Mitch's area. "Anchor eight is secure," he said. "Boy . . . that drill packs a punch, doesn't it?"

"What's the psi on your crampons?" asked Ira.

"Tenfold."

"Then you have nothing to worry about."

At the end of the seventy-two-hour training session— and with the CAPS it really wasn't a training session so much as going along for the ride—they were ferried up to the AviOrbit launch platform fifty miles above the Moon and installed in the *Prometheus.*

AviOrbit and the *Prometheus* did a lot of the subsequent work by themselves. In fact, having a human crew was really nothing more than a fail-safe, though determining the exact placement of the five big FMC Transit Collective drives on the surface of Gaspra would require a human eye.

Gerry watched through the window as the *Prometheus* approached the five Federated Martian Colony drives. A strong titanium alloy frame locked the drives together, two at the front, three at the back, in a triangular boom. The *Prometheus* docked with the frame in a classic orbital rendezvous. At that point, AviOrbit Control asked the crew to make a complete systems check.

"I'm reading a glitch on the starboard number five thrust conduit," said Ian. "Control, can you copy that?"

"We copy that, *Prometheus.* Please refer to Procedure 5-78a-11. It could be a misread."

Ian referred to the procedure in question, then initiated the steps via the onboard diagnostics computer. As Gerry watched his old friend, he felt a new admiration. Ian moved quickly and precisely, and looked right at home operating these complicated systems. After fifteen minutes, Ian finally had the system green-lighting him on the starboard number five thrust conduit. The pilot glanced at Gerry and gave him the thumbs-up sign. Ian's head was now shorn—in fact, he had decided to go for the completely bald look, and his scalp was as pink as the skin of a freshly washed piglet, as if shaving his head was just another way he was reinventing himself. His handlebar mustache, however, was still thick and, for the most part, brown, but with some silver.

"I'm sober three weeks today," he told Gerry.

"Congratulations."

"This thing we're doing . . . you have no idea what it means to me. I know you two are the ones with people back on Earth, but I finally feel as if I'm doing something . . . that really matters."

Gerry gestured at the control panel, then at the CAPS they were wearing. "All this AviOrbit stuff . . . I had no idea. AviOrbit deserves a lot of the credit."

"They've made it fairly foolproof," said Mitch. "Though that warning . . . on the starboard number five thrust conduit."

"It's fixed," said Ian.

"Are you sure?"

"I'm getting a green on it. And the procedure allows for a test fire. The test fire is a go."

"I've just never seen it before. Especially in an M-class freighter. And as that particular thrust conduit is supposed to link FMC Drive Five—"

Ian gave him a wry look. "We got red-lighted all the time back in the old days. The thrust conduit's just a minor system with a hundred redundancies in it. You don't have to worry about it."

34

They transited past Mars, which happened to be in closest opposition, a week later and the Martians sent them fresh oxygen, food, water, and the heartfelt best wishes of its citizens.

Then it was out to the asteroid belt.

The sun was no longer an orb but a gigantic star, a bright presence to their port side, bristling with jagged rays, like a dangerous and sharp object one could cut oneself on if one got too close.

They settled into their own Kirkwood Gap seven million miles away from Gaspra. The *Prometheus* performed exactly to spec and braked as it neared the asteroid, spinning round so that the log-boomed singularity drives were now behind it.

Over the next sixteen hours, as they got closer to Gaspra, Gerry kept looking out the window, hoping to get a visual on the asteroid, but it finally had to be sighted through the telescope apparatus, and he got his first view of the misshapen rock on the monitor eighteen hours later.

Twelve miles long and seven across, it reminded him, in shape, of a peanut—a giant stone floating through space, twirling like a gargantuan football, rotating once every six hours and fifty-eight minutes.

The approach procedures were fully computerized. Gerry sat back and watched *Prometheus* take control.

She approached the asteroid's "south pole," though such directions were entirely relative, and for mission convenience only. She brought herself within five hundred yards of the asteroid's surface, firing a final braking thrust to match Gaspra's orbit, then initiated two axial bursts so that she began to rotate exactly in tandem. What Gerry saw below him was a bleak, moonlike surface, with horizons that dipped alarmingly and craters that looked disproportionately big on what was a small celestial body.

With its orbit and rotation established in Gaspra's wake, *Prometheus* then fired three harpoons at the planetoid, instantly compensating for the force of the shots by five quick and perfectly timed blasts of its axial thrusters.

"She's red-lighted our axial number three," said Ian.

"Really?" said Mitch.

Ian quickly keyed in some queries on the diagnostics. "It's a bug," he announced a few seconds later. "Like the one we got in the number five starboard thrust conduit."

"That's suspicious," said Mitch.

The word choice startled Gerry. "Suspicious how?"

"One red-light I can accept," said Mitch.

"We used to get red-lights all the time," said Ian.

"And when was your last active mission?" asked Mitch. The question was rhetorical. Everyone knew Ian hadn't flown in five years. Ian looked away. "You see what I mean?"

Then Ian brightened up. "Look, she's green-lighting it."

"What'd you do?"

"I didn't do anything."

"Shit."

"Mitch, it's working fine. There's just some small bug in the diagnostics. There's nothing wrong with the basic equipment."

"We got every single Tarsalan?" asked Mitch. "There weren't any hiding out anywhere?"

Gerry got the drift of this with a jolt to his heart. "You think we're sabotaged?"

"Don't they want to stop us any way they can?" said

Mitch, looking at Gerry through his visor screen. "They don't want us to save the planet. They want to keep it bagged until their reinforcements arrive. They'll keep us locked away like zoo animals on Mars, Mercury, and the moons, and roll into Earth unopposed."

"Jesus Christ, Mitch," said Ian, "we've had two red lights, and they've both been resolved. AviOrbit whipped this mission together in record time. What do you expect? And yes, we got all the Tarsalans."

"But did we get all their macrogens? I don't trust those things. I never have. Especially the way they reproduce themselves."

"Gerry, I think he's having some mission stress. You're the medic proxy. Maybe you should give him something."

Gerry pointed to the screen. "Look. We have target acquisition."

The screen showed that the three harpoons had exploded deep into the rocky, sun-blasted dirt of Gaspra, and the panel was green-lighting them for rendezvous.

"There," said Ian. "You see? A green light. Are you happy? Let's roll this rig in."

Over the next fifteen minutes, the *Prometheus* pulled itself along the harpoon cables, traveling at no more than two miles per hour. The rock got bigger and bigger, and Gerry was somewhat comforted to see that it was green lights all the way. Still, the thought nagged. Macrogens. Devices no bigger than his thumb, capable of all kinds of nasty work, including the deployment of millions of nanogens. Had Kafis outplayed him after all? Were the number five starboard thrust conduit and axial number three just the start? Was the *Prometheus* slowly going to self-destruct as it got deeper into its mission?

The *Prometheus* touched down without any fanfare and hardly any dust.

The crew spent the next hour fastening her down with fluorescent green anchoring bolts, walking around on the surface with the special crampons on their boots so they wouldn't drift away.

The FMC Transit Collective drives towered above

them in an upside-down pyramid, an architecturally impossible structure anywhere but in the negligible gravity of a planetoid. The sun came up, the sun went down, all within the space of the first three and a half hours, but it was an odd sequence because the crew was on the south pole, and the sun didn't so much set as hide behind a ridge, slipping out of sight on the left side, then coming out on the right, as if it were playing hide-and-seek with them.

The surface of the asteroid was different from the Moon in that there were only scattered deposits of loosely clinging regolith, like the pockets of snow that hid in the shade when spring came. For the most part it was bare rock, the best possible anchor for their specially designed crampons.

The work was a lot harder than Gerry had thought it was going to be, construction work, really, and he was glad his suit had artificial muscles, and that the gravity was so weak, because he wouldn't have been able to take the strain otherwise. They jackhammered the *Prometheus* into the rock, and once all sixty-eight bolts were done, they stopped calling it the *Prometheus* and started calling it the PCV—the primary command vehicle.

After the PCV was established, they had a rest period of six hours.

At the end of that six hours they got up and launched a small survey probe—what the technicians at AviOrbit had christened *Smallmouth 3,* in Gerry's honor, even though technically speaking *Smallmouth 2* had been nothing more than a Styrofoam ball embedded with microinstruments.

Smallmouth 3 performed a complete survey of Gaspra, correlating the new topographical information to the known engineering tolerances of the five FMC Transit Collective drives, and feeding all this into a computer program that was meant to design, out of the misshapen rock that was Gaspra, the best possible spacecraft and, more importantly, the best possible planet killer. The program established five installation areas—these would be the five primary thrust bays, and operationally would be connected via laser through the PCV's thrust conduits.

The crew sledded the drives one at a time to their installation areas, riding the sled two hundred yards above Gaspra's surface. It was a bit like maneuvering an old-time zeppelin, as it had to be done with great care. The dual dangers were either that the drive would slam into the surface of the asteroid, or, barring that, would drift away into outer space. It had to be maneuvered through what Ian kept calling, with some nervousness, the "critical plane."

Despite the finickiness involved, they managed, over the coming days, to anchor the drives into the installation areas with glitchless monotony. Gerry's confidence climbed each time a new drive was installed. This was vindication. This was proof that he could do something like this. This told him that he was more than just Neil Thorndike's younger brother.

Their third day, they sledded Drive Four to its installation area, what they were dubbing the Norbert Plains, after Mitch's partner back on Earth. In fact, all the installation areas were plains of one type or another—the computer program had minimized the landform-thrust interference ratio as much as possible.

They maneuvered Drive Four over the selected area, then allowed the sled's ion pump to give it a shove groundward. The crew capitalized on this downward momentum and soon had their boot crampons biting into the asteroid's surface. Except for some minor irregularities, the surface was flat and devoid of loose particulate.

The stars swept by overhead as the short day counted out its two hundred and nine minutes. The three of them, like superheroes, held the drive above their heads, a unit that was fully the size of ten transport trucks but weighed next to nothing in Gaspra's weak pull.

Ian said, "Let's shift it a few yards to the left. We'll miss that swell over there."

So they moved it a few yards to the left, like three guys moving a big couch.

"Settle her down," said Ian.

Which they did.

The mission continued with seamless predictability until Mitch started working on anchor seventeen.

Then Gerry heard through his helmet radio the two most dreaded words any crew never wanted to hear during a space mission.

"Oh, shit."

Mitch drifted upward from Drive Four at a speed greater than escape velocity. His crampons had failed, and the force of his pneumatic drill had propelled him into space like one of the old Atlas rockets, his trajectory on an angle so that he didn't drift straight up but floated quickly over the short horizon like a stray cloud. Ian fired a line to him, but by that time it was too late. Gerry keyed over to Mitch's visor readouts and saw that the diminutive engineer had red lights not on one, but on both crampons. One he could accept. Two was . . . well, suspicious. Then both Ian and Gerry cramponed over to the sled. Ian interfaced the sled's computer with Mitch's CAPS computer to see if the two could arrive at a workable procedure. By this time, Mitch was well out of view beyond the short horizon.

"Mitch?" said Gerry.

"Jesus Christ . . . oh, shit! Where are you guys?"

Gerry and Ian looked at each other. It was Ian who delivered the bad news. "Mitch . . . the sled is giving us a negative on a rescue mission."

"What? Are you sure?"

"Affirmative."

"But that's impossible. The sled should have more than enough thrust to reach me. I can't be more than three miles away. Why's it giving you a negative?"

Ian hesitated. "Because I'm afraid that the particular code needed to effect the proper burns and trajectories . . . it's gone. Deleted. Not by me."

The silence that came to the three of them was like the turning of a page. Gerry felt a tightening in his throat, and the tightness quickly spread to his stomach as the claw of an overwhelming apprehension closed its grip. He heard Ian's voice through his suit radio, a few tense words, "What happened, Mitch?" but the words seemed to come to Gerry through thick cotton batting.

"Both my crampons red-lighted at the same time," said Mitch. "Do you know what the likelihood of that is?"

Mitch's voice sounded hurt. Ian responded, telling the technician, "Even in my day we never got two red lights at the same time. . . ." His words seemed unsure, as if the idea expressed was one Ian never expected to find in his mouth, especially in the current context. "And with the rescue software kaput . . . I don't know. What are the chances?"

All the while Gerry felt Mitch was on a big river, and that he was getting further and further away. His face tensed into a mask of anxiety; he liked Mitch, and couldn't believe they might lose him.

"Around one in twenty-five million," said Mitch, because Mitch was always a man for statistics. Gerry heard the AviOrbit technician's breath coming and going quickly. "It's them," he said, his voice going lower, dipping, like hanging onto the edge of a cliff and finally letting go. "They've done something." Then a pause, accompanied by a little rough static from the radio. "You guys need redundancy procedures."

Mitch might have spoken a foreign language. Redundancy procedures? Gerry was nonplussed. The man was going to *die*. "Mitch, just hang on. We're going to save you."

"That's it." Ian had gone into reckless mode, the damn-the-torpedoes Hamilton of old. "I'm getting on the sled. Just hang on, little guy. I'll be there in a minute."

"No! Listen to me! The two of you! My suit tells me I've broken orbit. There's nothing you can do. If the rescue software is deleted, that's . . ." Then, softer: "That's it. Let's face it, the delete is another Tarsalan trick. Ian, if you come after me in the sled, that's two of us gone. You're at work, Ian. Remember? The first job you've had in five years. Let's stay professional. Gerry?"

Gerry felt miserable, but managed to get the words out. "I'm here, Mitch."

"Have you confirmed the delete? Let's stick to procedure. Can you confirm?"

"It's a no go on all fronts."

"Then that's it. There's nothing we can do."

"I'm sorry, Mitch."

"I've got eighteen hours of life support."

"Mitch, we could still . . ." This from Ian, but the words came out in the defeated tone of a man who had reached that cusp where hope and hopelessness merge, and, balancing for an instance on the possibility of last-ditch efforts, the pilot finally teetered into the territory of lost causes. He gave the console a petulant smack with a half-closed fist and turned to Gerry. He shook his head.

"There's nothing we can do?" asked Gerry.

"There's zero chance of getting him back, and we risk the whole mission if we try."

Through his yellow-tinted visor, Gerry discerned his old friend's face. Here they were again; not the first time they'd been in extreme circumstances—though riding an asteroid bronco-style while a friend drifted to his death was perhaps the most extreme circumstance of all. Ian's lips had a curious curl, and his eyes had narrowed with resentment. Gerry, on the other hand, felt shocked into a kind of mild catatonia.

Mitch had guts of steel, though, because he was already on to the next thing, miles ahead of either of them. "There's only two of you now."

"Mitch, we're sorry," said Gerry.

"Think of the phytosphere."

The dark, ugly thing that was suffocating Earth.

"Right . . . right. Go ahead, Mitch."

"With me out of the picture, it means a lot more work for the two of you. Which in turn means new procedures. And if this virus thing keeps evolving, the framework for those procedures will constantly change." His voice was high, tremulous. "You've got to work the procedures up fast, because this thing might balloon exponentially."

And Gerry had to hand it to Mitch, because he went out like a hero, detailing the kinds of things they would have to do if they were going to get the mission accomplished against this increasingly growing threat, giving them guidelines and new timetables, interfacing with the PCV's main computer to model fresh mission dynamics, and at last logging the whole thing into the mainframe. Only then did Mitch get weepy. Only then did Gerry and Ian loosen their hold on their own grief.

Gerry asked Mitch if he could still see Gaspra.

"I'm facing away."

"Buddy, we're going to miss you." Ian's voice was rough.

And it was true. Mitch was one of a kind.

They covered a few more technical possibilities, contingencies, and what-if scenarios, then Mitch's voice got quiet. It was if the small man could already see the end of his life, was watching hours turn into minutes, minutes into seconds—those finite units of time that everyone had to measure eventually.

"You guys . . . make it count . . . that's all I ask. And if you see Norbert . . . if he's still alive . . . just tell him . . . you know."

"We'll tell him," said Gerry.

And rather than drift toward Jupiter for the next seventeen hours—the remaining extent and breadth of his current life support—Mitch had his med-pak deliver an untenable dose of barbiturates to him intravenously, even as the Tarsalan infection in the PCV and its external components ballooned—as the small man had feared it would—exponentially.

35

As Glenda and her children ventured onto the final stretch of Marblehill Road, Hanna's breathing grew more labored. Her coughing exploded into the still, hot air like small pneumatic reports. The trees in the forest loomed over them on either side, dead brown things. No cars, trucks, or people, just the awful silence. Glenda could barely see her kids in the dark. She looked up at the sky. No stars, Moon, or clouds—just the blackness of the phytosphere.

Hanna sank to the ground and coughed more violently. Jake kept looking down the road, gun held loosely in his hand. Glenda knelt next to Hanna. The perpetual darkness felt like something evil inside her body, a tumor she wanted to remove but couldn't.

"Hanna, we've got to keep going."

"I'm too weak, Mom. It's never been like this before. I'm going to die. I know I am."

"You're not going to die. We just have to get to Uncle Neil's. He has medicine."

"Yes, but I can't make it. I can't get enough breath."

"Get between me and Jake. We'll help you along."

"I can't, Mom."

"You've got to, Hanna. Buzz is going to come along."

Hanna coughed some more, then choked out the words, "Just give me a minute."

While Hanna rested, Glenda stood up and turned on her flashlight. She shone it up the road toward Marblehill, but its beam was weak and could barely penetrate the gloom. Still, it was strong enough to brighten a big tree that had fallen across the road. As the beam brought the tree's spidery brown branches into relief, she had the distinct impression of something darting by overhead in the darkness. She looked up just in time to see a large shadow, maybe twenty-five times the size of her car, disappear above the trees on the left-hand side, rustling above the uppermost branches.

"Did you see that?" she asked Jake.

"Yeah."

"What was it?"

"I have no idea."

But Glenda knew what it was, and didn't want to say because her children were already scared enough as it was. She switched off the flashlight. She looked around at the dark forest with a sudden sense that they weren't alone. That's when she heard the bump and rattle of Buzz's truck far down the road.

"Goddamn him," moaned Hanna between coughs.

"Come on, sweetie. Let's get up. Jake, give me a hand."

"Maybe we should go into the forest," suggested Jake.

"I'm not sure it's safe."

"Why?"

"Just give me a hand."

They each took one of Hanna's arms and lifted her to her feet. They struggled along with her as best they could, but she kept stumbling and they made slow progress. Glenda opened her eyes wide, something that was habitual now as a way to see as much as she could in the perpetual dark, and something that made her temples ache with a low throb.

She could barely see the left and right shoulders of the road. Her feet crunched through the gravel. Hanna started crying, getting her weeping done in between her explosive coughing. The bump and rattle of Buzz's truck got closer, the signature sound particularly noticeable on this potholed road. Glenda had the sense that she had already lost, and that dragging her daughter up this lonely rural road in the middle of this perpetual night would be the last thing she would ever do. The futility of her situation made her want to weep, but she found that, despite these self-defeating feelings, her body kept going, as if it had an internal agenda for survival and couldn't be bothered with the emotional fuss her mind was making.

"I don't see his headlights," said Jake.

"He's behind that hill," said Glenda. "He'll be coming over the rise any second. Just keep going."

They struggled and struggled, and finally came to the fallen tree in the middle of the road. The tree was huge and tinder-dry, and all the leaves had fallen off its branches.

"Let's go around the left side," she said.

She and Jake helped Hanna around to the left just as Buzz came over the rise. The dead branches, still thick, scratched her.

"Just push your way through. Hurry up. Hanna, lift your leg over the trunk."

"I can't see it, Mom."

Glenda turned on the flashlight. "There."

Her daughter climbed over the trunk, but it was as if death had already come to Hanna because, once on the other side, she collapsed.

"Just leave me here. Let him kill me. Maybe that will satisfy him. You two go ahead."

"Hanna, come on, get to your feet," said Glenda, her voice now panicked. "He's nearly here."

"I can't, Mom. I really can't."

And she simply lay there on her side coughing, too weak to move.

"Jake, let's drag her."

But Jake was looking over the tree. "I'm going to take him out."

"No, no . . . not with a handgun. Not from this range. You'll waste bullets like you did last time. Just grab her and let's go."

They dragged her—literally—so that her jeans scraped along the gravel and kicked up a small cloud of dust. Buzz's truck rattled to a stop on the other side of the fallen tree, and she heard Buzz open the door and get out of the vehicle. She didn't look back, couldn't look back, because her eyes were glued to the sky above the road, where she saw the dark shape again—huge, hovering silently, with no lights, no visible means of propulsion. Now that she listened more closely, she heard a faint hiss, like water being sucked down a drain.

The headlights on Buzz's truck shone through the dead branches of the fallen tree, making a wild tracery of shadows all over the road. She glanced at Jake and saw that he was outlined in the branch-broken glow of Buzz's headlights. But it was as if he didn't care, because he was looking up at the Tarsalan vehicle as well.

"Goddamn it, Glenda, why don't you let me kill you easy?" called Buzz.

The sound of a rifle shot rocketed through the air.

That's when lights exploded everywhere on the Tarsalan Landing Vehicle. Shaped like a clamshell, the TLV now glowed with a mother-of-pearl mix—violet, green, silver—and this light coalesced into a single beam, which quickly pinpointed Buzz's ramshackle old truck, while a smaller, separate beam outlined Buzz. She saw Buzz clearly in this small beam. He lifted his arm to his forehead to shield his eyes from the light, and squinted at its glare. Then a series of blue and green embers floated away from the alien landing craft and drifted, in no particular hurry, toward Buzz and his truck.

"Get off the road!" she cried.

She and Jake dragged Hanna up a small incline to the other side of a hummock. She got on her stomach and watched things unfold. As the blue and green embers got closer to Buzz they began to whine with a rising pitch until finally the sound was so painful that she had to cover her ears. Buzz figured things out quickly and, after a moment of drop-jawed scrutiny, ran away from his truck, rifle in hand, and disappeared into the forest on the other side of the road. Five embers drifted toward his truck and burrowed into it like hot little drills. A few seconds later, his truck exploded and was left a flaming heap on the asphalt.

Other embers pursued Buzz into the forest. She watched in horrified fascination. With all the underbrush dead, she kept fairly good track of Buzz. He ran from tree to tree as if pursued by a band of malevolent fairies. The embers cruised after him, closing the distance quickly. When they were a yard away, they pulled back, then dove into his body with the ferocity and quickness of bullets. Buzz cried out, an awful throaty scream. His limbs went stiff, his fingers splayed so that he dropped his rifle, and it was as if he was illuminated from within by high-voltage electricity. He shook violently. His shirt burst into flames, and he fell to the ground so that half his body was hidden behind a tree trunk, the other half still visible. Then came a small explosion and she got the distinct impression of a detached leg flying into the air. She turned away. She was saddened that it had come to this, but she was also relieved. And terrified that she now had to elude the Tarsalans herself.

At that point, the alien spacecraft descended to the road. It was wacky, a scene out of a science fiction movie, something she had never expected to see; visitors from another star at last landing on her planet, the spacecraft settling on the road like a giant glowing egg. It made a creepy sound, a sudden buzz with low-frequency harmonics that vibrated through her whole body, then that sucking sound again, like the last bit of water in a bathtub going down the drain. Then all sound faded.

In the ensuing silence, her body took over. She got her kids to their feet and helped them through the forest. Hanna didn't have to be dragged—fear was a great motivator. Glenda got all kinds of scratches from the thick, dead bushes, but continued to cajole her kids through the dark forest past the spaceship, and finally back out onto the road. Her mind, in its own separate universe, reeled from the terror of it all.

With Hanna in such a debilitated state, it took them a long time to get the rest of the way to Marblehill. Glenda looked at her watch in the dim glow of her flashlight, and wasn't sure if it was one o'clock in the afternoon or one o'clock in the morning.

When they finally reached Marblehill, she looked up at the three-story mansion and saw lights burning in four windows. In the glow of these lights she saw a helicopter sitting on the big front lawn. The building itself looked as if it had been under prolonged attack, with the east turret demolished and the rest of the various walls, dormers, and cornices badly shot up.

The three Thorndikes stood outside a big stone wall. There was a path outside the wall that led into the forest. In happier times, she had walked along this path, hand in hand with Gerry, down into the rugged limestone ravine that abutted the property where the trees used to grow. Hanna lay on the ground outside the wall. Her coughing sounded different: still persistent but not as strong, as if she had long ago ripped all her abdominal muscles to pieces and no longer possessed the muscular mechanics to cough the way she used to

"Jake, stay with your sister. I'm going to the gate."

But beyond that? She didn't know. What if this whole thing turned into a bust? What if everybody was dead inside? *Shut up, Glenda. Live a minute at a time . . . minute at a time . . . minute at a time . . .*

She reached the gate and turned her flashlight on and off three times. She waited, then repeated the signal, terrified that, somewhere out in the dead forest behind her, Tarsalan refugees watched her. She repeated the signal a third time, then saw someone run from the house, across the lawn, and toward the helicopter.

As the figure got closer, she saw that it was recognizably human, with normal human proportions, not short legs and long arms like a Tarsalan. She was so overwhelmed with relief that she felt dizzy and pressed her hand against the gate for support.

The figure resolved itself into a man. "Mrs. Thorndike?"

"Yes . . . yes, it's me. Call me Glenda."

"Where are your kids?"

The man closed the distance between them, and she

saw the name FERNANDES stitched above his left breast pocket.

"Just down here." She peered into the darkness. "Jake? Hanna? Come on." She saw movement in the shadows along the stone fence. She turned to Fernandes. "My daughter's really sick. I hope you have medicine."

Fernandes nodded. "We have all kinds. Let's get them across the lawn . . . before the Tarsalans come."

New anxiety shot through her chest like a lightning bolt. "It's bad?"

"We have five dead. Six including your sister-in-law."

"My sister-in-law?"

Fernandes nodded. "It's just three airmen left, Dr. Thorndike, and his three girls."

"Louise is dead?"

"One of the VMs got her a few days ago."

Her children appeared out of the shadows.

"Kids, Aunt Louise is dead. Just so you know."

"What?" said Jake. "Really? What happened?"

Fernandes was looking at the gun in Jake's hand. He then turned to Glenda. "He know how to shoot? I mean, really shoot?"

But Glenda was too upset about Louise to respond.

"I'm getting better," said Jake.

"Ever handle a Montclair?" asked Fernandes.

"A Montclair? What's that?"

Fernandes's face sank. "Come on. Let's get everybody inside."

Fernandes hustled them across the lawn.

The lawn was brown and had the texture of a piecrust, the sod seeming to have come loose in a single piece from the underlying soil, as if the lawn's root system had died at the same time, *en masse*. In a world where things kept getting worse and worse—where the sun could be extinguished by alien plankton, where Glenda could become a cop killer, and where mass famine took the lives of millions every day—Louise was just one more catastrophe, and it was hard for Glenda to immediately feel grief. She just felt shocked. How was Neil handling it? How were the girls handling it?

Fernandes led them under the great stone portico and up the steps. They went through the front door, and . . . there they all were, Neil and the girls, waiting for them, just like any other Marblehill visit, only this one was so different.

Neil was smiling in the oddest way. "Welcome to Marblehill."

His face was lit by a light that was hanging on a hook, a bare bulb in a cage, the kind mechanics used to look under cars. The greeting came out in a stiff, formal way, and the man standing before her didn't sound like Neil at all.

"Neil, I'm sorry about Louise. This fellow . . ." She glanced inquisitively at the airman. "Fernandes, is it?"

"Yes, ma'am."

"Fernandes told me."

Neil raised his hands—no need to make any fuss. "We're all right, Glenda. We're just glad you made it here okay. We were starting to wonder."

And that smile. Something wasn't right about that smile.

The cousins got to know each other again. They had something to eat—military-issue stew, just add water— and her nieces came and clung to her off and on through the next several hours, especially Morgan, who mistakenly called her mommy a number of times.

She got to know the two other airmen: Captain Leonard Aft, who was nominally in charge, and Lieutenant Yuri Rostov, who was always wearing a pair of headphones and seemed to be the technical man; he had a constantly abstracted look in his eyes.

They had a rest. Hanna got her medicine. Her coughing got better and she breathed, for the first time in several days, without a wheeze.

Later on, Glenda stood guard duty with Neil in his study on the second floor. He still had that odd smile on his face, the squeeze of the curve so tight that his lips were white. Light-gathering goggles sat hinged in the up position above his eyes on a strap, and he kept scan-

ning the grounds out front, his face lit by the dim glow
of the communications apparatus on the floor next to
him. He had lost weight. Not that he was gaunt, but his
customary paunch was gone, his clothes were too baggy
for his frame, and the usual fullness around his jaw had
melted away like wax around a candle.

Now that his face was thin, Glenda couldn't help
seeing the resemblance to Gerry: the way his brow
crowned around his eyes in a somewhat falconlike mold,
the same generous nose, and a similar rounded protuber-
ance to his chin. Her heart ached for Gerry.

And, as if Neil had read her mind, he said, "I'm sorry
about Ger. I'm sorry he's stuck up there."

She looked away. Tears came to her eyes. "It's a bit
much."

He reached out and put his hand on her arm. "Don't
worry, Glenda. I've got everything organized. We've got
listening posts reaching a mile in every direction. We've
got infrared cameras the size of your thumb up in trees.
We're tracking each new landing and plotting it on a
map. We've cataloged their movements and fed the results into a computer, and we're coming to a real understanding of how they think, at least from a tactical and
guerrilla standpoint. We've also made a fallback position
in the cave."

She dried her tears. "I forgot about the cave."

"We've fortified the first chamber, and provisioned the
second. We've got fresh water in there. Enough to last
a month. Medicine, too. Not to mention food. We go
out on patrol regularly. We search the area. And we
spray the house every day for bugs. Unfortunately, before we started spraying, the Tarsalans sent in bugs and
found out we had food. But don't worry about the Tarsalans. They haven't mounted a strike in the last three
days. We think they're starting to tire. As for the cave,
everything's buried under rocks so they don't know it's
there. And we go up there to spray, too."

And still that smile, the lid on something that was
simmering deep inside her brother-in-law.

She glanced out the front window. "I'm sorry about Louise."

He didn't say anything. She turned back to him. In the light of the communications apparatus, she saw that his face had turned red. She moved closer and put her arm around him.

"I'm okay. . . . I'm okay," he said.

"No . . . you're not."

He took a deep breath. The smile disappeared from his face. "Maybe not." And then he bowed his head, as if in shame, and closed his eyes. "I failed her, Glenda."

"You didn't fail her."

"And I failed the kids."

"No, you didn't."

"I finally realize what a big fool I've been all these years."

"You're not a fool. For God's sake, Neil."

After that, they lapsed into silence for a long time. She must have dozed. And Neil must have thought she was asleep—even when she opened her eyes around a quarter to eleven.

His shoulders heaved and he wept silently. The pain bristled off him like heat from a furnace. Her throat tightened with anguish and her own eyes filled with tears. God. What were they going to do? Here was the end of time. And Neil, once the world's hero, was nothing but a broken man who cried alone in the dark when he thought no one was watching.

36

Day now followed day. The sad, dark month of October crept slowly toward its close. Glenda occasionally tried to reach Gerry on her fone, but with the shroud constantly thickening, her signal never got through, and she didn't even get the message from AT&T Interlunar about service being down anymore.

At the start of their second week there, Neil got a call on his special phone from Assistant Secretary of Defense Fonblanque. When he was done speaking to her, he told Glenda about it.

"The United States Navy recovered a communications drop from the Moon three days ago south of the Solomon Islands. The Moon is telling us they've embarked on their own mission to destroy the phytosphere." And then, unexpectedly, after talking in official mode, Neil got choked up. "Gerry might have had something after all. With his stress band and flagella." He looked at the airmen, then at his daughters, then at Glenda and her family. "It seems they've conducted experiments that prove the phytosphere is . . . sensitive to gravitational pressure . . . and that the Moon, all this time, has been creating a tidal flux in the phytosphere—Gerry's stress band. Gerry says if he increases the gravitational pull of the Moon against the phytosphere by a factor of fifteen percent for a period of five days, the flagella will be overwhelmed and the phytosphere will break apart." Neil spelled it out in one blunt summation: "He's going to slam the asteroid Gaspra into the Moon, move the

Moon closer to the Earth, and use the resulting stronger gravity to shake the phytosphere apart." He then sketched in the technicalities.

When he was done, Glenda stared at her brother-in-law with unmitigated alarm. Colliding emotions rushed through her body. Her throat felt ticklish, tears sprang to her eyes, and her head swam. She stumbled backward and would have fallen if Rostov hadn't caught her.

"And he's going to be riding on this asteroid?"

"That's what Fonblanque says. At the last minute they're going to eject in a survival pod. The mission is already well under way."

"What's to stop the Moon from falling into the Earth?" asked Lenny.

"The Moon's orbit has been widening for millions of years. It's going to continue in that pattern. This will just be a momentary blip. Centrifugal forces will soon pull it back to its regular orbit."

"Is he serious?" Glenda couldn't seem to catch her breath.

"They've already gone. They've reached Gaspra. They're rigging it with AviOrbit's five biggest singularity drives." Neil looked away. "I've always chastised him for taking wild risks . . . but even I couldn't have imagined—"

"Is Daddy all right?" asked Hanna, her eyes like tombs after all the asthma, but showing some light for the first time in weeks.

Neil turned to Hanna. "*He's* all right."

The reservation Glenda heard in Neil's voice jabbed her like the point of a hypodermic needle. "And just what the hell's that supposed to mean?"

Neil hesitated. "It seems some Tarsalans escaped to the Moon after the TMS became unviable. Before Nectaris mounted its mission, it neutralized those Tarsalans, and they're now in detainment facilities on the Moon. This was to circumvent the possibility that the Tarsalans might sabotage the Gaspra mission. But it seems the Tarsalans had automatic sabotage procedures in place, and that all the equipment and software for the Gaspra mission has now been infected with a slow-burning virus. Systems are failing one by one. As a result, one of the crew members has already been killed. But Gerry and . . . and you'll never guess . . . Ian Hamilton—"

"Ian Hamilton?" The sudden appearance of this dark phantom from Gerry's past alarmed Glenda to the core of her being.

"Apparently he's been up there working as an AviOrbit test pilot for the last seven years. Now he's mission pilot."

"I've got to sit down," she said.

Rostov led her to one of the overstuffed chairs Louise liked to decorate her various homes with, and she sat down heavily, hyperventilating. The components of the disastrous mission paraded darkly through her mind. Gerry, millions of miles away in deep space, riding on a giant rocket that was falling to pieces, one crew member already dead, and the other—the god of good times, as Gerry used to call him—ready to wreak havoc on Gerry's life all over again.

"Did they take any alcohol with them?"

As ludicrous as the suggestion sounded, it was no joke, and Neil was sensitive enough to see that. For only Neil fully understood the pain Gerry's alcoholism had caused her, because who could she turn to but Neil when Gerry didn't come home for three days, or wound up in jail under Fulton's mocking gaze, or tried to be affectionate to the children when he was so repugnantly drunk he could hardly stand? She would never forget her long telephone calls with Neil, and how Neil had gotten her through the worst of it. And then what she called the New Sobriety had come along, the sobriety that had finally stuck, after so many times of Gerry trying to quit, but always falling back off the wagon. Was all that in jeopardy now? Surely Nectaris wasn't such a party capital that they'd allow their astronauts to take booze with them on a critical mission.

"Glenda . . . it's okay. For the first time in my life I actually believe in Gerry. He's going to do this thing. I know he is. I might be smart. But Gerry's the family genius. And I've finally got the guts to admit that."

She broke down completely after that. Her nerves were shot.

"How long till he makes it light again?" she asked through her tears.

Because, *God,* did she want daylight again.

"Eight days. Ten at the most."

So in ten days she would know if she was a widow or not. She wasn't sure how she was going to make it through the uncertainty.

She didn't have time to brood or think about it because Rostov, using the tiny state-of-the-art radar dish mounted on the roof, tracked seven TLVs landing within an hour of each other, all within a one-mile radius of Marblehill.

An hour later, Marblehill came under heavy attack. This attack was different in that it employed not only the regular VMs but also standard human weaponry.

"They must have found an armory somewhere," was Lenny's only comment.

So, amid the whining squeals of the VMs, there was also a lot of semiautomatic weapons fire. With all the gunfire, she was surprised that the surrounding dead forest, now dry as straw after all the heat, didn't go up in flames.

She was in a sandbagged position under the drive-through portico with her fellow soldiers, Jake and Melissa.

She watched Melissa in amazement. Here was a girl who should have been more at home in a shopping mall, or out on a prom date, but now she was firing her Montclair like a seasoned grunt, her face darkened by military greasepaint, her jaw clenching each time she pulled the trigger. She stood up over the sandbags and sprayed the yard with gunfire, her long blond hair jerking around her shoulders and her lips pursed against the clenching of her jaw, and when she was done she ducked back down daintily, as if she were practicing a move in a cheerleading squad.

Then Jake got up, and he had the curious habit of holding out both elbows when he was firing his Montclair, as if he were a bird about to take flight. He fired a burst of nearly forty bullets, and as he neared the end of this fusillade, his elbows rose higher and higher until they were nearly parallel with his shoulders. Then he stopped firing, and his head ducked to the left and right, as if he were inspecting the damage; he reminded Glenda of a dentist drilling a tooth—drilling a bit, then looking—but in Jake's case it was shooting a bit, then looking.

It was Glenda's turn. This wasn't like shooting Fulton from the rooftop. This was full-fledged combat shooting, and she was so scared she felt queasy. She flipped down her night goggles, scanned the yard, and saw two Tarsalans, ghostly figures in green, moving toward the helicopter, both carrying automatic weapons, man-made rifles. Hardly any VMs anymore, as if they were running out and had to make do with local resources. She took aim, just as she had taken aim at those partridges so many years ago, and fired, not a whole gusher of bullets the way Melissa had, but with her Montclair on its single-shot setting, believing she was more effective in sniper mode.

The first Tarsalan dropped dead. She aimed at the second. They had a dozen crates of Montclair rounds, including what could be made with the round-making kit, but someday even those were going to run out. Best to conserve. She squeezed the trigger and the weapon spit its bullet with a *phhitt!*, and the second Tarsalan went down; and now there were two lumps of green in her night goggles.

She saw five more come through the gate.

So began what turned into a long night. Glenda, Jake, and Melissa covered the front yard. Rostov and Morgan guarded the west wing. Neil, Ashley, and Fernandes manned the east wing. And Lenny and Hanna patrolled the rear, though Hanna really wasn't good for much fighting because she was still too weak from asthma. Glenda was glad the back was fairly well protected by the swimming pool and tennis courts. So far the Tarsalans hadn't mounted more than harassment strikes from the rear.

She heard a lot of fighting from the west wing and, as they had things fairly under control in front, she sent Jake—yes, her own son, because she wasn't about to send Melissa, not when Neil had already lost Louise—over to the west wing to help Rostov and Morgan.

"But, Mom, what about the three we keep seeing run by the gate?"

"Melissa and I will handle them. Go help Rostov and Morgan."

Children as soldiers. Hitler's Germany. Cheng's Hong Kong. And more recently, Ngaradoumbé's Chad. She remembered seeing a picture of a nine-year-old African girl kneeling with a machine gun, a teddy bear poking out of the knapsack on her back. And now it was happening here. At Marblehill.

After two hours, it didn't seem so strange anymore that children should be fighting. Glenda slowly lost her fear simply because she had to concentrate so hard on what she was doing. It was, in a word, *work*. Like a shift at Cedarvale, especially a holiday shift, when Whit would sometimes have her on for twelve hours at a time.

She got tired by the third hour. "Is this what the last one was like?"

Melissa nodded. "We fought . . . and then we fought some more . . . and after we were done fighting, we fought some more. It went on for eight hours . . . and it had these lulls." Melissa motioned out at the yard. "I hate these lulls worse than I hate the actual fighting. You don't know if they're done or not. You're always waiting for more."

"I don't see why we don't just give them food. Surely we can spare a bit."

"Dad says there's no point. They'd just want more.

We're probably the only food source around for miles. Plus, he's never going to negotiate with them now. Not since they killed Mom."

"Yes, but . . . there's going to come a time . . . we've only got twelve crates of ammunition left."

"Dad's had Yuri wire the whole house with explosives. If we have to fall back to the cave, the house goes up."

"You're kidding."

"If they get the house, there are all kinds of things they can use. We can't let it fall into their hands."

Glenda motioned at the sky. "Yes, but they keep coming."

And, in fact, over the next half hour Rostov radioed and told them he had another five confirmed landings in the general vicinity, that listening posts and tree-mounted cameras had picked up increased activity, and that they should be prepared for a renewed and stronger offensive at any time.

The offensive came fifteen minutes later, with an unexpected burst of VMs floating up from behind the wall like a Fourth of July fireworks display. The modules drifted toward them with their customary whine, flickering like pulsars. All Glenda could think of was that if she got touched by one of those things the intense vibrations would turn her internal organs to mush. She grabbed Melissa and dragged her away from the sandbags.

In the few seconds it took them to take cover behind the portico's granite pillars, two VMs drifted in under the vaulted ceiling and lit the dark space within—a space where luxury automobiles had once dropped off illustrious guests to Neil's various hoity-toity gatherings. Her pupils contracted painfully in the sudden sharpness of the light. The two VMs swirled around as if looking for them. But then they targeted the house, driving into double oaken doors that had been shipped all the way from Scotland. In moments, the doors burst into splinters and their stone casing disintegrated into rubble.

Melissa shrieked the way all young girls shrieked—it

didn't matter if it was a VM or a spider, the shriek was the same.

Several other VMs exploded throughout the Marblehill complex. Then the Tarsalans commenced a fusillade of regular gunfire from scrounged Earth-made weapons, and bullets ricocheted off the portico's granite pillars, creating sparks in the darkness. The few windows that hadn't yet been shattered burst into fragments. The hail of gunfire was so intense and nonstop that Glenda was too afraid to move. She also feared that under the cover of such heavy gunfire the Tarsalans might make a significant advance across the lawn.

Just as she was thinking that she had to get back to the sandbags and return fire, no matter what, Jake ran from the west side of the house dragging Morgan behind him. Glenda's first thought was to send him back immediately, because how could Rostov cover the west side all by himself? But a moment later she understood, and a moment after that, Jake confirmed it.

"They got Yuri, Mom! One of those VM things shook him to pieces!"

She told him to get down because he was just standing there looking too shocked to think straight. Then she glanced beyond his shoulder to the west side of the house, where she saw shadows moving among the dead ornamental cypresses. She flipped her night goggles down and counted five Tarsalans, their shaggy bison heads and misshapen bodies now making her think of Quasimodo—five hunchbacks coming toward them. She immediately switched her Montclair to repeater mode and fired in their direction. She got three of them, but the other two found cover behind the balustrade.

"Move!" she shouted, and pointed east.

Glenda, Jake, Melissa, and Morgan ran toward the east wing. As they ran, she glanced out at the front, and saw so many Tarsalans swarming across the broad front lawn that she didn't have time to count them.

She and the kids ran past the garden shed and around the corner, where they found Neil on his stomach by the lily pond, shooting with focused deliberation into the woods at the side of the house. Fernandes lay next to him, scattering gunfire into the trees as well. Ashley lay motionless, her brown hair matted with blood, her dress twisted around her waist, half on her side, half on her back, her legs scissored as if she were stepping into nothingness. Glenda felt suddenly woozy, and her grief was immediate, because here was just a child, fifteen years old, a year younger than her own Hanna, and she was dead. Her eyes clouded with tears. She glanced at Jake. Jake was staring at his dead cousin, a look of profound solemnity on his face, his eyes wide in the dark. Morgan wept as Glenda, getting a grip on herself, pulled both children to the ground. Melissa ran to Ashley and tried to shake her, but then, as more gunfire came at them from the woods, sank instinctively to the ground, pulled her own Montclair up in a petulant and angry gesture, and fired sporadic short bursts as she swore under her breath.

"Neil!" Glenda cried over the gunfire.

He glanced back. He looked like a phantom through her night-vision goggles, like something that had crawled out of a grave and now glowed radioactive green. And, in fact, with his daughter dead next to him, he looked as if he didn't belong here at all, and wasn't really part of this battle anymore, but was in a quiet place where none of it could hurt him. Fernandes, meanwhile, went about combat in his usual businesslike way, as if it were just a chore that he had to get done. Ashley's awful stillness, lying there half twisted on her side, gave the whole scene a surreal aspect. Morgan wept more persistently, but her weeping sounded different this time: resigned, accepting, just something her body had to do.

Glenda pointed out front. "There's a bunch of them coming this way!"

Neil nodded and got to his knees, then to his feet. "Help me with Ashley."

She stared at her brother-in-law through her light-gathering goggles. Didn't he understand that Ashley was dead, and that to carry a corpse would hamper their efforts; that they might be sacrificing themselves for the sake of a gesture? But in their mutual moment of indecision, Fernandes was already up on his feet, hunching over, taking a few steps toward the dead girl, lifting her, and tossing her over his shoulder, his small frame showing immense strength. And the decision was made; they were taking Ashley with them, whether she was dead or not.

The group ran crouching along the east side of Marblehill, the venerable old manse rising darkly beside them, Fernandes leading, then Neil, then the three kids, and herself at the rear. Tarsalan gunfire continued from the front of the house, but it was wasted because all the humans were back here now. Neil swung round the rear of the house and headed west, toward the metal fire escape that led to the third floor.

"Where are you going?" she cried.

"Up to get Lenny and Hanna. Go to the cave."

Another burst of VM fire came. It rose from the front of the house until it was high overhead, a total of nine modules altogether. They lit the tennis courts, the swimming pool, and the back of the house with a shifting green and blue light; and in this shifting light, Glenda saw Hanna, running as fast as she could down the metal fire escape, a look of unmitigated panic on her face.

"Where's Lenny?" Neil called to her.

"They got him, Uncle Neil! They're in the house! They came through the dining room window!"

"But Lenny has the detonator. Did you get it from him?"

"I couldn't, Uncle Neil. He's dead. I saw it."

Neil turned to Glenda. "I've got to get that detonator. Take the kids to the cave."

"Neil, if they're in the house—"

"I've got to get it. If they get their hands on all our supplies . . ."

He ran up the stairs, passing Hanna on the way.

Hanna joined Glenda and the other kids behind the tennis courts. She glanced at Ashley. "She's dead?" Her voice was without inflection, as if she were too shocked to react.

No one answered.

"Everyone up to the cave," said Glenda.

Everybody knew the way, having gone to the cave—the single most interesting landform anywhere around Marblehill—many times before. Melissa led the way. Then it was Morgan, Jake, and Hanna. Then Fernandes with Ashley over his shoulder. Ashley's head and arms flopped back and forth against his back. Hanna began to wheeze mildly as she climbed the hill, but was otherwise in much better shape than she had been while traveling to Marblehill. Tears came to Glenda's eyes as she stared at Ashley. How could things have gone so bad so quickly? She reached out and touched Ashley's head. Pulling her hand away, she saw blood. Glenda thought of Louise. And she spoke to Louise under her breath, telling Louise that she was sorry, that she should have tried harder, but that there was nothing she could do now. Louise's baby, her niece, was dead.

Glenda glanced back at the house and saw Neil disappear through the third-floor door at the top of the fire escape. The VMs came down. Five of them splashed into the pool, and their combined vibrations forced every last ounce of water into the sky, so that for several seconds it rained pool water, and the smell of chlorine filled the air. A couple of VMs fell into the middle of the tennis courts, cracks instantly appeared all over the ground, and three of the high fenceposts sagged toward the middle of the court. The last VM hit the slope behind the tennis courts, and shook loose a lot of the dead bushes, which then slid to the lawn in a mini avalanche.

Just as the path drew even with the roof of the house, Glenda saw Neil emerge from the third-floor fire exit carrying a large knapsack looped around one shoulder. She heard his footsteps resounding tinnily on the risers of the fire escape as he double-timed it to the ground. At the same time, she saw a half dozen Tarsalans coming around the west side of the house, all of them armed with Earth-made weapons, one of them running so fast he slipped on the pool water and fell on his hip. The others took aim at Neil and fired. Neil went down, but got on all fours and crawled toward the path leading to the cave. Coming on the heels of Ashley's death, Neil's wounding made her feel as if all that was good and decent in the universe had suddenly disappeared, and in fact had never been there in the first place. But it also filled her with the raw determination not to fail Louise again.

"Hold it . . . hold it! Take positions. Neil's been hit. Let's cover him."

Melissa, especially, followed this order instantly, as if the inadvertent boot camp at Marblehill had trained her well. She fired a withering hail of stinging Montclair ordnance into the advancing Tarsalans and killed all but one of them. The last one fled west and took cover behind the house. Morgan was already running down the hill, screaming for her daddy. Neil was up on his feet, but staggering badly as he climbed the path.

"Jake, go with Morgan. Help your uncle Neil. We'll cover you from here."

Jake went.

No more Tarsalans came, and they helped Neil up the hill without further mishap.

A perch in front of the cave overlooked the house from a little less than a quarter mile away. Fernandes finally put Ashley down. The girls, including Hanna, fussed over her, and they all cried to varying degrees. But the men, including Jake, were peering through their night-vision goggles at Marblehill, and Neil now had the detonater in his hand, his hand poised on the plunger. They were all waiting, the three of them, silently poised there, caught in one of those odd, still moments that sometimes happen in the middle of the most dire combat. Glenda peered past them through her own night-vision goggles. Dozens of Tarsalans entered the house. Neil's elbow flexed . . . flexed . . . and it all came down to the timing. . . . Neil, Fernandes, and Jake balanced there, as if they were team members engaged in a sporting event, waiting to place the puck in the net, or the ball through the hoop . . . waited . . . waited until at last Neil shoved the plunger down with a viciousness that seemed to be a summation of all the anger he felt over losing his wife and daughter.

The house went up.

Two seconds later, Neil sat down quickly, weakened by his own blood loss.

37

Gerry gripped the fifth and final singularity drive, conscious that if Mitch hadn't overdosed himself with barbiturates, his life support would have given out seventeen minutes ago. Gerry had a line around his waist, and this line, attached to Drive Five, slowly settled in a deep arc toward the surface of the asteroid, its fall slow in the weak gravity, as if it settled through molasses. Ian maneuvered around behind, gripping him, fearful of falling off the asteroid. Gerry's fingers felt stiff from holding the drive so tightly. He was sweating inside his suit, and his smell was ripe because the Tarsalan virus had sabotaged his personal hygiene unit and all his intragenic filters were off-line.

He heard Ian's stertorous breathing through his suit radio. The sun was to his rear, and Gerry's shadow was like a piece of black felt on top of the drive.

He glanced toward Ian and saw his old friend latch his safety belt to one of the drive's maneuvering rings. "How do your crampons feel?"

"Still holding." Ian sighed. "This is taking so long."

"Last one."

"I keep thinking of Mitch, drifting away."

"We stay professional, like he says."

"We've been going for eighteen hours. We're punch-drunk tired. We're going to start making mistakes soon."

"Last one. Go ahead."

"I wish we could fight this damn virus."

"It would be like two men trying to dike a flooding Mississippi."

Ian withdrew the pneumatic drill from his pack, like pulling a huge white arrow from a giant quiver, brought it down, maneuvered carefully, then glanced at Gerry. Gerry reached over and grabbed onto his arm. Once Ian was convinced Gerry was holding him tightly, he muttered under his breath, "Three, two, one," and fired the T-bolt through the brace. Both of them tensed up. Gerry watched his monitor as his crampon psi increased tenfold, and was glad that his feet felt as if they were stuck in deep mud. The last one. Ian started to laugh, first a few short guffaws, then a long run of ha-ha-has, as if they had just deviously outsmarted the virus. No sooner had he finished laughing than the right guidelight mounted at the side of his helmet blinked out. They both froze. They braced themselves. Little things were going wrong all the time now. As though everything was going through a quick aging process. Gerry's left guidelight blinked out, and the little red warning signal on his inside visor screen, retinally focused so that he could see it easily, told him that the virus was now checkmating his means of illumination.

"I don't get how this virus works," said Ian.

"And look, it's nearly night."

The terminator came at them like a quick and relentless black tide, spilling over the uneven surface like ink. He couldn't help thinking of the rising tide of barbiturates in Mitch's bloodstream. Funny the way it worked, but the second the terminator touched them, their remaining guidelights went out, as if the leading edge formed an invisible circuit. The darkness was so complete that he felt as though he was in a coffin. The stink of his own fear came to him like the sharp zest of a lemon. The red light blinked again, and in this darkness he was too afraid to move—because first it could be the guidelight, then it could be the crampons, and then they could fall off the edge of Mount Gaspra.

"What do we do?"

Ian's breathing came over his radio—uneven, stopping

at times—and it took him a full fifteen seconds to answer. "Wait for daybreak." This immediately seemed reasonable, because daybreak wasn't too far away, only three and a half hours, and they had worked so hard that they were considerably ahead of schedule anyway. Neither of them said anything for several minutes. The whole episode had a dreamlike aspect, especially when Gerry started thinking of the physical particulars: two human beings on an asteroid, desperately isolated from every other human being in the solar system, both of them gripping the last drive, neither moving nor saying anything. Because it was so dark, Gerry began to feel disembodied after a while. But then Ian, a man who always had to talk, gave way to that particular impulse, and the first words out his mouth had to do with Neil, and how Neil was going to have to eat crow when they got back.

"I'm not even thinking of that, Ian," said Gerry. "I'm just hoping it all works out."

"Whatever happened to Neil?"

"I guess he started believing in his own propaganda."

"I just want you to know, I admire the hell out of you, Gerry. I used to admire Neil, but now I admire you. Not only for this mission, but for the . . . the way you've turned your life around. Giving up drinking and all. It's really helped me."

"You should thank Glenda. Glenda's the one who made me see sense."

"It's seven weeks for me."

"Congratulations."

"I guess I didn't mention—I started going to A.A. meetings before we left."

"That's great, Ian."

"And I want to meet someone when I get back."

"I thought you had Stephanie. That night we went for a walk around the lake . . . I got the impression—"

"Stephanie doesn't know what she wants." He said this abruptly, with evident hurt in his voice. Gerry waited for him to elucidate, but he steered clear of Stephanie. "All I'm saying is . . . I believe in the future.

That might sound funny, considering we're up here, and we have one system failing after the other. But . . . you know what it's like. The drinking. Especially when you start doing the heavyweight rounds. And I was doing a lot of heavyweight rounds before you came up. I was a miserable human being, Gerry. I didn't believe in the future. And now I do. And I just want you to know that . . . even if things don't work out . . . all this has made a big difference to me.''

Sunrise ripped over the opposite horizon of Gaspra like a wild bushfire at the end of the asteroid's short night.

They found their way back to the sled.

The sled wouldn't start at first, and when Ian checked the diagnostics monitor, he saw that the number-three relay in the ion pump was misfiring, turning back on itself so that it was in danger of shorting out.

The pilot shut the number-three relay down, keying in the off-line sequence with a quick and practiced hand, and while this resulted in a lessening of drive power, and a concomitant reduction in speed, they still covered the ten miles from the end of the asteroid to the Primary Command Vehicle in under twenty-five minutes. They maneuvered through the critical plane and, looking down at the pitted gray-brown surface with its little freckles of shadow here and there, Gerry got the sense that they were not flying above a planetoid but passing a gigantic transport truck, this illusion created by the way the horizon sloped drastically in all directions.

The PCV came into view a short while later, its clean, angular planes, panoramic freighter windows, and fluorescent green anchoring supports a comforting sight to both of them. They were thankful to at last land the sled, untether themselves from each other, make the final risky walk to the air lock, and get inside the *Prometheus,* where the danger of falling off Mount Gaspra didn't exist.

Telemetry and orbital dynamics called for the ignition sequence three hours and twenty-two minutes later—in other words, Gaspra had reached that precise point in its age-old journey around the sun when it could most effectively be targeted toward the Moon. As Ian went through the sequence Gerry felt, like a presence inside him, the death of Mitch Bennett. The pain was no longer acute, but it was still there, a chronic ache. Through the freighter windows he saw the sun, a bright star, something that could easily be transplanted to a Christmas card as a stand-in for the Star of Bethlehem. Ian had his gloves off and his long fingers danced over the keyboard with virtuoso intensity. With the command patterns now encoded, he went to the engage sequence, something he had to do with a special key made of orange-tinted titanium. But when he turned the key the red warning light went on, and they learned that the spreading Tarsalan virus had hamstrung the ignition cascade.

"The PCV's main computer was supposed to fire engines one, three, and four but instead asked me to fire two, four, and five," said Ian. "I'm going to have to bypass the computer and make myself the interface."

Ian took out tools and fiddled with the key box, and got to the guts of the thing. There were some sparks and smoke, and finally a smooth hum. The position of the sun shifted as they began heading homeward in a steadily collapsing orbit.

But the ignition sequence was just the start of their troubles.

Three days later, communications with AviOrbit Control became intermittent. They sat together by the console, and while Gerry saw that the bits of information were coming in—they could be seen in a representative sawtooth pattern on the Vox interpretive software screen—the virus jumbled those sound packets so that the vocal result was the equivalent of a spilled jigsaw puzzle. They glanced at each other. It sounded like a bunch of ducks settling down for the night. Ian went into the background language and made adjustments, typing furiously, and they finally got Ira.

"What the hell is happening?" asked the AviOrbit boss.

"We're having further degradation," said Ian. "Maintain an open channel at all times."

Navigation blinked out for up to thirty minutes at a time and then would come back on, and Ian would scramble to recalibrate their fall sunward. Four days in, they sat by the navigational unit and Ian had his wristwatch up close to his eyes. They were both sweating because life support was making the temperature warm. Ian's face had gone red in the heat, and a small droplet of perspiration hung from the point of his nose.

"I hope my watch is right," he said, and fired another braking burn, having to use his own wristwatch for the timing because the navigational counter was currently off-line due to the virus.

The solar-activity warning system failed, and they were forced to use one of the backup radiation monitors to alert them to any possible anomalous radiation from the sun. Gerry climbed into the helm area to hold the wand in the air, and the little speaker crackled and the needle jumped into the red. They were forced into the radiation bunker for the next eighteen hours, having to strip down to their thermals, as the magnetized protection of the bunker allowed no metal of any kind. It was like sitting in the scoop of a backhoe shovel, the ceiling sloped and cramped, and the only light coming from a nonmagnetic phosphorescent strip that put out such a pathetic number of weak green lumens that only the edge of Ian's face was outlined with an ill-defined edge of olive murk. They were like two men in a dark steam bath, only there wasn't any steam, just the steady hiss of the monitor telling them that solar activity raged outside. At last the radiation passed and they came back out to take their posts at the command console.

Because the five FMC Transit Collective drives were the most advanced AviOrbit had ever built, and were able to accelerate, in theory, indefinitely, the trip sunward was quick, and after six days Gerry and Ian were halfway back to Earth.

But in that six days, a lot happened.

At one point, their life support began to behave erratically. They both huddled around the monitors and watched the temperature plummet, the little blue bar sinking and sinking. Ian went into the background language and tried to write some corrective code, but even as Gerry watched, new Tarsalan-generated code appeared, as if antiphonally answering whatever Ian might try. So at last they got into their CAPS. Gerry cranked up the heat and heard the little crackling noises of the conduction coils, and merciful warmth caressed his shivering body. But eight hours later he watched the blue bar on the life-support readout rise, and he got so hot, and his ventilation was by this time so riddled with virus, that he took off his CAPS and pressed himself against the polycarbonate pressure windows to keep cool. Ian came up and joined him.

"Remember the time we went to Mexico? That heat wave they were having?"

But all Gerry could truly remember of the Mexico trip was the tremendous amount of tequila they had downed.

The cabin pressure became too high, and his eardrums ached. The alarm dinged and told them that hull tolerances had climbed into the yellow, so they had to vent atmosphere in order to bring the pressure back down. Out the freighter windows Gerry saw a cold, blue cloud of the stuff drift away over the surface of Gaspra, like a tenuous and ill-defined band of ghosts, the color reminding him of the color of the blue marlins his brother caught at Trunk Bay.

Then, as they were nearing Mars, the virus locked the venting system into the open position and the air became so thin that it reminded him of the time he and Neil had climbed Mount Baker, back in the days when they actually still did things together. Ian sat at the console, his fingers clicking over the keys, and his blue eyes were a picture of concentration, predatory and birdlike as he finally managed to reroute air away from the vent manifold and into auxiliary tanks. By this time pressure was so thin that Gerry felt dizzy, and he was wondering if he might be suffering from altitude sickness. They broke out the emergency breathers—they wanted to conserve their CAPS for whatever emergencies might lie ahead. Once he had his breather strapped to his face, he didn't feel so light-headed anymore.

They again stopped at Mars, establishing a braking orbit around Earth's red neighbor, and approached the FMC's Phobos-Deimos Terminal, an immense structure fabricated out of the planet's two moonlets, the planetesimals joined by hundreds of luminous skywalks. PDT Control okayed them for rendezvous, stipulating a ten-kilometer limit, and Ian parked the craft in a tandem orbit behind Deimos. The two men got out and were ferried by taxi to a hotel on Deimos for the night. Meanwhile, the Federated Martian Colonies refurbished their ship with the necessary life support to get them the rest of the way to Earth.

Their room, in a hotel that resembled a stack of bubbles, much like the bubble nests Siamese fighting fish manufactured to breed, was made of a one-way material. Outside, looking in, Gerry saw an opaque blue sheen similar in color to a sapphire. But once he was inside looking out, he got a spectacular view of the Martian surface ten thousand miles below. (Phobos had been moved into a considerably higher orbit while Deimos had been maneuvered into a much lower one for the construction of the PDT.) Gerry beheld the red planet with a mix of awe and reverence. Its red, orange, and ochre shades reminded him of the flowerpots Glenda had in their backyard at home. And even though it was a dead world, it was at least a self-supporting world—if worse came to worst, they would always have Mars. He saw the volcanoes of the Tharsis Bulge. He saw Valles Marineris, and the whitish straining of the polar ice cap as it tried to finger its way south. A world without a phytosphere. As beautiful in its way as Earth. He couldn't help thinking of Luke Langstrom. Somewhere down there, Dr. Langstrom had his home. Spacecraft occasionally flew by. It was like a scene out of a futuristic dream, and he was thankful, because ordinarily he never would have gotten to see something like this.

It was while they were in their hotel room that Ian again broached the subject of trying to meet someone when he got back to the Moon—as if the future were a certainty, and the precariousness of their situation meant nothing to him.

"I was kind of hoping for Stephanie," he said. So. Stephanie, after all. "That is, if you don't mind me moving in on her."

"Why would I mind?"

Ian stared at the terra-cotta palette that was the Martian surface below. "Because, you know . . . you and her—"

"There's absolutely nothing between us, Ian."

"I was actually going out with her for a while."

The strain he heard in his friend's voice unnerved Gerry. "I kind of figured."

"But when you came along . . . well . . . you know . . . I stepped aside." And there was an admission in this, as if Ian understood that he must step aside, that his behavior, abominable for so many years by his own reckoning, disqualified his tenuous hopes for Stephanie's affections.

"Stepped aside? For what?"

"I didn't want to get in your way. Or in hers." He reached up and scratched the back of his head. Outside, a ground-to-orbit launch vehicle, filled with people looking out windows, eased by. "It was just like the Maggie Madsen thing all over again."

"Ian, I thought we weren't going to talk about Maggie."

"Anybody can see Stephanie's crazy about you, just like Maggie was. Matter of fact . . . Steph was the one who broke up with me . . . once she met you, that is. That's one thing I admire about her. She wasn't going to two-time me."

The sophomoric details of this astounded Gerry. "Ian, I had no idea." Five miles away, across the delicate network of transparent skywalk tubes, he saw Phobos. "She didn't mention anything to me." Phobos looked like an olive with the pimento missing—the Stickney Crater.

"She didn't?" He seemed to regard this as another

indication of his own spectacularly failed personal life. "No, I guess she wouldn't."

"You should have said something."

"I kind of mentioned it. In a backhanded way. That night I came to your room and broke the mirror. How you would never steal a girlfriend out from under me again? The whole Maggie Madsen thing?"

"That's what that was about?"

"In a way . . . but . . . that night. I want you to forget about that night. I was going through a lot that night."

Gerry frowned. "I had no idea you were talking about Stephanie."

"I didn't want you to . . . you know . . . get distracted from your work. Or feel uncomfortable."

"Ian, you know me better than that. And I could never go with Stephanie. I love my wife. She's the single most important thing in my life. I made that a hundred percent clear to Stephanie. She knows there can never be anything between us."

"So you don't mind if I move in on her, then?"

His friend seemed to be missing the point, so he let it go. "No . . . I don't mind." He lifted a citrangequat, a hybrid citrus fruit that for one reason or another had become extremely popular among Martian hydroponics growers, and began peeling the skin from the pear-shaped trifoliate, the peel coming off in blaze orange fragments that seemed to highlight the color of the planet below. "And I wish you'd forget about Maggie."

"With Maggie, it was a crush. With Steph . . . it's more." Ian looked up from his contemplation of the warrior planet and turned to Gerry, a wistfulness creeping into his blue eyes. "I was hoping that when we get back . . . you know . . . you can build me up a bit. Tell her what a hero I've been." He gestured in the general direction of Gaspra. "Because I'm having to drive that asteroid all by myself and it ain't like drivin' a bus. This is real test-pilot stuff. You make her understand that I'm worthy of her, and that I've been working real hard on being worthy, and that I don't mean to screw up on her or anybody else ever again."

Gerry recognized only too well what his friend was going through. This was alcoholic's remorse again, like on the night he broke the mirror. He gazed at Ian in a new light, and realized that Ian was no longer the god of good times but a man, like so many others, who had been transformed by a woman. Ian didn't even know if Stephanie loved him. Didn't even know if she would have him when he got back. Yet there was a new purity to the man.

"I'll make her understand, Ian."

38

Glenda wasn't a doctor, but she'd seen and learned enough working at the nursing home to understand that Neil's back wound was bad. Fernandes stood next to her holding a flashlight. She took a huge wad of dressing and pressed hard against the injury. She looked up at Fernandes and saw that his face was flecked with tiny spots of blood, maybe Ashley's. Neil moaned in pain.

"Some morphine?" asked Fernandes.

"Yes."

Fernandes went over to the kit and brought the unit back. He seemed to know how to use it well, because he jabbed it right into Neil, no hesitation, and a moment later Neil quieted down.

He weakened through the night, and even though they had a stockpile of dressings in the cave, Glenda went through them quickly, trying to stanch the flow of blood. Fernandes tried to comfort the girls as best he could, but he was awkward in this task and finally went to join Jake a little farther down the hill to keep an eye out for possible attacking Tarsalans.

By morning—if in fact it was morning—Neil's breathing grew labored, and his face was so pale that Glenda was sure they were going to lose him. Yet he hung on, hour after hour, and was even able to eat some military rations. At one point, she sent all four kids out to the ledge along with Fernandes to keep a lookout for Tarsalans, even though for the last several hours—ever since the destruction of Marblehill—the aliens had been eerily inactive.

That's when Neil started talking.

"In our will . . . Louise's sister, Joanne, and her husband, Lorne . . . are designated as legal guardians for the kids . . . should Louise and I die before they reach the age of majority, et cetera, et cetera. Grab Lenny's topographical map for scrap paper. Let's write a . . . a codicil to change that."

"Neil, you shouldn't even think of that now. You should try to rest."

"No, no. We've got to do this, Glenda. Joanne and Lorne . . . who knows if they're okay. I'm sure all of Atlanta has burned to the ground by this time. We've got to make it so . . . you know . . . you have the necessary resources to . . . raise Melissa and Morgan, and send them to college . . . and all the things . . . that the girls are going to need. And to bury Ashley . . . properly."

"Fernandes is talking of burying her up here . . . close by."

He turned from her and stared at the cave ceiling. His eyes closed partially and he exhaled, and finally nodded. "I think she'd like that. When I die, bury me next to her. I don't want her to be alone."

Glenda wanted to tell him that he wasn't going to die and that there was no need for him to think about his burial at this time, but she had extreme doubts that he would in fact pull through because he looked awful, white and clammy and ready to give up at any moment.

"Why don't you have some more water?" she suggested.

"I've got pens in that case."

"And how's your pain? Do you need more morphine?"

"I'd sooner stay clearheaded for this."

She saw he wasn't going to take no for an answer, so she got the topographical map, and a pen from the case. Neil dictated and she wrote the codicil in the light of a flashlight, and she couldn't help taking heart because he appointed not only herself but also Gerry, as if he firmly believed that Gerry was going to return and that Gerry's mission to destroy the phytosphere would succeed.

Ten hours later, when it was only Jake and Melissa standing guard on the ledge, and Fernandes, Hanna, and Morgan were trying to make themselves comfortable on coarse military-issue mats, Glenda heard a strange hissing sound up toward the cave ceiling. She shone the flashlight at the ceiling but all she saw was the rough limestone.

She shook Neil by the shoulder. "Neil. Wake up."

Neil groaned and opened his eyes.

"Listen," she said.

Neil's eyes grew more focused, and he finally lifted his head off the mat. "Get the spray. They've sent in some macrogens."

She quickly got an aerosol can and sprayed the air. Fernandes roused himself and helped her with a second can. The spray particles immediately tagged the macrogens, and they glowed with a dull green phosphorescence, fifty of them, flying all over the cave, several of them going into the second cavern, where the foodstuffs and medical supplies were.

The tagged macrogens eventually fell to the floor, like insects overcome by insect killer, but she was sure some must have already transferred their data to Tarsalan survivors in Chattahoochee.

She and Fernandes crushed the felled macrogens underfoot, like they were so many dead locusts. They then picked them up and threw them off the cliff overlooking the dry forest. They did all this, but she knew it wouldn't matter. From that point on, she understood a fresh Tarsalan attack was imminent. The aliens had to know she had food in the cave. And they were starving. It was the same story all over the world—everybody fighting over food, simply so they could live another day.

Neil settled and she sat up next to him. Fernandes, unable to sleep, joined her. He talked about his wife.

"Her name is Celia. She's in Denver. I haven't heard

from her since this whole thing began. But I got this strong feeling that I'm going to see her again. She's smart. Like you. She'll know how to survive through this. We always meant to start a family."

After that, they both slept for a while.

When they got up, they decided to bury Ashley. They got some shovels, went up the hill, and dug a pit through the soft forest mulch. They laid the girl inside. Jake stood next to them holding a flashlight, his Montclair slung around his shoulder. Once Ashley was settled in her grave, Fernandes went to get the others. He came back. Neil limped along, supported on one side by Fernandes, and on the other by Melissa. At the graveside, Neil managed to say a few words. Recounted Ashley's short life. Her interest in riding, tennis, and reading. How, though she didn't say much, everyone could tell that she thought a lot, that she was extremely aware of the world around her, and that she loved life. "She was too young," said Neil. "But at least she's gone to join her mother now."

The girls gathered some chunks of limestone and made a marker for her.

As they finally pushed the forest soil over the dead girl, Glenda couldn't help wondering how many similar scenarios were playing themselves out all over the world.

In the meantime, she was worried that the Tarsalans had spied on them with their little flying bugs.

Her suspicions about an imminent attack were confirmed when, over the next several days, she and Fernandes counted a combined total of seventy-three new Tarsalan ships landing in the vicinity. After two days of continuous sightings, the landings tapered off and the dead forest grew still. Glenda knew that it had to be the proverbial calm before the storm.

On the evening of that fifth day, she sat on the ledge overlooking the forest, cross-legged, bony knees slightly up, her Montclair resting on her lap, and her night-vision goggles flipped down over her eyes. Fernandes was somewhere off down the main road running reconnaissance. The forest was a collage of green trunks and branches. She saw no movement. But somewhere out there she realized there had to be hundreds, possibly thousands, of desperate Tarsalans who knew about her food. She hoped Fernandes would come back with exact numbers.

She flipped her night goggles up and looked at the sky. Why didn't Gerry hurry up? If the phytosphere were suddenly and miraculously destroyed, and the sun shone again, wouldn't that give everybody, including the Tarsalans, hope? Wouldn't there be born in the breasts of humans and aliens alike a new spirit of cooperation? She wasn't more than moderately religious, but she couldn't help thinking of the old Biblical phrase in Genesis: "Let there be light."

She repeated this phrase to herself, off and on, for the next half hour, chanting it like a mantra, but it did absolutely no good as the sky remained locked in darkness. She had to be frank with herself. Louise and Ashley were dead. Neil was going that way. Of the airmen, only Fernandes remained. Marblehill was destroyed. The world was forever enshrouded in darkness. And now she had to defend this cave against hundreds of alien invaders from a star forty light-years away. Worst of all, she had to do it with an army of kids.

A couple of days later, while she was sitting in the exact same spot overlooking the forest, waiting for the Tarsalan attack to come, Morgan came out of the cave and said, with zero inflection, "Dad's dead."

In another time, Glenda might have jumped up and raced into the cave. In another time, she might have said, "What? Are you sure? This can't be." But all she did was sit, her shoulders sinking, trying to pick out the features of Morgan's face, struggling to understand how this solemn and strange third child, who always went her own way on everything, must be feeling, now that she was an orphan.

Subdued at first, Morgan cried a short while later. So did Melissa.

Glenda and Fernandes gripped Neil by the shoulders, and Hanna and Jake each grabbed a leg—they couldn't have the remaining Thorndike sisters doing this—and they carried him outside, up the hill where the trail curved past three yew trees, venerable evergreen giants she remembered and identified from happier times. They took him to the same spot where Ashley had been buried. Jake and Fernandes hollowed out a shallow grave through all the dead leaves, having to cleave through some roots with the ends of their shovels. And as Jake and the airman dug, Glenda wondered about the nature of luck. As she had once told Gerry, Neil, a spectacularly successful academician, an investor of consummate skill, a presidential advisor, the man appointed to save the world, had been born with a golden horseshoe up his butt. But now it was up to Gerry—a reformed alcoholic who never had any luck, and who had faced setback after setback in both his professional and financial lives—to get them out of this mess. She decided Neil had to be overdrawn at the bank of good luck. The gods of misfortune had cashed in big-time.

They buried Neil. Morgan, Melissa, and Hanna gathered some limestone from the surrounding area and made a crude marker similar to Ashley's: just a pile of stones—hardly worthy of this great Nobel prize winner, with his five homes, eighteen cars, and magazine-perfect family.

Glenda said a few words. She didn't know much of the Bible, especially as it pertained to death, but she parroted the most obvious phrase that everyone knew: "Ashes to ashes, and dust to dust." And thought she'd better improvise something more so the girls wouldn't feel shortchanged. "May the Good Lord take our brother Neil into His arms." What else, what else? There had to be something solemnly appropriate she could say about Neil. "He was a loving father, and a good husband . . . and he was kind to me when I needed help . . . and I could always talk to him . . ."

She had such mixed feelings about Neil. On the one hand, she couldn't understand why Neil deserved to be so lucky, and got all the plum appointments, and was able to make such a killing on the stock market. Envy was a sin, she knew that, but it didn't seem fair that Gerry, who was really an extremely smart man, should have to suffer through a lackluster academic career, chronic financial embarrassment, and a serious bout of alcoholism that had nearly killed him.

So how to wrap it up? Melissa and Morgan wept. Hanna, emotional in any situation, had tears running down her cheeks. Jake was like a stone. Fernandes kept staring into the forest, on guard as always. Glenda looked at the grave. In this final hour, in this desperate last chapter, when Neil had been handed his greatest challenge and the stakes had never been higher, the gods of misfortune had indeed cashed in. And Neil's luck had finally run out. Her eyes moistened.

"May God bless him," she intoned, and then said what she really wanted to say. "He was like the rest of us after all."

A hot west wind rustled through the forest a day later, bringing with it the scent of a dead, dry land. The temperature had to be over a hundred. The sky was darker than ever. And the air seemed thin.

Glenda sat on the ledge overlooking the forest. The wind was so strong it kept blowing her hair in front of her face. Hanna and Morgan slept inside. Melissa and Jake were in position up and down the path. Fernandes was somewhere out in the forest doing reconnaisance again. Jake came running up the hill, breathless, skinny, and as pale from lack of sunlight as a fresh mushroom. She thought he was coming to tell her that Fernandes was returning. But it wasn't that at all.

"Three Tarsalans are coming up the path. They've got strange lights over their heads. They're unarmed."

Thirty seconds later, she saw the glow from down the hill.

Three Tarsalans, one in a jumpsuit made of papery material, another in something that looked as if it were stitched from orange and brown silk, and a third who wore blue jeans with the legs cut short to fit his short limbs, came up toward the cave. An egg-shaped beacon of light shone over each one, hovering in the air above them like halos.

As they got closer, the one in the middle shone an Earth-made flashlight up the path. Glenda immediately lifted her Montclair and pointed it at the Tarsalans. Hard getting used to them, the way they looked. In God's image, so to speak, as if human anatomical configuration was the evolutionary ideal for sentient beings throughout this sector of the galaxy, but with huge, bicephalic heads—big bulbs right and left on top of their craniums, each covered with shaggy black hair, so that, not for the first time, she was reminded of ostrich feathers. And the eyes. So large now, the special genetic part of their makeup actually changing the shape of them so they could see better in the dark—like loris eyes. Hard also getting used to the pale blue skin, a result, Neil had once told her, of a cyanogenic component in their blood.

The middle one had a headset and mike over his ears and mouth, one of those translating things. A small speaker-receiver apparatus hung around his neck, so small that it was like a piece of faucet mesh.

The Tarsalan spoke and the translation thing translated. "Please, my child, put your weapon down. We mean no harm. We've come to"—and here the translation device took a few seconds—"palaver, or at least to offer you an ultimatum."

Her face settled. She kept her Montclair trained on the middle one. So, an ultimatum. Just like the phytosphere.

The middle one was obviously the oldest, with thick crow's-feet around his eyes, a bushy black brow, and a steadiness about him that the other two didn't possess. The three kept coming, but they advanced slowly and it was hard to read their expressions. As they got closer, their approach became downright cautious, and she could tell they were frightened, wary of her the same way they might be of a wild animal.

"We don't accept ultimatums," she said, feeling as if she were speaking for the whole human race. "Haven't you learned that yet?"

She heard the faint sound of the Tarsalan language bubbling through the translation device, and it sounded not unlike a human language because the Tarsalan mouth, glottis, and pharynx, though producing a timbre a lot different than the human voice, were fundamentally based on the same design.

"Then let us palaver," came the response at last.

"You back off. You withdraw. And I might let you live."

She couldn't stop her anger. Louise dead. Ashley and Neil dead. And her children and remaining nieces threatened. The Tarsalans obviously had no idea what a human mother was capable of. Even as she spoke, a plan formulated itself in her mind. If they wanted Armageddon, they would get Armageddon.

"Human, you underestimate the forces ranged against you. We are over a thousand strong. And we are hungry. We demand that you give over your food and fresh water. We'll leave you with a day's supply of each. With this food of yours, we can feed our survivors in the command area for a week. Our metabolism utilizes food resources much more efficiently than the human metabolism. The human metabolism is a wasteful thing."

She was galled by the alien's hubris. "And this is a reason I should give you all our food?"

"In an absolute moral sense, yes, it is. It's better that you keep more individuals alive longer than a few individuals alive for a shorter period of time."

"And you're the experts on absolute moral sense?"

"When creatures such as yourselves fail to see reason—and we will admit that we ourselves failed to see just how vastly reasonless your psychology is—it is incumbent upon us, as the more advanced society, to try to teach you what is just and right."

"So murder is just and right. You see these girls here? They're orphans. And they're orphans because of you."

"That was a choice you made for yourself. Human, I give you this opportunity to save yourself. We are by nature negotiators. We have proven this to you over the last nine years. We are not fighters."

"No. You simply put us all in a big plankton bag and watch us fight each other."

"It is you who choose to fight. Cooperation would have gotten you much further. Cooperation is the model for all other civilized worlds, and a model we mistakenly assumed for you. Yet you are creatures of choice, just as all creatures are. Don't blame others for the choices you have made."

"You're trespassing on the property of Dr. Neil Thorndike. Does that name mean anything to you?"

A pause as the translator did its thing, and then, "Yes."

"Dr. Thorndike has died, and all his property has passed to me."

It took the Tarsalan a moment, but finally, through his translation thing, he said, "Ah, yes . . . his last will and testament. We don't have such customs where I come from."

"Do you understand what trespass means?"

"The human sense of it is slightly different than the Tarsalan one. And there is no concept or word for *property* in any of our languages." The word *property* popped out in English. "Or in our various cultures. But it is a concept that is obviously deeply ingrained on Earth."

"Then let me give you some advice . . . *Tarsalan.*" She hit the word hard. "Get off my property before I kill you."

She lifted the Montclair and pointed it straight at him. He shifted, took a step backward, and his pupils shrank to such a small size that she could hardly see them.

"My child, shoot me if you wish . . . but you have already signed your own death writ. We outnumber you more than a hundred to one. What can you possibly do to stop us?"

And Glenda realized that, yes, they weren't really so smart after all.

She watched them go. She felt sorry for them. The Cameron Chess Study was one thing, and Tarsalans might win against humans again and again in a situation where all the moves were circumscribed by game rules—

indeed, all the negotiations with the Tarsalans had possessed a gamelike quality, and she remembered how all of Kafis's actions seemed to be predicated on a kind of rarefied and arcane games theory—but there were no rules when it came to war, especially human war. There was only brutality.

She waited for Fernandes to get back, then told him her plan. "Let's get the kerosene. Jake, help us."

They went into the cave's second chamber and retrieved five big cans of kerosene, a primitive fuel that Lenny had had the foresight to stash away "For when our batteries fail." The wind was strong, though it changed direction often, and would act like a bellows. The forest was tinder-dry and would go up like a torch. Eight hundred and seventy thousand acres, all of it dead, providing the necessary combustibles to make her own firestorm.

They poured the fuel in great ribbons of vaporous liquid, venturing into the forest, down the hill, up the hill, until they had dumped every last ounce of kerosene into the brush. Then Glenda got the box of safety matches, scratched one along the side, and, keeping it shielded from the wind with her hand, lit the nearest bush. The flames ignited with a voracious ripple, and spread so fast she hardly had time to leap back.

Ten seconds, twenty seconds, thirty seconds, and the size of the conflagration grew alarmingly. Tongues of flame leaped yards into the air; she took glory in how bright everything was. She could *see*! The glow of the fire bathed her eyes with soul-refreshing illumination. All four kids looked on in fascination. She knew that somewhere out there in the dead forest the Tarsalans looked on as well. She thought they were feeling dread in their hearts, and that they were oozing the thick, musty odor they oozed whenever they were terrified.

The heat of the fire became too much for Glenda, Fernandes, and the kids, and they retreated into the cave, where it was cool and damp, and where a faint wind blew up from the bowels of the Earth, forcing smoke away from the cave entrance.

There they stayed as the firestorm raged around them. Glenda wasn't without guile when it came to the Tarsalans. Maybe they had an ingenious way of putting out the fire. Maybe they would just get in their TLVs and take off. Some ash drifted in through the cave entrance and landed on her foot. Then again, maybe, as with the attack on the mothership, and ultimately on the phytosphere control device itself, they would be caught unawares. They would see this fire, and they would get another lesson in how humans behaved, especially when they had nothing left to lose.

39

The following day Gerry and Ian eased away from the Phobos-Deimos Terminal, and Ian established a transit orbit toward Earth. He engaged thrusters three and one. The singularity drives showed no malfunction and Ian risked full power.

Four days later, the Earth-Moon system hove into view over the craggy nose of Gaspra. The phytosphere was a festering green cancer around Gerry's home planet, thicker than he had ever seen it, and he momentarily wondered if it would be enough—the shift of the Moon two thousand miles closer to Earth—but then decided it would, knew that he couldn't have been wrong in his calculations.

For a brief while, as they got closer, an automated Tarsalan probe, egg-shaped like most of the alien craft and wrapped in its own shimmering plasma of blue, violet, and pink light, orbited the asteroid, but the PCV's scans told them it was unweaponized, unmanned, and posed no threat.

"I'm sure they've exhausted all their military capability by this time," said Ian. "Looks like we're home free, buddy."

All that needed to be done now was fire Drive Five. This would initiate the slight change of angle needed for the final impact, and bring Gaspra crashing into the lunar surface.

But when Ian tried the modified key box, it was as if the alien virus had at last worked through to his initial fix and he got no response from thrust conduit number five. In other words, the drive that had given them their initial trouble previous to mission countdown was again flickering into the red. Ian maneuvered from his seat over to the navigation console and his fingers clicked over the keys, but he couldn't regain command of the conduit, nor secure access through some creative rerouting.

He worked frantically on the problem for the next five minutes. Gerry glanced nervously out the big freighter windows and saw the Earth, like a rotting wedge of lime, and the Moon, craters now fully visible.

"So there's no way to fix the problem?" asked Gerry, because in these most harrowing moments he had no choice but to defer to Ian.

Ian now had full schematics on screen four. The left side of the screen showed diagrams, while text filled the right side—script so tiny Ian had to tap his contact lenses to their strongest setting.

Ian didn't so much read as skim. He ignored Gerry as he went through the thick, turgid prose of the drive specs, the sweat beading on his shaved head and a thick vein sticking out like a blue worm over his temple. All the while their speed increased.

"I know these specs like the back of my own hand," he said. "But you never know. Maybe if I review it, something could jog and I might . . ."

Gerry felt helpless, frustrated, and so anxious to solve the problem that he kept fidgeting in his seat. "Couldn't we go to the drive itself and do something to fix it?"

Ian froze. He stopped flicking through the script and turned to Gerry. He looked like a man on a spirit quest who had just experienced the revelation he had been looking for, his blue eyes wide, his lower lip coming out, his ears shifting a fraction on the sides of his head. Gerry thought he had only pointed out the obvious, but Ian looked at him as if he were Moses coming down from the mount.

"You're a genius, Gerry." Then he swung to the timer up on the console. "We've got to move. We've got only a certain envelope to do this and, after that, it's a no go for good."

"What are you going to do?"

"I'm going to blow Drive Five sky-high. I don't know why I didn't think of it before. Am I ever glad you're on this mission. The resulting explosion will give us the necessary thrust to angle us into a collision trajectory. As I say, I know the specs inside out and I think this can work. Especially because all we have to do is collide with your so-called wide region of effectiveness."

"You're going to blow up the drive?"

"Yes."

"How are you going to do that?"

"I'm going to sled to the drive, crawl into its access bay, and manually cross the male and female thrust conduits so they reverse on each other and blow the singularity to pieces." He motioned at the screen of schematics. "I can't believe I was looking at a technical solution when all I really needed was the PCV's fire ax. You're brilliant, Gerry."

"But . . . you're going to blow up the drive?"

"Right."

"And then what?"

Ian frowned. "I already told you. The blast should give us the necessary thrust to make it all happen."

"And then you're going to come back here to the *Prometheus,* and we're going to escape in the survival pod?"

Ian's brow settled. "Maybe you're not so smart after all."

The two stared at each other. It was a pivotal moment for Gerry, because he suddenly understood that Ian was a hero after all.

"Ian . . . no."

Ian's face creased and he now looked irritated. "It's the only way, buddy. You'll have the pod all to yourself. There's no sense in two of us going down for this thing. Now, come on, we've got to *move*. If I leave right now it's going to take me at least twenty minutes to get there. That's going to give me only three minutes to reverse the thrust conduits. This is the only chance we have. If this doesn't work, the Earth dies. Glenda dies. Jake and Hanna die. I got no one. You got your family. This is my moment, Ger, and I mean to go for it. This is the only way I can make up for all the dismal things I've done to other people over the years."

"What about Stephanie?"

"Just tell her what I did. And that I love her, even though she might not love me."

"It's not the only way, Ian."

"God damn it, Gerry. I take back what I said about you being a genius. You're an idiot."

"Yes . . . but you're going to die."

"And so's everybody else if I don't do something to stop it. Listen to me, buddy. I'm fifty next month. That's long enough. I've done some interesting things in my life. But this is where I can really contribute. When this is all done, they're going to need you back on Earth. 'Cause there's going to be a lot of problems, and they're going to need people like you to solve them. There won't be any need for reformed-alcoholic test pilots. Now, come on. Help me. Before we lose our chance."

Gerry forced himself to shut down his emotions.

But as they went into the surface access bay and he helped Ian into his CAPS, he couldn't help thinking that he was aiding and assisting in suicide. Plus he thought of all the good times he had spent with Ian: the time they had gone to Japan together and made a pilgrimage to Hiroshima on the two hundredth anniversary of the atomic bomb; how they had nearly gotten swamped in a hurricane after stealing a boat from the marina near Neil's place on Trunk Bay; and how, miraculously, they had finally met up at the Buena Vista Hotel and Gambling Casino on the Moon. Now they were here together, old friends, true friends, two men trying to save the world, knowing the stakes couldn't be higher and that time was running out. What did you say to each other at a moment like that?

"I'll make sure Steph knows what you did," he said as Ian finally mounted the sled.

Ian's lips tightened, and he nodded. "Just tell her how I feel. I want her to know." Then he checked over the sled's console, made sure the fire ax was secure in one of the straps, and turned back to Gerry. "You're clear on the precise point you have to eject?"

"The angle-of-entry change."

"When precisely? You have to remember the survival pod's orbital limitations."

"When the asteroid's angle of entry has reached thirty-seven degrees."

"That should put you ten kilometers outside of Nectaris. The blast event is going to knock out all radios for a while, and control has everybody hunkered down for the strike anyway, so—"

"I know. I have to walk."

"You've got ample life support, so it shouldn't be a problem."

They said a rough good-bye, gave each other a hug; then Ian went into the air lock.

The air lock opened ten seconds later, and Ian was on his way—on the last journey he would ever make.

As the air lock finally hissed shut and Gerry was left standing there by himself, he felt the sudden change, the quietness that comes with solitude; but also the shedding of the particular persona he used whenever he was around Ian, as if Ian was someone he not only embraced but also a man he had to guard against, a reminder of his own alter ego. He turned from the sled access bay and yanked himself along by the handholds, essentially in free fall except for the weak pull of Gaspra that settled him groundward with the slowness of a dust speck. He went to his bunkette and packed a few personal items: his A.A. two-year medallion, photographs of his wife and children, and a bag of rocks from Gaspra. He then suited up in his CAPS.

He got a red light on his fresh-water valve, which meant he was going to be awfully thirsty by the time he got to Nectaris, but he knew he would survive.

He took one last glance out the big freighter windows, looked around the operations area, and had the same feeling a castaway might have when leaving his island; that here, in this setting, momentous events had unfolded, and that the place had made an indelible impression. He turned away and stepped into the void of the companionway hatch. He sank—with the slowness of a dust speck—down to the engineering level. He pulled himself to the back, where the corridors bifurcated and continued in a large circle. He took Corridor A until it joined with Corridor B, way at the back of the PCV. From here it was into the survival pod launch unit, an area much like a missile bay on a nuclear sub, housing two projectiles, the primary and the backup, like huge bullets standing next to each other.

He checked over the system of the first and got three red lights. On the backup pod, he got only one red light, life support, but as his CAPS was capable of life support, this wasn't an endgame obstacle. He pressed the latch buttons and the gull-wing hatch lifted. He moved with an air of unreality, and with a distant sadness clutching at his throat. He slotted himself into the middle launch bed, while those on either side remained empty.

He had a moment of doubt. Would Ian screw up, as he had so often in the past? He touched the necessary spots on the screen in front of him, the gull-wing hatch sank, and the launch bed braces closed over him. He remembered the time Ian had totaled his car, and how he and Glenda had then had to buy a much crappier one, the relic they were driving now. Would Ian, in the final desperate seconds, lose his judgment, as he had lost it so often in the past? Or would he simply chicken out?

He radioed control. "Ira, I'm ready to eject." Then he let control know what Ian was doing. Ira ranted because Ira was the orchestra conductor, and someone had played a wrong note, but Gerry didn't want to listen to it, so he switched communications off. The silence was sublime. It memorialized Ian's approaching death. He brought his gloved hand up to the screen. With a few flicks of his finger he had his telemetry readouts. The timer now told him Ian had only three minutes to make a course correction.

All Gerry could now do was watch the timer roll down, the digital numbers, counting back in bright amber. When the timer reached the two-minute mark, the numbers turned red. Red, the color of the eleventh hour—this whimsical thought passed through his mind, even as his body tightened, went cold, and nausea knocked at the back of his throat. A big loser: these words from Glenda, describing Ian, when she had reached her wits' end about his drinking. And yes, there was something of the loser in Ian. A man with a lot of bravado, confidence, and damn-the-torpedoes attitude, but one who had a history of choking at the last second. The time was now down to a minute and twenty-five seconds. A man who ultimately scored the touchdown, but missed the field goal. The numbers rolled relentlessly by and Gerry had the sense that he was in numerical free fall. Also a man who was desperate to make amends. Maybe the pressure of his own remorse would be too much for Ian.

"Think of Stephanie, Ian."

And in that moment, he knew that's exactly what Ian was doing. The digits seemed to slow their free fall, as if they had the presentiment of great change and, as the counter timed down to twenty-two seconds, the PCV began to shake as if in an earthquake, sudden g-force pushed him flat into his launch bed, and his stomach got the same feeling it got whenever he was going down in a fast elevator. He checked his screen and saw that the diagrammatic representation of the Moon, the Earth, and the asteroid had shifted, and that Gaspra was now establishing a tight and degrading orbit around the Moon. He watched the angle-of-entry numbers tip toward the region of effectiveness. On the screen, Gaspra looked like a big bee getting ready to sting the Moon, and was approaching its surface at an ever-accelerating rate. He felt a curious moment of elation, because this really looked as if it was going to work. Then again, if the Martians could shift moonlets around to form the PDT, why couldn't he shift the Moon to save the Earth? What was so difficult about it? It was nothing but operating heavy equipment on a gargantuan scale.

The angle of entry eased toward the target zone. Yet the vindication he felt for finally struggling out of his underdog position and coming up with a procedure that looked as if it was going to do the trick was tempered by a knowledge of just how close they had come. The rock screamed toward the Moon at a phenomenal rate of speed. Angle of entry reached deeper into the region of effectiveness, and within the next few seconds, at thirty-seven degrees, Gerry launched.

The survival pod shot upward through the tube and in seconds he was well above the PCV and watching it recede. Ten seconds after that it was like he was looking down at a mountain, because he saw the sloping curvature of the asteroid, and the curves looked like precipices. Then he got so far up that Gaspra became the big stone that it was, with all its tiny craters—a scarred old warrior that was about to be obliterated in its final battle.

The surface of the Moon was a blur of speed below, its craters shadowy blips. As his vehicle rose, the asteroid sank. His pod's movement soon carried him beyond the asteroid's path. He was on his stomach now, his head down as if he was going to dive to the Moon, and from this upside-down position he watched the asteroid get lower and lower, rolling end over end like a badly thrown football, until finally . . . it struck the Moon's surface.

By this time, his readouts told him he was nearly three hundred miles away, with the curve of the Moon fully visible, but it was as though the blast happened right next door. The asteroid threw up a small ring of debris, but the debris was moving quickly, and every piece of blasted particulate took on the same shape, an elongated, blurry lozenge. Outside this first small ring, a second ring developed. Then a third ring. Then a fourth. Each ring reached higher and higher into the dark vacuum above the Moon, until finally the rings were so gargantuan, tall, and violent that debris started flying around him and he grew concerned that he might be hit. Take a baseball, stick an upside-down thimble on its side, and that was the proportion of the blast size compared to the Moon. The ground surrounding the crater, covering an area of five hundred square miles, quivered like a bowl of Jell-O. He watched in horror and fascination.

He took a moment to think of his friend—but then had his own concerns to consider. The survival pod carried him up and over the rim of the Moon so that the asteroid strike disappeared behind him. His braking thrusters fired and the pod sank. The surface of the Moon came up fast. In minutes he no longer saw its curvature. Then it was as though he was looking out a jet window from thirty thousand feet. And in many ways it was like coming in for a landing in a jet, with the bleak, gray-brown landforms growing more and more distinct every minute.

When he was a thousand feet up, the pod arced into a vertical position and sank thruster-first toward the surface. As the pod reached the thirty-foot mark, and slowed its descent to two miles an hour, he got a red light on the landing gear—it wouldn't deploy. When the pod finally reached the surface, it fell over like a big tree.

Luck.

He and Glenda had talked about it often.

Usually, when a piece of bread and peanut butter fell to the floor, it always fell peanut butter side down. In fact, that was the story of his life.

But it seemed his luck had changed. With no radios working and everbody hunkered down, his death would have been certain if the pod had fallen on its hatch. The weight of the pod on top of it would have stopped it from opening and he would have been trapped until his life support ran out. But the pod had fallen hatch up. He keyed the necessary commands. The gull-wing unit lifted noiselessly.

And Gerry climbed out onto the surface of a Moon that was moving toward the Earth exactly according to his own equations.

40

Driven by strong winds, the fire raged all night. It first consumed the trees around the cave, then spread in all directions according to the wayward will of the fickle winds. Smoke came into the cave, finally forcing Glenda, Fernandes, and the kids into the second cavern. The fire's roar was like several trains rumbling by the foot of the hill. The oxygen got thin, as if the fire was consuming every last atom.

At times Glenda thought she heard screams outside. Once or twice she grew convinced she heard cries for help, as if the Tarsalans expected her to rescue them. Fat chance.

At last, the fire burned a safe distance from the cave. Glenda, Fernandes, and the children went out to have a look.

The world was ashy, and embers flew everywhere. The main body of the fire burned about a mile off, the flames sometimes leaping a hundred yards into the air.

"Cool," said Jake.

She glanced at her son. He was dirty from head to foot. He had Leigh's pistol stuffed in his pants and his Montclair slung over his shoulder, and even though he was only twelve, he now possessed a disconcerting maturity and a battle-hardened stare as sturdy as cement. Yet . . . yet he was still a kid . . . because this fire was *cool*.

Light. It flowed into her eyes with a calming influence. All of the dry underbrush and tree branches had gone up, but there were still a number of tall tree trunks, horribly charred by the fire, sticking out of the ground like black fenceposts, all of them now backlighted by the frenzied inferno a mile off. She looked for figures moving through this outpost of Hell, flipping down her night-vision goggles but, because of the heat, all she saw was a blinding wash of green.

So she went back into the cave, got the binoculars, and scanned the destroyed forest for miles around. She didn't see a soul—Tarsalan or human.

They all watched the fire burn for the next hour. No human first responders came to put it out, and no fire planes flew by to douse it with payloads of retardant. Chattahoochee, protected under law, just burned and burned.

She wondered how many Tarsalans had died.

After an hour, everyone got bored with watching the fire.

Fernandes went to poke around in the ashes, getting as close as he could to the main body of the fire. The girls went inside to sleep while Glenda and Jake stayed on the ledge to keep watch.

Four hours later, Morgan and Melissa came outside to stand guard. Glenda and Jake went inside. By this time, Fernandes had come back and was dozing in the corner.

Glenda fell asleep in minutes.

A couple of hours later she was awakened by a strange noise outside. She opened her eyes. She listened more closely. It sounded like hail. It thumped down all over the forest, and hissed in the embers.

"Aunt Glenda?" Melissa called from the cave entrance.

Glenda got up and went outside.

Thumb-sized chunks of hail fell from the sky, only this wasn't ordinary hail—this was green hail. It took her a moment to realize what was going on. Then she looked up at the sky. Jake and Fernandes came to the cave entrance. Excitement exploded through her body, but she suppressed it. Had Gerry done it? Had his crazy scheme to push the Moon closer to Earth with a big asteroid actually worked?

She walked out to the ledge and picked up a chunk of hail. By this time Hanna had appeared at the cave entrance as well. The hail melted in her hand, leaving behind a green residue, like cream of spinach soup.

Everybody started picking up their own chunks of hail. The sky was black as oil. But surely to God this had to mean something. How long would it take, she wondered? Would it all fall to Earth, or would some of it drift into space? And if it fell into their oceans, how would it affect things? Was it dead? Or was it still alive?

Over the next several hours the green hail fell with increasing rapidity, so fast that, despite the high temperature, there was some moderate accumulation.

When the sky finally brightened—as at last it did—the forest floor looked glazed in green Jell-O.

Morgan jumped up and down, clapping her hands together. "The stupid thing is gone, the stupid thing is gone," and she put the words to the tune of "The Farmer in the Dell," and soon Melissa and Hanna joined in, and even Jake at last got going on it, until they were all singing, "The stupid thing is gone, the stupid thing is gone, hi-ho the derry-o . . ." On and on, the way kids sang sometimes, just to hear their own voices. Fernandes, meanwhile, simply surveyed the surrounding devastation, as if he expected Tarsalans to emerge from the ashes at any second.

To Glenda, it was more than just the phytosphere falling to pieces. It was Gerry at last succeeding. After so many small and humiliating defeats throughout his life, he had achieved this biggest thing of all.

The hail continued for several hours, but finally tapered off around six o'clock. Clouds moved in under the thin green veil of the disintegrating phytosphere, but they were strange clouds because they were tinged with green.

After a while it started raining green rain. It pounded on the Chattahoochee Forest, and a green flood roared down the path and rushed past the cave. They had to rearrange sandbags to divert the flow from the cave. The sky darkened, and night—just a normal night, not a phytosphere night—came at last.

She tried calling Gerry on her fone, reasoning that if the phytosphere was falling she might get through. But there was no service, not even a message, as if all the people who operated AT&T Interlunar had indeed gone home to be with their families in this time of crisis.

She pulled out Neil's special phone, the one he used to communicate with various government officials, and tried to get through to an operator, any operator. This time she got something, but frustratingly, it was just a message telling her that service had been temporarily suspended during the current national emergency, and that only preauthorized numbers would be connected.

She looked for numbers in Neil's backpack because, yes, Gerry might have saved the world, but she was still stuck out here, amid the burned-down forest and possible Tarsalan hostiles. She had no car, and her ammunition was running low.

As much as she looked for preauthorized numbers in Neil's pack, she couldn't find any.

Dawn came, and it was an Earth dawn. The sky was blue, the sun yellow, and only stray wisps of phytosphere remained, like emerald floss way up high. The Chattahoochee was a wasteland of ash coated in green slime. In and amongst the black-sparred tree trunks, she saw nine burned-out Tarsalan Landing Vehicles, looking like tin cans that had been left in a bonfire all night. She saw no survivors.

She and Fernandes conferred for a while about what they should do and, when they were done, Glenda told the kids, "We'll stay here for a while and see if anybody rescues us. I'm going to keep trying the Moon. And I'll try Neil's phone as well. In the meantime, Fernandes thinks we should dig through the house to see if we can salvage anything."

After a breakfast of baked beans, Glenda, Fernandes, and the Thorndike kids marched down to the house. They had nothing but their hands to clear the rubble away with. The sun was bright, and it stung Glenda's eyes after so long in the dark, but she took great joy in it. The uneasiness of having something drastically wrong with the world eased from her soul, and the quality and quantity of the sunshine increased her hope tremendously. Hanna, still not in the best health, sat out much of the time, taking guard duty while the others did the heavy work.

They spent the rest of the day digging into the basement supply room, where they found many crated provisions intact, enough to last six months if they rationed stringently. This was a great relief to Glenda, as it bought her a measure of time she hadn't been counting on. They lugged the supplies up to the cave and packed them into the second chamber.

Now that all immediate danger had passed, her nieces again grew weepy at the loss of their parents and sister, and Glenda spent much of the afternoon comforting them.

Around five o'clock, the sun began its descent, and though she was made anxious by the approach of night, and was even illogically apprehensive that dawn might never come again, she still thought the sunset was the most beautiful thing she had ever seen. Despite her desolation over the deaths of Neil, Louise, and Ashley, she felt buoyed by it. Light. Was there anything so miraculous? In all its various permutations of color and shadow, was there anything so surprising, mood-altering, or restorative?

Morgan lay with her head on Glenda's lap, and Glenda stroked the child's brown hair. Jake ate like a pig in the corner, opening can after can of Irish stew— not rationing, as they had to celebrate their great find in the basement storeroom of Marblehill. Fernandes also ate. The sun would come up tomorrow, she decided. They would get through this. They would survive. Maybe they would survive in a vastly changed world, but they would go on. Gerry would come home. And her two children and two remaining nieces would live long, full lives. And Fernandes would go on as well. He would reconnect with his wife, Celia, in Denver. They would go on to have their family. She could sense this positive outcome in the light that was filtering down from the sky.

A placid and hopeful grin came to her face. She leaned over and kissed Morgan. She glanced at Melissa. She had two new daughters, and she would treat them like daughters, not nieces. She would have to do her best to be a mother to them.

Jake collected up his empty cans of Irish stew. "I'll throw these in the garbage." He went over and got Fernandes's cans as well.

"Come right back and get some sleep," said Glenda. "You're on at midnight tonight."

She watched him go. He now moved with a sureness of step that reminded her of a man's step. And though his clothes hung on him, she detected a new broadness to his shoulders. He ventured out into the maudlin tints of the sunset and turned left up the hill toward their midden. A breeze entered the cave and she smelled the charred scent of the forest. Her new sense of peace made her sleepy, and she closed her eyes. A comforting doze wrapped its fuzzy hand around her mind, and she nodded off with the rapidity of the truly exhausted. But not for long. Through the fog of her doze, she heard Jake cry out. Her eyes jolted open. His cry was oddly broken, coming in a series of yelps, breaking on the cusp of his changing voice, a cry not only of pain but also of annoyance. She sprang to her feet, at first thinking Buzz had miracuously returned from the dead. But as she hurried from the cave, with Melissa and Fernandes now behind her, she saw that her son had fallen from the cliff to a wide ledge below, and that the point of a broken sapling had skewered the extreme left portion of his abdomen underneath his rib cage.

Fernandes was quick with the orders. "Melissa, get the rope. Mrs. Thorndike, we need some pressure dressings, and some rubbing alcohol."

Melissa was off instantly to get the rope, but Glenda felt anesthetized. So far, she had dodged all bullets. But that was her son down there. And he had a sapling coming through his gut. And it wasn't Buzz or the aliens who had done it; it was just an accident, a stupid, stupid accident, one that could have been treated easily in a hospital. But they were out in the middle of nowhere. And who was coming to get them? Fernandes was already climbing down the rock face through the ash. Melissa came back, and she had the rope, the pressure dressings, and rubbing alcohol.

"Aunt Glenda?"

Glenda snapped out of it. "Let's get down there."

Aunt and niece picked their way down the cliff, coughing in the disturbed ash.

When Glenda got to her son, she saw that the wound was serious, bleeding badly, and that Jake was more or less stuck there because he was so thoroughly skewered. He was crying. He wasn't a man anymore. He was just a boy who had hurt himself.

Glenda tried to get her panic under control. "What happened?"

"I . . . I thought I saw a chipmunk." His voice was high, and his eyes were so wide with hurt amazement that they reminded her of Tarsalan eyes. "And then . . ." His emotion boiled over. "And then the edge of the cliff gave out and I fell." He cried again, gazing in horror at his wound, looking as if he wondered how something like this could happen to him. "And it didn't even turn out to be a chipmunk. It was just a rock."

Fernandes got down on one knee, took a wad of dressing from Melissa, and wiped some blood from around the wound. Glenda saw, to her relief, that the sapling, snapped perhaps by a falling tree, its point then tempered by the heat of the fire, had penetrated at the extreme left edge of her son's abdomen, just below the rib cage, not further in.

"Is it a flesh wound?" she asked Fernandes.

"I think so," said Fernandes. "We don't want any internal bleeding. Not out here." Fernandes looked at Jake and smiled reassuringly. "You're a lucky man, Jake. You've got a flesh wound—a serious one—but I think you're going to live. Another inch the wrong way, and it could have been much worse." Fernandes looked at Melissa. "All right . . . let's lift him off. Mrs. Thorndike, get ready with the pressure dressings."

Jake's wound, though, was a lot more serious than they first thought. Once they lifted him from the sapling and got him back to the cave, there seemed to be internal bleeding after all. They gave him morphine to control the pain. He weakened through the night, and no matter how many pressure dressings they put on the entrance and exit wounds, he still managed to soak them fairly quickly. Glenda desperately wanted to stabilize him, and couldn't believe that after everything they had gone through he would end up like this because of an accident, but he kept on deteriorating.

His condition worsened through the next day. Fernandes characterized the problem as a "slow leak somewhere," and was worried that if they couldn't stabilize him soon, they might run into "serious trouble."

Glenda was frantic to get proper medical attention, and called Gerry on the fone again and again—but the service remained down. She lifted Neil's special phone and punched in numbers randomly, but the phone kept flashing its message: *Preauthorized Numbers Only.* She finally gave up on the bulky government device.

Later, a ripe harvest Moon emerged from the east, reminding her of a pumpkin, rising into a spectacularly clear sky. Did the Moon look bigger? Perhaps it did. Were the tides along North Carolina's Outer Banks larger? Was her husband up there, in Nectaris, staring down at the Earth and admiring his great success? Or was he, too, a casualty?

The night was cool. Morgan came to her a little past midnight and slept beside her. Unexpectedly, so did Melissa, as if accepting Glenda as her new mother.

Around three in the morning, Jake began to cry, and she gave him another morphine shot. He felt clammy, and when Glenda re-dressed the wound, it looked angry

nd red. She had enough nursing-home experience to
know he needed antibiotics. Searching through the scav-
enged supplies, she found a bottle of Daprox tablets,
one of the new broad-spectrum bacteria-fighting drugs,
and gave him one.

After that, she slept.

At least until Melissa shook her by the shoulder.

"Aunt Glenda, it's my dad's phone . . . it's ringing."

It took her a few moments to rouse herself, but when
Glenda heard Neil's special phone burbling away, she
sprang up instantly.

She grabbed the bulky apparatus and pressed the engage button.

"Hello . . . hello?"

A pause on the other end of the line, then a woman's
voice. "Dr. Neil Thorndike, please."

She had no choice but to be the bearer of bad news.
"I'm afraid Dr. Thorndike has passed away."

Another pause, then, "And who am I speaking to?"

"I'm Glenda Thorndike. Neil's sister-in-law."

A pause. "Will you hold the line, please?"

"Who's calling?" But she got no answer. "Look, I
need help. My son's been hurt. He needs a doctor."

But she was on hold.

After thirty seconds a man's voice came on the line,
one she vaguely recognized, but couldn't immediately
place. "Is this Glenda Thorndike?"

"Yes."

"Dr. Gerald Thorndike's wife?"

"Yes, yes. Who's this? My son's been hurt."

"This is President Bayard."

She was, of course, floored. "Oh . . . I . . . I thought
I recognized your voice."

"Neil's dead?"

Her shoulders sank as the woe of Neil's death visited
her afresh. "I'm afraid he is. We've been under attack
here at Marblehill."

"You're at Marblehill?" The president sounded as if
he knew all about Marblehill.

"Yes . . . yes. By the Tarsalans."

By this time, Fernandes and Hanna had roused themselves.

The president said, "We were calling Neil to . . . to tell him that his brother . . . that your husband . . ." But then it sounded as if someone on the other end of the line was talking to the president, and Bayard muffled the mouthpiece with his palm. Her hand tightened around the receiver. What did the president want to tell her about Gerry? That he was dead? That he was never coming home? That he had ridden the asteroid right into the dark side of the Moon with that maniac, Ian Hamilton, and that he was now pulverized to atoms? *Come on, Mr. President, you're killing me.* Then the muffled sound disappeared and the president came back on. "We wanted to tell you that your husband's a national hero, Mrs. Thorndike. The country—in fact, the whole world—owes him a great debt of gratitude."

"Is he alive?"

The president seemed surprised. "Yes, he's alive. I was talking to him just five minutes ago."

Her throat closed up, and her blood must have done a wild thing, because suddenly she grew faint and collapsed to the cave floor. For several seconds she couldn't speak.

Hanna rushed over. "Mom?"

Through the receiver, Glenda heard Bayard's voice. "Mrs. Thorndike?"

Glenda looked at Hanna as tears sprang to her eyes. "It's the president."

Hanna's eyes widened. "*The* president?"

"Dad's okay. The president was talking to him five minutes ago."

"The president was talking to Dad?" Hanna seemed puzzled by this. Then she got businesslike. "Tell the president he's got to send a helicopter for Jake right away. He's getting worse."

"Mr. President?"

"I'm here, Mrs. Thorndike."

"My son's been in an accident. He needs medical attention."

"I'll dispatch a medevac helicopter to Marblehill immediately. Anything you and your family need or want, Mrs. Thorndike . . . We owe you a huge debt." At this point the president gave her his personal preauthorized number. "And if you want, I can arrange a connection to the Moon through this phone network. The commercial networks are temporarily down. But we've got a military one established. We've been talking to the Moon for the last eighteen hours. You stand by, Mrs. Thorndike. We'll get you talking to your husband in no time."

And the president was as good as his word.

41

From the time the phytosphere shredded into nothingness, Gerry's life was never the same.

He came home to a hero's welcome, which, because of the state of the Earth, and because of all the work that had to be done, was a subdued affair, but gratifying nonetheless. White House staff arranged a small ceremony in the Rose Garden, and the president thanked him personally. Ian Hamilton was honored, and so was Fernandes. Fernandes was there in a dress uniform, and had come with none other than Celia, a pudgy, short dynamo of a woman who looked as if she could survive anything, and who beamed with pride when the president presented her husband with the Air Force Cross.

It was from the president on this occasion that both Gerry and Glenda found out that all those Tarsalan refugees still left on Earth were succumbing to a strange new disease. As they stood in the Rose Garden sipping champagne—the president's gardeners had been hard at work, coaxing to life dormant samples kept in the vast cold-storage warehouses of 937—the president explained to both Gerry and Glenda that it was the Tarsalan-specific component in Neil's phytosphere virus that was killing the alien survivors on Earth.

"A micropercentage of the phytosphere consisted of Tarsalan DNA, and Neil's virus was essentially targeting that DNA. While the phytosphere was able to . . . uh . . . circumvent Neil's virus by utilizing its carapace component . . . when the phytosphere rained down on

Earth the virus escaped, and the Tarsalans didn't know what hit them. They're succumbing fairly quickly. We're trying to save them, but so far we haven't found a cure. And to tell you the truth, finding a cure isn't a major priority for us. Not after what they did to us. It's probably better that they all pass on. We've got more pressing concerns right now."

The president was blunt about his concerns. "Our population has been culled by about forty-five percent, and our best estimate is that it now stands at just under two hundred million. In less developed countries the figures are far more staggering. Of course, the environment has been severely degraded—for several months now we haven't had any plant life pumping oxygen into the atmosphere, or taking carbon dioxide out. Restoring our atmosphere is going to have to be our top priority. The phytosphere itself was replacing quite a bit of oxygen, but now that the phytosphere is gone, we've got to make up the shortfall quickly. Gerry, I want you to think about this. How do we start pumping oxygen back into the atmosphere? The neutralized xenophyta seem to be pumping *some* oxygen back into the atmosphere, enough to keep us going for a while. And many of the larger, heartier plant varieties—mostly trees of one kind or another—didn't die out completely. They're starting to come back, and that's helping with the oxygen situation. Still, it's a critical concern. The atmosphere has been badly compromised."

Over the coming weeks, Gerry became what his brother had once been—a special scientific advisor to the president.

Also, as financial institutions resurrected themselves and lawyers reopened their offices, Neil's codicil, written on the back of the topographic map, was deemed legal and binding and, overnight, Gerry became a rich man.

But none of this could bring his brother back, and Gerry grieved deeply for Neil.

To stabilize the atmosphere and restore its oxygen to normal levels—respiratory symptoms were now common in about half the population—Gerry surprised everybody by suggesting they dump iron into the ocean.

"Iron?" asked Bayard.

Gerry, still not comfortable in the Oval Office, nodded. "Iron is already a micronutrient in ocean waters, and with even a slight increase in its concentration, phytoplankton growth can be stimulated significantly. Because of widespread destruction of our forests and grasslands, CO_2 levels in the atmosphere have increased significantly. If we mass-create phytoplankton blooms in the oceans, they'll devour a lot of this excess CO_2, and replace it with oxygen. As the oxygen levels come back to their norms, the artificially created phytoplankton blooms will then die out because they'll have used up the available excess CO_2. Essentially what we're doing, Mr. President, is terraforming our own planet. I submitted a paper to the NSF about this particular technique during your first year in office, sir. I meant it to address the greenhouse gas problem, but it will work equally well in this situation."

The president turned to his chief of staff, Holden Gregory. Gregory raised his eyebrows and shook his head. "It never reached my desk."

In other words, Neil had quashed it.

"The great thing about this technique is that everybody can do it. Anything that has iron content can be thrown into the ocean. If we alert governments worldwide, and fast-track the production of artificial ferrous materials as an ocean fertilizer, we should see significant improvement in as little as six months."

The plan was put into effect.

Slowly the world came round.

Gerry and Glenda followed developments on TV, now resurrected on a limited basis, from their new three-story home in Nag's Head, North Carolina.

They followed not only the story about increasing oxygen levels, but all stories related to the aftereffects of the phytosphere.

For instance . . .

Some animal, bird, and fish species were now extinct, but many had survived, albeit in small numbers.

As for the Tarsalans, SETI apparatus monitored the

skies for signals, and because the Tarsalans had actually improved all this equipment during the honeymoon period of First Contact, upgrading it to send and receive instantaneously, Earth intercepted radio communications from many of the civilized worlds, but, oddly, none from Tarsala itself. Which Gerry thought strange, because the Tarsalans were always so full of well-meaning, if misplaced, advice.

Also . . .

In the months immediately following the destruction of the phytosphere, Neil's virus found its way to the Moon, no doubt because the Moon had endless visitors from Earth. One of the two hundred Tarsalan refugees on the Moon caught the virus, and that was it—in a matter of days they were all dead, including Kafis.

In the spring following the destruction of the phytosphere, Gerry and his new extended family were at their house at Nag's Head. They had just been to the beach. They were all in the kitchen, and Glenda was making lunch—not much of a lunch, because the whole country was on a draconian rationing system, even though the food-supply network was starting to come back fairly successfully now. (The Western Secessionists were cooperating.) Glenda was in the middle of mixing egg powder to make scrambled eggs. The four kids were playing Chinese checkers at the kitchen table. The window was open, letting in fresh sea air.

Glenda stopped stirring the egg powder. She looked up. She peered out the window, then exited the house via the back deck that led off the kitchen.

"Glenda?" said Gerry.

She didn't answer. He got up and followed her. The kids remained distracted by their game of Chinese checkers.

He went out onto the deck, down the steps, and into the yard. As with their house in Old Hill, a woods abutted the back. Glenda was now standing at the end of the yard peering up at the dead trees. Several young saplings, with the return of the light, had begun to sprout in between the dead trees. And even some of the bigger trees, apparently stalwart enough to survive the long stretch of sunlessness, were starting to come back. Grass and weeds were coming back as well.

Gerry reached the back fence and stood next to Glenda. "What's wrong?"

"Shhh. Do you hear it?"

"Hear what?"

"Listen."

Over the sound of the wind rustling through the dead branches, he now heard the sweet song of a . . . a what? He wasn't much of a bird fancier.

But his wife . . . Glenda's eyes lit up as if with the glow of celestial magic. "It's a cardinal. Look. There it is."

He looked. The bird's crimson plumage was like a dash of hope at the beginning of this new world. It was like a revelation. It told him that it was, at last, over. And when Glenda finally looked at him, he knew that all the trouble between them was finally over as well. The world was vastly different, weighted with tragedy and death. But like that cardinal up there, it was also a place of new starts.

For him, as well as for everybody else.

And he decided a new start was all anybody could ask for.